Coffee

in

Common

~

Dee Mann

~ ~ ~

Mason Marshall Press
Medford, Massachusetts

Also by Dee Mann:

Beginnings – Seven short stories that prove you never know where and when love will strike.

Plain Shane - With the help of her new roommates, and a new special friend, Shane overcomes her shyness and finds life leading her down paths she only once imagined.

Available at www.masonmarshall.com and amazon.com.

~ ~ ~

ISBN-10: 1632470071
ISBN-13: 978-1-63247-007-2

For information, please contact:

Mason Marshall Press
P.O. Box 324
Medford, MA 02155-0004
www.masonmarshall.com

PUBLISHED IN THE UNITED STATES OF AMERICA

I owe a debt of gratitude to the following fine folks:

Liana Peterson, who helped me discover I didn't understand certain people quite as well as I thought, and without whose eagle eye and verbal flogging, this story might still be bouncing around inside my head.

Catherine Oteri, and her musical instinct for finding the right songs with the right lyrics.

John Silveira, who was kind enough to let me steal one of his jokes.

Carol Henriquez, whose proofreading saved me from several embarrassing errors, both major and minor.

Thank you all!

~ Dee

For Marty

Points of Interest

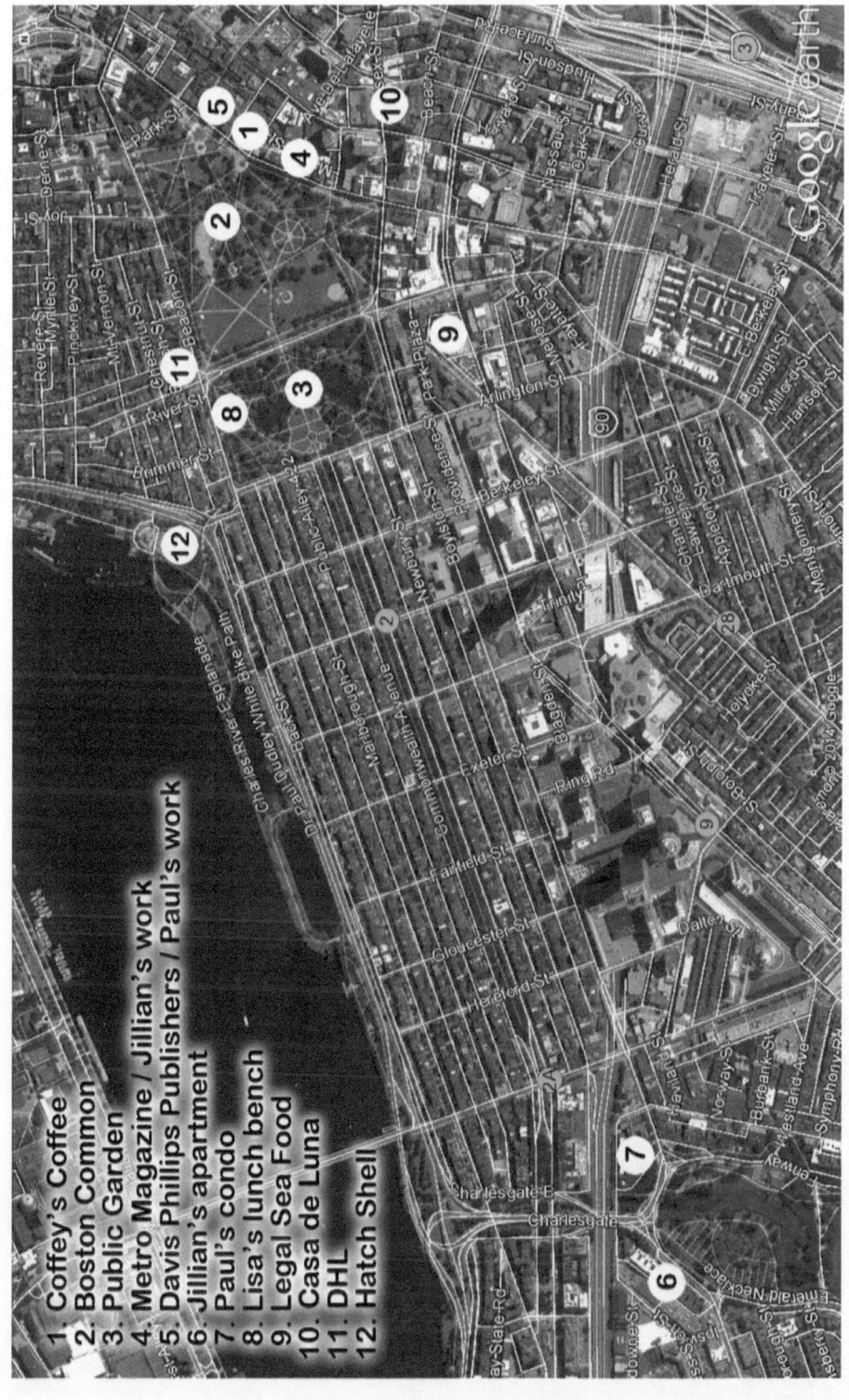

1. Coffey's Coffee
2. Boston Common
3. Public Garden
4. Metro Magazine / Jillian's work
5. Davis Phillips Publishers / Paul's work
6. Jillian's apartment
7. Paul's condo
8. Lisa's lunch bench
9. Legal Sea Food
10. Casa de Luna
11. DHL
12. Hatch Shell

Prologue

In the spring of 2004, a group of young Bostonians experienced the most incredible, life-altering month of their lives. I was privileged to observe much of what happened and to be able to fill in details after the fact so this story could be written.

If you've read romance novels before, please put aside your preconceptions. This is not a "bodice buster" and it does not conform to any romance or romantic comedy "formula." Rather, with a modicum of literary license, it lets you follow events from start to finish as if you were the proverbial fly on the wall.

If this could have been presented as a history or biography, you'd be reading about real people who you could probably Google or find on Facebook or Myspace. Unfortunately, despite modern culture's love of so-called reality entertainment, this story could only be told if presented as fiction.

So, dear reader, I hereby fulfill my obligations and state unequivocally, with the fervent hope you will believe me, that:

1. The story you are about to read is completely a work of fiction.

2. Names have been changed to protect the innocent and the guilty.

3. The characters, incidents, situations, dialogue, and story are entirely the products of my imagination and any resemblance to actual persons or events is purely coincidental.

And, of course, legal, ethical, and moral considerations absolutely prohibit me from claiming that it all really happened exactly this way.

But it could have...

WEDNESDAY, MAY 5, 2004

7:40 AM

Paul DiLorenzo and Roberto Tello stood in line at Coffey's Coffee as they did nearly every workday morning. It wasn't unusual to find the line of customers snaking around inside the shop and stretching out the door, even on the blustery, frigid mornings that frequently passed for spring in New England.

There were no lattés, or double mocha cappuccinos to be found at Coffey's. Seventy-two year old Gil Coffey didn't believe in trendy. For forty-nine years he'd been serving hand-made-on-the-premises pastry and bagels and the very best caffeine fix in downtown Boston, and didn't see any reason to change.

Rumor had it representatives of some large chains periodically bought Coffey's coffee, not to drink, but to analyze in an attempt to determine what made it so good. So far, they'd not succeeded.

In 1994, when Starbucks moved into Boston, one of Gil's employees took a marker to her name badge and became Barista Betty. Gil and the customers thought it a hoot. At the time, most folks in the area still thought *barista* was Italian for *barkeeper*. So Gil had new badges made for all the employees, a practice that now, years later, had become tradition.

"...but there was no *way* he was going to strike him out."

Paul was only half paying attention to his friend as he silently debated the merits of ordering one of Gil's amazing blueberry muffins versus a cinnamon-raisin bagel with cream cheese.

"He hasn't struck him out in three years. So why in hell would Francona leave him in there with the bases loaded?"

"Maybe he had a hunch." He watched Barista Akina bring three cups to the counter for the girl in front of them.

"No maybes. The guy needs his head examined. There's no way he should be managing a little league team much less the Red Sox."

Paul enjoyed baseball and the Red Sox, but Rob was one of those fanatical fans for whom Red Sox Nation was created.

Akina twisted the three cups into a cardboard carrier and asked the woman, "Will there be anything else today?"

"Whatever you're giving away for free," she said with a grin as she reached into her purse.

Paul was about to answer Rob, but instead whipped his head around and blurted out, "Hey, that's my line."

Her eyes met his when she turned to see who shouted in her ear. "Excuse me?"

Paul could only stare, captivated by her dark brown eyes, the smoothness of her skin, the gentle slope of her nose, the whiteness of her teeth, and the way her lips seemed to make him ache. He sensed the color rising in his cheeks and felt his heart quicken, unsure if it was his embarrassment or her amazing eyes making him feel suddenly very strange and self-conscious.

Finally he managed, "I ah, I'm ah, sorry. I said, 'that's my line.' I almost always say that when someone asks if I want anything else."

The woman's skeptical frown was followed by first one, then the other eyebrow arching to accentuate her disbelief. "You say 'that's my line' whenever someone asks if you want anything else?"

"No, no." He was so rattled he didn't realize she was joking. "I mean I always say *that*, what you said, when someone asks if I want anything else."

Her simple, "Really!" made it obvious she didn't believe him. He turned to Rob in desperation. "Tell her. Don't I always say that?"

Crap. That sounds so lame she must think I'm an idiot.

There was no longer any doubt his face burned from making a fool of himself.

Rob rolled his eyes and nodded as he turned to face the girl. "Yeah, he does. He says that *all* the time."

The girl added a wrinkled brow.

Are these two working on a new pickup line or are they simply demented?

"See." Paul tried to look hopeful.

Akina cleared her throat. "That will be nine dollars and twenty-one cents please."

The woman turned back, removed a ten from her red leather wallet, and handed it over. "Keep the change."

She dropped the wallet in her purse, picked up the tray, turned her head to smile briefly but dismissively at Paul and Rob, and headed for the door.

The two stepped up to the counter. Rob ordered his coffee and perused the display cases filled with rich, moist muffins, flaky, sweet pastry, and assorted giant bagels. Paul watched the girl until she walked through the front door.

No sooner did it close behind her than he turned to Rob, then back to the door, then back to Rob, who glanced over in time to catch his friend's brief ballet and knew what was coming. Paul broke for the door, calling back over his shoulder for Rob to get him the usual and that he would meet him at the office.

Out on the street, he performed another dance, twisting left, then right, then left again, finally catching sight of her in the morning crowd. She was walking slowly, gracefully, and he could not help but admire the gentle curves of her very feminine form as he hurried to catch up. Her dark-auburn hair shone in the morning light, swinging back-and-forth across her shoulders in a gentle counterpoint to the sway of her softly rounded hips.

"Excuse me," he said, touching her lightly on the shoulder.

She glanced back, then stopped and turned toward him, her face filled with curiosity.

Paul realized he had no idea what to say. Something was drawing him to this attractive stranger, but whatever it might be, it was not providing any dialogue.

"Hi. I'm Paul. I, ahh, well I couldn't let you go away without talking to you. I mean, I'm, well…"

What the hell is wrong with me?

The woman's curiosity morphed into mild amusement at his continued fumbling.

He took a deep breath, let it out, and shook his head, not wanting to believe he could be acting like such a dolt. He felt like he was fourteen again, facing Susie Quan, the girl who gave him his first lesson in rejection.

"Wait. Please, let me start again. I swear I'm not usually this much of a loser around women. My name's Paul. Paul DiLorenzo. And you are…?"

"Wondering how often you stop girls on the street to make yourself look foolish." Impatience mixed with the amusement in her eyes.

He grinned at her quickness. "Thankfully, this is the first time. And please. Lord, let it be the last."

As before, he found her eyes hypnotic, even though they were now almost laughing at him. He shrugged.

"I really don't make a habit of accosting women on the street. It's just…back there in the coffee shop was the first time I've ever heard anyone else use that line. I've been saying it since I was a teenager and when I heard you, something sort of clicked. Then, when you turned and our eyes met, something clicked again. I know it sounds crazy, but as I watched you walk out the door, this feeling came over me that I had to come after you, that I had to get to know you or I'd miss out on someone…something really important."

"You mean, like, the universe or God or something was telling you to chase after me?"

Clearly confused, Paul replied, "Well…I don't know, but, yeah, I guess."

The woman chuckled, shook her head, and asked, "Does this line usually work for you or are you trying out new material today?" Without waiting for a reply, she turned and resumed her slow stroll down the sidewalk.

She's blowing me off. Why the hell am I acting like this? What is it about this girl that has me so off-balance?

He hurried to catch up, desperate for a miracle, a way to salvage this mess.

"Wait. I mean, can I walk with you. Walk you to work or wherever you're going? I really don't ever do this…approach someone on the street like this. But what I said back there was the truth. Please. I won't even ask your name. If you don't think I'm worth a chance by the time we get to your building, or wherever, I'll leave and you'll never see me again."

She paused and appeared to weigh his offer. Then, with a playful half-smile, she said, "Okay. It's a deal. You have until we get to my building. Go."

She started walking slowly again. Paul kept pace on her left, again feeling hopeful.

"As I said, I'm Paul DiLorenzo. I'm an associate editor at Davis Phillips publishers, and…" He turned his head to stare at her as they walked. "…I can't believe how attracted I am to you when I don't know a thing about you. My…"

They'd traveled about 30 feet when the woman stopped and turned to face him.

"Well, here we are," she said, interrupting him.

Huh?

He expected to have more time to make an impression.

"Thanks for walking me," she said as she started toward the office building behind him.

Completely crushed, Paul could only stand there, frozen and speechless.

A quick glance at his face as she passed startled her, but she continued toward the building. Shoulders slumped, Paul stared after her, a poster boy for total defeat.

She reached for the handle, pulled open the door, then turned and stared at him for almost twenty seconds, her gaze hard and appraising. Then her eyes softened and she said, "I usually have coffee at lunch, usually around 12:30." She began to turn away but glanced back again, smiling.

"And my name is Jillian."

10:01 AM

Davis Phillips Publishers, the nation's third largest producer of beautiful coffee-table books no one ever reads, occupied the fifth floor of the nine-story O'Malley Building on the corner of Tremont and Winter Streets, across from the northeast corner of the Boston Common and two blocks north of the Heritage Building into which Paul watched Jillian vanish a few hours ago.

Paul shared an office with the three other members of his team, his best friend, Rob Tello, team leader Thomas Driscoll, and the recently hired Priya Kumar.

"Geez, I hate those meetings," Paul whined as he and Priya walked away from the conference room. "Sixty minutes of my life wasted. You'd think…ah, who cares. Let's go get coffee."

"Shouldn't we tell Tom, first?"

"Nah. He won't care, as long as we bring him some."

Passing by the company coffee room, they headed for the elevator. Neither saw any reason to drink brown sludge when Coffey's was only two minutes away.

The ride down was silent, but as the elevator doors opened to the lobby, Priya asked, "Mind if I ask you a personal question?"

"I don't know. About what?"

"Rob."

"Priya, trust me, you don't want to go out with him. Besides he's…"

Her laughter echoed off the marble walls. "Lord, no. It took me about two minutes to figure him out. Besides, remember my first day?"

Paul grinned and nodded.

"I was just wondering how long you've been friends. It's pretty clear you knew each other before working here."

"Oh, yeah. We go back to high school. We were best friends. Played ball on the same teams, dated cheerleaders, did stupid stuff together.

"We sort of lost touch after high school. I was going to Tufts and he ended up at Florida State. Then just before the end of his freshman year, his dad landed a great job near where the Red Sox have spring training, so his parents moved south." He laughed. "While all the other kids were heading to party places for spring break, Rob was watching the Red Sox every day at training camp."

Priya shared the laugh. "I can see that. He does seem to like his baseball. So when did you connect again?"

"About three years ago, not long after I started here. This girl Jody in accounting brought him to the company Christmas party. I tell ya, Pri, it was like I'd just seen him the day before."

"That's the hallmark of a true friendship," she said, walking through the door Paul held open for her.

"I guess so," he agreed as they approached the end of the short line. "He was teaching high school English at the time but hated the politics and bullshit. So when his predecessor announced she was resigning when her baby was born, I got him to apply for the job." He laughed again. "I think a lot of women in the company rue the day he started."

"Why? He seems like such a nice guy."

"He is. But you've only known him since he started going out with Lisa. You wouldn't know it to look at him, but he's always been a wicked player. In high school, he developed this kind of...mystique, I guess, as a party animal and chick magnet. Girls seemed to find his personality and charm and sense of humor irresistible despite his looks. I probably shouldn't admit this, but the best part of being friends with him was the leftovers."

"Leftovers?"

Paul nodded, looking sheepish. "The friends of the girls he went out with, the ones he broke up with after a few weeks."

"*You called them leftovers?*" Offense blazed in her eyes, but he was saved from having to answer when Barista Manny asked what he could get for them.

Four minutes later, as the door to Coffey's closed behind them, Priya punched his arm hard enough that he almost dropped the cardboard cup holder. "Leftovers! What is it with men and their need to objectify and demean?"

She stomped off, leaving him rubbing his arm as he hurried to catch up.

"Priya, I'm sorry. That's what we used to say in high school. We were stupid kids with too many hormones. Come on, don't be angry."

An hour later, Paul was still getting the silent treatment, much to the amusement of Rob and Tom.

Priya glanced at him.

I suppose I should let him off the hook. After all, it was a long time ago, and he is such a gentleman now. And I guess I was really taking out on him all the crap from other guys.

Tom clearing his throat drew her eyes across the office to the desk that faced hers. She took in his familiar round freckled face, bushy orange-red hair, and trim but stocky five-foot eleven-inch build.

He could change his name to Mahatma Chang or anything else and you would still know he was of Irish descent. Rob, on the other hand, has that everyman look. He really could come from manywheres.

Her eyes returned to Paul as she let her thoughts drift back to her first day at DPP.

* * *

Priya was very nervous. She arrived at the office early, but stayed out of the way until all three guys were safely at their desks. Then she walked in, closed the door, placed her bag on her desk, lifted her arms over her head in a swimsuit pose, and said, smiling, "Good morning, guys. Let's see a show of hands. Who wants to see me naked?"

The men were stunned into silence. They stared, unblinking, unmoving, like clichéd deer transfixed by the bright headlights of an oncoming car. She stared back for a few seconds then started laughing as she pointed to each in turn and said, "Liar, liar, and liar."

Her laughter relaxed them a bit and Rob's hand inched up slowly until it was above his head.

"Ah," she said, "an honest man." Slowly, she shook her head from side-to-side, turned to face him and said, "Rob, it will never happen. Ever." Her hands moved to indicate her attractive, but conservative business suit. "This is as close as you will ever get to seeing heaven."

Shoot. That sounded awfully conceited.

"Look guys, I had to leave two really good jobs in the past year because the men I worked with either wouldn't take me seriously or couldn't keep their eyes, and other parts, to themselves. I'm good at what I do, and this seems like a really nice, friendly place, but I came here to work, and that's all I came here to do. If that's going to be a problem, please tell me now before I get comfortable in the job."

Her new coworkers were grinning broadly. Tom stood and gave her a slight bow of appreciation. "Well done, ma'am. Well done."

* * *

In the three months since then, she never once caught any of them looking at her in anything but a friendly and professional way. Even when the office banter turned suggestive, or even sexual, she was just one of the team.

She sighed, decided it was time to forgive Paul, and tossed a paperclip at him to get his attention. "So what happened with the girl this morning? Did you get lucky?"

Paul grinned, happy things were back to normal, then glared at Rob. "I should have figured you'd start blabbing the minute you got here." He turned his attention back to Tom and Priya. "To answer your question…oh yeah…I was on my game."

"Sure you were," Rob jeered, remembering his performance in the coffee shop. "Did you get her number?"

"Number, ha! Who needs a number?"

"He struck out," Priya said. "He got nothing and now he'll be getting nothing. Poor Paul."

Tom snorted his agreement, holding up his right hand with thumb and forefinger forming an 'L'.

"Lady, gentlemen, please. You forget to whom you are speaking. I was so smooth, so charming, *so* damned irresistible, I didn't even *ask* for her number.

"See, I told you…" Priya began.

"But," Paul continued, "I did make a date for lunch today."

11:30 AM

11:30! How can it only be 11:30?

Paul hadn't been this anxious for lunchtime to arrive since high school, when he'd skip the entrée in the cafeteria and head right outside to meet Sue Ellen for a little lip-locking dessert.

He studied Rob, sitting at this desk across the room, engrossed in whatever he was editing.

I wonder if he remembers the night we went to the Sheepfold with Suzy and…what was her name…the redhead with the big boobs…and he got out of the car in his boxers to take a whiz and…what the hell is her name…convinced Suzy to drive off toward the entrance as if we were leaving him there. Man, I can still hear us all laughing, still see him running across the parking lot by moonlight, cursing and pleading.

As he forced it from his face, he was glad none of his co-workers caught his evil grin.

Hmmm…did I ever thank him for introducing me to Suzy?

His gaze drifted right to Priya.

She really looks hot today…I wonder if she has a boyfriend. She must. Probably some muscle-bound face with a big dick. Girls like her can get anyone they want. But she never talks about dating anyone…and she doesn't seem like the superficial type…unless she's a great actress…but that stunt she pulled the first day…no way…she's okay. Just private, I guess. I wonder if

*Jillian will really show up? Damn, what was wrong with me this morning?
Must have been those eyes…great eyes…maybe she…*

Tom's voice rang out. "Hey, DiLorenzo, you working or dreaming over there?"

12:15 PM

Jillian hurried toward the coffee shop. A curious anxiety nibbled at the back of her mind. She wanted to be there before he arrived but wasn't sure why. The wind blew her hair around and though she tried to keep it in place, she knew she would need to fix it once inside.

The lunchtime crowd, like the wind, all seemed to be coming toward her, making it difficult to move quickly. As she drew closer to the shop, she realized she was actually nervous about meeting this guy.

Paul DiLorenzo. Nice name. And he is kind of cute. But he was so flustered this morning. Do I really want to sit through a whole lunch with some spaz? What would Liz say to do? Be cool. Just be cool and detached and make him work to impress me. But lord, that look on his face this morning. If it hadn't been for that look… Come on, girl, get a grip. You've shot down plenty of come-ons before. But that look…not just disappointment… almost…devastation. How can you not at least give a guy a chance when he's devastated at the thought of not seeing you again? And I guess it was kind of sweet the way he was stumbling over himself to impress me. I never did that to a guy before.

She reached the shop, pulled open the door and stepped inside. It felt good to get out of the wind.

Mmmm…smells wonderful in here. Coffee mixed with the pastry…I sure wish someone would figure out how to capture it in a bottle, so I can spray it around the apartment.

She was standing a few feet inside the door and when it opened again, the cold air roused her from her reverie. With a contented sigh, she turned to find a table and saw Paul sitting at the one in the corner, his back to the front window. He was reading from a stack of papers and there were three or four cups on the table.

Damn.

She quickly finger-combed her hair.

How long has he been here? And what's with all the coffee? Are other people coming? Is this some kind of game after all? Maybe I should just get out of here before he sees me.

She hesitated, still trying to smooth out her hair but, without a mirror, not having much success.

What the hell…he takes me as I am or not at all.

She removed her scarf and started toward the table. Holding the scarf in her left hand, she used her right to unbutton her coat. When she was closer, she saw she was correct about the coffees. There were three sitting unopened in the center of the table and one, obviously his and already half empty, near the edge.

"Hi," she said with a neutral smile as she reached the table.

"Hi," he replied without thinking. Then he looked up and jumped out of his seat.

"Oh, hi!" he repeated, this time with genuine enthusiasm. "You're early."

"Not as early as you, I see."

Her eyes flicked to the table, then back to Paul. "Have you been working?" She gestured reflexively and her scarf caught his cup, spilling this coffee all over the papers.

When they heard the cup go over, they looked down at the mess and simultaneously groaned, "Oh crap!"

Their heads snapped back up at the matching exclamations as all through the shop, heads turned to see what was happening.

Jillian was mortified. "I am *so* sorry. I..."

"That's okay," he said, interrupting, as he grabbed the few napkins on the table and started blotting at the drenched manuscript. "Just...can you get me some more napkins?"

He continued to blot at the spilled coffee but it was futile now. The napkins were saturated. Jillian hurried off, trying to ignore the stares from other customers, and returned with a napkin dispenser. She pulled out three small napkins which emptied the dispenser. Quickly, she turned it around to find the other side empty as well.

"I don't believe this," she moaned, silently cursing her decision to stay.

She hurried off again to return with two handfuls of napkins. Dropping them all over the spill, she began sopping up the coffee, so embarrassed that she could not look at him.

"I really am *so* sorry. I can't believe I did that. I've probably ruined your work and now...now..."

She wadded up a pile of saturated napkins, still not able to meet his eyes.

"...I...I'm sorry. I should go. Really, I'm sorry."

She turned to leave.

"Wait! Where are you going? You just got here."

Paul finished mopping up the coffee and piled the wet napkins on the edge of table against the wall.

"Please, calm down. Didn't your mom ever tell you not to cry over spilled coffee? Or was that milk? No matter. Come on, sit down. It's okay."

He could see how embarrassed she was. Gently he said, "Really, Jillian.

No harm done."

He moved to the other side of the table and pulled out the chair for her.

Jillian forced herself to face him and saw he was grinning.

He rattled the chair a bit, his eyes pleading with her to stay. "Please?"

She forced a weak smile and took the offered seat. As he moved back to his chair, she shrugged off her jacket and nervously ran her fingers through her hair again, suddenly hoping it didn't look too horrible. They stared at each other for a few moments, neither one really sure what to say. Then Paul started to chuckle. He tried his best to contain it but couldn't and a full-fledged laugh burst through.

His laughter was infectious. Jillian noticed her mood growing lighter as the corners of her mouth curled into a smile.

He is so strange!

"What's so funny?"

Paul took a few seconds to get the laughter under control. As he did, she again took in his thick, brown hair with its reddish highlights, his brown eyes flecked with gold, his straight nose, and his full, laughing lips. She remembered from this morning how he carried himself with a casual straightness. She noticed he sat that way, too. His shoulders were not exceptionally broad, nor his arms particularly muscular, yet he seemed to exude a quiet physical prowess.

"Well, think about it. Our first meeting this morning was somewhat of a disaster, with me acting unbelievably foolish. And now our second meeting starts with another, ahh...small blip, but this time it's you who..."

He began laughing again, quietly this time, enjoying the irony of the situation. Jillian started to say something but he stopped her.

"Wait, please. Before you say anything else, before anything else happens...what is your last name?"

Somehow, that simple question relaxed her and Jillian grinned at his urgency.

"Marshall. Jillian Marshall."

Paul began to extend his hand over the table to shake hands but retreated a bit and hooked it around the coffee cups.

Jillian feigned indignation and extended her hand straight over them. As their hands approached, a small jolt of static electricity made them both jump. Startled, each wondered if the spark was an omen and, if so, what sort. Then, as they shook hands, a spark of a different sort passed between them.

"Paul DiLorenzo," he said. "I am *really* happy to meet you Jillian Marshall."

"And I'm still a little embarrassed, but happy to meet you, too. I hope I didn't destroy anything really important."

Paul picked up one of the wet sheets of paper.

"No, don't worry about it. It's just the only copy of a recently discovered manuscript by Ernest Hemingway. It'll dry." He paused, looking worried. "I hope."

Jillian's wide-eyed stare vanished when she saw him grin again.

"Jerk. I almost believed you for a second."

"Sorry. I couldn't resist. How long do you have for lunch?"

"I should be back by one."

Paul nodded. "Me too." He paused for a deep breath. "You know, I probably shouldn't ever bring this up again, but I really am sorry I was so clumsy this morning about meeting you. I'm usually a fairly articulate guy."

"That's okay. You were nervous. Nervous can be kind of cute. And let's be honest here, your clumsy this morning doesn't come close to my clumsy a few minutes ago."

"Okay then, we're even. I hope you won't mind me saying this so soon, but you are the second most beautiful woman I've ever seen in person."

Jillian blushed, pleased and flattered by the compliment.

"Come on, I know I'm not a beast, but the second..."

"No, really. You are definitely the second most beautiful woman I've ever met.

Her blush deepened.

"Okay, but just the second? Who's the first?"

Paul looked right into her shining, beautiful brown eyes and said. "Everyone else."

Stunned at the unexpected reply, Jillian stared at him for a second before she burst out laughing.

"You really are a jerk. I owe you big time for that."

Looking pleased and a little relieved, Paul glanced up, thankful she was laughing.

"I'm sorry. I couldn't stop myself. And I figured that if I'm on trial, I might as well let you see who I really am. If you hadn't laughed just then, well...I'd have been heartbroken, but I'd have known we'd never really get along."

"What do you mean 'on trial'?"

"Didn't you come here to decide whether you liked me enough to give me your number and try me out on a real date?"

Jillian looked as if she was about to protest, but Paul continued on.

"That's okay. That's what you should be doing when a strange guy embarrasses himself on the street. I mean, anyone can act like a fool for a few minutes in order to charm a beautiful woman, but it takes a special kind of guy to sustain it for a whole lunch. And you don't strike me as the type of girl who would waste much time on that kind of guy."

"And how *do* I strike you?"

"Right through the heart, so far."

Jillian's blush had faded, but rose anew at this latest compliment. Desperate to change the subject, she nodded toward the three cups.

"Are these all for me?"

"Yes."

"*Three* coffees?"

"Well, I didn't know how you liked your coffee, but I figured one of the three you bought this morning had to be for you, so I talked to Akina and…"

"Akina?"

"The barista who waited on you this morning."

"You're on a first name basis with the people here?"

"Not really. Just Akina. And only since noon when I got here. I took a chance she might remember you, which she did, since you come in all the time with the same order. Or so she said. So I asked her for the same three coffees and here they are."

Pointing to them one-by-one, he said, "Decaf regular, black two sugars, and milk dark no sugar."

Jillian started to reach for one but Paul stopped her. "Wait. Let me guess."

He studied her for a few seconds, then picked up the milk-dark-no sugar and handed it to her with a hopeful look on his face.

"I'm impressed. How did you know?"

"I didn't. I guessed. Or rather, I hoped."

"Hoped?"

"Uh-huh. That's how I take mine."

Her disbelief was unmistakable.

"Really! I told you this morning I had a strange feeling when I first saw you. It was like I knew you, even though I didn't know you. It…but this is all getting a little too heavy."

Paul picked up his empty cup. "How about sharing some of that coffee?"

Jillian poured half of the coffee from her cup into his, then handed it back.

"I don't think it's hot anymore," she said.

"That's okay. I'm used to cold coffee. Besides, just looking at you will keep me warm."

"Oh *please*," she muttered, rolling her eyes.

Paul laughed. "Okay, I guess I *am* laying it on a little thick." He checked his watch and realized time was getting short. "As much as I'd like to sit here with you all afternoon, we only have about twenty-five minutes left before you have to decide and all you know about me is how I like my coffee, that I can act goofy, and that I have a strange sense of humor."

He locked eyes with her, his gaze never wavering as he continued.

"So fire away. Ask me anything you want to know. Job, school, shoe size, favorite Backstreet Boy. Anything. Because when I walk out that door in a little while..." He reached across the table to move a tuft of hair away from her eye. The touch of his finger against her skin sent another spark through her, a warm, welcome one. "...I'll either have your phone number, or a huge hole where my heart used to be."

6:20 PM

Jillian closed the door to her apartment, dropped her keys in her purse, shrugged off her coat, and hung both on the wooden pegs on the wall next to the door. The scarf she held up, smiling with the memory of the chaos it caused.

It had been a long, eventful day both in and out of work, but she was still full of energy. Happy and excited her lunch with Paul went so well after its disastrous beginning, she was dying to tell her friends all the details. But it was still too early. Neither Liz nor Jenna would be home from work for at least fifteen minutes.

The golden glow of the afternoon sun streamed through the four oversized, Victorian-era double-hung wood sash windows that formed a bay overlooking the street. It cast curious shadows in the two alcoves, one that held her bed, nightstand, and dresser, and the other, an efficiency kitchen.

She took the big feather duster from the umbrella stand by the door and moved around the room dusting the photos, prints, and posters that brightened the room and, even on a gloomy day, made visitors feel welcome. Then she fixed the pillows on the floral print sofa and two overstuffed chairs that reminded her of the wallpaper in her room as a child, all the while, thinking of him.

Suddenly in the mood for music, she loaded her special mix CD into the player.

Always and forever
Each moment with you
Is just like a dream to me
That somehow came true, yeah

The sweet sound of Luther Vandross filled the apartment. Her eyelids drooped, half closed as she conjured an image of Paul smiling at her the way he did when he was holding the chair for her, urging her to stay.

Something about him, even the thought of him, made her feel strangely comfortable. He was so nice, so easy to talk to once she got past the humiliation of spilling coffee on his work.

She grinned, remembering the exasperation on his face as he tried to sop up half a cup of coffee with a few small napkins. Then her face softened, almost glowed, as she remembered the light in his eyes when he moved that wisp of hair and said those sweet things.

Lost in her fantasy, she ambled to the windows to close the curtains, flopped on the sofa, then almost immediately jumped up and headed for the kitchen where she grabbed a bottle from the fridge. Sipping the water, still swaying with the music, she strolled to the bedroom alcove and sat on the edge of the bed, recalling yet again the events of the day. The last strains of the song faded and were replaced by another Vandross standard, *Here & Now*. She giggled out loud at the memory of how goofy and desperate he'd been when they first met, but was startled out of her reverie by the shrill ring of the phone.

Hoping it would be him, but knowing it was probably some telemarketer, she screwed the cap back on the bottle and rolled backward over the bed to grab the cordless phone on the nightstand.

"Hello?"

"You forgot to take your cell phone off silent again. It's a wonder you have any friends at all since you make it so hard for people to reach you."

"Hi, Liz." She tried to keep her excitement out of her voice. "You're home early!"

"Jenna and I both got out early. I just talked with her. We were thinking about Piazolla's for dinner tonight. Lucy from work said she was there twice last week and there were lots of mighty fine guys hanging and…"

Unable to contain herself, Jillian blurted out, "Liz, stop. I have to tell you something. You won't believe what happened to me today."

Liz heard the particular excitement in her friend's voice and knew only one thing could have put it there.

"Don't even tell me his name. I promised Jenna I'd pick her up in ten minutes and if you start talking now she'll be waiting on me for an hour. We'll be over as fast as we can get through traffic. And forget about Piazolla's tonight."

"Okay, okay. But you and Jenna hurry. And bring Thai."

7:10 PM

DHL sat on the corner of Charles and Chestnut Streets, two blocks north of the Boston Common. Named for the writer D.H. Lawrence when it first opened three decades ago, it quickly became a trendy,

English-pub-style watering hole. Today, it attracted a loyal clientele who were more interested in a relaxed atmosphere than being seen in the vicinity of whomever happened to be hot at the moment.

Paul and Rob liked DHL because it was never so crowded or loud you couldn't carry on a conversation. That the place offered thirty-six beers and ales on tap, with another three dozen in bottles didn't hurt much either.

"Your favorite Backstreet Boy? You didn't really say that." Rob's incredulous stare conveyed more than his words.

Paul surveyed the long mahogany and brass bar that ran along the left wall and the lacquered pine tables surrounded by wood chairs comfortably padded with dark, leather cushions that filled most of the rest of the space. "I swear. It just came out. And I can't figure out why. I never even liked the Backstreet Boys." He shook his head. "But it didn't matter. We hit it off, man. We really hit it off. She was so uptight and embarrassed after spilling my coffee but then she just seemed to relax. And after that, there were no games, no posturing. We were just talking and laughing. Really connecting."

Rob screwed his face into a grimace. "Geez, man, you realize you're starting to sound like a girl."

"Up yours. Are you telling me you and Lisa never talked about stuff?" He knew Rob suggested drinks for a reason and figured it was time to start the poking and prodding.

In response to silence, Paul said, "Look, buddy. I really didn't want to come here tonight. I wanted to head home and call Jillian. If you hadn't practically begged me...you know?"

Rob sighed. "Well, yeah, of course. We talked about movies, and food, and sex, and things to do. Stuff like that."

"Maybe that was the problem. Maybe she wanted to talk about more than that. Feelings and stuff. Chick stuff, you know?"

Rob stared into space for a few seconds then sighed, nodding slightly. "Yeah, maybe."

"So what's going on there?"

"Same as yesterday. Same as last week. We're on a break. She wanted a break to think about us."

He paused for a few seconds, again shaking his head. "What's there to think about? We go out, we have fun, the sex is great." He grimaced. "It's her friends, I know it's her friends. They don't like me much. They think I'm a troll."

Caught off-guard, Paul almost choked on his beer as he tried hard not to laugh. "A troll?"

"They don't think I'm handsome enough for her. They want her to find some guy who's more in her league. I'm too ordinary for them, which would be okay if I had lots of money, but I don't. I guess I embarrass them. When all the beautiful folk get together they don't want to have to look at commoners."

"Come on, Rob. Lisa is *not* that shallow. She…"

"I know, I know. But her friends are. And they're at her all the time about me."

"How do you know? You've heard them?"

Rob fidgeted with discomfort. "Two months ago we were at a party. It was a benefit thing for some beavers or possums or something like that. Anyway, I'm standing at the bar waiting for our drinks. Lisa's off with some museum people she knows. These two girls come up behind me talking."

* * *

"So how long has she been seeing him?" Kiki asked.

"Like, a couple of months," her friend Rachel replied. "I can't believe you didn't hear."

"How would I hear? Four months I'm in Paris and did anyone call me? *You* didn't call me."

"Yes I did. Two weeks after you left. You said you were having *très* much fun and met this guy François, and just *didn't* have time to talk because he was waiting for you in the lobby and…"

"Oh…well…yes, now I remember. Well…"

"I decided you'd call if you got lonely. Not that I could imagine you *getting* lonely in a country full of hot guys."

"Girl, you can not imagine. But that's for another day. So you say she's been seeing him for two months?"

Rachel nodded. "Two or three."

"But why? Does he have this enormous package or something? Or is he, like, really rich? He certainly doesn't dress it if he is."

"I don't know about his package, but he can't have much money. Nobody ever heard of him." She shrugged. "None of us can figure it out."

"Has anyone asked her?"

Rachel didn't even try to hide her disdain. "Of course," she said, then added in a mocking tone, "She said he treats her nice and makes her laugh."

"And that's supposed to make up for his looking like a truck driver? What *is* Lisa thinking?"

Rob didn't usually listen to chatter or gossip but his ears perked up when he heard Lisa's name. He paid close attention now, as the women continued their conversation.

"I don't know. But she's, like, totally into this guy. Everyone keeps telling her she should dump him and find someone in her own league, you know, because this guy is just so far beneath her. Oh, and you haven't heard the worst yet."

"What could be worse than no money and no looks?"

"His name's Roberto something. I think he's from Mexico, or Puerto Rico, or someplace like that."

"No!"

"Yes!" Rob's voice mocked her exclamation.

The bartender had just placed the drinks on the bar. Rob grabbed one in each hand, turned, and smiled at the women.

"Actually, my family is from Ecuador."

Smiling, he introduced himself. "Roberto Tello. It's *so* nice to meet you. It's good to know Lisa has such warm, caring friends who look out for her best interests even when she's so obviously out of her mind."

Both girls were embarrassed to discover the subject of their gossip overheard them, but neither appeared contrite. Just the opposite.

"Well, I'm sorry you heard that," Rachel sniffed, "but maybe it was for the best. You have to know you're just a fling for her." She smiled viciously. "I mean, we all go slumming once in a while."

"Really? We all do that?"

"Those of us who...well, you know."

"Yes, I think I do know."

Not to be left out, Kiki chimed in. "You really should, you know, save yourself a lot of future pain and move on to someone who's more your type. I mean, this thing with you and her can't last. She'll get tired of people making fun of her because of you."

Rob's smile disappeared. Worry lines creased his forehead. "People, her friends you mean, make fun of her because she goes out with me?"

"Yes! All the time!" Her voice lowered as she confided, "You know, people at our level can be, well, mean sometimes."

"No!" Rob appeared confused. "I haven't noticed that at all since we've been together."

"Oh you wouldn't. I mean, we're not uncouth or anything. No one would come right out and say anything if you or she were, like, around. But people do talk and the talk certainly gets back to Lisa."

"Yes, I can imagine." He could no longer hide his contempt. "I guess it *is* a good thing she has friends like you two who she can count on to keep her abreast of all the mean and hurtful gossip your little minds produce."

Being chastised by someone she considered beneath her was unthinkable and Rachel's glare could have melted steel. "Sure, as if you never say anything about anyone. See, that's what I mean. You think you're as good as she is but you're not. Lisa should have someone who's her equal. Both socially and, ah, visually. You are not that person. And you'll never *be* that person."

Rob was growing tired of the two snobs, but his honor had been offended, something he could not let pass.

"Well...this was very enlightening. Very enlightening indeed. If you'll excuse me."

He started to walk between them, but appeared to stumble, sending the contents of one of the glasses spilling down the front of Rachel's dress. "Oh my. I'm so sorry. How clumsy of me."

Rachel was livid. "You did that on purpose. You..."

Rob interrupted her. "Please, let me get something to dry you off."

He turned to Kiki and said, "Here, hold this, while I get a towel."

He handed her the drink, which slipped from his fingers, bounced off her hand, and spilled on the front of *her* dress.

Kiki gave a short scream of dismay.

"Oh dear!" Rob said. "Again! I really *am* sorry." He turned to the bartender, who winked at him. "May I have some towels please?"

Both women were beside themselves now with fury. They could not believe any man, especially one like him, would treat them this way.

"You asshole!" Rachel seethed, her voice dripping with venom. "You stay away from us. Just remember, Lisa *will* dump you. And I'll be standing next to her laughing at you when she does."

* * *

Paul's raucous laughter caused a few heads to turn their way. "Are you serious? They really said that stuff? You really did that to both of them? Why did I never hear about this?"

"They did, and I did. When I told Lisa what happened, she couldn't believe I'd actually do something like that."

"I can understand. I'm having trouble believing it myself."

"Well, she made me promise never to do that to anyone again, no matter what the provocation, and not to tell anyone else about it." Rob shrugged. "You know Lisa. What else could I do but promise?"

Paul was still chuckling.

"I guess I see why you think her friends may have something to do with it. All I can say is, I wish I'd been there to see it."

Paul extended his hand, palm open, and they exchanged slaps twice.

"Do you have to hang around a lot with these people?"

"No, not really. They're not friends like we're friends. Not any more. They're the kids of people in her parent's social circle. They all used to hang out when they were in high school, and I guess many of them still do, but Lisa doesn't really see them much…once in a while at some social thing."

"That would be once in a while too much for me."

"Me, too. But Lisa feels like she has to be friendly for her parents' sake."

"So, you haven't heard from her at all?"

"Not a word. And it's been, like, almost two weeks now. I called a couple of times but got her voice mail. I left a message once, but she never called me back."

"That's tough, dude."

"Yeah, well, she said she wanted time alone to think, so I probably shouldn't be surprised. But I miss her, man, you know? We were so good together. I loved how proper she was in public and how wild she could be when we were alone."

He glanced away for a few seconds, trying to gauge whether to risk ridicule by continuing.

Paul read the indecision on his friend's face. "I know what you mean, buddy. It's like a big hole, a big empty place she used to fill, but now…nothing."

"Exactly." He decided to take the risk. "You know when you were talking about coffee girl before, and you said that when you saw her the first time you felt something click. Well, that's what happened to me when I first met Lisa."

"Did you ever tell her?"

"Tell her? No. I don't think I ever really acknowledged it to myself, much less to her. I mean, you know me. I've always been free, having a good time, one girl after another. Do you realize I'd been with Lisa for over five months before this break. Five months! That's the longest I've been with one girl since high school. Even then, I wasn't really exclusive with anyone. But with Lisa, it's different." He sighed. "You know, I realized last week that since I've been with her, I never even think about other women."

Paul looked skeptical. "Man, I've seen you ogling…"

"Yeah, yeah, I know. I look at pretty girls. But it's the damnedest thing. I look, but I never fantasize about what it would be like to be with them anymore."

"Sounds like the 'L' word to me," Paul said. "Sounds like you have it bad. Did you ever tell her you loved her?"

"Of course, like when we were doing it and stuff."

"That's it?"

"What do you mean?"

Paul was shaking his head. "Rob, how can a man with Latino blood in his veins, a man who's had more women than most men dream of…how can you know so little about them? Are you seriously telling me you only told Lisa you loved her while you were doing her?"

"No. Sometimes I'd tell her afterward, or before."

Rob was beginning to regret taking that chance. He wasn't comfortable talking about love and emotions. And he really didn't like talking about sex, although he'd engage in bragging banter with other guys when it seemed to be called for.

Paul noticed his friend withdrawing.

"Rob, Lisa is the steadiest, most unassuming girl I've ever met. She's smart, funny, looks great but doesn't seem to care, and…well, you know I could go on and on. Five months ago, for whatever reason I'll never know, she chose you. And until this taking-a-break thing, I thought you two were made for each other. So did everyone else, which is why none of us can figure out what the taking-a-break is all about.

"But now I think I understand. You believe it was her friends dissing you, but from what you say, they'd been doing that right along. No, this is not the fault of her friends, buddy, it's all your fault."

Paul took a swig of his beer, sat back, and waited for a reaction.

Rob looked dazed. After a minute he mumbled, "My fault?"

"Your fault," Paul shot back. "Man, if you want to keep a woman like Lisa you have to work at it. She can have any guy she wants in this town. Hell, she can probably have any guy she wants in the world. But she chose you. Why would she do that?"

"She said I made her laugh, and that I'm nice to her."

"Okay, that's what hooked her, but what kept her coming back for five months?"

"I don't know," Rob replied. "Good times, great sex?"

Paul signaled the bartender to send over another round.

"Rob, she can get that anywhere, and probably in greater quantity and quality."

"Hey…"

"Yeah, blah, blah, I know. I've seen you in the shower, buddy. You ain't that special. Look, Lisa saw something in you, something that made her want to stick around. But you never gave her any reason to do so.

Women want, no, they need to be told, to be reassured all the time. They need to hear the words, and not just when you're in bed with them. I'd bet money Lisa's trying to decide if you'll ever wake up and realize being together involves more than just fun and games, especially if she's thinking long term. You know what I mean about long-term?"

Rob nodded. "Yeah, I guess so. But it's too late now. I can feel it. If she hasn't called in two weeks, she's not going to. Not until she gets up the nerve to tell me it's over for good."

"You don't know that."

"Yes I do."

"No, you don't. But what have *you* done the past two weeks to help her decide? You've done nothing but leave one message on her machine. What do you think that's telling her? It's telling her you don't care enough to pursue her."

"She said she didn't want to talk to me, she wanted the time alone."

"Bullshit. She wants you to come after her, to show her you really want her, and not just for sex and smartass. She's waiting for you to decide if you really want her for the long haul. She's waiting for you to *do* something, you dope."

"Do what? What can I do?"

"What can you do? Are you serious? Send her flowers, call her and tell her how much you miss her. And leave that message if she doesn't answer the phone. Camp out on her door step. Invite her out to talk. Tell her you love her, stupid."

Paul punched Rob in the arm. "Tell her and *show* her how much you love her."

7:35 PM

Jillian opened her door and waited for her friends to hike up the twenty-one stairs to her floor.

She spent the forty-five minutes between hanging up with Liz and her friends' arrival vacuuming her already clean rugs, washing and polishing her already spotless bathroom fixtures, and setting dishes, glasses, and chopsticks on the burled oak coffee table she rescued from the trash last year and spent an entire weekend restoring to beauty. It rested in front of the sofa which was nestled in the large window bay.

The girls bounced up the stairs whispering to each other, then hurried down the short hall when they noticed her waiting for them.

"Jilli's got a boyfriend, Jilli's got a boyfriend," Jenna sang as she pranced through the door and hung her jacket on a peg. "Liz and I discussed it on the way over and we decided we really don't want to know anything about him. We'd rather watch a movie."

Liz nodded her agreement as she set the bag full of aromatic Thai food on the bar separating the kitchen from the rest of the studio.

"Oh, well, if you really don't want to hear about him…"

Just then, the CD Jillian started earlier played the last chords of *I Believe In You And Me* and restarted with *Always and Forever*. The dreamy expression returned as her eyes slowly closed, and she began swaying slightly with the music, her thoughts suddenly far from friends and food.

Liz and Jenna exchanged astonished stares. Jillian was the practical one, not usually given to overly romantic flights of fancy. They watched her for a minute, grinning and pointing, mouthing silent questions and replies to each other.

"Okay," Jenna said, no longer able to keep silent. "Enough of this game. Anyone who can make her do *that* I *have* to hear about."

7:45 PM

Halfway through their third beer, the Lisa situation was pretty much talked-out, so they sat quietly for a few minutes, each lost in his own thoughts before Paul glanced at his watch, ready to split.

Man, I hate leaving him here like this, but I really want to get home and call Jillian. Why the hell is he just sitting there? I'd have been out of here long ago looking for her. It's like he really doesn't think he can do anything. But how can he not at least try?

He was about to tell Rob it was time to go when he noticed two women walk in. The shorter one waved their way as they approached the table.

"Hi Rob. Sorry we're late. We took the train and something happened and we sat there, stopped, for almost twenty minutes."

She leaned over to give Rob a short kiss. Perplexed, Paul's glare demanded to know what was going on.

"Hey, Debbie." He turned to the other girl. "You must be Marianne." When she nodded, he said, "Hi, I'm Rob and this is Paul."

"Pleased to meet you both." Forcing the glare from his face, Paul rose to shake their hands.

Introductions completed, Debbie said, "Pardon us for a minute. We need to find the little girls room."

The glare returned and as soon as the girls were out of earshot, he blasted Rob. "What is this? Did you set me up or something and not bother to ask me?"

"Take it easy, man. Debbie said her friend was staying with her for a few days and asked if I could find her a date for the evening. She wasn't even sure Marianne would want to come out, so I didn't say anything in case she didn't show. I didn't want to get your hopes up, you know?"

"Get my hopes up? Are you kidding? What if I already had a date tonight?"

"But you don't."

"But *you* didn't know that. Besides, I'm not interested in a date tonight. I want to go home and call Jillian."

"Who?"

"Jillian. Focus, Rob. The girl from the coffee shop. The girl I've been talking about all day. And who's Debbie?"

"I met her yesterday at the gym. If you think she looks good now, you should see her in spandex."

Paul's head moved slowly from side to side, unbelieving.

"And what about Lisa? You just finished telling me how much you love her, how much you miss her, how you never think of other girls, and now you're ready to date this Debbie? Was that a joke? What if she sees you with her?"

"Hey, she's the one who wanted to take a break. Am I supposed to sit around and wait for her to make up her mind?"

"I don't believe this. Did you hear *anything* I said before? I told you to go after her, to convince her she wants you back. Do you think going out with someone else will accomplish that?"

"I don't know."

"Man, I really don't want to spend the night with…oh crap, here they come."

Rob glanced over his shoulder as girls emerged from the ladies room.

"Come on, man, be a friend. Be nice to her for a few hours so me and Debbie can get to know each other. I'll owe you one."

"A big one."

"A big one what?" Debbie asked.

Paul raised his hand and wiggled his little finger. "We were discussing Rob's desire to find a way to overcome his, ah, shortcoming."

7:55 PM

Laughter rang through the room. Jillian was on the sofa between Liz and Jenna. The table in front of them was littered with dishes, chopsticks, open take-out containers, and water bottles.

"I'm telling you, he was so goofy and cute and he was trying so hard, but I really thought it was some kind of totally bad pick-up thing, you know?"

Liz and Jenna nodded.

"So my evil twin took over and I was *so* mean to him. But then, when I saw his face as I passed him, I started thinking maybe it wasn't just a line. So I let him know where I'd be for lunch and he, umm, he looked like he'd won the lottery."

"The lottery?" Jenna asked.

"Uh-huh, all happy and excited. I spent all morning debating if I should really go, you know. I mean, he could have been a good actor or some weirdo, but I went."

Jillian's eyes closed as she smiled again.

Liz grinned. "Jeez, she's at it again." She poked Jillian's arm. "Come on girl, snap out of it."

Jillian made a face but resumed her recitation. She reported everything that happened at lunch. Her friends interrupted frequently with questions, for clarifications, and to laugh out loud. They analyzed every sentence, every word, every inflection, gesture, raised eyebrow, scratched ear, and twitch of the lunchtime conversation. They chewed it all up and spit out every possible shade of meaning of every minute point until there was simply nothing left to scrutinize.

"So how ugly is he?" Liz asked.

"What do you mean?"

"Well, so far, we've heard how goofy he was and then how charming he was and blah, blah, blah, but not a word about how he looks. What's the matter with him?"

"I already told you he was cute."

"No you didn't," Jenna said. "You said he *acted* goofy and cute."

"Well my mistake. I'll tell you..." Jillian took several long sips from her water bottle before checking the various containers to see what morsels might remain. Then she said, "You know, I really should go pee. I'll be back in a minute."

Liz grabbed her left arm. "You're going nowhere." She motioned for Jenna to hold her right.

"Yeah," Jenna said. "Pee your pants if you have to but you're not getting up until we know what he looks like."

Jillian pretended to struggle for a few seconds, until all three were laughing again.

"He is sooo cute. He's about five-ten, has brown hair, cut short, and these incredible brown eyes that seemed to see right inside me. He's thin, but not skinny and has a really nice smile with a dimple right here." Jillian pointed to a spot on her left cheek a little less than an inch away from the corner of her mouth. "Satisfied?"

"He sounds really great," Jenna told her. "Is he cuter than Aiden?"

Jillian flinched as Liz glared at Jenna, who just shrugged.

"I'm sorry. It's been so long I didn't think his name was still verboten."

"Well, it is," Liz barked. "And you should..."

Jillian laid a hand on her friend's arm. "It's okay, Liz, it just caught me off-guard." But her dreamy smile had vanished. She turned to Jenna.

"Neither one is cuter, really. They're too different to compare like that. Paul has a kind of Mediterranean look while…the other one had that blond, Nordic thing going."

Jenna nodded. "I remember."

"But when's he supposed to call?" Liz asked, to change the subject.

"I don't know," Jillian replied, as her smile returned. "I was hoping he'd call tonight. He said he would, but it's after eight already so maybe not."

"Could be he had to work late." Jenna said.

"Or had a date," Liz teased.

"Maybe." Jillian shrugged. "I'm not worrying about it. If he calls, he calls. If he doesn't, he doesn't." She jumped up from the sofa and headed for the television. "Let's watch a movie."

10:05 PM

"The guy had been knocking over jewelry stores for six months," Marianne said, her eyes on Paul but aware of Rob and Debbie playing darts behind him, at the end of the room. "Mostly smash and grab, although once he showed a knife when a store manager started to chase after him. Anyway, we're taking lunch, and my partner's sitting in the car while I run in for some stuff I needed. I'm almost at the drugstore when an alarm goes off and this guy comes barrel-assing out of the jewelry store, knocks down two teenagers, and flies off away from me. I yell, 'Stop, police' and take off after him. He was fast, but I was faster.

"So I chase the guy through the mall and into the parking garage. I'm only about twenty feet behind him and closing when he decides since he can't outrun me, he's gonna whoop me. He stopped so abruptly my momentum carried me right in front of him before I could stop, too. Now he figures to get in a quick punch before I can set myself, so he throws a roundhouse."

She paused half-a-second, giving her head a quick shake. "I reacted without thinking, you know? I've had some martial arts training and it just kicked in. I grabbed the arm and used the momentum to pull him forward and off his feet as I twisted. But somehow, as he's flying by me, he reaches out, grabs at me with his free hand and suddenly the front of my shirt is ripped open and one side of my bra is up here."

She ran a finger across her chest from the opening in her v-neck, across the top of her left breast, to her armpit. "Now, the guy is down, but scrambling to get back on his feet, so I pull my weapon and yell 'Freeze asshole.' Well, he looks up, sees the gun, then sees my boob waving in the breeze, and his eyes kind of bug out and start flitting back and forth from one to the other. I swear, despite the adrenaline and being pissed and everything, I almost started laughing."

Paul grinned, but said nothing, not wanting to interrupt her.

"Well, by this time, there's about a dozen civilians watching, so I yell at them to stay back, then order the guy face down on the ground. Holding the gun on him with one hand, I get the cuffs on him with the other. Now I can holster the gun, get myself back into the bra and pull my shirt closed, even though most of the buttons were gone. And as I'm doing that, the civilians start applauding."

Paul was laughing, loving both the story and the easy way in which she was telling it.

"Sure, laugh at the poor cop's embarrassment," Marianne said. "But you haven't heard the best part yet.

"When I ordered him to get on the ground and he was going back and forth between the gun and my boob, you know what the jerk said to me? He said 'Man, I wish I had a camera. Nobody's ever gonna believe this in the joint.'"

By now Paul was howling and it took him a minute to get his voice back. "You're an amazing woman, Mare." He started chuckling again. "I'm sorry, but I can't get the picture of you and the gun and the guy looking at you out of my head. Somebody should put that scene in a movie."

That drew a laugh from Marianne. "Well if you ever write the script, remember to give me credit."

She swallowed some of her beer. "The strange thing was, even though it was a little embarrassing while it was happening, it wasn't all that big a deal until I started writing the arrest report. Then I had to think about whether to put those details in. Technically, I'm supposed to, but it was too much to think of the report being copied and passed around for some cheap chuckles, so I said the guy tore my shirt and left it at that."

"And nobody found out?"

"Oh, they found out. When the uniforms arrived, they took statements from the civilians who witnessed the arrest. I took a pile of crap from the guys for almost a week. But it was worth it. Catching the guy was a real coup. They couldn't give me a promotion so soon after the last one, but they did ask me if I'd be interested in a special two week training seminar in Boston. I hadn't seen Debbie in almost a year since she took the job here and these seminars are like paid vacations, so I jumped at it."

She paused to take another sip from her beer.

"Hey, ummm...I want to thank you for being so nice tonight. It was obvious you didn't know you'd been set up to baby-sit. Yet you stayed and listened to my stories and had some pretty good ones of your own. You even made me laugh and I really appreciate it."

Paul started to protest. But she cut him off.

"Stop, please. You don't make detective at my tender age without being able to read people and situations. So who is she?"

"Who is who?"

Doing her best to sound like a TV cop, she said, "Hey, I'm asking the questions here. Who's the girl you've been thinking about all night while you've been paying attention to me?"

Paul's grin told her she'd been on target. "Was it that obvious?" he asked. "I'm sorry."

Marianne waved off his apology. "It wasn't obvious at all. Just an educated guess. So, who is she?"

"You really are good at your job, aren't you? I'll have to remember never to commit any crimes in Seattle. Her name is Jillian. I met her this morning in a coffee shop."

"A coffee shop? Good coffee? You know how we cops like our coffee."

"The best in Boston. It's across the common on Tremont Street. Coffey's Coffee."

"You're kidding about the name, right?"

"Nope. It's been in the same location forever. Way before either of us were born. If you go there, try the blueberry muffins."

"I will. Thanks. Now tell me about Jillian."

Paul spent the next ten minutes relating the story of how he and Jillian met, his pursuing her out of the coffee shop, and their lunch date.

When he was done, Marianne's hand was at her cheek, her face and eyes soft with emotion.

"What a great story," she said. "What a great way to meet. So when's the first date?"

"I don't know."

"You don't know?"

"Well, I'd planned to call her when I got home tonight, but, ahh, something came up."

"You mean..."

She abruptly stood up and waved. "Yo! Debbie, Rob, over here now."

"Mare, you don't have to..."

"Oh yes I do."

Hearing the tone of her voice, Rob and Debbie hurried back to the table.

"What's wrong?" Rob asked. "Did he..."

Marianne cut him off with a glare. "You are in *big* trouble, pal."

She turned to Debbie.

"Deb, we have to go. Paul has something important to do and it can't wait any longer."

She turned to Paul, leaned in, and kissed him on the cheek.

"Thank you again." She said. "You were very sweet. Jillian is a lucky girl, even if she doesn't know it yet."

"Jillian? Who's Jillian?" Debbie asked as Paul said goodbye and headed for the door.

"I'll tell you later." Marianne turned back to Rob. "As for you…"

10:45 PM

The windows of Paul's third floor condo on the corner of Charlesgate East and Boylston Street looked out across the busy intersection onto the north end of the Fens, a beautiful, peaceful park of ponds, flower beds, and manicured lawns as well as a running track, basketball court, and a baseball field.

He let himself in, dropped his coat on a chair, and headed for the bathroom.

Man, Marianne was something else. Who knew cops could be so hot? And funny. I really had a good time with her tonight…and she seemed to like me…maybe I shouldn't have said anything about Jillian…but she knew…damn she's a good cop. And there is something about Jillian…

Three minutes later, his mind was still racing as he walked back into the living room.

…but there's no way I'm moving to Seattle or she's staying in Boston, so forget about her and call Jillian.

He flipped open his wallet, retrieved a small slip of paper, and held it before him with reverence. On it was written *the number*.

A glance at the clock as he fished his phone from his pocket told him it was 10:50.

Is it too late to call?

He sat on the edge of the recliner, next to the table that held a small lamp. After switching on the light, he studied the clock again for half a minute.

Geez, why am I so nervous?

He jumped up and grabbed a beer from the fridge. After a long pull, he checked the clock yet again as he paced in front of the sink.

Come on, get on with it. She's just a girl. But what if she's sleeping? Will she be upset if I wake her? Maybe I should wait and call her in the morning. Maybe…

He shook his head. "What is wrong with me? This girl's got me so freakin' off-balance I can't think straight. Is this some cosmic joke or something? We've both been going to the coffee shop for years and now, suddenly, there she is, right in front of me, stealing my line. I wouldn't even have noticed her if she hadn't…maybe it *is* fate or something. Damn! She even has me talking to myself!"

He shook his head to clear it.

"Call. Just call her before it gets any later."

His thumb started punching numbers.

10:55 PM

Less than 350 yards away, Jillian was saying goodbye to her friends. Her second floor apartment at 1171 Boylston Street was across the Fens from Paul's condo.

"Don't worry," Jenna said as she and Liz donned their jackets. "He'll call tomorrow for sure."

Liz agreed. "For sure. He obviously likes you."

Jillian repeated her earlier contention. "If he calls, he calls. I really don't care one way or the other."

Liz chuckled. "Sure you don't. That's why we spent the past four hours talking about him. 'Cause you don't care one way or the other. HAH! You are so in denial girl. Do you even remember what movie we were watching? This guy has you bad, girl, really bad."

"Bad," Jenna mimicked, laughing. "*Really bad.*"

Liz turned the knob and opened the door, but before she could move, the phone began to ring. Jillian made no move to answer it.

"What are you waiting for?" Liz asked. "Go get it. It's probably him."

Jillian stood her ground.

"Well if you won't answer it, I will."

Liz started toward the phone on the table but Jillian rushed by her and grabbed the receiver.

"Don't care one way or the other my ass," Liz muttered, heading back to the door.

Jillian pressed the talk button and said, "Hello?"

"Hi, it's Paul. Please tell me it's not too late to call."

Jillian's face lit up. She pointed to the phone and mouthed 'it's him', then waved goodbye to the girls as they closed the door on their way out.

"Hi. It's not too late. Two of my friends just left."

"Sorry to call so late. I was with Rob. Remember him from the coffee shop this morning? I got tied up with him after work and just walked in a few minutes ago. I'm glad you're still awake."

"And I'm glad you called. Did the manuscript dry out?"

"Sure. After you left, I took it to the Laundromat and put the wet pages in the dryer."

"You did not!"

"No, not really. But it sounded good, didn't it?"

Jillian laughed and realized she'd been laughing a lot since lunch today.

"Are you like this all the time?"

"Like what?"

"Funny."

Paul thought for a few seconds. "I try. I like to laugh, and I like to make other people laugh. Especially people I like."

"Oh, so you're saying you like me?"

"Yes, I'd definitely say I like you. The big question though, the one on which the future of this whole conversation rests is..." He paused for effect. "...do you like Italian food?"

"It's my favorite."

"Whew. Okay. Everything's fine now. I was really worried. I could never date a woman who didn't like Italian food."

"Really?"

"Absolutely. You see, Italian food is more than just food. It not only nourishes the body, it nourishes the soul. It makes your tonsils dance and your heart sing. It fills your stomach, yes, but it also fills you with a sense of peace and contentment. Especially when accompanied by a couple of bottles of Chianti."

Jillian was laughing again. "My, my. Is it only food, or are you this passionate about everything?"

Paul knew what he would have liked to say, but instead offered, "I think I'll let you discover that for yourself, a little at a time. So, tell me about your friends."

Jillian's eyebrows arched at the unexpected question. "You want to hear about my friends?"

"Of course. If they're over there this late on a work night, I'm guessing they're a big part of your life and someday I hope to meet them, so why not get to know a little about them now. Unless you'd rather not talk about them."

Someday I hope to meet them? Someday I hope to meet them! Does he know what he just said? Is he actually thinking that far ahead? How could he be? We just met.

Jillian thought she should be feeling funny about his self-assurance, his presumption he would be around long enough to meet her friends. Instead it made her feel warm inside, peaceful and happy.

What is it about this guy that keeps making me feel so opposite to what I should be feeling?

"So you're serious? You really want me to tell you about Liz and Jenna?"

"Of course. I wouldn't have asked otherwise. How did you meet them?"

"Okay then," she said, reclining on the sofa. "I hope you're sitting down.

"Liz is Elizabeth Farrell. She's my oldest friend. We met in the third grade and hated each other until half-way through the fourth grade. Then this pint-sized terror named Eddie Lepage started picking on both of us, so we called a temporary truce so we could figure out a way to get back at him. We schemed for almost a week before deciding on a plan. Are you bored yet?"

"Not at all. I love revenge stories."

"I see. Well, one day during recess, I started taunting Eddie until he started to chase me. I ran halfway around the yard, then around the back of the school where Liz was waiting. As soon as he turned the corner, she jumped out and screamed at the top of lungs, which didn't bother Eddie at all, but did get him to stop. That's when she threw a glass of water at the front of his pants, soaking them.

"The two of us ran back out to the yard where all the other kids were playing. When Eddie came around the corner to get us, we started laughing and pointing, telling everyone Liz scared him so much he peed in his pants."

She could hear Paul chuckling softly.

"Eddie's denials were long and loud but to no avail. From that day, until his family moved away the following year, he was known as Eddie LePee."

She heard his chuckles become laughs. "Eddie LePee! That's a riot. I bet his folks moved to save him from the humiliation."

Jillian matched his laugh. "Maybe so. Anyway, with our mission accomplished, we found we had a lot in common and since neither of us could remember why we hated each other, we decided to be friends, instead. That was eighteen years ago."

"Whoa…eighteen years! My oldest friend is Rob and I met him in high school. What about the other one? What's her name?"

"Jenna. Jennafer Williams. Liz and I met her freshman year in college."

"Which school?"

"Boston University."

"Oh! Good school. I went to Tufts."

"That's a pretty good school, too."

"It was close to home. And I got a discount because I lived in Medford. Hmmm…I wonder if they still do that? Anyway, Jenna?"

"She was the third girl in a triple dorm room."

"Holy crap! Three girls in one room? With one bathroom?"

"You have no idea! But anyway, we'd all won scholarships…or rather, the school gave Liz and I scholarships. Jenna got hers by winning some national science contest."

"Wow, she must be pretty smart."

"She sure is. But she's such a goofball you'd never know it outside the lab where she works."

Jillian found herself telling him things about Liz and Jenna, what they did, what they liked, things she might have expected to tell a new girlfriend, but not some guy she just met.

"Man, I wish I had a friend like Liz. You two sound more like sisters than friends."

"I guess we are, really."

"At our age, it's hard to imagine having had a best friend for eighteen years. And speaking of age, if I've done my math correctly, you would be 25?"

"Your math is correct," she replied. "Now, to get your age, how much should I add or subtract from mine?"

"You should add three."

"Twenty-eight! You're twenty-eight? I never would have guessed. I thought you were my age, or younger."

"It's my boyish good looks. They're a curse, really. But it's true, I'm only two years away from the big three-oh. Can Social Security be far behind?"

As the conversation continued, each offered tidbits of information, about work, friends, likes, dislikes; the things two people usually share at the beginning of a new relationship.

Paul was charming, constantly making her laugh. Both were so caught up in the dialogue, time flew by.

When Jillian thought to check, she was shocked to see it was well after midnight.

Didn't the phone just ring a few minutes ago?

"You know I was so embarrassed at lunch today, I just wanted to go hide somewhere."

"I remember," he said, chuckling, "but there was no reason to be embarrassed. You were nervous. So was I. Heck, if you hadn't knocked it over, I probably would have. Actually, I was more relieved than anything else."

"Relieved?"

"Sure. After all, I made such a fool of myself this morning, and I had this vision of you as, you know, so cool and calm and detached. I had no idea what to say or do to impress you. I just knew I had to. And when the coffee went flying, and you got all flustered...well, I knew we were okay. I knew you'd laugh at my 'most beautiful' joke and I knew we'd hit it off."

"You knew that? How?"

"I'm not sure. I guess because if you really were the cold, aloof type, you wouldn't have reacted that way to the spill. And to tell the truth, by then I had a feeling, but it was probably more hoping than knowing how you'd react to the joke."

Jillian found herself nodding, pleased that his answers were so honest and unguarded.

"Since we're doing *True Confessions* here, I had planned to come in all cold and aloof, what you were expecting, just to test you. I was really afraid you were playing me and I didn't want any part of it, if that's what it was. Knocking over the coffee and you being so nice about it sort of reset my attitude I think."

"Well I'm very glad it did."

"Me too."

Her eyes flicked to the clock again. "You realize it's way after midnight, and I have to get up for work in the morning."

Paul sighed. "I know. So do I. I just don't want to let go of your voice…"

That warm, comfortable feeling flowed through her again.

"…but I will. So now the moment of truth has arrived. Would you like to go out with me Friday night?"

"No."

There was dead silence on the phone line. Paul's face had drained to a ghostly white. Was she really turning him down?

"I'd *like* to go out with you tomorrow night but I can't because I have yoga class and then dinner plans with some friends. So I guess I'll have to hold out until Friday."

It took a moment for Paul to recover his voice and for the color to return to his face.

"You know you almost gave me a heart attack. Was that…"

"Payback for the jolt this afternoon? Yes it was." Jillian laughed. "Still want to go out with me?"

Paul was laughing now as well. "Oh yes. I have a feeling getting to know you will be the most interesting thing I'll ever do."

THURSDAY, MAY 6

7:35 AM

Paul and Rob stood near the window of the coffee shop sipping their morning caffeine as they scanned the sidewalk.

"I'm glad to hear it, man." Paul's eyes never paused as they swept back-and-forth.

His friend nodded. "It was weird. Debbie was so nice, you know? She really has her act together, unlike some of us. We seemed to hit it off and all, but the more I got to know her, and the more I realized how great she was, the more I missed Lisa. Even worse, though, is that I'm pretty sure Debbie would have invited me home if I'd shown even the slightest interest. But I knew it would have felt like I was cheating on Lisa. Besides, I think Marianne might have grabbed her gun and shot me had I dared set foot inside Debbie's apartment."

"I'm guessing you two didn't get along well after I left?"

"Man, she started in on me as soon as you were out the door. She all but tore me a new one because I dragged you there rather than let you get home to call coffee girl. She went on and on and on about it. Whatever you told her made one hell of an impression."

"I told her about meeting Jillian and what happened at lunch, the same things I told you."

"Well, she obviously read more into it than I did, because she reamed me good."

Paul laughed. He could picture Marianne berating Rob. "In your defense, you *were* a little preoccupied with your own problems with Lisa."

"Maybe so, but she certainly liked you. When I said goodbye to them at the subway, I got the impression they'd be talking about you and coffee girl all night."

"Jillian."

"What?"

"Jillian. Her name is Jillian, not coffee girl."

"Oooo, touchy, touchy. Jillian it is then, but I don't think she's coming."

Paul glanced at his watch and sighed. It was quarter to eight. He really wanted to see her again this morning.

Last night, after saying goodbye, he tried to sleep but found he could not get her off his mind. Her face, her voice, the way she looked from behind as he chased after her that morning, it all kept playing back, over and over. He guessed he finally fell asleep sometime after two, and when his alarm clock buzzed at 6:30, his first thought was of her and how she might look in the morning.

"Let's give it few more minutes. So what are you going to do about Lisa?"

"Well, last night I burned a CD with a bunch of songs to tell her I'm sorry, and I miss her, and all. I was up until almost two-thirty figuring out what to put on it. And I'm sending flowers to her at work this morning and including the CD and a letter I wrote last night."

"A letter? You wrote a letter?"

"Well, I do have some skills in that area."

"What did you write?"

"None of your business."

Paul turned from the window to stare at his friend. "You know this may be your last chance."

He continued to stare until Rob relented.

"I basically told her I was an idiot, that I've been thinking about all the things I did wrong, or didn't do, or should have done, that I miss her a lot, and all the things I miss about her, and that I really hope she'll give me one more chance."

"That's it? Didn't you forget something important?"

"No, I didn't forget," Rob said with a pained expression. "I told her how much I love her and all that."

Paul nodded. "Good. I hope it works, I really do. I like you two together. You fit. So, when are you sending them?"

"I figured I'd call as soon as we get to work. There's a florist over on Newbury Street that opens at eight. I'll have them stop by the office first to show me the arrangement and so I can attach the CD and note."

"Very nice plan," Paul said, formulating one of his own.

"Come on, man. She's not coming. If we don't get our asses in gear, we'll be late for work."

Paul took a last peek at the sidewalk.

"Maybe she went in early or didn't want coffee today," Rob offered.

Paul sighed again, nodded, and followed his friend out the door.

As they crossed West Street on the way to the office, Rob asked, "So what's up with you and Jillian? Did she put a spell on you or something?"

"I think so. I don't know what it is. I mean I've only talked to her three times, but I feel like I've known her forever. Remember when you and Lisa first hooked up? Remember how you couldn't think or talk about anything else?

"Well..."

"Don't even try to deny it. Nobody could stand you for the first month."

"What do you mean?"

"Rob, it was bad enough all you did at work was talk about how great she was, and that she was all you talked about on those suddenly rare occasions after work when you found time for your friends, but man, once you even brought her to the poker game. Even *she* thought you were nuts that time."

"No way. She..."

"She left after twenty minutes. Why the hell would she want to hang out with five guys drinking and playing cards? And then, after you spent fifteen minutes in the hall saying goodbye, you came back in and spent the next three hours telling us how much you missed her."

"Okay, okay, so what's your point?"

Paul came to an abrupt halt, grabbed his friend's arm, and turned to face him. With an almost forlorn look on his face, he said, "I think I have it worse than that."

10:10 AM

The eight foot square that defined Jillian's workspace at Metro Magazine was lined with file cabinets, bookcases, a drafting table, her desk, and a long table that held her computer and the other state-of-the-art electronics a graphic designer uses.

It was one of eighteen work, storage, and utility spaces that filled the cavernous graphic arts room, along with an office for the Design Manager, and a break room that doubled as a meeting room. Jillian's desk and computer were arranged to face away from the goings on, allowing her to focus on her work.

Her reputation for concentration was legendary in the workgroup, so it was no surprise she didn't hear the deliveryman call her name.

After the second call, several heads popped up and the occupant of the space nearest the door indicated where Jillian could be found. Half-a-dozen people, including Shandra and Marie, Jillian's closest work friends, followed him down the aisle.

"Jillian Marshall?"

"Yes?" She didn't look up from her computer screen.

He placed the vase in the center of her desk and held out a clipboard and pen. "Sign here please."

Jillian turned, saw the flowers, then the clipboard, then the deliveryman. "Those are for me?

"If you're Jillian Marshall they are. Sign on line two please."

Jillian took the clipboard, signed and asked, "Who are they from?"

"As if you didn't know, girl," said Shandra.

"There's a card." He plucked it from the holder, handed it to her as he retrieved the clipboard, and said "Enjoy the flowers" as he turned to leave.

The crowd in the aisle grew to an even dozen, including her boss, Cathy, who had been lured from her office by the commotion. Comments and questions were coming to Jillian from all sides.

"Open the card."

"Nice flowers."

"No one ever sends me flowers like that."

"What's his name, Jill?"

Finally, Shandra said, "Come on girl. Don't keep us all in suspense. Open the card."

Jillian surveyed the expectant faces, then slid the card from the envelope, read it, and smiled, covering her mouth as she did so.

Marie couldn't stand the suspense. "Well what does it say?"

"I miss your voice," Jillian replied softly.

"That's all?" asked Shandra.

"That's enough. That's perfect."

Reaction among the crowd ranged from rolling eyes to shaking heads as everyone but Shandra and Marie dispersed.

"They're from coffee guy, right?" Marie asked.

Jillian nodded.

"I knew it. You saw him last night, didn't you? You two hooked up late and now he's sending you flowers. You're bad, girl."

Jillian tried to feign offense but was too happy to pull it off. "No. I swear. I was with Liz and Jenna until almost eleven. He called as they were leaving and we talked for about an hour. That's all."

Clearly, the two did not believe her.

"No man ever sent me flowers just for talking to him," Shandra said.

Implication filled Marie's accusing gaze. "Me neither. Just what kind of talking did you two do last night?"

"I told you. It was all completely innocent. Now go away, I have work to do."

Shandra and Marie flung skeptical looks at their friend before they retreated down the aisle, whispering and glancing back at Jillian, who returned to her computer.

She stared at the screen for a few seconds, then turned and reached for the flowers.

Callas. He sent me Calla lilies. How could he know?

She was all smiles and dreamy looks as she first studied the vase of creamy white flowers and then the card on which he wrote the note and his work number. She picked up the phone and dialed.

"Paul DiLorenzo."

"Thank you for the flowers, Paul. They're lovely."

"What?"

"Thank you for the flowers. They're lovely."

"Who is this?"

"Jerk," she said, laughing.

"I'm glad you liked them. I thought they might be a bit much since we've only talked a few times, but I really was missing your voice, especially since you didn't show up this morning. I thought the flowers might be a good way to get you to call."

"Show up?"

"At the coffee shop."

"Oh! It never occurred to me to tell you. It was Shandra's turn to get the coffee this morning. Three of us take turns. I hope you didn't wait too long."

"Nah, just long enough to almost be late for work.

"Poor guy."

"But it's okay now that I've heard your voice. Any thoughts on where we should go and what we should do tomorrow?"

"Well, I am partial to food. After that, surprise me."

"Surprise you, eh? Any limitations?"

"Nothing illegal."

"Shucks."

"Or immoral."

"Damn. You're killing all my good ideas."

Jillian laughed again. It was getting to be a habit whenever she talked to him.

"Poor baby. I guess you'll have to think a little harder."

"Now I like the sound of that."

"Bye Paul."

"How about lunch today?"

"Can't. I already have a date..." Jillian paused for a few seconds, grinning as she listened to the silence, "...with my boss and three other people from the department. The publisher wants to do a special issue next week and wants some design suggestions."

"Hmmm. I think I owe you one for that. Call me when you get home tonight?"

"It'll be very late. You might be sleeping."

"Doesn't matter. I can't think of a better way to wake up than to the sound of your voice."

10:25 AM

A happy Paul hung up the phone, grinned at Rob and said, "My flowers worked."

"I could tell." Rob was pleased for his friend, but anxious about his own delivery.

The florist's driver stopped by forty-five minutes earlier to pick up the note and CD. It cost him an extra forty dollars, twenty for the pick-up and twenty as a tip to the driver to ensure he placed everything right in Lisa's hands, but he didn't care. It would be worth every penny when the phone rang.

Rob stared at the pages on his desk, hoping nobody noticed he wasn't really doing anything.

Why did I put that song first? Maybe I should have put our song first? What if she doesn't like the mix...or doesn't get what I was trying to say...or doesn't even listen to it! Damn! What if she doesn't even read the letter! No, she'll read it. But will it work? Will she want me again? What am I going to do if she doesn't? Hell, what am I going to do if she does? I'll change...I'll have to change...I can do it...

"Earth to Rob." Tom upped the volume when Rob didn't answer.

"What? What's wrong?"

"That's what I'd like to know. Priya just asked you a question. Twice. What's wrong with you today?"

"I, ah..."

"He's waiting for a phone call," Paul said. "About the flowers from before."

"It must be pretty damned important for him to be that distracted," Tom said. "When is this call due?"

"We're not really sure. It's..."

Interrupting, Rob said, "Just tell them."

So he did. Paul explained about the break, about Rob's feelings about it, and about his last ditch effort to win her back.

"Geez, Rob," Tom said, "no offense, but you've always been such a player, it's hard to imagine you this hung up on one girl. I mean, I know you've been talking about her for months now, but I never figured...well...I never imagined you getting serious about anyone."

"You're not the only one. I hope this works. If it doesn't, I don't know what I'll do. I never realized how hung up on her I was and if she doesn't..." He didn't finish the thought, not wanting to make real with words the thought of never seeing her again.

Priya stood and walked over to perch on the corner of Rob's desk. "Look, if a guy sent me what you sent to her, and I had any feelings for him at all, well, he'd be one lucky boy tonight."

Rob smiled. "So you think I have a chance?" He could see the compassion in her eyes.

"Rob, I can't predict what she'll do, but I can say she'd be a fool if she didn't give you another chance."

Paul and Tom voiced their agreement.

"Women are funny, Rob. We like to think we're always logical and reasonable, but the truth is we more often listen to our hearts than our heads when it comes to relationships. We want to know we're wanted, that we're appreciated."

She glanced over at Tom and Paul. "Are you two bozos paying attention? You're not likely to get this kind of lesson again anytime soon."

Turning back to Rob, she continued. "It sounds to me as if you've been taking her for granted. It's not enough to just be there, to go out, get laid, whatever. You have to let her know she's important, the most important person in your life. If you don't, eventually some other guy will.

"When was the last time you sent her flowers, or wrote her a note, or sent her a funny card? We love that stuff. It lets us know you're thinking of us, that you care about us enough to take the time to do something out of the ordinary.

"When was the last time you surprised her with a sexy negligee or a weekend on the Cape or took her to some pretty little Bed & Breakfast? How often did you give her a pat on the butt or a kiss on the top of her head or stroke her cheek as you were walking by her? Not often, I'll bet.

"Stuff like that lets us know you care. You guys seem to think love is all about grand gestures, expensive jewelry, fancy cars, and such. It's not. Sure, those things are nice, but love is really about the little things, the sweet little intimate things we do for each other. Anyone can plan a vacation or buy a necklace once in a while, but only someone who really cares about you does the little, everyday things.

"As for grand gestures, if you really want to show her how much you love her, next time she's sick or drinks too much, sit on the bathroom floor with her, hold her hair back, and comfort her as she pukes her guts out. *That* is real, true love."

Rob sat mute, stunned for the second time in two days.

Could Paul have been right yesterday? Do I really not know anything about women? Listening to her, it sure seems that way. Oh man, this is not good. What if I really did screw up the note or the CD?

"Maybe I should call her."

"No, give her time to call you. Give her time to read the note and listen to the CD, time to think about it all, to figure out what she's feeling. If she's really the kind of girl you and Paul told us about, and she still has feelings for you, she'll call"

"And if she doesn't."

"Then you'll hurt for a while and move on, as I'm sure we've all done a time or two."

The men nodded, remembering those painful times in their past.

"I guess this means you won't be worth two cents today, eh?" Tom asked.

Rob grunted. "I don't know. Give me something mindless to do, something that doesn't require any heavy thinking."

He smiled at Priya. "Thanks. Why is it that women always know the right thing to say?"

"We don't," she told him with a playful grin as she sashayed back to her desk. "It's just that anything sounds good when it comes from a hottie like me."

12:15 PM

The warm spring sun made Paul wish he was walking with Jillian instead of Rob. They were eating sausage sandwiches as they strolled along the sidewalk.

"Did you know Boston Common is the oldest public park in America?" Rob asked. "Dates back to 1634."

"And you know this...why?"

Rob grinned. "Lisa told me once. I guess when you're the function manager, the Ritz makes you learn all that stuff. Did you know the place is fifty acres? And they used to use it for grazing cows?"

"Really?" Paul surveyed the grass and trails. "All I see now are grazing people."

As they ate and walked, Rob casually led Paul onto a path that cut diagonally across the Common to Charles Street. He was re-telling, in greater detail, the story of last night's chastisement by Marianne.

"You have no idea how pissed she was at me," he said. "She even threatened to arrest me if I ever had the poor sense to do that again in her jurisdiction."

Paul's expression made clear he thought Rob crossed the line from mere embellishment to outright fantasy.

"I swear. Those were just about her exact words. As if I would fly out to Seattle to keep you from calling your new honey."

"I'm not sure she qualifies yet as my honey. And to tell the truth, I actually had a pretty good time last night. I never talked with a cop before. She was pretty interesting. Real smart. And she was funny! You never think of cops as being funny. At least I don't. And let's face it, she was pretty easy on the eyes."

"Hmmm...sounds like coffee girl has some competition."

"No. No way. Marianne was nice but Jillian is something special. Like I said this morning, I have it bad."

Paul looked around and realized where they were. "Where are we going?"

"Hey, it's a nice day. I thought we could take a walk over to the Beacon Street side."

"Wouldn't it have been easier to walk straight across? Or is there some special reason we'll be walking up Charles to Beacon?"

"Reason? Besides this glorious sunshine?"

"Are we planning to turn left when we get to Beacon? Are we hoping to run into anyone we know sitting on her favorite bench eating lunch in the Public Garden?" Paul sighed loudly and shook his head for effect. "Didn't Priya tell you to give her time to make up her mind?"

"I know, I know. But I want to see her. From a distance. I haven't seen her in almost two weeks and I miss her. I miss the sight of her. You know?"

Paul nodded. "Yeah, I know." He felt the same way about Jillian and it was only twenty-four hours since he saw her.

Neither of them spoke now that the real purpose of the walk was revealed. Paul hoped she wouldn't be there. He trusted Priya's judgment and was afraid if Rob saw her, he would not be able to resist approaching her.

As he walked, Rob conjured Lisa's image in his mind; her brilliant smile, sapphire-blue eyes, long blond hair, and delicate, creamy skin; the five-foot ten-inch body that turned heads wherever she went.

"You know she's loaded, right?"

"Well, I suspected with two uber-lawyers for parents, she might be well-off."

"Her parents do okay. But they both come from old money. Lisa has this huge trust fund...I'm talking eight figures before the decimal point...but she never touches it except to write checks to charities and stuff. She lives off her salary. I mean, she could be some ditzy playgirl like ...what's her name...Paris Hilton or something, but that's not what she wants. I mean, she really is so...what's the word you used yesterday...unassuming and straightforward. And she's way more interested in other people than herself." He sighed. "I guess that's why everyone finds her so sweet and charming."

Paul just nodded, knowing his friend was mostly talking to remind himself of all the things he loved about the woman who might soon shatter his heart.

Lisa's favorite bench was about 100 yards ahead, diagonally across from the Bull & Finch Pub, the inspiration for the 1980's television comedy *Cheers*. Set back a few yards from the sidewalk, the bench was still hidden by the shrubs and trees that lined the park.

Paul was on the street side of the sidewalk so his view cleared the trees a split second before Rob's did. He reached for his friend's arm, but it was too late. Ahead, seated on her bench, Lisa was engaged in animated conversation with a man. She was laughing at something he said and reached out to touch his arm. As she made contact, she glanced over his shoulder and noticed Paul and Rob, who came to an abrupt halt. Paul watched Rob as Rob stared at her, shoulders slumped. He looked like he'd been punched. Then, before she had time to react, Rob turned on his heel and walked away. Lisa's gaze shifted to Paul, who sighed, pursed his lips, and with a slight shake of his head, turned and hurried to catch up with his friend.

When he matched pace, he said, "Hey, slow down. It's…"

"Forget it, man." Rob's head was shaking so fast it seemed to be shivering. "I should have known. What an idiot I am. Taking a break. Right."

Rob's cell phone rang. He didn't even glance at the display before turning it off.

"Why didn't you answer it? She might…"

Again Rob cut him off. "Hey, I have no right to complain. She can see anyone she wants. Hell, I was out with what's-her-name last night, wasn't I? Fair is fair. What did you think? She'd sit around like a nun?"

"Well, I hadn't…"

There was no mistaking the despair in his voice as he said, "She's a great girl. And she can have anyone she wants." And then a few silent steps later. "Anyone she wants."

3:30 PM

Jillian and six of the crowd who witnessed the delivery of the flowers that morning sat around the oval table in the break/conference room. One of the perks of working at Metro Magazine was management's laid-back attitude. As long as the work was done on time to meet deadlines and you showed up bright and cheery for meetings, they didn't much care whether you stayed glued to your desk all day or wandered the halls. It made for a relaxed atmosphere where creative people could work and rest as needed.

Pumping Jillian for information about Paul seemed to be the day's sport. Her co-workers alternately sighed, smiled, laughed, and cooed with appreciation as she told them about how they met, the fateful lunch, and of the late night conversation.

Finally, Marie asked the question that was on everyone's lips. "So when's the big date?"

"Friday. Tomorrow."

"Where's he taking you?"

"I don't know." She repeated what she'd told Paul.

Dave Webber, one of the layout guys chuckled. "Now that could be dangerous. Giving a guy carte blanche to surprise you! How bold! And here we all thought you were so quiet and conservative. You know, some men might take that as an invitation to, let's say, some interpersonal relations."

Jillian shook her head. "I'm not worried, Dave. You have to remember, most men aren't like you."

He clutched at his chest. "Argh, you wound me. Although it's true, of course."

Everyone laughed. Dave had a well-deserved reputation. Every new female employee received a warning about him from one of the other females, although many times, the warning came with stories and the kind of praise for his attributes and talents that made the new girl want to sample for herself.

"To tell the truth," Jillian said, "I really don't care if we just grab a burger and sit and talk all night."

Shandra grunted. "You know *that's* not happening, girl. This boy sent you flowers after only talking to you. My money's on a fancy restaurant, some quiet place for drinks, or maybe the theater, then drinks, then a night-full of the hot and nasty. Yes! Jilli's gonna be gettin' *dowwwwn*! Woo!"

Her slow, sultry bump and grind elicited peals of laughter from everyone. Jillian could feel the heat rising in her cheeks.

Time to change the subject, I think.

"Anyone else have plans for tomorrow?"

"Why?" asked Lucinda, one of the copy writers. "Are you inviting us all along on your date?"

That brought more laughter.

"What a great idea!" agreed Marie. "We can all meet him and share all the gory details about our girl here."

Jillian groaned. "That is soooo *not* gonna happen. I knew I should've kept my mouth shut. This is what I get for blabbing to a bunch of mental misfits."

Again laughter rang through the room as everyone congratulated themselves on their collective wit.

Jillian rose to pour herself another cup of coffee.

"Sounds like fun over here." Cathy O'Hara stuck her head full of long, red hair through the door. "Am I missing a party or something?"

Shandra explained as the others drifted off back to their workspaces.

"Oh, that's right. I forgot about you leaving early for lunch yesterday. Okay, now I have to hear the story, too."

Jillian didn't mind the re-telling. Cathy was older, thirty-two and married, and Jillian was interested in her take on the whole thing. She began again as Shandra waved goodbye.

Cathy found her heartstrings tugged as the tale unfolded. When it was over, she sat quietly for a few seconds, then smiled. "Jillian...I have a good feeling about this."

"Really? I mean, I've been having all these feelings that don't seem quite right yet. I hardly know him, but just talking to him makes me all warm and tingly. It sounds stupid, I know. Stereotypically girly, like every guy's impression of how we go all soft and mushy when they deign to talk to us. But I can't help it."

She looked sheepishly at her boss, hoping she wasn't sounding too much like a kid caught up in her first crush.

"Did I ever tell you how Mike and I met?" Cathy asked.

Jillian shook her head.

"I was twenty-three, a year out of college, and had been laid off from my first job when the company merged and downsized. Nobody was hiring, I was almost out of money, and my roommates were hinting that they couldn't carry my share of the expenses for very long. In short, I was miserable.

"I had visions of having to move back to my parents' house in Chicago. I knew lots of people were doing it, but I hated the idea. Just the thought of it made me feel like a loser."

Jillian nodded. As much as she loved her parents, she, too, never wanted to have to go back home to live.

"I'd been making the rounds of employment agencies for almost two weeks without so much as a hint of a position. I was an English major with a minor in business, but evidently everyone and their sisters had also majored in English and seemed to be after the same jobs I was."

She grimaced as she recalled that time in her life.

"It was a Tuesday afternoon and I was waiting my turn at yet another agency. When I filled out the application, I indicated I'd consider any entry-level position in publishing. I was sitting and reading some trashy novel when I heard the woman at the desk call out 'O'Hara, room three twenty-two'

"I stuffed my book in my purse and hurried down the hall. The door was open, so I knocked and walked into the office. This gorgeous guy was sitting behind the desk reading what I thought was my résumé."

* * *

Without glancing up from his reading, the interviewer said, "O'Hara, I'm Marcel Henriquez. This may be your lucky day. We just got a call from Metro Magazine. They want some fresh blood to write ad copy and they pretty much take whoever we send over. Interested?"

"Yes, sir," Cathy said as enthusiastically as she could. "It sounds exactly like what I've been looking for."

At the sound of her voice, his head snapped up and did a double-take.

"Who are you?"

"O'Hara. The woman at the desk called my name and said to come here."

"I don't think so."

"What do you mean? I'm Cathy O'Hara and she told me to come to room three twenty-two."

Before he could respond, a voice at the door said, "I don't think he was expecting anyone so pretty."

She turned to see a man standing there, briefcase in hand. He'd been grinning, but she saw his face change as their eyes met. He seemed suddenly nervous or ill as he stared at her for a few more seconds.

"I'm afraid O'Hara is a pretty common name in Boston. I think he was expecting Mike O'Hara."

"Right, Mike O'Hara," Henriquez said.

Cathy realized what happened. For a split second, she thought her job worries were over. Now it was all being snatched from her.

She could feel her spirit collapsing inward. Her whole body drooped with the weight of her disappointment. All the while, Mike stood there, transfixed, unable to tear his eyes from her.

"You don't have to gloat," she said to him. "You were here first, it's your job."

"No...I'm not...I mean...I was just...look, have we met before? Because I feel like I know you."

Oh great. Could this get any worse? Not only does he take my job, he's hitting on me, too.

"I don't think so." She turned to leave.

"Wait!" He sounded frantic. "It's obvious this job is important to you. Why don't you take the interview? I'm really not all that interested in publishing anyway."

Cathy was surprised, but shook her head. "No, I can't take your job." Again she started to leave.

"Please, I want you to." He turned to the headhunter. "I don't want the job. I already found one. I just came to see if there was anything better. Please give her the interview."

He turned back to find Cathy stopped halfway out the door.

"Why would you do this?"

"I'll make you a deal. This guy is on commission. Time is money to him.

Take the interview. Get the job if you can. I'll wait out in the reception area. When you're done, I'll tell you. Deal?"

He could see the uncertainty in her eyes.

"Please?"

There was something about the way he was looking at her, something about the way he said 'please.' "Okay. But don't you dare leave."

"I promise. I'll go flirt with the receptionist while I'm waiting."

She wasn't sure if he was kidding, but, curiously, she didn't like the idea. She watched him leave, then turned back to Mr. Henriquez, her hand extended.

"Hi. I'm Cathy O'Hara."

Twenty-five minutes later, she was walking on air as she entered the lobby. The interview went well, helped along, she thought, by what happened earlier. She wanted to find Mike and thank him for what he did for her.

She saw him on the other side of the lobby, gazing out the window as he talked on his cell phone. She walked quietly up behind him and sat on a chair so as not to disturb his conversation.

"It doesn't matter," he said, then listened for a bit. "I know I needed the job, but she needed it more, I could tell. And, dad, she was so, so...I don't know. There was something about her. Something special."

What? He lied! He doesn't have a job at all. And he gave this one to me? Why would he do that?

"I know, dad, I know. Look, I promised I'd wait for her. Heck, I'd have waited even if she..."

He'd evidently been interrupted by his father.

"I told you, she's special, dad. I know it. I don't know how I know it but I felt it the first time I saw her."

"Geez, dad, no, not *that* way."

"Yes, she's pretty, but it's not that. I don't know what it is but I have to find out."

"Okay, I will, I promise. But I have to go. She'll be coming out soon. Say hi to mom. Bye"

Mike closed the phone and continued to stare out the window.

Cathy rose, walked up behind him, touched him on the shoulder, and said, "Hi."

Startled, he spun around to face her. She could see on his face he was concerned she may have overheard his conversation.

"I saw you talking on the phone as I came over. Were you talking about me?"

"I, ah..."

"I'm kidding. Why would you be talking about me? It's none of my business. But, as I recall, you owe me an explanation."

They stood, inches apart, each intent on the expressions of the other. Her eyes took in every curve, every facet of his face, the way his nose seemed to be slightly off-center, the way his chin dimpled when he smiled.

"Do you think there are people who are fated to meet?"

"I'm not sure," she replied. "Maybe."

"I know this sounds crazy, but when I walked into that office and you turned toward at me, something happened inside me, like a switch being thrown or, hell, I don't know, but something. It was like my whole life had conspired to lead me to that moment, when I'd meet you for the first time.

"Suddenly, the job wasn't important anymore. The only thing that felt important was that you not go away. What I did, it was all I could think of at the moment to keep you from leaving. Or maybe 'think of' is the wrong phrase. I don't know."

He grinned and she blushed.

"But it worked. You're still here"

"Yes, I guess I am. And I really want to thank you. I needed a job so badly and you...you..."

She smiled at him, and when he smiled back, the warm feeling engulfed her again.

"I don't know how I can ever repay you for..."

"Have coffee with me."

"Coffee?"

"Have coffee with me and give me the chance to convince you to have dinner. After that..."

He let the sentence dangle, but his eyebrows arched to accentuate what he left unspoken. Her eyes searched his and what she saw both frightened and excited her.

She smiled. *Yes. After that...*

* * *

Cathy drained the last of her coffee.

"And the rest, as they say, is history. We've been together almost ten years now, and not a day goes by that I don't love him more than I did the day before. And to think I might have simply walked out that day."

Jillian could see the shiver course through her.

"Jilli, I know Mike and I were meant to be. I don't know if Paul is your Mike, but the signs are certainly there."

She reached over and touched her hand.

"It's okay to be cautious and it's okay to be a little scared. I certainly was. For the whole first year I kept expecting it all to fall apart. But I was being silly, really, because I knew, the night of our first date, when I looked into his eyes after we kissed goodnight that we really were meant to be together. And I think he knew it, too."

She rose to leave. "If he's the one, you'll know soon enough."

"And if he's not?"

Cathy shrugged. "I wouldn't worry too much about that. As I said before, I have a good feeling about you two."

5:45 PM

Priya, Paul, and Rob stepped off the elevator, still arguing about the fonts for their next project. Ultimately, Tom would decide, but he preferred to let the other team members narrow down the choices. Not only did it make his job easier, it forestalled any chance of them starting to feel as if they were not really contributing.

Halfway across the lobby, Rob was making his case when he saw Paul's mouth fall open and felt him grab at his arm but miss. He turned his head and froze so suddenly the other two were two paces past him before they, too, could stop.

Lisa was standing by the front doors. Next to her, looking very uncomfortable, was the guy they saw with her at lunch this afternoon.

A tentative half-smile curled the corners of her lips. She touched the man's arm and they started toward them.

Paul half turned to Rob, then turned back as Lisa approached. Priya never met Lisa but watched with great curiosity, deducing from everyone's actions what was happening.

"Hi, Lisa," Paul said as she neared him.

"Hi, Paul," she replied, her gaze never shifting from Rob.

For his part, Rob stood there, numb, his feet glued to the floor, his eyes flicking back and forth between Lisa and the guy.

Oh, no. Oh crap. What am I going to say? What am I going to do? What if this is it...the big goodbye?

Lisa stopped in front of him, the guy on her right, standing close. "Hello, Rob," she said softly.

Rob stared for a few seconds before croaking out a greeting in reply.

"I received your flowers, the CD, and the letter this morning." Her voice remained low and steady. "We need to talk."

Rob continued to stare, his mouth half-open, his expression reflecting his feeling of impending doom.

"I would have come alone," she continued, "but I thought it would be a good idea if Hector came along, since you saw us together at lunch."

Rob's heart sank deeper into his chest with every word, his face mirroring every twist of his emotional nosedive.

Please...don't introduce us. How cruel are you going to be about this?

"Hector, this is Rob Tello, the guy I've told you about."

"Rob, this is my friend Hector Fernández. He and his partner Frank have been on a break similar to ours."

Rob blinked rapidly, not sure if he really understood what she just said.

Hector and Frank? Hector and Frank? That means…

Lisa saw understanding come into his eyes and smiled. She reached up and touched his cheek with the palm of her hand.

"Hector and I have been helping each other through our recent relationship problems and I needed to talk to him about what you did. That's why we were eating lunch together. Then you showed up and when you didn't answer your cell I knew what you were thinking. I felt terrible, especially since you just sent those sweet gifts. I wanted to come after you, but we took an early lunch because we had an important meeting and couldn't be late. We had to run back to make it on time and didn't get out until after five. On the way back to work I made Hector promise to come with me tonight because, well, I didn't know how you'd react. From the look on your face when you saw us, I wasn't sure if you'd believe me if I told you he and I were just friends."

Thank you, Lord, thank you. She's not seeing another guy.

His face clouded.

But just because she isn't seeing some other guy doesn't mean she still wants to see me.

He managed to mumble, "So, you wanted to talk?"

"Yes," she said, looking around. "But maybe we could go somewhere a little less busy?"

She thanked Hector, gave him a short hug, and told him she would see him tomorrow at work. Rob, remembering Paul and Priya were standing six feet away, glanced over to them.

"Priya and I are going over to DHL for a beer," Paul said with a wicked grin. "You and Lisa want to join us?"

Rob's glare made it unnecessary for him to respond. Nevertheless he said, "No thanks. We're going to…"

"I know. I was kidding."

He gave Rob a nod and a thumbs up as he and Priya turned to leave.

Rob turned back to Lisa and asked, "How about a walk?"

Outside, the evening air was still unseasonably warm. The sidewalk was packed with people hurrying; going home, to late meetings, to bars or restaurants, or simply because that's how they lived their lives.

They worked their way through the throng, crossed the street, dodged the crowds on the opposite sidewalk, and strolled into the Common.

Silently treading the same paths they followed so many times before, they soon found themselves crossing Charles Street and entering the Public Garden.

They walked straight now, heading to the place where they shared their first lunch together. As they crossed the bridge over the Duck Pond, Lisa reached over and took his hand.

Startled, Rob turned his head toward her.

If she wants to hold hands…

Lisa sensed his gaze and smiled. "Did you think I came to say goodbye?"

Lisa liked to get straight to the point, something that made Rob uncomfortable early in their relationship. She generally knew what she wanted and was never shy about telling him, whether it was which movie to watch or in which position she wanted to make love. She was so unlike any other woman Rob ever knew. Perhaps that was why he fell for her and why it hurt so much when she announced the break.

Rob nodded. They were approaching the statue at the main entrance to the Garden.

"I'd been thinking about it," she said. "No, that's not quite true. I pretty much made up my mind, but couldn't find the nerve to tell you."

Rob was dumbfounded.

Made up her mind? Wait. Had been? She said had been!

Out loud, he said, "What, I mean, why? Why did you want to end it?"

"Because I didn't think we were going anywhere. I'm not a kid anymore, but it seemed as if you still were. Well, not a kid, but it was like you still had the frat house mentality. It was fun…lord knows we always had a good time…but it was time to move beyond parties and sex and fun all the time, you know? Time to grow up. I never felt like you understood that. And when I tried to talk to you about it, you always found a way to change the subject."

"I thought it was your friends. I thought they finally convinced you to find someone who, well, who wasn't me."

"My friends! You mean, like, Kiki and Rachel?"

Suddenly, she did not sound happy. She stopped walking, her hand sliding out of his as she turned to face him.

"Do you mean to tell me you think I'm so shallow I'd listen to those two airheads? After five months together, you think that deep down, all I care about is pretty wrapping? Is that really what you think of me?"

"No, not really. No!"

"Then why would you say that?"

"It's just…I've been so miserable, Lisa, and a part of me knew it was my fault you left, or took a break, or whatever. But I couldn't face it. I couldn't admit to myself I'd been such a screw-up that I lost the best person I ever met. In my head, it was easier to blame them."

He seemed to be on the verge of tears, afraid he messed up once again, but his eyes never wavered from hers. She could see he was telling the truth and he could tell she wanted to hear it.

Lisa opened her purse, removed an envelope, unfolded the paper inside, and began to read aloud.

Dearest Lisa,

If you look in a dictionary for the definitions of the words blockhead, bonehead, dolt, donkey, dope, dunce, fool, halfwit, idiot, imbecile, jackass, jerk, nincompoop, nitwit, numskull, simpleton, twerp, and twit, you'll find the first definition for each is Roberto Tello.

I have been all of those things these past five months and because of it, I am on the verge of losing the most amazing woman I am ever likely to know, the only woman I have ever loved with all my heart and all my soul.

I am so sorry it took you leaving me to make me understand what I was losing. And I'm sorry it's taken almost two weeks for me to realize you might be waiting for me to wake up. But I am awake now, and I see how I held you at arms length, how I never told you how I really feel about you and about us, how I let my insecurities and fears keep me mired in a mindset I should have outgrown long ago.

If I live to be a hundred, I'll always regret the pain and frustration I've caused you. I can't change the past, Lisa, but I can try to make the future be whatever we want it to be. All I need is a chance.

I can only pray it is not too late, that you still hold a part of me in your heart, and that you'll give me a second chance to show you how much you mean to me, how much I need you in my life, and how much I love you.

And I do love you, Lisa, more than I can find words to express. And I miss you. I miss the way you look in the morning and the way you wrinkle your nose when you smell fish. I miss seeing you in that long red dress. I miss your hand in mine when I'm walking, and the way your icy toes always find me in the middle of the night. I miss your pantyhose on the shower rod, the notes you leave around my apartment, and the way you whisper dirty jokes in my ear. I miss you so much I ache when I think of you.

Without you there's a huge hole in me and in my life, a void only your smile, your laughter, and your love can fill.

Please call me. Please give us one more chance.

Love always,

Rob

"Did you mean all that?" she asked.

"Every word. Every single word."

He reached for her hand and she let him take it as they resumed walking.

"Lisa, I've never really understood what you see in me. I mean, I'm grateful as all hell, but the fact is, the airheads were right that day. Someone as smart, and funny, and kind, and talented, and decent as you are could have anyone. And I knew that.

"It's always been in the back of my mind haunting me, telling me one day you'd wake up and realize what you were settling for and that would be the end. So I guess I tried to keep it all fun and games. I figured if you were having a great time, you might not notice who you were having it with, at least for a while longer. And when you tried to talk about us, about the future and stuff, I panicked. I never really believed someone like you could want someone like me for the long term. I never let myself believe I was good enough for you because I knew how much better a person you are than me.

"There were times I ached to tell you how I felt, how much I love you, but I didn't. I couldn't. Despite everything, I was scared to death you'd leave me if I ever really tried to tie you down."

He grunted, disgusted with himself.

"What a fool I was. If you only knew how tired I am of all the clubs and the partying, of all the late nights, of having to drag myself to work the next day, of the whole scene. But it made you happy, or seemed to. So I kept going. It was all I knew to do to keep you near me. I didn't want to take a chance and rock the boat."

Rob squeezed her hand a bit tighter as they reached the main entrance to the Garden. "I could have told you six times a day how much I love you and it wouldn't have been enough for me, but I...well, now you know it all. And if you'll give me one more chance, if you let us start over, I promise..." He nodded toward the statue. "...as George Washington is my witness, you will never, ever regret it."

Lisa's eyes glistened. Tears rolled down her cheeks. This was the first time he ever really opened up to her, the first time he ever let her see behind the armor he wore, the first time he ever made himself really vulnerable to her.

She threw her arms around him and hugged him, her head resting on his shoulder, her tears wetting his jacket. She felt his arms move around her.

"I love you, Lisa," she heard him say softly, his lips near her ear. "Lord how I love you."

They stood there, bodies pressed close, hearts beating as one for long, loving minutes. Then she broke the embrace and used her fingers to wipe the tears from her cheeks.

Then she smacked him hard on the chest with the palm of her hand.

"That was for being such an ass for so long."

She leaned in to kiss him, their lips touching softly at first, but with growing fervor as the seconds ticked on. After a minute, she broke away. "And that was for realizing it before it was too late."

6:50 PM

Paul and Priya walked back to their table after she embarrassed him in a best-of-three darts match. Though they played many times since she began working with him, Paul beat her only twice – two single games. Both wins came after Priya consumed more than a few drinks. Even still, she managed to take the best-of-three series both times, despite her inebriation. Paul was never sure if that said more about her skill at the game or about his lack thereof.

"I can't get over that you never played darts before coming to Boston."

"It's true."

When the crew took her to DHL to celebrate the completion of her first week, several people thought they found an easy mark in the new girl. That was when they discovered her amazing hand-eye coordination. By the end of the second game, she figured out how to throw the darts and now few at the company would play her.

Paul never minded losing to her, though. He was fascinated by the way she could pop the darts pretty much anywhere she wanted them to go. Plus, she was fun to hang with. She could talk about movies, music, art, literature, even politics, and always seemed to be in good humor. Plus, she shared his appreciation for really bad puns and jokes, especially the risqué kind.

"By the way, what's the definition of moron?"

Paul grinned. "I'm afraid to ask."

"What a father tells his teenage daughter to put before she goes out on a date."

His groan elicited a fit of giggles.

"I wonder how things are going?" she asked once they were seated.

"With Rob and Lisa?"

"Uh-huh. It was so strange. I've never seen Rob like that before. He's usually so cocky and cool. But when he saw her standing there, he seemed to turn into someone else."

"I know. The threat of losing her really upset him. He's always been such a dog; never getting serious about anyone or anything. From day one though, it was different with Lisa. He knew it, too. I think it scared him and he let his fears cloud his judgment."

"Well I'm glad to see he's finally come to his senses."

"Me, too. Underneath all the bull, Rob's a great guy. And he and Lisa just seem to work together. You know?"

"I do. One of these days I'd like to find someone like that. I guess everyone would."

"Well, I hope he keeps it all together tonight. If he blows this chance…"

Priya nodded as Paul signaled for another round.

"More beer? We've already had two. Are you trying to get me drunk, sir? Or should I say, drunkerer?" Her grin turned into a soft giggle.

"Drunkerer? Is that another of your quickly-becoming-famous made-up words?"

"How about tipsier? Does that sound better? Are you trying to get me tipsier? I hope you're not planning to take advantage of me?"

If you only knew how many times I've dreamed about it.

He set his shoulders and tried to look hurt. "Madame, you wound me. I would never take ungentlemanly advantage of a lady. Unless, of course, she convinced me she's no lady." He tried to leer, but two beers on an empty stomach turned it into a wide-eyed, goofy grin.

Priya enjoyed flirting, but she could see the conversation heading in a dangerous direction.

"So why are you here killing time with me instead of out with Jillian?"

"She has a yoga class on Thursdays and then I guess she and a bunch of her friends go out afterward. And for your information, I am not killing time. I enjoy your company, even though I've never quite forgiven you for raising my hopes to previously unheard of heights on your first day of work, and then dashing them most cruelly and completely."

Priya giggled again. "Oh, if only you all could have seen your faces when I struck that pose. I'd give heavy odds none of you could have stood up without discomfort and embarrassment."

His abashed grin told her she was correct about at least one of them.

"Weren't you worried we might not have been so amused and accepting? I mean, with the whole sexual harassment thing and all…that was a heck of a chance you took."

She took a long drink from the just arrived mug.

"I *was* worried. But I had to find out if I could be part of the team, not just some eye candy for you guys. Once I came up with the idea, I debated it in my head all night. I even called my brother Raj to ask what he thought."

"You called your brother? And he liked the idea?"

"Hell no! He was ready to come and lock me in my apartment. And he might have if he'd been able to get a flight here in time.

"But his objection was not so much that it might backfire, but that his chaste little sister would be doing something so overtly sexual."

Paul's ears perked up.

"Chaste?"

Priya felt the blood rushing to her face.

"Did I say that?"

"Yes you did. Did you mean it?"

"Paul, you're a nice guy, but I really don't care to have my personal life become the subject of office gossip."

"Priya, I would never tell anyone something you told me in confidence. I swear. No, I swear on my soon-to-be relationship with Jillian. No sex? Really?"

"It's a long story."

"Pri, I have nowhere to go and nothing to do but listen."

None of the added color faded.

I can't believe I let that slip. Damn beers. Can I trust him? He's never made me think I couldn't. And he is a pretty decent guy. Damn!

Deciding, she said, "If you ever..."

"Never, Priya. On my life."

She sighed, then nodded, wishing she had the good sense to eat something before drinking.

"I didn't start developing until I was fourteen, but when I did, it happened quickly. My mother never had *the talk* with me before she passed away, so it was left to my father to help me through my first period, and to tell me the facts of life."

Her face softened as her eyes lost focus for a few seconds. Paul could tell she was remembering the event.

"He was so gentle and kind about it. Even though it was only two months after my mother died, and even though he was devastated by it, he sort of sucked it up and focused on me.

"I was so embarrassed about the whole thing when I told him, but he came to the store with me and stood there helping me read the various packages of pads and tampons as we tried to figure out which would be best for me.

"When we got home, we sat down to talk. Both of us were hideously uncomfortable, but even so, he managed to make me feel like I was the most special girl in the world as he told me what was happening to my body.

"Then he started in about sex.

"Looking back on it now, I guess it was kind of funny and sweet at the same time. He was so clinical about it at first, as he described the mechanics of it. But then he started talking about feelings, and love, and making love, and how sharing my body with someone was the most sacred gift I could give.

"As fascinated as I was to finally hear the straight dope on sex, I was relieved when it was over. I think he was relieved, too, but he made it clear that despite our embarrassment, I should always come to him and ask whenever I had a question, or whenever something didn't sound or feel right to me. And I did a few times, in the beginning. But mostly I thought about what he said about me being special and about giving myself being sacred. So I started reading all I could about love and sex and the more I read, the more I realized how many people were messing up their lives because of sex. At least it seemed that way to me at the time. So I made a vow that I wouldn't give myself to anyone until my wedding night. There were other things to do – school, sports, writing. You know.""

Paul's eyes bugged out. "Wait a second! You mean you're a…"

"Shush!"

Priya glared. Her hand smacked at his shoulder as her voice sank to a whisper. "What do you think 'chaste' means?"

"I thought you meant you'd sworn off it, you know, like you were taking a break. I never…wow. And you've never had any regrets? Never been tempted?"

"Oh, I've been tempted. Many times. But I've never really regretted my decision until recently."

An evil grim spread across his face, "Well, if you're regretting the decision, I'd be happy to…"

Glaring, she held up her hand to stop him. "*Do not* even go there."

"Sorry. Really, I'm sorry. Totally inappropriate, but I couldn't resist. But seriously, what's happened to make you regret it?"

"Sometimes I worry that I'll be a..." She glanced around. "...you know, forever. It wasn't a big deal when I was still in school. Guys would ask me out, and I'd go now and then, but there was always studying to do to fill the time, to keep me from thinking about what I might be missing. This last year, since I've started work, it's been different. I'm ready to get serious with someone, but in this day and age, it seems like if you don't put out you get shut out.

"Did you know I've gone out with three guys since I came to DPP?"

"No! I think we all figured you didn't date."

"I thought as much, which is what I wanted you all to think, I guess."

She looked sad, almost pained.

"All three dumped me when it became clear I was serious about my vow."

"Geez, what assholes. How come you never said anything to us? Hell, we'd have been happy to find them and beat some sense into them for you."

Priya laughed.

"Thank you. I think I believe you all would. But, you know, as much as I kid and joke with you guys, sometimes I really feel like an outsider being the only girl. Not that anyone has ever done or said anything to make me feel uncomfortable. On the contrary, you've all been great. You treat me like one of the guys, which is what I want. And we're all close, in a way, but I really wouldn't feel comfortable talking about guy problems with you all the way I would with another woman."

Almost as an aside, she mumbled, "Of course, I've never really had many close girlfriends. And none here, yet. " She sighed. "Anyway, as I said, you guys are great and all, but you have the wrong hormones and plumbing to be able to really understand certain things."

Paul nodded.

"I guess that's true, but have you considered that we can provide a perspective you simply cannot get from someone without our particular plumbing."

She thought about that for a bit, then grinned.

"Perhaps you're right."

"Try me. Come on, the promise is still valid. In fact, I hereby make it valid for eternity, or until I croak, whichever comes first."

"Thanks, you're very sweet, but you don't really want to hear me chattering about my boyfriends and such."

"Priya, have you ever known me to lie? Please, just this once. If it doesn't work out, what have you lost but some time."

She paused for a few seconds, then shrugged.

"What the hell. After..." Again she glanced around before whispering, "...*virginity*, how much more personal can you get? But I'm getting pretty hungry, and I really don't feel like eating bar food. You want to get some dinner?"

"Sure. What are you in the mood for?"

"Lobster. I really can't afford it, but I've been craving it for a week now."

"Lobster it is, then. My treat."

She started to protest, but he cut her off.

"I make more than you do and I can afford it and it would make me feel good to treat you as a way of saying thank you for placing your trust in me this evening."

She still was not convinced.

"And you can treat me next time, okay?"

She smiled and nodded. They stopped by the bar to pay their tabs then headed toward the door.

"You know," Paul said. "I still can't get over your...ummm...well, never having experienced sexual pleasure."

Priya shot him a sly grin.

"I never said I haven't experienced sexual pleasure." She raised her arm a little, then rotated her hand and wiggled her fingers. "I only said I've never been with a man."

Paul clutched his head and staggered against the doorframe.

"No no, no!" he said in mock anguish. "Why did you tell me that?

Now I won't be able to sleep all night thinking about it."

7:10 PM

Jillian spread her mat next to Jenna's.

"Where's Liz."

Without waiting for an answer, she began her warm-up routine.

"She had to work late. Said she'll meet us here if she finishes in time and if not, she'll meet us at Legal's."

Jillian was surprised to see the class nearly full. A virus was making the rounds in New England and for the past few weeks, nearly half the class was missing.

"How did the phone call go with the coffee guy?" Jenna was eager to hear the details.

Jillian's answer was a coy smile.

"Come on, you know you want to tell."

Actually, Jillian was dying to tell, but she knew she would be telling everyone about Paul later.

"Sorry, you'll just have to wait until dinner later when I tell everyone else. Besides, you should be warming up."

Jenna scrunched her lips into a pout as she started to stretch.

"Will you at least tell me when you two are getting together?"

"Tomorrow. I'm not sure of the time yet. He said to call him tonight when I get home."

"That late? Or are you planning to leave early?"

"No, I told him he might be asleep by the time I got home and you know what he said?"

Jenna cocked an ear.

"He said he couldn't think of a better way to be awakened than by the sound of my voice."

Jillian sniffed when Jenna's eyes rolled skyward. "Well *I* thought it was sweet."

"I bet you did," Jenna replied, then leered at Jillian. "But I'll bet *I* can think of a few *other* ways he'd prefer to be woken up."

"You're awful!"

Jillian felt her cheeks growing hot, and then hotter as the things Jenna meant, and then others, filled her head. In seconds, her face looked sunburned and Jenna laughed at her friend's embarrassment.

Just then, the instructor, Maureen, asked everyone to take their places. She began the class as she always did, with some breathing exercises.

Jillian tried her best to concentrate on her breathing but found Jenna's suggestive remark had planted itself firmly in the forefront of her consciousness. The thoughts excited her at a time when she should be relaxing, clearing her mind of worldly things, and focusing on her center. She was so distracted by mental images of herself and Paul she did not hear Maureen call for everyone to assume the first asana.

"Jilli!" Jenna whispered, then whispered again, accompanying it with a poke that succeeded in breaking through her reverie. "Hero."

When her eyes snapped opened, Jillian found she was the only one still standing.

"Well," Maureen said, catching her eye, "it's good to see one of my students has mastered the art of total concentration. Now if only we knew what she was concentrating on."

As she said that, she touched her cheek, glanced at Jenna, and winked to let Jillian know she noticed her blushing and understood why, which caused the poor girl's face to reach a shade of scarlet Maureen never saw before.

Jillian spent the next forty-five minutes struggling to focus on what she was supposed to be doing. She cursed her friend half-a-dozen times, twice out loud, much to the amusement of Jenna and several of the people around them.

Finally, the class was over. As she rolled up her mat, Maureen approached.

"I'm pretty sure you didn't get your money's worth tonight, and I wanted to apologize for embarrassing you earlier. Sometimes my mouth runs faster than my brain."

"No, it wasn't you."

"Perhaps it was the guy Jenna was teasing you about?"

Maureen caught the surprise in Jillian's face. "Good acoustics in here. Not so much side-to-side, but great from front to back and back to front. I've never been able to figure out why. This guy must be pretty special to get you that worked up."

"I think maybe he is. I can't stop thinking about him."

She offered a condensed version of the past two days.

"And you two are going out tomorrow night?"

"Yes."

Maureen grinned. "It sounds to me like Paul's going to get *very* lucky tomorrow night."

Jillian pretended offense. "I am not that kind of girl."

Maureen clucked ruefully and patted Jillian on the shoulder. "Of course you are, honey. We're all that kind of girl for the right guy."

8:05 PM

Rob shuffled uncomfortably down the hall, following Lisa who was fishing for keys in her purse. They were making out in the elevator and now Rob's constrained, but very visible excitement required him to move carefully to avoid inflicting pain upon himself.

As the door clicked shut behind them, Lisa flowed into his arms, her lips anxious and demanding. The time for soft, gentle kisses passed quickly in the elevator. Now, their lips ground together with a hungry urgency, their tongues twining in a dance that served to further inflame their passions.

His lips kissed their way across her cheek, moving toward the spot on her neck that always elicited a shiver of pleasure.

Thank you, Lord, thank you. It feels so good to hold her again.

He felt himself shudder.

I can't believe how close I came to losing her.

"Mmmmmm."

His lips reached the spot and her body grew softer against his.

Lisa felt his arousal throbbing against her thigh and sensed herself growing moist in anticipation.

They returned to her apartment to discuss their future together, but a simple kiss as the elevator doors closed became an aching need for both by the time the doors reopened.

She felt his hand slide between them, then under her thin shirt and silky bra to caress her breast. Again she moaned with pleasure as he toyed with her. His lips returned to hers while his hand stimulated the hard softness beneath his fingers. His tongue pressed urgently between her lips. Then, suddenly, he stiffened and pulled away.

"What's wrong?" she asked breathlessly.

He wrapped his arms around her, pulling her close.

"We're doing it again," he said softly, his voice quaking from the effort of suppressing his need for her.

She looked up at him, into his eyes.

"We're doing it again," he repeated, and then, in answer to her unspoken question, "We're putting the pleasure first."

He couldn't believe he was actually stopping them but felt her arms encircle him and squeeze as she nodded.

"You're right. You're right. After all I said, after all I blamed you for things, I couldn't even control myself for an hour or two. One kiss and all I wanted was to have you inside me again."

"That's true. But in your defense, you *were* kissing *me*, and how could *any* mere mortal be expected to control herself when tasting the lips of a love god."

She smiled, but it died quickly.

"Is this what our life will be together. Uncontrolled passion all the time?"

"I sure hope so."

He broke the embrace and led her by the hand to the sofa.

"Or, maybe not all the time. But enough of the time."

They sat quietly, her head resting on his shoulder, his arm holding her close.

After a minute, he said, "I don't ever want to lose the way you make me feel when we're together. It's all that keeps me going when we're apart. Just knowing I'll see you again in a few hours keeps me smiling all day. And the thought of touching you...well...there are times during the day that an image of you will pop into my head, an image of you in the shower, or lying in bed, or walking across the room in your underwear, and I'll get so hot I can't concentrate on my work. Lord help me if I ever have to stand up during one of those episodes."

She laughed softly and smacked him lightly on his thigh. "Is that all you think of me?"

"No baby. You didn't let me finish.

"There are other times, when something will remind me of you, of something you said, something you did that made me feel proud of you, and for a few seconds, the whole world fades away and all I can see in my mind is your face smiling at me. And let me tell you it can lead to some embarrassing moments if someone asks me a question during a meeting."

Again he heard her soft laugh, but this time felt her hand caress his chest.

"And then there are the times I think of you for no reason at all other than I love you so much. *That* only happens a few *dozen* times a day."

Lisa lifted her head from his shoulder and kissed him on the cheek. Her eyes were moist as she told him how much she loved him, too.

"But things have to change, Rob."

"I know. And they have. That's why I stopped us before. Do you think I would have done that, could have done that, three weeks ago? Right then I wanted you naked more than almost anything in the world. The one thing I want more, though, is to never, ever have to live without you again."

Lisa disengaged herself and sat up. She turned on the sofa to face him, searching his eyes as she crossed her legs and leaned back on the armrest.

"But what can we do, Rob? What happened a little while ago has made me realize how unfair I was to you. We were the way we were because I let us be."

"Maybe. Or partly. But it was mostly me being afraid of what I knew in my heart I really wanted. We were having fun, Lisa, and I didn't know how to move beyond it. Remember that old song by the Eagles, *Life in the Fast Lane?* In a way, that was us. We were rushing down the freeway and I was too blind to see the exit. You tried to show me at least a half-dozen times, and each time I..."

"You're right," she said, interrupting. "You did what you did. But I let you. And when it got to be too much, I simply took the exit by myself rather than fight for what *I* really wanted."

There were tears in her eyes again. "If you hadn't done what you did today, I would have walked away from us, Robbie. I would have let myself blame you for everything and walked away. And I think I would have regretted it for the rest of my life."

The tears rolled silently down her cheeks. Rob reached over to wipe them away.

"Stop," he pleaded in a whisper. "Please don't cry. It doesn't matter who did what. That's all in the past. What matters is now, tomorrow, and all the other tomorrows after it. What really matters is us, that there is an us, and that we make sure they'll always *be* an us."

8:37 PM

When Jillian and Jenna arrived at the restaurant, everyone else was already seated.

Thursday night dinner with the girls started several years ago, when Jillian, Jenna, and Liz were sophomores. At first, it was the three of them and Mary Louise Beaumont, a genuine southern belle and friend of Jenna's. Over the years, women drifted in and out of the weekly gathering which usually numbered eight to ten.

They took turns selecting the restaurant and this week, it was Gloria's turn. No one ever had to wonder what they'd be eating when it was Gloria's turn. She grew up on the coast of Maine and loved seafood of all kinds. Her favorite place in Boston was the Legal Seafood at Park Plaice. Gloria insisted the food at that Legal's was "a whale's tail better" than at any of their other locations around town, although no one else could taste any difference.

It appeared most of their friends been waiting for awhile. Gloria, Holly, Shandra, Marie, and Maggie were each working on their second drink while Liz and Marissa had only one half-full glass each in front of them.

All eyes turned to Jillian as she and Jenna approached the table. Before she could even remove her coat, she was peppered with questions about Paul. Obviously, Liz, Shandra, and Marie were comparing notes and filling in the others.

"Please!"

She held up a hand as she took her seat.

"I just finished my yoga class and must remain focused on my center for a while. My thoughts have to remain relaxed and pure."

This elicited a round of raucous laughter from the whole table, but especially from Jenna.

"Girl, are you forgetting I was there with you. The thoughts you had were anything but pure and the only center you focused on was between your legs."

"Jenna!"

Jillian felt her face grow hot yet again as the laughter renewed.

"Don't play innocent with me, girl."

She proceeded to relate what happened during yoga class.

"And then Jilli says 'I am not that kind of girl' and Maureen pats her on the shoulder and says, 'Of course you are, honey. We're all that kind of girl for the right guy.'"

Laughter rang out again from her audience.

"Well, she's right about that," Maggie said. "Of course, if a man can walk and brushes his teeth he's the right one for me."

Maggie was, by far, the most sexually liberated of the group. She was twenty-nine, soon-to-be-thirty, and considered *Sex and the City's* Samantha Jones a role model. She once confided that by the time she turned twenty-four she lost count of the number of men she slept with.

Although she played well the part of the slut who would screw every man in sight, she was actually quite choosy about who she let share her bed. So much so, she could honestly say she only had one bad experience in the fourteen years since giving her maidenhood to Billy Fontaine, the boy who lived across the street.

"Well I think it's the most romantic thing I've heard in a long time," said Holly.

She was twenty-six and the only married member of the group. Although happy in her relationship, a part of her missed the excitement of those chance meetings, first kisses, and new loves. She regularly lost herself in romance novels, much to the benefit of her husband, Jamal, who was always game for any fantasy his wife might want to act out.

"So do I," Marissa agreed, feeling a tinge of jealousy at Jillian's good fortune.

Marissa, a senior at Northeastern University and the youngest of the group at 22, was between boyfriends. She joined them about eight months ago after a work-study stint at Metro Magazine led to a regular part-time job and a friendship with Marie.

"Where's he taking you?" Holly asked.

"I don't know. When he asked, I told him food was good and after that to surprise me. So I guess we'll be having dinner somewhere."

Shandra had the next question. "Are you planning to do the I'm-not-too-hungry-I'll-just-have-a-salad thing? I know I wouldn't be able to eat if he's really as great as you're making him out to be."

"More important, though," Marie interjected before Jillian could answer, "is...what are you going to wear?"

"Oh! You're right," Jillian said, "I haven't even thought about it."

"What about your red pantsuit?" Liz offered. "You look great in that."

"Yes," agreed Jenna, "or maybe that long black skirt that's slit to the thigh. You could wear it with that lacy white top you keep saving for a special occasion."

The conversation became almost frenzied as the women discussed clothes, shoes, accessories, hair, nails, make-up, what to eat, how to eat, what to talk about, and so much more that after ten minutes of it Jillian's head was spinning.

8:50 PM

Paul was blushing. He'd been blushing on and off since they left DHL and each time Priya noticed she broke out in another fit of giggles.

"You're loving this, aren't you?"

"You bet! I can't wait to see what happens tomorrow at work. You better get a handle on your imagination or you'll have to make up some pretty interesting explanations."

Paul groaned. "I know, I know. But every time I look at you I see you...you know."

"Naked on a bed having fun with lefty?"

She watched his already red cheeks burn scarlet.

"Come on, Priya. You have to stop that."

"All right, all right. I'll stop." She sounded more contrite than she looked. "I'm being mean and you've been so sweet tonight. I really do appreciate you listening to me, and it really did help to hear a man's point of view."

Earlier, as they walked the half-mile to the restaurant, they talked all the way. The conversation continued during dinner, with frequent breaks for Priya's deliberately embarrassing innuendo, and worse.

Now, as they enjoyed coffee and dessert, Priya was sure her decision to trust Paul was correct. Over the course of the evening, she confided much of her past, including the men she dated, and how she felt about meeting, and ultimately losing each of them. She spoke of her loneliness, her difficulty in making female friends. There was nothing too personal to discuss.

As she sipped her coffee, thinking, Priya appeared worried.

"Paul, did I mess things up between us tonight telling you about...?" She lifted her left hand. "I'll never forgive myself if I let having a little fun wreck a really good friendship."

"No, you didn't wreck anything."

"But now you'll always have that image of me in your mind and..."

"Priya, if I tell you something about myself, about guys in general, will you promise not to hold it against me?"

"Of course."

"No, I mean, you have to actually promise. Seriously."

"Okay, I promise not to hold against you whatever you are about to say."

"Right. Well then…Priya, almost every man you meet imagines you naked. Many probably go home at night and dream about you. Or worse, if you know what I mean."

It was Priya's turn to blush.

"That first day, as you struck that pose, I guarantee all three of us were imagining you standing there *au naturel*. I don't think any of us do it any longer, but once in a while I still wonder. I can't help it. Men can't help it. You're an exceptionally beautiful woman.

"You have this amazing face and an even more amazing body to go with it. A man would have to be dead not to notice you, not to want you based only on your physical attributes.

"But if a guy is lucky enough to get to know you it's even worse! If he finds out how bright, and funny, and talented you are, how decent a person you are…well…he'll imagine himself with you even though he knows he'll never have a chance.

"Those guys who dumped you recently are idiots, Priya. They're little boys with raging hormones and no brains. They scored big by convincing you to go out with them and then all they could think about was a quick piece of ass."

He stopped and shook his head. He appeared to be considering something.

"The only reason I'm telling you what I'm about to tell you Priya, is because you trusted me so much tonight I know I can trust you in return."

Priya's eyebrows arched as her head tilted slightly in curious anticipation.

"Do you remember about two weeks after you started working with us, there was a period where I kept having to leave early, or had some appointment during the day."

When she nodded, he continued.

"I was interviewing for another job. I wanted to leave Davis Phillips so I could ask you out. I was so enamored of you I was having a hard time sitting in the same room and not staring all day. I didn't get the job and I did get over the crush, but that's how much you affect people."

"My gosh, I never realized. I never noticed even a funny look from you."

"And that's the way I wanted it. Especially after what you did and said that first day. But it illustrates the point I've been trying to make this whole time. We can suppress it, we can even hide it well, but men are men and we cannot help wanting a beautiful woman. It doesn't matter that we're in love with someone else, we still feel the urge. That's why so many men cheat on their wives and girlfriends. They feel the desire and go for it. That doesn't excuse them, of course. But those jokes about the little head leading the big head are often true, Priya. Fortunately, they're not always true."

"I can't believe this." She held his eyes. "Are you telling me that all the men in this room right now are fantasizing about doing me?"

"No, of course not. Not all the men. Odds are some of them are gay."

She burst out laughing and reached over to lay her hand on his.

"You, too?" she asked.

"Nah. Right now I'm still focused on you and lefty."

Again she shook with delight.

When the laughter subsided she told him, "All this laughing has made me need to pee. Will you excuse me for a minute? Why don't you see about getting the check."

8:54 PM

The date-talk had shifted from the practical to the hypothetical. Speculation about where he would take her and how they would get there grew so fantastic, Jillian was desperate to move the chatter away from her and Paul. She turned to Holly and asked, "So how did you get Jamal to let you out this week?"

It was a running joke that Jamal had to be bribed to let his bride out of the house for her night with the girls. Each week, Holly would come up with one outrageous answer or another.

"I told him if he let me go I'd bring you all home tonight for a nine way. The poor guy couldn't even stand up to give me a hug when I left."

"Holy Mr. Happy, girl," Maggie said. "You mean that man of yours could satisfy all of us?"

Holly's wicked smile and raised eyebrows started a round of comments that had patrons at nearby tables wondering if they were dining in the company of a group of porn stars.

Speculation about Jamal's length, girth, talent, and ability was still going strong when a party of six across the restaurant rose to leave. On the other side of the now-vacant table, previously hidden from her view by the diners, sat a guy and the most beautiful Indian girl Jillian had ever seen.

Oh...is that him? It looks like him from the side. What's he doing here? With her! Are they on a date? Look at her...she must be a model or something...or an actress...maybe it's not him...maybe its just someone who looks like him from the side.

She shook her head slightly as if to clear it, willing the guy to turn so she could be sure. The stunning girl she could see full on. When she laughed at something the guy said, then reached over and laid her hand on his, she actually became more beautiful.

Jillian's throat was suddenly dry and her chest felt strangely empty. Again the guy said something and again the girl laughed.

Are they just friends? Business associates? No, they seem too close, too intimate. But it can't be him…it's just a side-view look-alike.

At that moment, the woman rose. Jillian saw the man turn his head to follow her as she walked away.

Oh lord, it is him…getting cozy with…a centerfold or a cover girl or…why would he be chasing me if he has her? Why would he call me…send me flowers…maybe…maybe…

She saw Paul catch the eye of the waiter and make a check mark in the air with his finger. Oblivious now to the discourse around her, she continued to stare at him, her mind racing with questions for the few minutes it took the waiter to bring the check and take his credit card.

Liz, who sat across from her, glanced over and was startled to see Jillian staring over her shoulder, the color drained from her face.

"Jilli! What's wrong? Are you sick? Are you…"

"It's him," she said, her voice not much more than a whisper.

Liz couldn't hear her over the conversations. She quickly shushed everyone.

"What'd you say, Jilli? I couldn't hear you. Are you okay?"

Everyone's attention focused on Jillian, who was still staring at Paul. The girl was returning to the table.

"It's him," she repeated. "He's here." She paused, then added, "With *her.*"

Everyone followed her gaze in time to see a gorgeous woman rejoin a man at a table across the room.

"Who's here?" Holly asked. "You mean the guy over there with the Playboy model?"

Liz suddenly realized what was happening.

"That's Paul, isn't it? That guy with the knockout is Paul."

Jillian nodded. She watched the waiter return with the credit slip. Paul signed it and pocketed his card and receipt.

Why is this bothering me? What does it matter if he's here with someone else? We've never gone out. Just talked a few times. I have no hold on him, no rights to him, no reason to feel betrayed. But I do. I do. He said all those things to me. And the Callas.

"That's Paul?" Marissa asked. "Wow, he really *is* cute."

Half the table glared at her.

"Are you okay, Jilli?" asked Maria.

Recovering her composure, she said quietly, "Yes, I'm fine. I was just taken by surprise. Everyone, please don't all stare at once, but that's Paul, the guy you've been hearing so much about." Then the tone of her voice took on a razor sharp edge as she added, "I don't know who...who *she* is."

And how can I ever compete with her.

Everyone rushed to say something, but she stopped them. "It doesn't matter who she is. I don't own him. I don't even really know him."

Her friends heard the sadness in her voice.

"Look," Marie said.

They all turned and saw Paul and his companion rise. They certainly seemed to be very friendly as he helped her on with her coat, donned his own jacket, then headed for the door.

The focus returned to Jillian, who was staring down at her drink. An unnatural quiet fell over the group as each considered what they just saw and what it might mean for their friend.

9:10 PM

Paul and Priya headed toward the subway station on the corner of the Common at Boylston and Tremont. They said little as they walked side-by-side. Each was trying to digest the way the evening played out.

As they turned left at Stuart, neither was in a hurry to say goodnight. When they reached the subway, they found themselves lingering at the entrance.

Finally, Priya said, "If you're not in a hurry to get home, would you like to walk off some of those calories we just enjoyed?"

"Sure!"

Both recognized their friendship was becoming something more, though neither really understood yet exactly what that "more" was.

For her part, Priya never before spoke so intimately with a man. Such conversations were always reserved for her few female acquaintances, and even then, not to the depths of intimacy she reached with Paul tonight.

How did this happen? Am I so desperate for friends that one boozy slip of the tongue made me bare my soul like that? Or...is there something about him I never noticed before, something that just put me at ease? Oh no! Is it more serious than that? Am I starting to fall for him? No, he's not interested in me. But he sure was right about seeing things from a different perspective. Even his questions. It was like he was trying to get me to consider alternatives, not just be supportive like girls usually do.

And he was so attentive. He listened...really listened. No guy ever focused on me that way before...like...like I had his complete attention...like I was the only thing on his mind. Maybe that's was what made me blab so many personal things.

Now I really feel bad about all those comments. The poor guy was red-faced all night. But it was so great to let go for once. I never felt so free before! I never let a man get that close to my center. Why did I do it tonight? I don't know...there was just something about him that made me feel safe. Oh Shiva! Of course! He made me feel safe. And comfortable. Those other guys would have been all over me if I'd been so free, so suggestive with them. Ugghh...that pig Mike especially. He could never understand me the way Paul does. Paul is such a...Oh! Oh dear!

As they ambled along the path, Paul kept stealing sideways glances at Priya.

She hasn't said much since we left the restaurant...but I guess neither have I. Maybe she regrets telling me so much about herself. Man, I can't believe it...no girl's ever opened up like that before...it was freakin' amazing. Who knew women thought about that kind of stuff? And she's a virgin! A freakin' virgin! Man, what a waste of a great body. Ah, crap. Now you're thinking like those jerks she went out with. Damn...she really laid it all out there tonight. It was like...like seeing her naked without taking off her clothes. Man! I can't freakin' get over it.

He was incredibly flattered at her trust, but realized he was also nervous about the responsibility he now felt toward her. Another part was still in shock at the things he learned. Then there was that other part, the primal part, which still could not drive from his mind the image of her pleasuring herself.

Strangely, although that image of her excited him, he found it did not really arouse the kind of lust for her he expected and he didn't understand why not. There was a time not long ago that just the thought of her smiling at him would start it throbbing. But now, nothing.

Oh crap!

He came to an abrupt halt, startled by his epiphany.

Priya turned to see why he stopped and was, herself, startled by the melancholy she saw on his face.

"What's wrong?" she asked, her voice anxious.

"You've ruined it for me." His eyes drifted to the cloudless sky. "You've completely ruined it."

Priya was genuinely worried now.

What's he talking about? Our friendship? Our ability to work together?

She walked back two paces to stand right in front of him.

"Paul, please. What's the matter. What have I ruined?"

He lowered his eyes to meet hers. Then, without warning, he threw his arms around her and pulled her into a close embrace. Instinctively her arms encircled his waist and returned the embrace. They stood there for almost a full minute before his arms released her and he stepped back.

"Nothing. Not even a twitch."

Although it would seem to be impossible, he appeared depressed and elated at the same time. "Paul…"

His smile interrupted her. "Come sit for a few minutes."

He led her to a bench a few yards away. Seated next to each other, he rubbed his neck as he thought about what to say.

"Priya, remember when we were talking earlier, and I told you men will always fantasize about you, that they generally won't be able to help themselves?"

"I remember."

"Well, watch this, watch my face."

She saw him close his eyes. His face and whole upper body relaxed a bit. He sat that way for about fifteen seconds, then opened his eyes.

"What did you see?" he asked.

"Well, you seemed to relax a little, but other than that, nothing."

"Exactly. Nothing. You've ruined it for me." He sighed. "You know what I was doing? I was sitting there imagining you spread-eagled on a bed in the throes of a tremendous, self-inflicted orgasm."

"Paul!"

"Wait, let me finish."

"Did you see my face flush? No. Did I get a hard-on? No. Did my dick even twitch a bit? No."

She started at his language, but he just smiled again. "Priya, come on. After the stuff you told me tonight, I think we're past being shocked by references to our respective body parts, don't you?"

She laughed a little and nodded. "I guess you're right."

"Something really special happened tonight and I know you felt it, too. Some kind of connection, some bond was formed between us. At first, I thought it might be the beginning of a romance, but then, as we were walking I realized that despite my embarrassment whenever I thought about what you'd said, I wasn't getting turned on by the image.

"Suddenly, I realized that all these years I've been wrong about something. I realized a man and a woman *can* be friends, even intimate friends, without the sex thing getting in the way. At least I *think* that's what's happening here."

Priya looked thoughtful as she processed what he said. Then her face changed, not much, but enough for him to wonder what entered her mind.

"Stand up," she said, taking his hand and pulling him off the bench as she rose. She stood so close he could feel the heat from her body.

"Just so we don't spend our whole lives wondering…" Priya threw her arms around his neck, leaned into him and kissed him, really kissed him as few women had ever done before.

When she was done, she pulled away and said, "You're right. Nothing." She plopped back down on the bench. "So how does this work?"

"Hell, I don't know. I guess we'll figure it out as we go along."

They considered the possibilities, oblivious to others walking by.

Finally, Priya broke the silence. "Well, since I pretty much told you all the intimate details of my life, how about you sharing some of yours?"

"I guess that's fair. What would you like to know?"

"Hmmm, I suppose we should start with some basic stuff. What do you call your, ah…you know?"

She felt herself blushing and was glad he wouldn't be able to notice in the dim light.

"My, what?"

"Your thing."

"My thing? What thing? My index finger? My navel?"

"You know what I mean."

"Maybe. But I like to hear women talk dirty, so if you want to know, you have to say it."

Priya smacked him lightly on the arm.

"Your penis. What do you call your penis."

Laughing, Paul said, "Darn, I was hoping you'd use one of the more earthy euphemisms. I call it Mr. Johnson."

"Hello Mr. Johnson," she said brightly, waving at Paul's lap. "So tell me more."

Paul didn't respond immediately. Again, he rubbed his neck as he thought. Then he sat up straight and caught her eyes. "You know how yesterday, when I met Jillian in the coffee shop for the first time, I told you I felt like something clicked between us?"

Priya nodded.

"Well, ever since then, I've had this feeling my life is changing direction. At first, I thought it was because I met a new girl, and certainly that's part of it, because I've never felt this way about anyone before, despite not really knowing her. But it's like I do. At lunch yesterday, after the initial awkwardness, we were like old friends. The conversation came naturally for both of us. I seemed to understand her, to know the exact right thing to say, which was really weird given how tongue-tied I was a few hours earlier. And she could almost read me, too. I tell you, Pri, it scares me a little."

She put her hand on his shoulder. "What is it you're scared of?"

"I don't know. Maybe it's the intensity of it all." He shook his head. "But that can't be it. I've had pretty intense relationships before." His frustration was clear. "I know something is different this time. I just don't know what."

"Maybe it's a control thing."

"What do you mean?"

"Well, you've always struck me as a take-charge kind of guy. But now you're facing this new relationship and it's coming too easy, as if someone or something was making it all happen. Maybe you're scared of not really having control over where all this is headed."

Paul was quiet for a minute, then grunted. "I should have thought of that. You may be right. But it occurs to me it's even more than this new thing with Jillian. I think this new thing with *us* is part of it, too. My life really *is* changing."

They sat and talked a bit longer before deciding to walk again. Paul told her more about himself, about his family and past girlfriends, his passions and goals, answering her questions with a casual frankness that surprised him. Time flew by, and as they strolled, sharing more and more about themselves, they further cemented the growing bond between them until, realizing it was getting late, they steered themselves toward the entrance to the subway.

"Too bad our names aren't Harry and Sally," Priya said. "They were best friends in that movie without the sex getting in the way."

"For a while. But if you recall, they wound up in bed, split up, then ended up falling in love when they realized they didn't want anyone but each other."

"That's right. And you do have Jillian."

"I don't know about that yet. We haven't even gone out on a real date yet."

"I think deep down you do know. I think that may be part of what's scaring you." She grinned and bumped him with her shoulder. "And why Mr. Johnson isn't interested in me."

Paul bumped her back.

It certainly would explain a lot of things.

"Priya, I, umm, I wanted to say thank you for tonight. I've never before had a woman trust me and confide in me the way you did tonight. And I've never really had a girl I could talk to like this, where I could say anything without having to worry how she'd take it or think I was coming on to her.

"This…I don't know what to call it…this thing of ours means a lot to me. In a different way it means as much to me as my new thing with Jillian."

Priya closed her eyes as a sudden rush of warmth filled her. Her life, too, was changing, and she knew Paul would play a role in that change. A part of her worried all night that she'd made a mistake opening up to him, but her fears were gone now. "It means a lot to me, too."

More than you know. More than you'll ever know.

They strolled in silence again, each contemplating what such a friendship would mean in their futures.

For Paul, it meant having someone who could help him understand women in a way he would never have been able to accomplish on his own. It meant having someone who was like a sister, but more than a sister.

For Priya, it meant having someone to whom she could honestly and openly reveal herself without fear of her words being misconstrued or parsed for hidden meanings; someone to whom she could confide the embarrassing thoughts and feelings, who she could allow to see her inner warts and flaws without worrying they would be used against her.

As they neared the station, guilt nagged at her.

A lie is not a good way to begin a friendship. But I really had no choice. And he'll never find out.

Paul took Priya's hand and led her past the station to the curb.

"It's too late for you to be riding the subway," he said as he hailed a taxi. "And it's still my treat."

He opened the door and helped her inside. She smiled and thanked him and told him she would see him tomorrow at work.

After paying the driver, he started to close the door, then stopped, leaned his head inside and said quietly with a salacious grin, "Since we've been so honest with each other tonight it's only fair you know that just because we're tight now, and just because I might have a new girlfriend, doesn't mean I've given up on my dream of seeing you naked."

He laughed as he pulled his head back and slammed the door before she could respond.

Priya laughed too, but as the taxi pulled out into traffic she wondered if one day, perhaps on his birthday, she might have a bit of fun and surprise him with a gift he would never, ever forget.

11:05 PM

Lisa wiggled her toes. She and Rob were again sitting on the sofa, their feet resting on the coffee table. They talked for well over two hours, talked as they never had before, sharing hopes and dreams, fears and regrets, and setting the foundation for the relationship and the future they hoped to build together.

Then they made love, sweet, tender, passionate love, right there on the sofa. Now they sat naked, huddled under a comforter, still savoring the recent passion.

"This is nice," he said, rubbing his shoulder against hers.

"Yes, it is."

He moved a foot and started ticking the soles of her feet with his big toe.

"Stop that!" she shrieked, laughing.

"Why should I?"

His toes chased her feet around the table until she pulled them back and planted them on the floor.

He gave her a look of mock contempt. "You think *that* will save you?" In seconds, his toes were trying to wiggle under her feet.

Laughter filled the room as she counterattacked, tickling his kneecap and the area behind it until he ceased his attack and called a truce.

Eyes closed, Rob's head resting atop hers, they cuddled as they caught their breath, savoring the closeness and intimacy they missed during the break.

His voice became serious. "You know, you never answered my question earlier. I poured out my soul to you in words and in writing and then we came back here and all you wanted to do is jump my bones."

"How could I help myself, being, as I was, in the presence of a love god? But what question didn't I answer?"

"If you recall, at some point I told you that I never understood what it is you see in me."

"You did. But that was a statement, not a question." Her bright, challenging grin dared him to disagree.

"Sure, get all technical with me." He kissed her hair before continuing more sedately. "Seriously, Lisa, I want to know."

"You really want to know what I see in you?"

"Yes, of course."

She snuggled closer.

"Do you remember earlier, in the Garden, when you were describing me, telling me why I could have any guy I wanted?"

He nodded.

"You said I was smart, and decent, and funny."

"And some other things."

"That's right, you said I was many things, but you never said I was pretty."

Rob was confused. "But you are. You're gorgeous."

"I know that, fool. But when you were listing all my good qualities, it didn't occur to you to mention that."

Rob was more confused. "Are you saying you like me because I didn't tell you you're pretty?"

She chuckled. "Sort of. I like that how I look has never been a big deal to you.

"If you contacted all the guys I dated before I met you and asked each of them to describe me, every one would start out with 'she's hot' or 'she's gorgeous' or, in the case of a couple of them, 'she has a great body.' Then they might throw in a few other things so you wouldn't think they were shallow.

"When I met you, I'd just broken up with this guy Lenny. I told you about him."

Rob nodded.

"All he could ever talk about was how great I looked. Whenever he introduced me to someone, he always referred to me as his '*Playmate* girlfriend Lisa' and people assumed there was nothing else to me. One jerk even asked what issue I was in so he could get a copy. It didn't matter who I was, what I did, or anything else. It made me feel empty, shallow, and alone. Lenny set the tone for their thoughts about me and that was that. And that was why I showed him the door after two weeks.

"Not everyone was as bad as him, of course, but I'd had my fill of guys with pretty faces and no character or great bods but no brains. I wasn't interested in vain, self-absorbed guys anymore. I wanted substance. And I found that with you.

"Looks fade, Rob. People may think I'm pretty now, but ten years from now, when the wrinkles begin and my boobs start to droop are you going to care?"

"Of course not."

"Of course not. But all those other guys *would* care. They'd be hinting it might be time for some nip and tuck so I could look like I was twenty-five again. And if I told them I didn't want to, that I was a person, not a doll, and didn't want to feel like a trophy, eventually they'd find someone else to show off."

Lisa took a deep breath and held it for a moment before continuing. "In the time we've been going out, do you know how many times you told me I was pretty? Other than when we were fooling around, which doesn't count because guys will say anything in bed."

"Uhh, a lot?" he asked, hopefully.

"Four. Four times. And three were times when I was really dressed up because we were going somewhere special."

"Four times? Only four times? And you're happy about this?"

"Rob, you only told me four times how pretty I was, but you must have told me a hundred times how smart I was, how nice I was, how proud you were of something I did. Almost every day you found something nice to say to me and it never had to do with how I looked. You made me feel special, Rob. Every day you made me feel special for who I am on the inside, not for what's on the outside. Do you have any idea how much that means to a woman?

"We kill ourselves trying to look good for our men when what we really want is for them to notice what's inside us. You notice, Rob. You notice without even trying." Tears welled up in her eyes. "It broke my heart when I decided we had to take a break. I hated that you could make me feel so good about myself at the same time you were making me so depressed at you not wanting to grow up."

Rob put his arms around her. "I'm sorry. I really am. All I ever wanted to do was make you happy."

"I know." She wiped her eyes and kissed him on the cheek. "You're crazy if you think I can do better than you. Let me tell you what I see when I look at you.

"I see a guy who sees me for who I am, for who I want to be. I see a guy who's decent, and loyal, and funny. A guy who'd do anything for me if he could, who'll always be there for me when I need him, who'll love me, and care for me, and let me warm my feet on his butt when we get in bed on cold winter's nights.

"I see a guy who won't even notice when my hair starts to turn gray. I see a guy with whom I can share a life and not be insecure about how my body's changing as time goes by. I see a man I can love with and laugh with and cry with for the rest of my life."

She turned so she could see his eyes. "Rob, you are the nicest man I've ever known. And I thank God I met you when I did. If I'd met you much sooner, I never would have given you the time of day. I wouldn't have been ready."

He tried to look hurt, but Lisa just smiled.

"Before Lenny, I was still in my bad boy phase. Now, would you like to know why I got you to ask me out?"

Rob frowned. "You got me to..."

"Please. Don't pretend you didn't notice me throwing myself at you. Want to know why?"

He nodded.

"Think back to the night we met. When I first saw you, you were talking music, or trying to, with one of those girls who are the cause of all the world's blond jokes."

"That's right! Sandi. I think her name was Sandi and she was a model or something." He chuckled, remembering the conversation. "Yes, she wasn't one of the brightest bulbs in the pack that night."

"I could tell. I was standing to the side of you with some people and could hear you. You never once talked down to her, even when she made some really loony comments. But even more than that, during the whole time I was watching, your eyes never once dropped down to her huge boobs.

"At first, I thought you were gay, but I asked around and discovered not only were you *not* gay, you were something of a hound dog."

"Who told you that?"

"Pretty much everyone. But forget it, it doesn't matter. I was intrigued that a guy with your reputation would act so contrary to it, so I sort of shadowed you for a while, eavesdropping, watching...getting a feel for you. Twice you hit on women that night. Neither one was what you'd call model material but both had other things going for them, which you picked up on. Both turned you down because they were in relationships, but even then you were gracious and sweet, leaving each with the thought that their boyfriend was the luckiest guy in the world. I mean, what kind of guy gets rejected, and then takes the time to make the person rejecting him feel good about doing it?

"After the second time that happened, I decided I had to get to know you, if only to find out if it was all an act, or if you were the real deal."

"And what have you decided?"

His hands began to wander beneath the comforter.

"I don't know," she replied breathlessly, squirming as his fingers made it hard to think. "The jury is still...ah...deliberating. I...ohhh... Mmmmmm...I'll have to let you know in the morning."

11:25 PM

After seeing Priya safely on her way, Paul decided to walk the one and a third miles home. He really needed time to think about all the incredible things that happened to him since yesterday morning.

It's unbelievable. Two days ago there were no women in my life I'm not related to. And now there's this incredible friendship with Priya and tomorrow, with some luck, I'll have a new romantic thing with Jillian! Two great women now. Two very different relationships. Am I really this lucky?

As he walked through Copley Square, he considered what Priya said.

It makes sense, I guess. Still, no matter how close we get, there'll always be that one thing we'll never share. We'll never be a When Harry Met Sally *thing. And what a shame. Sure would have been nice to get a look at her as nature intended, but there was nothing. Damn! Even a little spark and I could have talked myself into it, maybe. But no. Me and Pri are destined for friendship. At least that much was clear tonight. I get the feeling we're going to end up closer than if she was my sister.*

He groaned inwardly at the possibility of one day actually thinking of her as a sister, then started to laugh out loud at himself and at the whole situation, drawing curious looks from passersby.

As suddenly as he started laughing, he stopped.

Oh crap! If things work out with Jillian, she might not like me having such a close friendship with another woman, especially one as hot as Pri. Damn! If things go well tomorrow night, I'll tell her about Priya right up front, tell her the whole story, from the day she first started work right up to when we said goodbye earlier. I want both of them in my life and the only way that'll happen is if I can make Jillian understand that Pri will never be a threat.

He massaged his scalp with his fingers as he passed the Prudential Center.

Am I crazy to think the fates will really let me have a lover like Jillian and a friend like Priya?

He groaned softly and shrugged.

Que sera, sera. Whatever will be, will be and all the worrying in the world ain't gonna change it.

I wonder how her yoga class went. She must go with friends. She looks pretty good…must have been going for a long time. Hmmm…does she wear one of those spandex body suits? Man, I bet she'd be smokin' hot in one. Maybe I should look into taking a yoga class myself.

He glanced at his watch.

I wonder where she is now. Probably still out with her friends. Girlfriends…I'm pretty sure she said she was going out with her girlfriends. Hmmm…I wonder if women think of gay men as girlfriends of a sort. Seems that way in movies. Hey! I can ask Priya! And Jillian! I wonder if she told her girlfriends about me.

He flashed back to the first time he saw her smile and the way it made him feel so warm and excited. He could hear her voice in his head, the sound of her laugh, the way it would suddenly climb an octave when he said something a little naughty and she pretended to be shocked; the way it sounded when she said his name.

Then he shook his head, suddenly realizing he was acting like a schoolboy.

"So what?" he muttered.

Thinking about her makes me happy. And if just thinking about her makes me feel this way, is my heart gonna be able to stand it when I'm with her?

Again he shook his head.

Cripes! I'm going off the deep end. I really do have it bad.

He was running on auto-pilot as he unlocked his front door, stepped inside and threw the deadbolt. A quick glance at the clock told him it was almost midnight.

I wonder if she called yet?

He checked the answering machine. There were two calls, one from his brother Steve and another from one of those annoying sales machines.

Why the hell didn't I give her my cell number instead of this one?

Despite her promise to call, he wondered if she would really feel free to phone at this hour. Just in case, he picked up the handset and dialed her number. On the fourth ring, her voicemail answered.

"Hi. I only sound like Jillian. If you want to talk to me anyway, here's the beep. Beeeep."

"Hi, it's Paul. I guess you weren't kidding when you said you'd be getting in late. I was about to get ready for bed and was thinking of you, which is not to imply that the two are connected, I just happened to be doing them at the same time."

Damn. Did I really just say that?

"Anyway, I thought I'd try you in case you thought it was too late to call. I hope you're having fun wherever you are. It's okay to call when you get this, whatever the time. Really. I miss your voice. The machine was okay, but I'd much rather hear the real thing. Okay, enough of this. Talk to you later."

11:58 PM

Jillian sat on the edge of her bed, crying, as she listened to Paul leave his message. Her eyes felt puffy and she could only imagine what the rest of her face looked like.

Why didn't I mind my own business? Why didn't I listen to Liz and stay at the restaurant? At least then I could have fooled myself and gone out with him one time.

Despite everything that happened, I still feel him tugging at me. Just like it was with Aiden.

Her brain sped out of control, rushing from thought to thought

How can I still feel something for this guy? He lied to me. Didn't he? Lied by omission. He never told me he was involved with someone else. But would it have mattered if he had told me?

"Of course it would."

But I still could have gone out with him. No! But what if he isn't serious about…about her. What if he was breaking up with her. What if it was just a business thing. Or they were just friends. But it couldn't be. Not after…

Jillian grabbed her pillow and screamed into it all her anger, frustration, and hurt.

He made me feel special. In less than a day he made me believe in him, made me care. Is that his game? Does he make every girl he wants feel this way? Did he make her feel this way, too?

She took the pillow from her face and hugged it to her chest.

Why does this always happen to me? Why do I keep attracting men who hurt me? Ever since Aiden…

Her phone rang again. When the greeting was done, she heard Liz's voice. Her hand was halfway to the receiver when she let it fall away.

"Hey Jilli. I was going to call your cell, but then I figured you might not want to talk, and this way, you'd at least hear me." She paused. "I wanted to make sure you're okay. Just remember he probably has a tiny little dick to match his tiny little brain. So stop crying, get some sleep, and call me when you wake up in the morning. You know I love you sweetie. Goodnight."

Jillian fell back on the bed as tears flowed anew. They ran down her cheeks creating small wet spots on the patchwork quilt her grandmother made for her when she was 16.

Earlier, at the restaurant, after she and her friends watched Paul and the woman leave, nobody wanted to say anything. If only someone had, perhaps she wouldn't have been so impulsive.

Instead, after half-a-minute of quiet, she jumped up, grabbed her coat, told the other girls they'd be back in a while, and practically dragged Liz toward the door. It all played back in her head as she wept.

*   *   *

"Jilli!"

Liz tried to button her coat as she hurried through the front door.

"This is a mistake. You don't know who that was, and all this can do is lead to trouble."

"I don't care. I'm *not* getting involved with another guy who'll hurt me. No more players, no more cheaters, no more jerks of any kind. I'd rather find out the truth now than have to deal with the hurt after I've let him get close to me."

Jillian looked left, then right, just in time to see them turn onto Stuart Street. She and Liz followed them, watching from a distance as they walked and talked. From halfway across the Common, they watched them hug, then sit and talk, then stand up and kiss in a way that made clear they were anything but friends. And when the kiss ended, so did Jillian's hopes for her and Paul.

"Asshole."

She felt Liz's arm across her shoulder as they trekked back to the restaurant. They were gone a while, but their friends were still there, all dying to know what happened.

*   *   *

For two days he made me feel so wonderful, so special. But if I'm so special, why was he kissing another girl? It was all a game. He was playing me after all and I fell for it.

She breathed deeply, trying unsuccessfully to fight back the tears as she slid off the bed and walked into the bathroom. She cringed at the lost soul she saw reflected in the mirror.

She thought a nice hot shower might make her feel better and reached into the tub to turn on the water. Slowly, she undressed, dropping each piece of clothing in a pile next to the sink.

Steam rose over the curtain as she slid down her underpants and dropped them on the pile with the toe of her right foot. Standing in front of the mirror again, staring at her reflection, she touched her face, then her breasts. Her hands slid down, over her stomach and below, then around to cup the cheeks of her backside. Then she straightened up and threw out her chest.

"Look what you missed asshole. Look what you gave up."

Jillian's feelings overwhelmed her. Despite the steamy warmth in the bathroom, she started to shiver and shake, her knees suddenly weak.

She sat down on the toilet, arms wrapped around herself, head bowed, and rocked.

And cried.

FRIDAY, MAY 7

7:40 AM

Paul stood by the window in the coffee shop, nervously scanning the sidewalk as he did the previous morning, the coffee in his hand all but forgotten.

"I don't understand it," he told Rob. "She said she'd call last night and I even left a message letting her know it was okay to call late, but she never did. And she didn't answer her phone this morning either."

Worry lines creased his forehead, though he wasn't sure what to worry about. All he could think to do was to wait here and hope she stopped by. If she didn't, he planned to call her at work.

"You're Paul, right?"

He spun around to see a lanky, dark-haired girl clutching a take-out tray that held three coffees and a bag. She stood four feet away with a look of utter contempt on her face.

He was taken aback but acknowledged, "Yes, I'm Paul."

"I just wanted to see what a real asshole looked like up close," she said with a sneer before she turned and headed toward the door. Rob turned away from the window, interested to see what would happen next.

"Hey! Wait! Who are you and what are you talking about?"

The woman stopped and faced him again.

"She saw you last night. We *all* saw you with that bimbo."

"Who *are* you?" Paul wondered if this woman had a screw loose or something.

"Marie. I work with Jillian."

"Jillian?" Now the three coffees made sense, but was she saying Jillian saw him last night with Priya?

"She saw everything last night. Everything. She liked you. She liked you a lot. She thought you were different, really special. And then to find out like that that you're just another dickhead."

"Are you telling me that you and Jillian and...some other people saw me with Priya last night?"

"You were out with Priya last night?" Rob was even more interested now.

"We went out after work. We...later, for Pete's sake."

He turned his attention back to Marie. "Where did you see me?"

"In Legal Seafood. We were sitting across the room. And you were so into what's-her-name you never even noticed Jillian watching you."

"But she's just a friend. I work with her."

"What a jerk." She spit out the words with vehemence. "You guys are all alike. You think we'll believe anything, don't you. Well eyes don't lie. We all saw how you two were in the restaurant. And Jillian saw you two hugging and kissing on the Common. I hope you know you blew the best thing that will ever happen to you for the whole rest of your miserable asshole life."

Rob's voice rose an octave in astonishment. "You *kissed* Priya?"

Paul ignored him and started to say something but Marie didn't give him the chance.

"All you had to do was be honest. All you guys ever have to do is be honest. But you're all alike. Oooo, I think you're so nice. Oooo, I've never known anyone like you. Oooo, I miss your voice."

"But..."

"Forget it. I don't want to hear your excuses. Jillian's my friend and you hurt her. So leave her alone. Go play your games with the slut you were with last night."

With that, she turned and stormed out of Coffey's.

"Oh shit! Oh shit!"

That's why she didn't call last night. What am I going to do?

He gave Rob a capsule review of the previous night as they walked quickly to the office.

"You kissed her? You really kissed Priya?"

"Rob, you can never let her know that you know. And never tell anyone else at work. She'd be so embarrassed. It was nothing, an experiment to prove a point, that's all. And she kissed me. I only hugged her. Promise me, man. Promise me on our friendship you will never mention it to anyone, ever."

"Okay, okay, I promise. But you have to at least tell me how it was."

In response, he received a sulfurous glare that left no doubt he would never get the answer to that question.

Paul was frantic. He had to fix this and fix it fast. In two minutes, Marie would be telling Jillian what just happened, giving her a name to attach to the girl she thought Paul wanted more than her.

She must really think I'm a total asshole. That I was playing her or something. Damn, damn, damn!

He rushed into his office and barked, "Where's Priya?"

"Ladies room, I think," Tom said, evenly. "She should be back in a few. What's wrong?"

Paul couldn't wait. He picked up the phone and dialed Jillian's work number. A strange voice answered on the second ring.

"Good morning. May I please speak with Jillian Marshall?"

"I'm sorry, but Jillian is tied up at the moment. May I take a message?"

The voice was polite, but didn't sound too friendly. He left his name and number and could swear he heard the sound of paper crumpling as the line went dead.

Priya was all smiles when she walked into the office, but the smile vanished when she saw the panic on Paul's face. "What's wrong?"

"Come on." Paul rose from his chair. "Let's take a walk. I need to talk to you about something."

"Does it have to do with last night?"

Paul nodded.

"Then sit down. I know I should have asked you first, but I pretty much told Tom about what happened last night. I mean, we all have to work together, and it would be hell if we had to pretend we weren't more than just co-workers. Eventually one of us would say or do something that would cause them to wonder and, well, it wouldn't be fair."

"So you told him, ah, everything?"

"Pretty much."

"Okay then, here's what happened a few minutes ago."

Paul told her about the confrontation in the coffee shop and about the call that went nowhere.

"I don't know what to do. I can't even go over there. She'll never believe me. And given the way Marie was acting this morning, I'd probably get killed if I even showed my face on her floor."

Tom shook his head. "Oh you are so *screwed*. I feel for you, man."

Priya stood quietly for a few minutes, her head bobbing slightly back and forth as it always did when she was concentrating on a problem. Then she smiled at Paul and turned to Tom.

"Tom, Paul and I need some time off this morning. We have some repair work to do."

8:20 AM

Shandra was on her way back from the ladies room when she saw Paul and the bimbo step off the elevator right in front of her.

Hoo-mama! This should be good!

"Good morning," she said to their backs. "I'll bet you're looking for Jillian."

Paul turned to see who spoke.

Good lord, does everyone in the company know who we are?

"My name is Shandra. Jillian works right through there." She pointed to an opening flanked by a set of huge wooden doors.

Paul recognized the name as the third person who took turns bringing the coffee in the morning.

"Hi, I'm…"

"Paul. I know. And I have to say you must have one big set of brass balls to show up here with her." Shandra nodded toward Priya. Despite her words, she seemed calm and pleasant, not at all like Marie was earlier.

"Look, I…"

Shandra held up her hand. "Not my business. But you better be nice to her. She has lots of friends in there."

As they entered the huge room, Shandra pointed to an open door to the right.

"Check in there with Cathy O'Hara. She's the manager."

Paul cleared his throat at the doorway, introduced himself and Priya, and explained they needed to speak with Jillian.

Her first instinct was to tell them Jillian couldn't be disturbed, but the look on his face, plus the fact they both showed up here so quickly after Marie confronted him made her think this mess might not be as straightforward as everyone thought.

She rose from her desk. "Follow me. I'll show you to her space."

Nothing spreads faster than a new Internet virus except juicy news, and it was evident the news had spread here. When they emerged from her office, almost everyone in the room was standing, waiting for a glimpse of the bastard and his whore. Paul felt like a criminal being escorted past the media on a perp walk as Cathy led them down the left aisle, nearly to the end, past assorted nods, glares, and appraising stares.

Jillian was seated at her desk waiting for them. Paul's heart sank when he saw her. She had obviously been crying, probably all night judging from her red, puffy eyes. Priya's hand shot to her mouth when she caught her first glimpse of the distraught girl. She felt like crying in sympathy, understanding completely what Jillian was feeling.

"What do you want?" Her cold eyes locked on Paul.

He started to answer, but Priya interrupted.

"Jillian, my name is Priya Kumar. Is there someplace a little more private we can go to talk?"

Jillian didn't move. "I don't think…"

"Please?" She noticed a big aluminum straightedge on the drafting table. She pointed to it and said, "And bring that. When we're done, if you think we've wasted your time, you can bend it over my head."

Jillian's lips twitched at the corners, not really into a smile, but enough to let Priya know she convinced her for the moment.

She stood, took two steps, turned back to grab the straightedge, then walked out of the space without even a glance at Paul as she passed him. She led the way to the break room, casually tossed the straightedge on the table, and sat in one of the chairs.

Priya walked in behind her but turned and blocked the door.

"Not you," she told Paul. "You wait out here."

"But…"

"Don't argue. This is between us girls. You'd only get in the way and mess things up like men usually do."

With that, she closed the door in his face and took a seat next to Jillian.

"I don't know what he told you, but we're nothing to each other. We just talked a few times."

"And had a most eventful lunch."

"You know about the lunch? You must have had a good laugh over that one." She sounded bitter.

"Laugh? I don't think so, Jillian. I thought that was one of the sweetest stories I ever heard. I was so excited for him when Paul told us what happened."

"Us? Who else did he tell? Is this his…"

"Jillian, please listen to me. He told me and Tom and Rob. We all work together in one small office. We're close. We share things. Especially when we're happy and excited. And girl, I have never ever seen anyone as happy and excited as Paul was when he returned from lunch Wednesday. The man literally floated into the office. He accomplished nothing all afternoon because he was thinking about you."

Jillian felt her fury abate the tiniest bit.

Is it possible she really is only a co-worker? But the kiss!

As if she was reading her mind, Priya said, "Look, I came here today because I care about Paul, but not in the way you think I do. And despite what you think you saw last night…no, that's wrong. You saw what you saw. But it was not what it looked like. Anyway, Paul's become one of my very best friends. But we are not into each other the way he is into you."

Jillian sat quietly, listening closely as Priya gave a detailed account of her relationship with Paul, beginning from the first day she started work. She told her almost everything, even her parting thought last night about someday surprising him on a birthday with a glimpse of her naked. She knew it was important for Paul that Jillian believe all the way down to her soul that she was hearing the complete truth.

As the story wound down, Jillian realized her anger and the ache in her chest were gone. She made a terrible mistake. She allowed her assumptions to almost ruin things with Paul when she should have confronted him about what she saw.

Still, Priya was enough to make anyone jealous and Jillian still felt a bit uneasy.

"I feel especially bad about having kissed him as I did. I'll bet that right up until that moment you were giving him the benefit of the doubt."

Jillian's face betrayed her.

Am I that transparent to this woman?

Priya continued. "I know I said this before, but it's really important you know that I kissed him because I had to make sure he was telling the truth about not being attracted to me anymore. I had to really know I would be able to trust him, that he wouldn't be tempted to use our friendship to try to manipulate me into bed."

"I suppose I can understand that."

Jillian found herself warming up to this straightforward person with the polite manner and quick humor.

I want to believe her...I...I think maybe I'm even starting to like her a little...but she's so damn beautiful...I feel like an ugly duckling sitting next to her. If she's going to be Paul's friend, how long will it take before he notices how bad I look in comparison?

"So what happens now? You and Paul are like buddies or something?"

"I guess so. This is new for both of us."

"And you share everything? I don't know if I'm all that keen on the idea of you two talking about me. If anything ever happened, I mean."

Priya smiled. "Well, think of it this way. Let's say you two get together, and one day you have an argument. You go storming out of the house because he acted like a jerk but refuses to admit it. What's he going to do? He's going to call a friend for advice. Now, who would you prefer he call? One of his guy friends who's as simple-minded as he is and who'll tell him he's right and that you'll soon come running back ready for some make-up sex? Or should he call me, who'll listen to what he says, find out what *really* happened, and then tell him he acted like a jerk and he'd better buy you flowers and jewelry pretty damn quick before you come to your senses and realize what an idiot he is?"

Jillian felt her fears dissolving as she laughed.

Maybe this girl isn't so bad after all, despite her looks.

"Can I ask you something, Priya?"

"Of course. Anything."

Jillian pursed her lips into a little half-grin. "How was the kiss?"

Priya lay her hand over her heart and said, "You have to promise never to tell him this and never to hold it against me."

Jillian nodded. "I promise."

"It was a wonderful kiss. He's a great kisser. When it was over, I told him I hadn't felt any spark and that was true. But Jillian, spark or not, I've not often been kissed that well. And you know what the worst part is?"

"What?"

"I don't think he was really trying. I think he was kissing me back... well...to be polite. But wow. That kiss was my fifth real temptation. I'm ashamed to say this, but if there *had* been something between us I might have broken my vow last night. I might have given myself to him and worried about the consequences later." A deep sigh punctuated the thought. "I guess it was for the best, though."

Jillian stared at Priya in amazement. "Vow? Given yourself? Are you a nun or something?"

Twice in two days. Unbelievable. What is going on with me lately?

Priya shook her head. "I guess if I can trust Paul with it, and he's falling in love with you, I can trust you, too."

"What do you mean 'falling in love with me'?"

"Oh please girl. You know exactly what I mean. Don't you dare sit there and try to pretend you and Paul don't mean anything to each other. I know for a fact that's not the case on his part. And as for you, well, no one gets that angry and spends the night crying over someone who means nothing to her."

Jillian felt the heat rising to her cheeks and wanted to change the subject. "So are you really...?"

"A nun, no. A virgin, yes."

Jillian's eyes widened at the unexpected revelation.

After extracting a promise not to reveal her secret to anyone else, Priya shared with her an abridged version of what she confided to Paul the previous night.

"Look Jillian, if things work out between you and Paul the way I think they will, you and I are either going to have to get along or I'll have to move far away. And I don't want to move.

"Paul and I shared something incredible last night, something I don't want to lose and that I think Paul doesn't want to lose, either. But if it meant ensuring his happiness with you, I'd quit my job and move to California tomorrow. That's how much he means to me."

Jillian couldn't help letting the skepticism show. "Come on. You'd move away if I didn't like you?"

"No, but I'd move away if you made Paul choose between us.

"I don't have many real, true friends, and I've never had one, not even a girlfriend I felt as close to as I feel to Paul. But when I do make a friend, I'm fiercely loyal to them. And I used the word fiercely on purpose. I'll do almost anything for a friend.

"So yes, if it came down to him being with the woman he loves, or remaining friends with me, I'd take the decision out of his hands and move away to spare him the pain of choosing."

Is she serious? Would she really move away if it came to that?

Jillian held the woman's eyes for long seconds.

My lord, I think she really would!

She found herself envying Priya's inner strength and commitment.

"I don't want that to happen," Priya continued, "but to ensure it doesn't, it means you have to know, really know, that there will never be anything more than a very special friendship between Paul and I.

"And I suppose you also should know that he and I share an affinity for humor, especially bad puns and sexual humor and innuendo. We discovered that last night, although I kind of suspected it from the banter around the office. So if I kid him about Mr. Johnson when you're around, you have to know there is nothing more to it than face value."

Jillian looked puzzled. "Mr..."

"Johnson. That's what he calls his thingy."

"Really? And here I thought guys all called it Butch, or Spike or some other silly macho name."

They chatted for a while longer, getting to know each other, sharing intimacies, and laughing, mostly at Priya's anecdotes about Paul and the other guys at work, until Jillian noticed the time.

"Yikes. We've kept him standing out there for almost an hour! He must be going crazy." She smiled at Priya. "Thank you for this. I feel so foolish now, but I'm really grateful you came this morning." She reached over and picked up the straightedge. "I guess I won't be using this after all."

Priya laughed and gave Jillian a hug. "Thank you for understanding and for giving Paul another chance. I hope we can be friends regardless of how things work out between you two. Now, I'm going back to work. I'll send him in. Please be nice to him."

Priya opened the door to find Paul pacing back and forth between the break room and the manager's office. He was heading away when he heard the door and whipped around so fast he almost lost his balance. Worry and expectation contorted his face before a wave of relief coursed through him when he saw her smile. Still rooted to the spot where he turned, he waited for her to approach him.

"She's a nice girl, Paul. You treat her well or you'll answer to me. I'm heading back to the office. Don't be long. We have lots of work to do today if you want to get out in time for your date tonight."

"Thank you, Priya." He kissed her on the cheek before she disappeared into the hall.

Jillian was standing next to the table when Paul appeared in the doorway. The corners of his mouth turned up into a tentative smile. "Hi," he said softly.

Jillian felt tears welling up in her eyes, but fought them back. This wasn't the time to be crying.

"I'm sorry." Her voice trembled. "I'm so, so sorry. I completely misjudged you and treated you like…" Her head drooped and shook slightly. "I don't know why I acted like that. It's not…" She sighed and raised her eyes to meet his. "Look, I'll understand if you're…if you'd rather not keep our date tonight."

"Rather not…are you crazy? Do you think I dragged Priya down here and grew three ulcers outside there pacing because I don't want to see you anymore?" His head tilted before an amused smile reached out to reassure her. "Jillian, tonight will be the best first date you've ever been on. That I've ever been on. You think I'd pass that up because you did something I probably would have done myself?"

He took a step toward her, arms outstretched, and she moved into them. His arms closed around her and pressed her close as the tears broke through and ran silently down her cheeks. She squeezed him tighter, mashing the softness of her breasts into his chest. She felt a stirring against her thigh, then it was gone as Paul broke the embrace.

His eyes locked on hers, his cheeks slightly flushed, and she knew he was searching her face for signs she noticed his arousal. She realized he was embarrassed and did not allow her gaze to betray the elation she felt inside. For right then, she knew with absolute certainty she had no reason to fear Priya or be jealous in any way. Merely hugging her started to arouse him while the long kiss he shared with Priya did not.

"I really am sorry," she whispered, still not sure what else to say to him.

"Forget it." His tone let her know he meant it. "I told you, if the situation was reversed, and I saw what you saw, I'd have reacted the same way. Maybe worse."

Jillian smiled, his sincerity reassuring her. "Paul, do you realize we've only just met, and so much has happened. I wonder if this is a sign of some sort."

"Maybe it is. Maybe the fates are testing us, trying us to see what we're made of, to see if we're really supposed to be together. I don't know. I guess only time will tell.

"And speaking of time, I have to get back to the office. As it is, I'll need to work straight through lunch to finish everything I have sitting on my desk. You see, I have a really big date tonight, and I absolutely do not want to be late."

She hugged him again. This time, there were no tears, only whispered plans for him to call around 4:30 to let her know what time he would pick her up.

She felt warm and optimistic for the coming night as she walked with him to the double doors and watched as he headed for the elevator.

Cathy appeared beside her. "Everything okay?"

Jillian nodded, still watching Paul.

Cathy followed her gaze for a moment, then whistled softly. "Nice butt!"

10:10 AM

Jillian was dropping shadows behind the graphics of suits she was using in the ad for a local clothing store when her phone rang.

Earlier, as the elevator doors closed behind Paul, Shandra, Marie, and a few others gathered around, anxious to know what happened between her and Priya, and with her and Paul. She gave them a capsule review, leaving out the personal details Priya confided, but soon had enough and told them all she needed to get back to work so she could get home in time to prepare for the date.

"Where the hell have you been?" Liz's voice was shaking with anxiety.

"Oh Lizzie, I'm so sorry. I know you asked me to call this morning but I was feeling terrible and I way overslept and I just wanted to get to work and not have to think about anything. But…"

"Well I've been dialing your house and your cell all morning and you didn't answer. I was really worried about you." She paused for a second and Jillian could hear her friend take a deep breath. When she continued, her voice softened. "Are you okay?"

"I'm fine, Lizzie. I…"

"Yeah, sure you are. After what he did to you? I'm gonna find that asshole and…"

"Liz, stop. Please. I was wrong, all wrong. I should have listened to you last night." Jillian chronicled everything that happened that morning. "I planned to call you at lunchtime to tell you. I figured you'd be busy."

"I am busy, but how could I concentrate not knowing where you were or if you were okay." She sighed. "Are you sure this is all on the level? It sounds so strange, the two of them showing up like that."

"I thought so too, at first. But really, Liz, Priya is nothing like what I imagined someone who…who looks like that would be. She's like this regular person. And she was really upset that her kissing Paul made me think the wrong thing."

"Which wouldn't have happened if you had listened to your best friend."

"I know, I know. But I tell you Liz, this whole thing with Paul has been so strange right from the start. Maybe it *is* fated to happen. Think about it. If I hadn't said that silly 'whatever you're giving away for free' thing, which just sort of came to me, Paul and I would never have met. And if I didn't rush out to follow them last night, against the better judgment of my best friend, I might never have met Priya.

"I feel like I should hate her for kissing him and for looking so good but I don't. Well, maybe I do a little for being so damn pretty, but I really do like her, Liz. And once I didn't despise her anymore, I kind of sensed she liked me, too. I don't think she has many friends here and she seems so smart and funny and really nice. I can't wait for you and Jenna to meet her. I think you guys'll like her, too."

"Sure, that's exactly what we need, a friggin' Playboy model hanging around to make us look worse than we already do."

"Oh stop it. What are you talking about? You're beautiful."

"Yeah, right. Compared to her we're all flat-chested, dog-faced skanks. Who needs to compete with someone like her? And the way she was all over Paul last night? She's probably like that with every guy."

"Come on, Lizzie."

Hearing the venom in Liz's voice, she found herself growing a little frustrated with her old friend at the same time she wanted to defend her new friend.

"I'm sure she's not like that. She spent over an hour with me this morning and I think she would have spent all day if that's what it took to convince me she wasn't interested in him. Do you know anyone else who'd do something like that? Or who'd tell a guy's girlfriend that she'd move away rather than jeopardize her friend's relationship?"

"Oh, so you're already his girlfriend?"

"No. Of course not. Not yet anyway. But you know what I mean. You have to respect someone who'd do that for a friend. And aren't you the one who's always going on and on about not judging people by their looks?"

Liz didn't respond right away and Jillian let the silence drag on. After almost a minute, she heard her friend sigh.

"I guess you're right. I don't know why I'm being like this. It's probably just leftover from hating her all night for you."

Jillian laughed softly. "That's okay. It took me almost half an hour to get over it. You've only had five minutes."

"Do you know where he's taking you?"

"Not yet. He's calling me this afternoon. Maybe I'll get a hint then. But he told me this morning it would be the best first date I ever had."

"Well that sounds promising! What are you going to wear?"

'I don't know. I sort of stopped thinking about it last night and I haven't had time this morning."

The two spent the next ten minutes trying to figure out what she could wear, but nothing seemed right for the best first date of a lifetime.

"Maybe I'll try to get out a little early and hit some shops. And I guess I should call Jenna and tell her what happened."

"You can't. She's in the lab all day running some big experiment. She won't take any calls until it's finished this afternoon. Don't worry, I'll call her and tell her."

They talked for a few more minutes, speculating about where he might take her. And before they said goodbye, Liz told Jillian she'd call her cell tonight around eight-thirty, just in case the date wasn't going well.

11:50 AM

On the walk back to work, Paul vowed to keep his promise. Tonight's date had to be beyond exceptional. He plotted and planned as he worked, but found himself so distracted he had to go back and re-edit things three times after realizing he had no memory of what he saw, read, or did.

A few minutes before noon, he gave up, threw his pencil down on the desk and explained his problem to the team. "I want to pick her up in a limo and take her to a quiet, romantic Italian restaurant. But which one? I'll never get a reservation anywhere nice on such short notice."

"Maybe I can help with that," said a voice from the doorway. Lisa walked in holding a huge basket that could only contain the fixings for a picnic lunch. She placed it on the corner of Rob's desk and walked around to kiss him.

"Hi baby," she said as their lips met.

Priya noticed the kiss lasted a bit longer than strictly necessary for such a greeting and smiled.

I wonder if that was conscious or not? Letting me know Rob's taken. I guess I'll have to have lunch with her too one of these days. Rob's been though enough lately. He doesn't need her wondering about me.

Rob introduced Lisa to Tom and Priya. After a short exchange of pleasantries, Lisa turned to Paul. "I take it you're really trying to impress coffee girl?"

Paul glared at Rob, who looked innocently away.

"Yes. I want to knock her socks off tonight. And her name is Jillian, by the way."

Lisa caught the glare and realization struck. She smacked Rob on the shoulder. "Fool. You set me up for that, didn't you? Coffee girl indeed. What if I said that in front of her someday?" She turned to Paul. "Sorry about that. He told me it was your nickname for her."

"That's okay. I'll make him pay one day soon."

"No, no. Don't you worry," she told him, a devilish gleam in her eye. "Leave it to me. I can make him suffer in ways you can't begin to imagine."

That cracked up everyone except Rob, who just sat silently, trying his best to appear repentant.

"So you want someplace quiet and romantic. What price range?"

"Doesn't matter. But it has to be *really* romantic."

"My, my. This Jillian must be something special!"

"You have no idea," Tom said, giving up on the team getting any meaningful work done for the rest of the day.

Lisa's quizzical smile had everybody eyeing each other.

"Well, you might as well hear the whole story." Paul said, and proceeded to tell her everything that happened since Wednesday morning.

When he finished the monologue, Lisa's hand covered her mouth and her eyes were misty. For the second time, she smacked Rob on the shoulder. "All this happened and all you tell me is that Paul met a girl?" Shifting her gaze back to Paul she said, "That is so romantic. Now I see why... Okay, let me make a phone call."

She flipped open her cell and dialed a number as she headed out the door. "I'll be right back. Start thinking about what happens after dinner."

When she returned ten minutes later, she was all smiles. "Okay, how does this sound? You have a seven o'clock reservation at Casa de Luna. You know the place? When you get to the restaurant, ask for Gino. He'll take good care of you. You also have a New England Coach limo and driver for the night so you won't have to deal with taxis."

Paul stared at her, completely flabbergasted.

Casa de Luna?

You would expect the finest Italian restaurant in Boston to be in the North End, home to all things Italian. In an area roughly one-quarter mile square, you can find more than sixty restaurants and cafes, many of them world famous. But the most famous of all, the restaurant it was impossible to get into unless you made a reservation many weeks in advance, was located not in Little Italy, but on Boylston Street, right on the edge of Chinatown.

"How did you..."

"Anthony DiBenedetto, one of the owners, is a friend of my dad. And his daughter's wedding reception was at the Ritz, where yours truly is the function manager. So I called him and told him about you and Jillian. I was hoping he'd be able to squeeze you in for an early reservation or something. I should have known the old softy would...well, you'll find out later. Just be sure to ask for Gino, okay?"

"Okay? Are you kidding? Casa de Luna is perfect! I can't believe it! Thank you, Lisa!"

She wrote something on a scrap of paper and handed it to Paul. "That's the number for New England Coach. Ask for Davie. Your car and driver will be available from six o'clock until whenever. The driver's name is Gary, he's prepared for an all-nighter if it comes to that, and his tip will be up to you, but the limo itself is being covered by your good friend

Rob."

"W...What?" Rob sputtered. "What do you mean? Why am I paying for it"

Lisa smiled sweetly at him. "Oh honey," she began in a tone usually reserved for small children, "don't be like that. You're doing something special for your friend. And I'll bet it will also help you remember that it's not nice to play tricks on the girl who loves you."

His workmates erupted in laughter.

"I like your style," Priya said. "I *really* like your style."

"And I like yours. What you did for Paul this morning was amazing. Not many people would have put themselves on the line like that. We have to have lunch one day real soon."

Tom glanced at his watch. It was nearly twelve-thirty. Motioning to the picnic basket, he suggested Rob and Lisa might want to head off on their picnic. Then he asked Paul and Priya if they wanted to join him for lunch. He told them all he planned to take the rest of the day off and they should do the same. Everyone was too caught up in the date drama to concentrate on work.

"Why don't you guys join us on the Common. There's plenty of food in here, although we may have to share plates and glasses. I know *we'll* be talking about the big date and I'm pretty sure that's what you guys will be talking about, so we might as well make it a party."

"Thanks, Lisa. Sounds good to me," Tom said. "And don't worry about plates and such. I'll grab some plastic stuff from the lunch room."

Forty-five minutes later, Paul swallowed the last sip of his now-cold coffee. He was too nervous to eat anything, but everyone else thoroughly enjoyed the crudités, cold meats, cheeses, breads, and fruit.

All were in good spirits as they ate and discussed the various places he might take Jillian after dinner.

There were several good plays running at the Colonial and Shubert Theaters, the Stuart Street Playhouse, and the Wang Center, but none started late enough to avoid having to rush dinner.

Tom suggested they stop by Mike's Pastry but Priya reminded him the place was so famous it was always packed with locals and tourists.

Tom nodded. "I forgot about that."

"Besides," Paul added, "I have a surprise in mind for right after dinner that pretty much eliminates the North End."

"Oh, you romantic devil," Rob kidded after Paul explained his plan. "You are getting lucky *for sure* tonight."

They kicked around ideas for a while longer. Various bars and lounges were mentioned for drinks, clubs discussed for dancing, even some unusual things like stopping at a local bookstore so he could see her work in the magazine and show her some of the books he edited. In the end, Paul decided on a plan everyone agreed was a good one.

"You do realize this date will cost you more than the annual budget of some small nations," Tom said.

"Oh stop exaggerating," Priya chided. "I think it'll be very romantic and I'll be feeling very jealous tonight thinking about it."

"The cost doesn't matter," Paul said. "It's only money. I'll make some more tomorrow. Or Monday. I just want to make this date one she'll never forget."

Lisa leaned over and put her hand on Priya's arm. "You know, I think we'll both be feeling a little jealous tonight."

2:15 PM

Seated at her drawing table, Jillian combed her hair back with her fingers, then grabbed a handful in both fists and let out a screech of frustration. This was the fifth mistake she'd made today.

"Don't pull too hard or you'll have to do some fancy hairdressing for your date tonight." Cathy stood at the entrance to her work space. "Let's see now, how many times have I heard that sound today? Three? Four?"

Jillian groaned. "Five. It's horrible. I can't concentrate. I keep thinking about what a fool I made of myself. He knows I was spying on him. I acted like a suspicious, clingy, insecure girlfriend...like he was cheating on me or something, and we've never even gone out." She groaned again. "What man in his right mind would want someone who acts like that?"

"I can think of one." Cathy laid her hand on Jillian's shoulder. "This boy likes you Jilli. I saw him when you and that girl, what was her name?"

"Priya."

"That's right. I watched him when you and Priya were locked in the break room this morning. Honey, that man all but wore out the tiles on the floor with his pacing. When he came into my office to ask to see you, he looked like someone just died. You didn't notice that when you first saw him?"

Jillian shook her head. "Maybe I was too angry to really see straight."

"You were angry all right. But I think it was more than that, if you'll admit it to yourself. You were heartbroken. Heartbroken over a guy you've never gone out with. How do you explain that?"

"I don't know. *I don't know!*" She was so frustrated she couldn't stand it, and it was showing. "I haven't been able to figure out any of this. Two days ago I meet this guy who acts like a goof, so I shoot him down, but something happens when I see his expression, so I tell him where I'll be for lunch, and then he's so charming at lunch where *I* make a fool of myself, and suddenly I'm all starry-eyed and can't think of anything else, and then… It's crazy, just crazy. I don't act like this."

"Maybe it's time you started," Cathy said gently. "You know, it's possible this guy is just a big loser who's so desperate to get laid he'll put up with anything for a date with a pretty girl."

Jillian's nostrils flared with anger. "He's not a…"

Cathy cut her off, laughing. "I know he's not a loser. But see how you reacted when I suggested it." She watched Jillian's face flush. "You like this guy as much as he likes you. Who knows why? Is why *really* all that important?"

She let the question sink in for a few seconds before she continued. "What *is* important is there's something special happening between the two of you. Maybe it's hormones, maybe it's destiny. Maybe you two will be shooting stars or maybe you'll build a brave new world for yourselves."

"Brave new world?"

"I know, sorry. I read the book again last week and couldn't resist." She sat in Jillian's desk chair.

"Did you consider that he may have found it charming you cared enough to follow him? Perhaps he realized you wouldn't have been so upset if you didn't feel something for him. There's no way to know, Jillian, and worrying about it will only make you crazy.

"Go out with him tonight. Go out and see what happens. Worst case, you wasted an evening, best case…"

She was interrupted by the sharp ring of the phone. Jillian glanced at the clock. It was too early for it to be Paul. "Please. I don't want to talk to clients right now. Will you…"

Cathy was already reaching for the phone. "Jillian Marshall's desk. May I help you? … Hold on a minute, please." She pressed hold, held out the receiver and said, "It's him. Now talk to him like last night and this morning never happened."

Jillian closed her eyes for a few seconds to compose herself, then nodded to Cathy who pressed the line button. "Hi, Paul!"

"Hi. Look, I know it's early but something came up and I didn't want to wait to call you."

Cathy saw Jillian's face and shoulders droop as she anticipated hearing Paul cancel their date tonight. "Uh-huh."

"Is something wrong? Is this a bad time? I can call back at four-thirty if you want. It's just that I'm kind of anxious about tonight. I've made some interesting plans and…"

Jillian straightened up, beaming. He wasn't canceling at all!

"Plans? What plans?"

"Oh no. You said to surprise you so now you'll have to wait. But the thing is, we have an early reservation somewhere and, well, I'll need to pick you up around six-thirty. I know that's awfully early and I'm sorry but I, well, I can't tell you why." He paused for a second. "Will that be okay? Will you have enough time to get ready after work?"

"Six-thirty is fine." She started to panic inside, wondering how she'd be able to get home, shower, and get dressed and everything in time.

"Great!" There was no mistaking the excitement in his voice. "I'll see you then. Oh, and you might want to wear something a little dressy. Bye."

Jillian filled in her boss on the side of the conversation she didn't hear.

"See, what did I tell you? He probably already forgot about the whole thing." She stood up to return to her office. "Why don't you leave early? That ad can wait until Monday morning. If you stay until five-thirty you'll never be ready by six-thirty. Go home now. Have a nice hot bath and relax for a while." Her eyes bright, she grinned and added, "And when you're walking in front of him tonight, make sure your cute little backside puts on a nice show for the boy! I have a feeling he's going to earn it."

2:40 PM

As the elevator descended, Jillian surveyed her nails, then pulled a small mirror from her purse for a peek at her hair.

Maybe I'll lose the clear polish and add some color. And I could put my hair up. But maybe he'd like it better down. Or maybe...

The door opening interrupted her thoughts. She stepped out and started across the lobby, mentally rummaging through her closet, searching for something she and Liz might have forgotten earlier. One by one, she dismissed each outfit, even the skirt and blouse combination mentioned last night.

No, they're nice, but nowhere near special enough. I need something fabulous...something simple but elegant. I want him to drool when he first sees me.

Her soft giggle turned some heads.

He said to wear something a little dressy. That's guy talk for 'don't wear pants.' So he wants to see me in a dress. Hmmm.

Once outside the building, she glanced at her watch.

Plenty of time. Thank you, Cathy.

She cut across the Common and Public Garden to Newbury Street and spent nearly forty minutes hopping in and out of boutiques.

She found a really hot, red, scoop-neck dress with an open back and criss-cross straps in the second store. When she tried it on, she almost blushed at how much cleavage showed. She loved the way it clung to her hips, but it was right on the cusp of being slutty, so she kept it in mind and continued her search.

As she strolled down the street toward the next shop she heard a familiar female voice call, "Jillian! Hey, Jillian!"

She was surprised to see Marissa scoop up a small boy and hurry to catch up with her.

"Hi! Are you cutting classes today? And who is this handsome guy?" She reached over and tried to pat him on the cheek but he squirmed around to avoid her hand.

"This is my nephew Christian. Mary and Frank are at the D-O-C-T-O-R, so Chris and I are having a fun afternoon."

"Is everything okay?"

Marissa grinned and patted her lower abdomen. "Oh sure. Three month ultrasound."

"Ooo, that's wonderful! Give her my congratulations!"

"I will. Now what are you doing out of work? Did you take the day off? I can't blame you after what happened last night."

Jillian gave her a quick update.

"That's unbelievable! And you still don't know where you're going?"

"Nope. He wants to surprise me. But I have a feeling it'll be pretty special, which is why I'm looking for a new dress."

Just then, her cell phone rang. She fished it out of her purse, flipped it open, and checked the caller ID.

"Oh shi…" She remembered Chris. "…ah, shoot. I forgot."

"Hey, Jills. How's it going?"

"Hi Patrick. I'm fine."

"I am *so* glad to be back in Boston. I've been craving stuffed calamari for a week now. How about I pick you up after work and we can find someplace in the North End for calamari, pasta, and a couple of bottles of wine. Then, when we're feeling good, we can go wherever you like. What time should I pick you up? Or did you want to go home first to change or something?"

"Patrick, I'm sorry, but I didn't know you were getting home tonight and I've already made other plans."

"So cancel them. Besides, you made plans with me two weeks ago."

"I know, but they weren't for any particular night. I made plans with my girlfriends and I can't let them down."

Damn, I hate lying, but how can I tell him I'm canceling to see another guy.

Patrick let her know he was not happy about being stood up. When he finally rang off, she found herself hoping he'd never call back, even if things didn't go well with Paul tonight.

As she closed the phone she heard, "Juggling two boyfriends, I see. This is a new side to you. Who's Patrick?"

Jillian wrinkled her nose. "I met him at a party two months ago. He's a sales-rep for some drug company. Used to play basketball in college. After about fifteen minutes of mostly meaningless small-talk, he claimed to be, and this is a quote, 'completely smitten. I've never experienced love at first sight before. It's amazing. You're amazing.'"

Marissa giggled. "You're kidding. He didn't really say that."

"I swear. But he was tall and good looking and dressed well, so I let it go and gave him my cell number, a mistake, by the way, from which I learned a valuable lesson – only give a new guy your regular phone number. It's much easier to control when you talk to him.

"Anyway, we went out a few times, but it turns out his love at first sight was more like lust at any opportunity. He was always charming, and attentive, and he took me to some nice places, but he was always, ummm, putting on a full-court press to get me to come home with him.

"I was sort of tempted after our third date 'cause, you know, it's kind of been a long time since the last time, and I thought maybe he'd relax and stop trying to close the deal all the time if I let him, but it just...I don't know...it just didn't feel right sleeping with him when that seemed to be the only reason he was seeing me. You know what I mean?"

"Yeah. But...you're still seeing him?"

"Not really. Two weeks ago, he told me he had to attend a training session in Chicago and wouldn't be back for a fortnight. He actually said fortnight, mind you. Honestly, I was relieved. He's just too pushy. I've been half-hoping he'd lose interest by the time he returned." She held up the phone. "Evidently he hasn't."

Marissa grimaced. "Yeah, I hate guys like that. They think they're doing you a favor by trying to get you naked. Northeastern's full of guys like that. Maybe you'll get lucky and he won't call again."

"I wish. No, I'll have to tell him goodbye eventually, but I didn't want to get into it now."

"Absolutely. Why get yourself upset before a big date. Hey, want some company shopping?"

Marissa stroked her nephew's hair and stage whispered, "Want to help Jillian find a new dress so she can be all pretty for her date tonight?"

Chris just snuggled closer and held on tighter, drawing laughs from the girls as they continued on with the search for the perfect dress.

By four o'clock, Jillian was about to give up and go back for the red one when, right in the only window of a tiny little walk-down shop, she spotted a black, silk, v-neck with spaghetti ties. When she tried it on, she knew this was the one. The silk clung to her in all the right places, as if it was custom made for her. The neck dipped just low enough to entice, as did the half-open back, and the hem fluttered two inches above her knees.

As she walked out of the dressing room, Marissa whistled. "Oh girl, you look *sooo* great in that. You have to get it." Then she held one side of Chris's head to her chest, covered his other ear with her free hand. "Of course, you *know* that when Paul sees you in that dress all he's gonna want to do is take it off you."

Jillian blushed but was pleased at the thought of such a reaction. She was still in front of the mirror, admiring the way the dress fit, when she heard, "Jilli, look at this!"

Marissa held up a lovely, black, cashmere wrap with delicate gold embroidery near the ends that would add the perfect touch of elegance to her new dress. It was wide enough to cover her back and shoulders and heavy enough to keep her cozy should the day's unseasonable warmth vanish with the setting sun.

Standing again in front of the mirror in the boutique, Jillian imagined herself with her hair up, wearing her black, strappy heels, and her diamond teardrop earrings and was pleased. She really wanted to look good tonight and wondered what Paul's reaction would be when he first saw her.

In a few hours, she would find out.

6:25 PM

Damn! It's almost six-thirty. He'll be here any minute.

Since arriving home two hours earlier, she dusted and straightened the whole apartment, showered, put her hair up three different ways, painted her fingernails and toenails to match the lipstick she selected for the night, agonized over which scent to use, and, finally, dropped the towel she was wearing and slipped into her new dress. All she had left was to put on her earrings, underwear and shoes and she'd be ready. Naturally, the doorbell rang.

"Damn!"

She ran to the speaker, determined it was Paul, and told him she was almost ready and that she'd leave the door unlocked. Then she buzzed him in and ran back to the bathroom.

Look at me...rushing around like a teenager getting ready for her first date. Why am I doing this? Why does it feel so important? It's just another first date. I've been on plenty of them. But...somehow, this one is different. It feels...right. He feels right. But why? The flowers? The misunderstanding? Is it guilt that's making me feel this way? Or is this what people talk about...the knowing, before there is any way you could know? The certainty you feel when you've met the right person? Stop it, girl. You can't think like that. He's just another guy...but what if...

"Stop it! It's too confusing and you don't have time to think about it now."

Her earrings went on in a matter of seconds. Then she stared at the silk pantyhose and panties. Which one? On the one hand, her legs looked great and she really didn't need to wear pantyhose, but on the other hand, is was only May, and if the night turned cold and the wind whipped up, she didn't want to find herself literally freezing her ass off.

She was reaching for the panties when she heard a knock, followed a second later by "Hello."

"I'll just be another minute or two. Please make yourself comfortable."

She picked up the black undies and slid them on. Pushing the dress back down, she inspected herself in the long mirror.

Damn! Panty lines. It ruins the effect of the dress. I'm sure there's some silky shear ones in the dresser, but there's no way I can go out and pull underwear from a drawer with him standing right there.

With a sigh, the panties came off and the pantyhose went on. When she checked the mirror again, she smiled.

No lines. Perfect.

She checked her face one last time, slipped into her heels, then quietly opened the bathroom door and stepped into the room.

Paul was dressed in a black *Donna Karan* three-button suit with a white shirt and a black and gray patterned silk tie. He was admiring the evening view out the window when he heard her softly say, "Hi. You look very handsome."

He turned and his mouth simply dropped open, his eyes blinking rapidly, as if they could not believe what they were seeing.

"Holy..." he whispered after a few seconds, "You look..."

He stood, unmoving, afraid if he even twitched, the spell would be broken and the vision in front of him would vanish.

"You look..."

Jillian lifted her arms above her head and executed a slow, graceful pirouette. "You like this dress then?"

"You..."

"I'll take that as a yes." She walked across the room to stand in front of him.

"Jillian, I, ahh, I'm sorry. I'm making a fool of myself again."

"Oh, don't you worry about it. Finding yourself speechless at the sight of me was exactly the right response."

Paul cleared his throat and remembered what was in his hand. He held out a small bouquet of the same white Calla lilies he sent yesterday.

"They're lovely, Paul. Thank you."

Callas twice in two days. How could he know?

She donned her wrap, eliciting another exclamation of appreciation from Paul.

"Wow. I may need to hire armed guards to keep other guys away from you tonight."

Jillian felt a quiver of satisfaction.

I don't know how this evening will end, but it's certainly starting out perfectly.

Paul offered his arm and a smile, and they set out on the date.

As they walked through the front door of the building, Jillian saw a limousine with a young man standing next to it. She turned to Paul, her face glowing. "You didn't!"

He merely smiled, satisfied she was pleased, and introduced her to the driver, who opened the rear door as they approached.

"Pleased to meet you," Gary said to her. "And if you don't mind me saying so, you look absolutely lovely tonight."

Jillian didn't mind at all and told him so as he helped her into the car. A moment later, Paul was beside her and the door closed.

Once in the driver's seat, Gary turned so he could see his passengers.

"You have the phone?" he asked Paul, who patted his jacket pocket and nodded. "Parking can be difficult and I may not always be able to stay close, so try to signal me at least five minutes before you're ready to leave, okay? Pound-7-7 sends a page. If you need to speak with me, press star-2-7 then the TALK button."

Paul nodded again. "Got it."

"A few other things. Help yourself to anything you find back there. The fridge is stocked with a variety of beverages as is the mini-bar and if you open the small door below the mini-bar, you'll find an assortment of snacks. The controls for the audio/video are above your head and if you slide open the top cabinets on the left and right, you'll find an assortment of CDs and DVDs. However, given our itinerary tonight, I took the liberty of loading a special CD I burned. I was listening to it on the way to pick you up, so it's all ready to go. The case is in that little drawer to your right if you want to check out the songs.

"Also, if you need me while we're on the road, pick up the phone on the armrest and press the star button."

"Thanks, Gary." Paul reached for the CD case. He scanned the titles and smiled. Looking up, he caught Gary's eyes in the rear view mirror and gave him a 'thumbs up'. Then he passed the case to Jillian. "What do you think?"

Jillian studied it for a minute. Five of the songs were also on her special mix.

"I think Gary knows how to create a mood."

She reached up to press the play button on the CD section of the controls.

The window between the driver and passenger compartments began to rise as the soft, sultry voice of Linda Ronstadt filled the air.

There's a saying old says that love is blind,
Still we're often told, "seek and you shall find"
So I'm going to seek a certain man I've had
in mind...

Jillian raised her eyes to meet Paul's. She could feel her heart quickening. Was this song another sign, she wondered, a good one?

Their eyes remained locked, each lost in the moment as the song played through.

...to my heart he carries the key.
Won't you tell him please to put on some speed,
Follow my lead, oh, how I need
Someone who'll watch over me
Someone who'll watch over me.

Neither noticed when Ronstadt's voice faded away to be replaced by Barry White's deep, sexy bass. Both were a little afraid of the intensity of what they were feeling. Was it the song or did the song merely channel to the surface what lay hidden in their hearts? Unsure, neither said anything, but both somehow knew that no matter what happened in the future, this was a moment they would never forget.

The spell was broken when Jillian's hand relaxed enough to let the flowers slip from her fingers.

Shoot. Why did I bring them? I should have put them in water.

She snatched them up, relieved to see they were undamaged. "Paul, these flowers are very beautiful. May I ask a question?"

"You may ask a thousand questions and I'll give you a thousand answers. They may not all be the right answers, but I guarantee they'll sound good."

Jillian giggled. "Just one for now, thank you. Why did you choose these lilies to send yesterday and to give me today?"

He was expecting something personal, something one usually shared on a first date. "I don't know, really. I went online to see what the florist had to offer and when I came to the Calla lilies they just felt right. They reminded me of you, I guess. They looked soft, and delicate, but hardy at the same time and when I *googled* them and found they represent innocence, purity and beauty, well...I knew they were the right flowers."

Jillian was more than pleased with his explanation. "They're perfect. Thank you again."

She wanted to tell him they have always been her favorite flower but held back, partly afraid it would sound phony, but mostly because she was feeling overwhelmed. At every turn, there seemed to be another connection between them. She sighed.

I guess there's no way to know what's going to happen. But it looks like it'll be fun finding out.

6:45 PM

Priya leaned back in the tub, letting the warm water and clouds of bubbles envelope her up to her chin. A single vanilla candle cast a soft glow as it filled the bathroom with its delicious scent.

I hate feeling jealous like this. He's a friend now...a very special friend. I should be thankful the fates have allowed that. And with luck maybe she'll be a friend, too. He wants her and that's all there is to it so stop acting like an irrational fool and get over it.

A long sigh split the bubble mountain she built above her chest.

Be happy for them. If you're happy for them it will make the envy go away faster.

She tried to clear her mind but her guilt kept nagging, refusing to let her be.

Two lies in two days. What's wrong with you, girl? Daddy would be ashamed if he found out. But I had no choice. He didn't feel it. I couldn't let him know about the fire. And I certainly couldn't tell Jillian. That kiss...nobody's ever made me feel that way before. The burning...the ache...I see now why girls give themselves with such abandon. Is it like this for guys, too? Do they feel this way when they want someone?

Priya sighed again and moved her hands gently beneath the surface, circulating the warm liquid over her skin. The sensation felt good and she tried to concentrate on that instead of imagining she was with Paul tonight or that he was here with her in the bath, but it was no use. He was in her head, and would stay there until her passion for him faded and only their friendship remained.

Silently, she cursed the fates for toying with her. She finally found someone with whom she could let down all her barriers, someone who could know all her secrets and not use them to his advantage, someone she knew she could count on for help and comfort whenever it might be needed, someone who could make her feel like a woman *and* a person, but she was only allowed to discover he was right under her nose for months a day after it was too late.

I wonder if he knows what kind of friend he's found? Probably not. Men are so clueless. They really aren't very good at sensing feelings or reading body language...unless the hints are as obvious as rocks hitting them on their stupid, hard heads.

Again, she sighed.

I guess it's for the best. He'd probably get all weird if he knew. And that would be the end of the friendship. And kill any chance of being friends with Jillian. I wonder where they are now? They must be on their way to the restaurant. Will he think of me at all, tonight? Right. Don't be stupid.

Again, she tried to relax and clear her mind, but memories of that kiss kept intruding.

It was a mistake to kiss him...no...it was wonderful, and now I won't wonder every time I see him. I'll get over it soon...and neither of them will ever know how I felt.

Priya realized she would not be able to get him out of her thoughts tonight, so she stopped trying. With the toes of her right foot, she turned on the hot water and let it run until the bath was toasty warm again. Then she closed her eyes and indulged in her favorite fantasy, only this time, her lover wasn't faceless.

6:55 PM

Jillian knew they could not have traveled far when the limousine rolled to a stop.

Paul jumped out when Gary opened the door, then reached a hand inside to assist her. As she stepped out, she saw a red carpet leading up to massive wooden doors on which had been carved a beautiful, detailed moon.

Ohmygod he's taking me to Casa de Luna! How? It takes weeks to get a reservation here.

She turned to him in disbelief, but Paul offered only a smile and his arm.

The inside was even more wonderful than she heard. If she had not just walked through those famous doors, she would have sworn she was standing in an outdoor café somewhere in Italy.

At first, it appeared the only light in the room came from the candles in fancy lanterns casting a soft glow on each table. But when her eyes adjusted, she noticed the high domed ceiling twinkling with hundreds of points of light, like stars in a night sky, complete with a softly glowing moon. The effect was breathtaking.

Scattered around the fountain that commanded the center of the large room, were square, wrought-iron tables, spaced far enough apart to ensure conversations were not overheard. They were covered with crisp, white linen tablecloths, and set with fine china, crystal, and silver. Each had four sumptuously padded wrought-iron chairs around it.

The floor appeared to be stone and brick. On three sides of the room, false stone facades rose to meet the sky while the fourth was a magnificently detailed fresco that gave the impression the whole room overlooked a large bay partially ringed by hills.

Even in the dim light, she could see all the tables were occupied.

"Mister DiLorenzo, Ms. Marshall, *buona sera!* Welcome to our humble café. My name is Gino." The heavily accented greeting came from a slender, distinguished looking man in a tuxedo who approached them from an unnoticed doorway to their right.

"Thank you, Gino," Paul replied as Jillian removed her wrap and draped it over her arm. "And please thank Mr. DiBenedetto for his kindness."

I wonder how he knew who we were. Must be the time we arrived.

"*Si, certo!* Of course. Please, give me a moment and then I will show you to your table."

Jillian watched as he spoke with a tall, similarly tuxedoed young man, then turned, the wonder still in her eyes. "This is amazing, Paul. How did you..."

"I'll tell you later," he promised, nodding to indicate the maître d' was returning.

Gino led them across the center of the room. Paul was aware of the many male eyes following Jillian. Part of him felt proud to have someone so lovely by his side. But another part wanted to bare his teeth and glare as a warning to stay away from his woman. Fortunately, the civilized part kept him moving forward, calmly ignoring the stares.

Jillian could not imagine where Gino was leading them since it was obvious there were no open tables. Her question was answered when he led them to one of the false building fronts and opened the double doors to reveal a cozy, private dining alcove constructed to resemble a *terrazzo*.

The table was set for two. In keeping with the walls of the main room, these appeared to be wide, ivy covered arches and railings with beautiful frescos of lush gardens overlooking the same bay as did the main room.

"Oh my! It's so lovely." Jillian's head was spinning. Paul said this would be a memorable date, but she never imagined he'd be taking her here, and to a private room!

She slid gracefully into the chair Gino held for her as Paul took the seat to her right. Gino stepped back a pace and, as if they had been signaled, several waiters appeared to fill water glasses from a crystal pitcher, place on the table a silver basket of warm breads and breadsticks and a matching tray with assorted olives and dipping oils, and to present them with beautiful leather-bound menus.

As quickly as they appeared, the waiters vanished. "Please, take your time," Gino said. "Nothing is ever hurried here. When you are ready to order, or if you need anything, anything at all, just press the button at the base of the lantern in the center of the table."

Paul nodded. "Thank you, thank you very much."

Gino bowed slightly before he backed out, pulling the doors closed to give them complete privacy.

Jillian's gaze drifted slowly around the room again before focusing on Paul. She felt like she was dreaming. "This is so lovely, Paul. It's like a fantasy. How did you ever get reservations?"

"I wish I could say it was because of my charm and good looks, or that I know powerful people in important places, but the truth is, Rob's girlfriend knows the owner. She overheard me talking about where to bring you tonight and offered to help. When she told me she arranged reservations here, I thought she wrangled us a table near the kitchen or something. I had no idea she managed this."

A gleam came into his eyes.

"You're right, though, this is a lovely room." He reached over and traced the line of her cheek with his finger. "But it's nothing compared to how beautiful you are tonight."

Jillian could feel herself getting all soft and fluttery inside and it made her a little nervous.

I shouldn't be feeling this way so soon. I hardly know him. Sure he's...

A short knock interrupted her thought. A few seconds later, Gino entered carrying an ice bucket and two champagne flutes. He set one down in front of each of them, removed the bottle from the bucket, and displayed the bottle for Paul's approval. It was a 1996 *Dom Pérignon*.

"Thank you, Gino, but we didn't order this."

"*Si*, I know. It is a gift. I am not permitted to tell you from whom, but I am to tell you..." He paused and removed a small card from his pocket. "If you do not behave like a perfect gentleman tonight, instructions will be provided to Ms. Marshall on how to make you suffer in ways you can't begin to imagine." He shrugged apologetically.

Chuckling, Paul shook his head. "Thank you, Gino." He turned to Jillian. "It has to be from Lisa. She said something similar this afternoon."

After Gino opened the bottle and filled their flutes, Paul explained Rob's 'coffee girl' joke, Lisa's threat, and how she made good on it.

"I am liking this Lisa more and more," Jillian said when she stopped laughing. "Rob. That's the guy who was with you in the coffee shop Wednesday?"

"Yes, ma'am. He's my best friend."

"I would think he'd have to be to pick up the tab for the limo."

"Well, Lisa didn't give him any choice, but I don't think he'll care right now." He chuckled at her quizzical expression. "It's kind of a long story. How about I tell you later, while we're eating?"

Jillian agreed and they picked up their menus.

Casa de Luna served a classic Italian six-course supper – appetizer, soup, pasta, main course, salad, and coffee and dessert. There were no prices on the menu because there was only one per-person price that included everything except beer, wine, and spirits.

The menu changed irregularly, but frequently. Each of the four brothers who owned the restaurant took turns scouring the cities, towns, and countryside of Italy for new recipes. The current menu featured dishes from Tuscany, particularly the cities of Florence, Sienna, and Pisa.

"I'm having trouble choosing," Jillian confessed. "Everything sounds so delicious."

"Me, too. If it wouldn't completely bankrupt me, I'd have them bring one of everything so I could take a bite of each."

Jillian laughed and touched his hand. "I'm afraid if you did that, by the time we left here this dress would be tighter than spandex on me."

"And that would be a bad thing?"

The implication pleased her even as it caused her cheeks to take on a rosy glow.

Jillian planned to play the game Shandra mentioned at dinner last night and order a salad and maybe a piece of fish or something. But as she read the menu, she realized she wasn't experiencing the same anxiety, the same need she usually felt on first dates to make the guy think she ate like a bird. Paul was a virtual stranger yet she sat with him as if they were old friends. Despite her misgivings, she could not help feeling comfortable with him.

She snuck a glance at him studying his menu.

He seems so relaxed. Why isn't he nervous? He's the one who chased me. He's the one who has to make a good impression...who's being judged here. But he looks so calm, so...content. Maybe that's why I feel like this, like I can just be me. No games, no watching every word like with Patrick. This is nice!

She returned her attention to her menu, and a few minutes later, they compared their selections.

Jillian decided to start with *Involtini di Melanzane e Zucchini*, eggplant and zucchini slices wrapped around a filling of bread, ham, pine nuts, currants and cheese then covered with a light tomato sauce and melted cheese. For his appetizer, Paul selected *Formaggio con le pere*, diced ripe pear tossed with small cubes of pecorino romano cheese and sprinkled lightly with freshly ground black pepper.

Both selected the same second course, *Pappa al Pomodoro*, a tomato and country-bread soup with sweet onion and basil. Paul's pasta choice was Cavatelli with a spicy bolognese sauce. Jillian decided to try the potato gnocchi with a simple marinara sauce.

Her main course would be *Pollo in Porchetta*, chicken stuffed with ham, bacon, and herbs while Paul would enjoy *Stufato Manzo e Funghi*, a thick beef and mushroom stew prepared with garlic and white wine. Both dishes would be accompanied by *Spinaci alla Fiorentina*, spinach sautéed with olive oil and garlic, and *Risotto all'Uva e Chianti Rufina*, rice sautéed with onion, butter, and red wine, then mixed with parmesan cheese and ripe red grapes.

They each opted for a simple garden salad and shared a smile when they discovered they selected the same dessert, *Zuccotto*, a rich cake made with chopped toasted almonds and hazelnuts, cognac, maraschino liqueur, Cointreau, semi-sweet chocolate, and whipped cream.

"Shall we order?" Paul reached for the button.

Paul found the champagne bottle getting low as he refilled their glasses. "Would you care for some red wine with dinner?" he asked, picking up the wine list.

There was a knock on the door and Gino entered. After taking their orders he said, "Wonderful selections, wonderful! I think you will be quite pleased..." A look of rapture came over him. "...especially when the *Zuccotto* arrives. Be sure to save room for it."

Both assured him they would.

"Would you prefer your salads before the main course or after?"

"When would it be served in Italy?" Paul asked.

"Almost always after."

Paul glanced at Jillian who nodded her approval. "After then, please. And would you also bring us a bottle of the '96 *Ruffino Chianti Classico*?"

Gino's eyebrows shot up in appreciation of the choice. "Of course. It is an excellent wine! You will find it perfectly compliments the meals you've selected."

He excused himself and retired to place their order.

When the doors closed, Jillian asked, "Are you a wine aficionado or just a lucky guesser?"

She didn't think the question all that funny, but Paul, who was taking a sip of his champagne, had to choke back his laughter so he wouldn't spit out the bubbly liquid. Then Jillian couldn't contain her own soft laugh as she watched him blotting the drops of wine dripping down his chin.

"So suave, so sophisticated," she teased.

With his mouth and chin free of wine, Paul glared and grinned. "I am so going to get you back for that."

Jillian threw him a sassy *oh see how frightened I am* look, then touched his hand. "I'm sorry. I didn't mean it to be funny. I really *was* curious if you knew a lot about wines or just happened to pick a good one."

The glare softened but the grin remained. "I know a little about wines, but mostly I like to drink them. All that 'nose' and 'legs' and 'finish' and stuff doesn't really interest me. The tastes interest me. I can usually tell the difference between a good wine and a cheap wine, but for the life of me I can't tell you what flavors I'm supposed to be tasting." He raised his hands, palms up, and shrugged. "I guess I'll never be much of a wine snob."

They kept the conversation light and filled with humor until the arrival of the wine and their first course detoured attention back to the food.

The appetizers were delicious and they found themselves sharing commentary and bites – either one feeding the other or simply reaching into the other's plate with a fork – as naturally and effortlessly as if they had done it for years.

The soup, too, was marvelous and they both drained their bowls, using small pieces of bread to sop up the last drops.

Jillian set down her spoon and glanced at her watch. Eight-twenty! How could the time have flown by so quickly? She told Paul she had to powder her nose and he rose as she did. She suppressed a smile at the old-fashioned courtesy and wondered if he would be so gallant the next time they went out. As she opened the door to the room, she realized what she was thinking.

The next time? I'm already wondering about the next time? Will he even want there to be *a next time?*

She entered the ladies' room and sat on one of the cushioned chairs. Removing her cell phone from her purse, she dialed Liz and could hardly contain herself when she answered.

"Girl, you will not believe where I am. Casa de Luna. He picked me up in a limo and took me to Casa de Luna."

"No way. On your first date? That place costs a fortune! Either this guy has a serious problem or he really, really likes you. Or maybe that *is* his problem."

"Ha ha ha. You're *sooo* funny.

"Oh Lizzie, it's so beautiful. It's almost like being in Italy. And get this, we have a private dining room."

"A private…"

"And he's been so charming and funny and sweet. And the food is unbelievable." She paused. "Lizzie…"

"What?"

"I, ahh, I think I'm glad I shaved my legs."

"Hold on girl. It's way too early to be thinking like that. It's only eight-thirty. Anything can happen and…"

"I know, I know, but I can't help it. It keeps getting better and better."

"You be careful girl. Just because he drops a pile of cash on you doesn't mean he's worth dropping your pants for."

"Hah. You're one to talk. Need I remind you about a certain blond Adonis named Timothy?"

"Okay, point taken. But seriously, Jilli, don't rush into anything. Don't let him hurt you. You've had enough hurt for…"

"I'll be careful. I promise. But I have to get back. I'm sitting in the ladies room and I haven't even peed yet."

8:30 PM

With a well-practiced smoothness, Liz's thumb released the *END* button and speed-dialed Jenna. On the second ring, she heard, "Hello?"

"Hey! I expected voicemail. I thought you and Roy were going to a movie tonight."

"We were, but he's sick. He didn't even show up at work today. What are you doing?"

"Nothing. Kevin had to work a double tonight."

"Bummer. You want to do something?"

"Sure. Beats sitting around thinking about Jillian and... Oh! You will not believe where coffee boy took Jilli tonight!"

"Where?"

"Casa de Luna."

"No way!"

"That's what she told me not five minutes ago. She called me from the ladies room and told me he picked her up in a limo and they were in a private dining room at Casa de Luna."

"Holy crap. Is this guy rich or something? But that is *soooo* romantic. Casa de Luna." Jenna grunted. "Looks like coffee boy's getting laid tonight."

"Don't laugh. She told me she was glad she shaved her legs." Her voice became serious. "But I'm worried about her. She's had such a run of bad luck with men since college. I don't want her to jump into something with this guy and end up hurt again. Especially after what happened last night." She paused for a second and sighed. "I think she feels really bad about spying on him and everything. I hope she won't end up sleeping with him because she thinks she owes it to him or to make up for some guilt."

"Jillian's not like that."

"Not usually, but something is different with this guy. I mean, she hadn't even gone out with him and she was crying over him last night. Whatever *is* going on, I...well, I hope this guy isn't playing her."

"I know, I know...but there's not much we can do about it now. So what do you want to do tonight?"

They ran through several options before Jenna said, "Hey, you know I talked with Holly a while ago and she told me she and Jamal, and Gloria and Chuck were going for drinks and dancing to some new place Chuck found. She asked me and Roy to go, too, but with Roy sick, I didn't want to go alone. What do you think?"

"Drinks and dancing. That sounds like fun. Sure, why not. Where is this place?"

"I don't know. I'll call Holly after we hang up and find out where it is and what time everyone's meeting there."

"Any idea what it's like so I'll know what to wear?"

"All I know is that it's supposed to be dark and romantic. I'm thinking maybe my blue pantsuit. Or...oh!." She started laughing. "I have a great idea! Do you still have that suit you bought for the costume party last Halloween?"

"Sure, I have the whole outfit."

"Excellent! How 'bout I dress up all slutty and you dress up all butch and I'll be your girlfriend for the night?"

8:35 PM

As she returned from the ladies room, Jillian realized heads were turning to follow her. It made her feel both sexy and self-conscious.

I wonder if he'd be jealous if he saw all these guys checking me out?

Her self-consciousness vanished as she reentered the alcove to Paul's appreciative gaze. She could see the wonder in his eyes...and something else...hunger. Hunger for her. A thrill ran through her as she imagined what he must be thinking.

Oh yes, he'd be jealous.

The thought pleased her.

Paul jumped up to hold her chair. As he returned to his seat, his finger trailed lightly across the back of her neck and shoulder, sending a shiver of excitement down her spine.

Liz was right. I have to be careful.

"You were going to tell me about Rob and Lisa."

Paul began the saga of Rob and Lisa, from how they met to his talk with Rob Wednesday night, and the surprise blind date.

"That was why I called so late. I was ready to leave when the girls showed up. I really didn't want to stay, but I couldn't abandon him. And I kind of felt sorry for Marianne. If I'd gone home, she would have been the third wheel. She was pretty cool, though. She told me she knew right away I was her babysitter and once we both realized there were no expectations on either side, we had an okay time."

"Just okay?" she asked, surprised to feel a slight, green twinge.

"Just okay. She's a cop in Seattle, and had some really good stories to tell, but she knew my head was somewhere else. She even asked me who I'd been thinking about all night. I guess she really is good at her job."

"So who were you thinking about."

"Some girl I met in a coffee shop. Some girl who played me like a violin, broke my heart, and then gave me a reprieve a few seconds later."

The green became guilt at how she treated him that morning.

"Why did you, by the way? You were walking away. Why did you tell me where you'd be for lunch?"

"It was the look on your face. When I said goodbye and started walking by you, I saw your face and I knew it wasn't the look of a player who hadn't scored. You looked like a wounded puppy." She saw the color rise in his cheeks. "And I guess I decided if meeting me was that important to you, I should at least give you a chance."

A knock signaled the arrival of the pasta and main course but Paul's eyes remained fixed on her. "I'm really glad you did."

He was rewarded by a shy smile. "Me, too."

They attacked their meals with gusto, once again sharing and stealing bits and bites. After Rob and Lisa, their conversation remained light, but focused on learning about each other. In between morsels, they explored likes and dislikes. They discovered both preferred baseball to other sports, shared a strong distaste for Brussels sprouts, and dreamed of one day, living in the country.

"Yellow, Cherry Garcia, *The Godfather*, *Claire de Lune*, shower, and Italian cold cuts with everything and extra hot peppers," Paul said in answer to Jillian's asking his favorite color, ice cream flavor, old movie, song, bathing preference, and sandwich. "And you?"

"Red, Heath Bar Crunch, *Groundhog Day*, *Always and Forever*, 80/20 shower, and grilled pastrami on dark rye with American cheese and dark-brown mustard."

"Mmmm." Paul regarded her with imaginative eyes. "Yes, you'd look good in red. Really good. I can see you sitting on a sofa next to me wearing a red dress, eating Heath Bar Crunch ice cream while we watch *Groundhog Day*.

"Yes indeed, but, oops, you have a little ice cream right here." He reached over and caressed the corner of her mouth with his finger, trailing it along the bottom of her lower lip.

She almost gave in to an impulse to grab his hand and hold it to her cheek, but was saved by the knock that presaged the arrival of their salad.

Get a grip girl! You shouldn't even think like that on a first date.

Both thoroughly enjoyed, but only ate half of their dinners. Each was uncertain where this date was going or how it would end, but neither wanted to chance feeling bloated and lethargic from overeating, no matter how good the food.

They picked at their salads as they traded stories of their high school and college years. Although they felt comfortable together, comfortable enough to confide, to confess, to share their most intimate thoughts, they each held back a little, sensing it was too soon.

When coffee and dessert arrived, they found their fingers intertwined, although neither remembered actually taking the other's hand.

"Oh my!"

Paul watched Jillian's eyes slowly close as the sinful flavors of the *Zuccotto* blended in her mouth for the first time.

Whoa! I wouldn't have believed it possible she could look lovelier than she has all night, but look at her enjoying that first bite! I wonder how much more beautiful she'd look stretched out in bed, in the middle of a giant...Stop it. You're getting yourself all worked up and it's way too early for that. Just eat your dessert.

At his first taste of the rich cake, he understood her rapture.

Slowly, respectfully, they savored each bite as a silent homage to the genius who created the masterpiece. Jillian finished first and felt a loss that could only be assuaged by reaching over and stealing a forkful from Paul's plate.

"Hey!"

"I'm sorry, but it's sooo good and mine is all gone and I just *had* to have one more bite."

He understood and told her so. He took another bite then offered her the last luscious nibble. She refused, but he brought the fork back, gently kissed the sweet confection and offered it again.

How could she say no?

Together, they sat back in their seats, completely sated. Neither could remember ever having enjoyed a meal more. Their eyes and thoughts were on each other. Silence stretched out as each realized they didn't feel the usual compulsion to fill every second with chatter.

Paul drank in the vision next to him and marveled at how comfortable he felt with her. Usually he was nervous on a first date, but tonight, with Jillian, it was effortless.

She, too, wondered at the ease with which it all came; the conversation, the little jokes, the touches, the sharing; all of it. In three short days, his face was so familiar to her she was sure she could draw it from memory. The sound of his voice echoed in her mind and she found herself longing to hear more of it.

With an impish grin, she said, "Priya told me this morning you two like dirty jokes. Is that true?"

Somewhat timorously, Paul replied, "Well...yes, I guess we do. Of course, everyone in the office likes them."

"So tell me one."

"Ahh..."

"Come on. I've heard them before. Tell me one. Please?"

"Well, okay."

This was an unexpected turn of events. In fact, it was the last thing he might have imagined doing on a first date. But she did ask

"A mother and father took their 6 year old son to a nude beach. As the boy walked along the beach, he noticed some of the ladies had breasts bigger than his mother's, and asked her why. She told her son, 'The bigger they are, the dumber the person is.'

"Pleased with the answer, the boy ran off to play in the ocean but returned to tell his mother that many of the men had larger members than his dad. His mother replied, 'The bigger it is, the dumber the person is.'

"Again satisfied with the answer, the boy ran back to the ocean to play. Shortly after though, the boy returned again and told his mother, 'Daddy is talking to the dumbest girl on the beach and the longer he talks, the dumber he gets.'"

Jillian groaned.

"Well, you didn't say it had to be a good one. And that's about enough with those jokes…" He paused for a beat, then added with a mischievous grin, "…at least until I know you a little better."

He glanced at his watch and asked, "Did you want to sit here all night and chat or, perhaps, find out what else I have planned?"

"There's more?"

"I did promise you the best first date of all time, although if you really want to stay and talk, we can do that, too."

When Jillian assured him she was game for anything, Paul reached over and pressed the call button. In less than a minute, there was a knock and Gino appeared at the door.

"Was everything satisfactory?"

"Everything was wonderful, Gino," Paul said. "Just wonderful."

"May I bring you something else? More coffee? Anisette?" He looked at Jillian. "Another piece of the *Zuccotto?*"

"Oh lord, no! That dessert was *so* good it should be illegal. If I eat another bite of that tonight I'll have to spend the next month, at least, atoning for the sin."

Paul and Gino laughed appreciatively.

"If there is nothing else, then…" Gino placed a leather folder containing the check on the table next to Paul.

"Wait." Paul slid a credit card from his wallet and laid it on the folder without looking inside. Then he removed a small cell phone from his inside breast pocket, flipped it open, and paged Gary.

Jillian touched his hand and said, "Thank you, Paul. This has been so wonderful, so unbelievable. It was the nicest meal I've ever eaten."

"You're welcome. And I agree. But honestly, as good as the food was, it was the company that really made it special for me."

Her heart leapt.

Always the right thing. He always says the right thing.

His hand caressed hers as they chatted aimlessly, waiting for Gino to return.

What else does he have planned? Is it as extravagant as dinner? This was nice, but it's too much for a first date. Is he expecting something in return? Why doesn't that bother me? It should bother me. Shouldn't it?

Gino entered the room holding the folder and a white bag. "I brought some *Zuccotto* to take with you," he said, smiling broadly. "You can share it later, or tomorrow perhaps." His eyebrow lifted and his smile became a knowing grin. "It was our great pleasure to have you dine with us tonight."

They thanked him as he bowed one final time before leaving.

Paul opened the folder to sign the credit slip.

Jillian's curiosity got the better of her and she tried to surreptitiously peek at the total. She couldn't see it, but her artist's eye for detail could follow the movement of the pen as he added the tip and then totaled the slip. It appeared he'd written a one-something-zero-zero-zero – over one hundred dollars for the tip! Then it looked like he'd written five-something-seven-zero-zero.

Suddenly, she felt guilty about being so nosy, as if she had intruded on his privacy. She looked away, but could not get the numbers out of her head.

Five hundred dollars! He just spent over five hundred dollars on dinner! For me! Is he mad? Or is the one I've dreamed about? But all that money! But maybe…maybe he really is the guy…the one who'll care…who'll make me happy again…the one who…

"Jillian?"

Paul was standing next to her chair.

"Sorry. I was thinking about something."

"Something good, I hope. Me, perhaps?"

He pulled the chair out as she rose, smiling.

"Perhaps," she replied with a saucy giggle.

He lifted her wrap from the chair back and draped it over her shoulders. Then he offered her his arm and they strolled slowly toward the exit to the accompaniment of dozens of jealous stares.

9:55 PM

"Oh, Paul, you didn't!"

At the end of the red carpet stood a white horse, with a light gray mane and tail, attached to a white carriage trimmed in gold, with plush red velvet seats. The driver, in his black suit, ruffled white shirt, bow tie, and top hat completed the scene.

His grin gave the answer and Jillian dashed across the sidewalk. "It's so beautiful! I've always wanted to ride in one of these."

Paul helped her in, then he, too, was seated and the clomp-clomp of the horse's feet drifted up as they began moving.

Oh, Lizzie, I know you'd disapprove, but I just can't sit here with all this space between us. Not after that dinner. It's just too romantic.

"Okay, now don't go getting any ideas, but…"

She slid across the seat until she felt his leg against hers, then settled back and rested her head against his shoulder.

"Uhh…well…sorry, but I do have one idea."

With a small sigh of approval, her head settled back against him as his arm encircled her, making her feel warm and safe.

They rode in silence for a few minutes until the carriage approached the Public Garden and Common. The fragrance of flowering crab apple trees permeated the air.

"Mmmm…it smells wonderful here." She glanced up to see if there were any stars. "And look, the moon is full. This is perfect."

"Yes, it is," he agreed in a whisper, though he didn't mean the ride, the fragrance, or the moon. It was the feel of her head on his shoulder, her breast against his side, the scent of her hair, the comfort of having her close to him that made the moment special for him.

This is great. I could easily get used to this.

"Tell me about your family," he said, partly because he wanted to know, and partly because, despite her warning, he was getting ideas that would only get him in trouble this early in their relationship. "Do you have any brothers or sisters?"

Immediately, he regretted opening his mouth because she moved away and sat up, facing him.

It's just as well. Having her so close made me want to stay that way forever and I have more surprises in store for her before this date is over.

"I have four. Three sisters and one brother. Julia's the oldest. She's twenty-seven. Then me. Then Joanne, twenty-three, James, twenty, and Jessica, who turns eighteen next month."

Paul laughed. "Your parents really had a thing for the letter J, eh? I'll bet you lunch tomorrow both their names begin with J."

Lunch? Tomorrow? That sounds promising. Too bad I already have plans.

"No bet. But you're right. Mom's name is Jolene and my dad's name is Jeffrey. They were high school sweethearts. Never even dated anyone else. They've been married thirty-two years."

"Wow. That's amazing. Thirty-two years! Did they let you in on their secret?"

"Actually, they sort of did. Or my mom did. When I was eighteen, two weeks before I was to leave for college, Mom and I were talking, girl talk, you know?"

Paul nodded.

"One of my friends just broke up with her boyfriend because she wanted to be free to experiment while she was away at school. The poor guy was devastated. He *really* loved her. I saw him one day, about a week after the breakup and…oh my…he looked exactly as you did Wednesday morning." She gave a little grunt. "I wonder if that was why your expression made me… Well, it doesn't matter.

"Anyway, Mom and I started to talk about relationships and things and I asked her how she and daddy stayed so happy all those years. And she told me."

Paul waited a few seconds, but nothing more was forthcoming. "Are you going to share what she said?"

Jillian flushed. "Well, some of it's kind of embarrassing to talk about with a guy on a first date."

"It can't be any more embarrassing for you than it is for me that you know about Mr. Johnson."

"Oh…! Oh…!" Jillian was mortified. She could feel her cheeks catch fire. Her hands shot up to hide her face.

Paul gently pulled them away. "I'm sorry. I didn't mean to embarrass you like that. Priya told me she let it slip this morning and, well, I thought you'd find it funny." He paused, but she continued to stare at her lap. "Really, honey, I'm sorry."

Jillian lifted her eyes to meet his. Her face was still hot, but she could feel the fire fading and forced a weak smile. "That's okay. I just embarrass easily. I've always hated that I do that."

"Don't." His voice was gentle, his hand still on her warm cheek. "I think it's sweet. These days, it's like no one is ever embarrassed about anything. Even when they should be. So please, don't ever be embarrassed about being embarrassed. At least not with me. Now come on, tell me. What secrets did you learn from your mom?"

Jillian took a deep breath and composed her thoughts. Then the realization struck her.

He called me honey. And he did it unconsciously, like he said it a thousand times before. Or is that what he calls all women?

"I can't believe I'm telling you this." With a sigh, she began. "Mom told me that over the years, she and dad came up with these rules. They seem to have worked for them, at least as far as any of us can tell."

"So what are they?" He was anxious to hear what her mother, and by extension Jillian, thought were the keys to a good marriage.

"Okay." She covered her eyes with her hand as her head swung slightly back and forth. Then she took the hand away and looked him straight in the eye. "First and most important, according to mom, never pass up an opportunity to make love."

"Oh ho!" Paul's voice and eyebrows rose in unison.

"Stop that! It's hard enough to think about my parents, you know, that way, without you…?"

"Sorry. Really. I know just what you mean." He shook a little, as if a shiver had run up his spine. "I promise I'll be good. No more joking."

"Alright then. This is exactly the way she told them to me."

"First, never pass up an opportunity to make love.

"Say 'I love you' at least once a day.

"Never bring inhibitions into the bedroom.

"No matter what the fight was about, always make up before bedtime.

"Touch each other often.

"Surprise each other often, in bed and out.

"Say something nice to each other every day.

"Never argue about money.

"Always be a team.

"Always remember the other person can't read minds.

"Always treat your partner better than you treat yourself."

When she finished, she watched for his reaction, but he sat quietly, rocking slightly, as if his whole body was nodding.

After a minute, he said softly, "I'm sorry I made fun before. You're parents are pretty wise people. I think I'll enjoy meeting them someday."

He shifted slightly, draping one hand across the back of the seat while absentmindedly rubbing his neck with the other as he lapsed back into thought.

Meet my parents someday? Is he saying these things on purpose or is he really so comfortable with me he speaks without thinking?

When he broke the silence again, he had a funny look on his face. "So tell me, do you subscribe to these rules, too."

Jillian realized the look was him trying to suppress a grin and smiled sweetly in return. "I think I might someday, if I ever get married. After all, who am I to argue with such a good example?"

It suddenly occurred to Paul where this turn in the conversation could lead. He deftly segued. "Are any of the other kids married?"

She, too, realized what she said and was happy to move to a safer subject, but before she could answer, they heard a loud voice call, "Jillian! Jillian! You stop right there."

The carriage was circling the Public Garden and was now on Beacon Street. Jillian searched for the source of the voice, then saw him. "Oh damn."

Standing on the curb in front of the *Bull & Finch Pub* was Patrick Fowler.

"What's wrong?"

"It's a guy I went out with a few times. He called today and wanted to go out tonight and I told him I had plans with my girlfriends." She turned to check on Patrick. "Oh no. He's following us."

Patrick ran after them and soon reached the carriage. "Hey, you," he yelled to the driver. "Stop this thing. I want to talk to her."

"I can't do that, sir. I can't stop in a lane of traffic."

Patrick appeared to have been drinking and was not happy to hear his command refused. He started banging on the side of the carriage.

"Hey pal, what the hell's your problem?" Paul started from his seat.

Jillian grabbed his arm, pulling him back. "Patrick, stop it!"

The unhappy drunk glared viciously at Paul, then turned his attention back to Jillian. "I want to talk to you," he bellowed, "You lied to me."

"Back off, buddy," Paul ordered. Again he moved to get up but again Jillian grabbed his arm. This time, Paul glanced over and saw the pleading in her eyes. Unhappily, he settled back in his seat as Jillian again asked Patrick to stop banging on the carriage, then asked the driver when they would be able to pull over. He told her there would be space once they turned onto Arlington Street, just ahead.

"Go wait on Arlington," she told Patrick. "The driver will pull over there and we can talk."

He was still furious but he did stop banging and trotted the fifty yards to the corner, looking back several times to make sure they were really following.

"Paul, I'm so sorry." Her face was a mask of worry. "I shouldn't have lied to him, I should have just told him I don't want to see him any more. Damn!"

"Are you sure you want to talk to him? He's obviously had a few and he's a big guy. Guys like that in his condition don't usually respond to reason. Really. Maybe I should talk to him."

"No, I have to do it. I'm sorry. If I don't deal with this now, he'll probably keep following us...or worse."

The carriage reached the corner. When the light changed to green, it turned left and pulled to the curb.

Patrick was at the side of the carriage waiting. "You lied to me," he hissed with real venom in his voice as he sneered at Paul. "He don't look like any girlfriend."

Paul stood and moved to the side of the carriage. He unlatched and opened the door quickly, making Patrick jump back to avoid being struck.

Warily, he stepped down, then looked back at Jillian. "Are you sure?" When she nodded and rose, he helped her down.

As soon as she stepped onto the sidewalk, Patrick grabbed her arm, causing her to wince in pain. "Come over here," he growled, almost dragging her away from the carriage to the middle of the sidewalk.

Paul saw the wince and moved quickly in front of the large man. Evenly, without raising his voice he said, "Take your hand off her now."

Patrick was in no mood to take orders from some shrimpy guy. He squeezed harder, causing Jillian to cry out, and yelled at her, "This is what you want to go out with instead of me?" Then he turned to Paul and said, "Get the fuck away from me before I hurt you." His free arm swung out to push Paul away.

In what seemed like an instant, Paul had grabbed the attacking arm and forced it behind Patrick's back, pushing it high enough to cause maximum discomfort without really damaging anything. Patrick yelped at the sharp pain. Paul's other hand firmly gripped the man's collar.

"Move one inch and I'll break this arm," Paul told him in a low, even, menacing voice. "Now let go of her." He applied a little pressure to reinforce he command.

Patrick's fingers sprang open and Paul asked Jillian if she was all right. She rubbed her arm, but nodded.

"Then please wait by that bench for a minute." He smiled at her. "Patrick and I need to have a little chat about manners."

"Paul…"

"It's okay. Really. We're only going to talk for a minute."

As Jillian moved away, Paul felt his captive tense. "Don't even think about it. Your arm will be broken before your head turns five degrees." He felt the man relax. "Now, here's what's about to happen. I'll let you go in a few seconds. When I do, you *will* apologize to Jillian."

"I'm not…"

Paul cut him off with pressure on the arm. "I didn't tell you to talk yet.

"I've studied martial arts since I was a sophomore in high school. You need to understand that because when I let you go, if you try anything, I'll put you down fast and hard. I don't want to do that. I don't want to hurt you, but I will if I have to. Do we understand each other?"

"Yeah."

"Good. Now you *will* go and apologize to Jillian for hurting her and for acting like an asshole. Then you'll talk nicely to her and listen to whatever she has to say. If I hear you raise your voice once, or move your hands within a foot of her, you'll wish I was only a gang of bikers beating you with chains. Understand?"

Patrick nodded and Paul released his arm. He stood by the carriage and watched as Patrick walked slowly over to Jillian, rubbing his arm and shoulder. He glanced at Paul as he stopped three feet away from her.

I guess I made my point.

They spoke for three or four minutes, then Jillian moved closer to Patrick, kissed him on the cheek and walked back to the carriage. Patrick watched her for a few seconds, then, shaking his head, turned and walked away. Tomorrow at the gym, he would tell his friends how he caught the frigid bitch he'd been dating with another guy and dumped her right in the middle of Arlington Street. He would also praise himself for his restraint in not beating the pansy she was with.

As Jillian approached, Paul realized she was shaking. He took her in his arms to comfort her.

"I'm sorry, Paul. I'm so sorry. I've ruined the whole evening now, all because I was afraid to tell him the truth."

"Nonsense! How is the evening ruined?" His voice took on a deep timbre. "I just rescued my woman from a mean, giant ogre. I'm feeling great. What more can a guy ask for on a date?"

She heard the pride in his voice and looked up. He was grinning like a fool. "Well, I guess you *did* save me."

After he helped her back into the carriage, she asked, "Where did you learn to do that?"

He told her about studying Karate, Judo, and other martial arts in high school and college.

"I still work out regularly, both to stay in shape and to keep the skills sharp. I never thought I'd actually have occasion to use it, but this one time made all the effort worth it. He could have really hurt you. But now it's over. I say we pretend it never happened and enjoy the rest of the evening. Okay?"

Jillian smiled and caressed his cheek with her hand. "Okay." She was overwhelmed by the whole experience.

First he treats me like a princess and then he actually fights for me! It's just too good to be true, like a fairy tale or a dream I'm going to wake up from any minute.

"So, you were about to tell me about your siblings," he reminded her. "Are any of them married?"

If it is a dream, it's the best one I've ever had.

"Julia and Joanne are both married. Julia has three boys, four, three and two years old. Joanne just had her first, a girl, in February.

"James is a sophomore at my alma mater and Jessica graduates from high school in three or four weeks."

"Are you all close?"

"We are. We all talk on the phone and see each other whenever we can. Actually, I'm meeting my sisters tomorrow for a shopping and girl's day. But holidays are the best. We all get together at my parent's house…" She started chuckling. "…and it's like we're kids again, laughing and squabbling and sharing secrets."

Paul saw her eyes get misty as a wistful smile curled the corner of her lips.

"I really love my family. I forget sometimes, you know. I'm always so busy, and, well, it's good to be reminded." She brushed at one eye, where the mist had threatened to become a tear. Then her voice brightened. "What about you? Any siblings?"

"Three, all boys, all older than me. John is 32, married four years to

Elaine, and has two boys, Jacob and Lawrence. He's a software engineer. They live in Winchester. Marcus is 30 and still single. He's a Marine. Right now, he's stationed in Japan."

"Japan!"

"Uh-huh. He's been all over the world. England, Germany, Korea, Thailand, and all over the US, too."

"That's amazing."

"That's the military! After Marcus is Steven. He's a year older than me. Well, actually, he's only 11 months older than me. We were born in the same year."

"Really! How did that happen?"

A gleam appeared in Paul's eyes. "Well, about two months after Steve was born, my mom and dad evidently started feeling…"

"Paul!" Jillian smacked his arm as her face contorted. "That's *soooo gross*."

Paul's mirth at her horrified expression rang out over the sounds of hooves and passing cars. It took him more than a few seconds to compose himself, by which time it was he who was wiping away tears.

"If only you could have seen your face. I wish I had a camera." He did his best to suppress his laughter, but it took a few more seconds before he was able to continue.

"Steve was born January 5th. I came along December 12th. When we were kids, we used to tell people we were twins. Got away with it, too, for a long time, until puberty hit him and he grew five inches in a year."

"Steve lives in Medford, two streets over from my parents. He's a Math teacher, has been married about six years now, and has a boy and a girl. And his wife Vikki is the second nicest person I've ever met."

Jillian grinned. She wasn't about to fall for it again. "I suppose everyone else is first."

"No," he said softly, seriously, his eyes meeting hers. "You are."

There are moments and there are *moments*. Jillian knew this was the second kind.

All night, from his brain freeze when he first saw her in her new dress to the absentminded reference to meeting her parents, Paul said and did little things that told her he thought she was special.

But she knew this was different. This was something more. His eyes, his voice, his manner, his body language, everything told her his simple declaration meant much, much more.

Neither of them said a word. The attraction between them grew stronger and stronger until Jillian could no longer resist its pull. She slid over, encircled him with her arms, and hugged him. Eyes closed, her head rested on his chest. She could feel his heart pounding as he returned the embrace. She felt his cheek rub against her hair and the close contact sent thrills of excitement through her.

Jillian was in the arms of other men in her life, but never before did she feel so safe, so much at peace as she did here, now, with Paul. The urge to tilt her head up for a kiss came and went quickly. She wanted their first kiss to be special and as much as she wanted to feel his lips on hers, something told her the right moment had not yet arrived.

10:10 PM

Rob's feet hung lazily over one arm of the sofa. At the other end, his head was nestled in Lisa's lap. Her fingers played aimlessly with his hair. Occasionally, they'd scratch his scalp, each time drawing a low 'Mmmmmm.' In the background, a song ended and the voices of Peter Cetera and Cher filled the room as they began to sing *After All.*

Earlier in the evening, they cooked a simple pasta dinner for themselves. After cleaning up, Rob suggested trading backrubs, which soon became full-body massages.

During the second month of their relationship, Lisa signed them up for a four-class course in massage. Both so thoroughly enjoyed the experience, after the third week, Rob bought a portable massage table, which now stood open in the middle of the living room.

Before the backrubs began, Lisa popped into the player the special "I'm Sorry" disk Rob burned for her. She treasured the CD. It was the effort he put into making it even more than the letter he wrote that convinced her he really had changed and really did love her. She could tell he spent hours carefully selecting and arranging the songs, some old, some new, so the lyrics would tell her all the things he expressed in the letter, and more.

He began his apologies on the CD with Frank Sinatra's version of *I'm Sorry I Made You Cry*, then followed it with *Please Forgive Me* by Bryan Adams, *Baby I Was Wrong* by Jennifer Hanson, and Brenda Lee's *I'm Sorry.*

He chose the next four, *When I Am With You* by Johnny Mathis, *Baby I Need Your Loving*, by Johnnie Rivers, John Lennon's *Woman*, and Mathis' *All The Time* to tell her how much she meant to him.

John Denver's *I'm Sorry* expressed his despair at having to live without her, and *After All* told her how much he needed her, and that he really wanted a future with her. Then he ended with their special song.

"I wonder where they are?" Lisa was so into the music she wasn't aware she said it out loud.

Rob turned his head so he could see the time display on the DVD player across the room. "Probably on the carriage ride, unless dinner made so much of an impression she's doing him in the back of the limo as we speak.

"Owwww!"

Lisa released handful of hair she just gave a playful yank. "You're terrible. Jillian's a nice girl. Priya said so, remember?"

"Maybe so, but nice girls do it in limos, too. Remember the ride back from your cousin's wedding in March?"

"We were both drunk. And that wasn't our first date." She wrapped her arms around his head. "But it *was* fun, wasn't it?"

The memory of that night brought wistful smiles to both their faces.

"So what's the deal with Priya?"

"What do you mean?" Rob had been expecting this question.

"Why did you never tell me how beautiful she is?"

"I don't know. It never occurred to me. I mean, the way she looks was never really an issue after her first day." He told her about Priya's stunt and how she was now just one of the guys.

"How could you not tell me that before?" Her tone made it more of a demand than a question.

"Because I didn't want you to get all worked up over it, like you are now."

"I *am not* getting worked up," she huffed. "I'm..." She laughed. "Okay. Maybe you were right. Did she really do that, though? She seems so prim and proper."

"She did and she is and she isn't. It's weird. She looks like a model, but she's so damn bright and talented, you don't even notice after working with her for a while. It's like with you. Once you know the person, you see the person, not the packaging."

Lisa leaned over to kiss his forehead. As she did so, the beautiful ballad ended and after a two second pause, Leann Rimes began to sing their special song, *How Do I Live Without You.*

Clad only in plaid boxers, Rob jumped up from the couch and extended his hand to his love, who was wearing only his v-neck tee shirt. Their arms encircled each other as they came together and began dancing.

Rob closed his eyes, still not believing this incredible woman really wanted him, really loved him. He mouthed a silent prayer to the God who brought them together, and then a thank you to Paul, whose words of wisdom Wednesday showed him the light and saved the relationship.

Lisa's head rested on his shoulder as they danced. Her hands caressed his back as she thought again how perfect the CD was, and how much she loved her Robbie.

Her pet name for him made her smile because he hated being called Robbie in public although he tolerated it when they were alone. The only place he really liked it was in bed, and the thought of what would happen later made her tingle. They almost always made love before they went to sleep.

The song came to a close, but they stood there holding each other for almost a minute longer, each loving the warm feeling of the other against them. Finally, after sharing a lingering kiss, they moved apart and resumed their previous positions on the sofa.

With her fingers again playing in his hair, Lisa asked, "What's Priya's boyfriend like?"

Rob hoped that subject was forgotten. He should have known better.

"I don't think she has one. At least she's never mentioned one I can remember." A waggish grin turned up the corners of his mouth. "But she does have this really special friend who's a guy."

"Really? And who would that be?"

"Paul."

"Paul? Our Paul?" She felt his head nodding in her lap.

"As of last night. Something happened last night and I don't quite understand all the details, but Priya and Paul are tight now, sort of like he and I are tight."

"Wow. I wonder what Jillian will think about that."

"If Paul pulls this whole date off the way he planned tonight, I'm not sure she'll care."

Lisa laughed. "She'll care. Trust me. Then again, that much romance in one night certainly could turn a girl's head."

Rob agreed. "I sure hope she knows how to dance."

"Why?"

"Paul's a pretty good dancer. When he was a freshman in high school, he tried out for every sports team. His brother Steve was a year ahead of him and a helluva jock. Paul really wanted to follow in his footsteps. Trouble was, he had lots of heart and determination, but two left feet. He kept stumbling over himself. So the coach told him to take dance lessons to improve his coordination and try again next year.

"He wasn't too keen on it, but he did it. Took a lot of crap for it, too, especially over the summer when he'd have to take off for his lesson. But he stuck with it and in the fall, made the Junior Varsity football team. So he kept up the lessons and started taking karate and stuff, too. And in his junior and senior years, he made varsity in football, basketball and baseball."

"Geez, that *is* determination. But he doesn't seem like a jock."

"He was, but he's not anymore. He played one year of football in college, then realized there was no future for him in sports so he gave them up and concentrated on studying."

"No kidding. Say, how is it that after five months together, I know so little about your best friend?"

Rob flipped onto his side and pushed himself up until his arm was resting on the arm of the sofa and his face was right in front of Lisa's.

"What are you talking about? You know everything about my best friend."

"No I don't. I..." She caught the look in his eyes. Her own eyes softened with understanding and love and she tenderly whispered, "Oh."

Once would not be enough tonight.

10:45 PM

There was no more talking after they settled back in the carriage, just the occasional murmur of pleasure. With eyes closed, their thoughts were of each other and dinner, of ogres and possibilities. They even wandered into flights of fantasy. So comfortable were they, it took several minutes, and the driver clearing his throat, before they realized the carriage stopped.

Paul groaned softly, not wanting the moment to end. When her eyes opened, and she saw they were stopped in front of the Franklin Hotel, she broke their embrace and sat back, her eyes full of questions.

What's this? Did he reserve a room here? Did he just assume I'd just go up and sleep with him? Has this whole evening just been a big seduction campaign?

Paul noticed the change in her and realized what she must be thinking. "I thought you might like to go dancing."

"Dancing? At a hotel?" Now she was confused.

"At the Candlelight Lounge inside." His voice assumed a conspiratorial tone. "It's the best kept secret in Boston. Thursday through Sunday nights they have a great band that plays all kinds of cover tunes. Lots of soft rock..."

Damn! Again I've misjudged him.

"...some jazz, new stuff, old stuff. Things you can dance to without getting all sweaty."

"But what if I want to get all sweaty?"

Did I really just say that out loud?

She tried to grin in a way that would let him know she wasn't serious, but his face lit up with mischief.

"Well...that would depend on whether you wanted to get sweaty vertically, or horizontally."

They both burst out laughing as she wagged a finger at him. "I guess I deserved that."

I can't believe I said that. And without thinking! How? I never joke that way with guys. Not even with...oh...oh my!

She recognized a change in herself, in her attitude and her expectations for herself and for this...this thing, this budding relationship. She sensed a familiarity, a nascent intimacy that wasn't really sexual, although she couldn't deny the heated attraction she felt for him in the carriage.

Paul stood, took out his folding money, and generously tipped the driver. Then he stepped down from the carriage and extended his hand.

Once on the sidewalk, Jillian noticed their limousine parked right behind them. "Has Gary been following us around all this time?"

"No. He knew where we were going and about when we'd get here. He was probably waiting somewhere close by."

Jillian smiled and waved to Gary, who returned both.

The Candlelight Lounge was aptly named. Except for a few dimmed spotlights that illuminated the dance floor and stage for the band, and the minimum of electric candles necessary for the bar to function, all the light in the room came from the small votive-style candles on each of the round tables.

The room seemed to glow with islands of soft light shining through the darkness. Jillian understood why Paul brought her here. It was beautiful, warm, and very romantic.

The hostess showed them to a table in the far corner of the room. Paul again held the chair for her then moved another around so he could sit next to her, both of them facing the large dance floor. Almost immediately, a waitress appeared with a bowl of pretzels, ready to take their drink orders.

Jillian thought it wise to stick with wine, having previously experienced some unpleasant aftereffects from mixing alcoholic beverages. Paul ordered a Captain n' Coke.

The dance floor was about half full as the band, three guys playing lead guitar, keyboards and drums, and a girl playing bass guitar, performed the old Commodores standard *Three Times a Lady*.

Jillian loved to dance. She took dance for eleven years, starting when she was five. Ballet, modern, ballroom, swing, western, Latin, everything. She never met a dance she didn't enjoy.

Dinner, a carriage ride, and now dancing. It's like he knows all my favorite things. He only missed one and given the time, there's no way we'll be going there tonight.

Paul held her hand, fingers entwined, as they sat, listening to the music and watching the dancers.

The waitress returned with their drinks and told them she would run a tab for them. As they lifted and touched glasses, the song ended to appreciative applause.

After a quick sip, Paul asked, "Would you like to dance or did you want to sit for a while?"

In answer, Jillian tabled her glass and all but jumped to her feet.

As they navigated between tables to the dance floor, the bass player moved to the center microphone and the band began to play *Could I Have*

This Dance. When they stepped onto the oak parquet, Paul surprised her by twirling her around once then moving smoothly into the one-two-three steps of a waltz. Jillian beamed at him.

I can't believe it. I thought he'd just hold me and sway, but he actually knows how to dance!

They moved effortlessly across the floor, Jillian following his lead as if they danced together for years.

When the song ended, he led her into a Cajun Two-Step as the spotlight switched to the keyboard player, who began to play and sing *Jambalaya.* Then the band slowed things down with *I Only Have Eyes For You.* Jillian only had eyes for Paul and could not have told you if the dance floor was packed or empty at the moment she was bumped hard twice, from behind and then from the left. The bumps threw her off her rhythm and she stopped. Hearing giggling behind her, she turned and saw them.

"Jenna! Liz! Look at you two! What are you doing here? And why are you dressed like that?"

When they saw the confusion on her face, the girls doubled over with laughter. Jenna was wearing a scandalously short fire engine red dress that was cut so low Jillian wasn't sure how her boobs kept from falling out. Fishnet stockings and matching red, knee-high boots made her look more like an expensive hooker than a brilliant chemist. But it was Liz's outfit that most startled her. Dressed in a gray pinstripe suit, blue shirt, paisley tie, and with her hair slicked back under a fedora, Liz looked like a very masculine woman or a very feminine man.

Effecting a deep voice and gangster accent, Liz said, "Ayyy, can't a guy take his best goil dancing?"

That started them laughing again. When they recovered, Jenna explained and told her Holly and Jamal and Gloria and Chuck had similar reactions when they first saw them in costume. Then she shifted her gaze to stare at Paul, who stood there, amused, listening to them talk.

Jillian realized she left him hanging. "Oh! I'm so sorry, Paul. I was so shocked at seeing them here and dressed that way that..."

"No apology necessary. However, to atone for you forgetting I was here, you have to allow me one dance with each of them tonight. I don't think I'll ever again have the opportunity to dance with a gangster *and* his moll." That started the two giggling again. He turned to them, hand out. "Hi, I'm Paul DiLorenzo. You must be Bugsy Segal and you must be the lovely Virginia Hill."

After more proper introductions, he said, "Jillian's mentioned you both and I'm happy to be able to put faces to the names now. Where are you sitting?"

"Over there." Liz pointed to a table on the opposite side of the floor from where Paul and Jillian were seated. Then, with a mischievous grin, she asked, "You guys want to join us?"

Jillian glared at her for a few seconds before she turned to see what Paul thought of the idea.

"It's up to you. But I wouldn't mind meeting some of your friends."

They grabbed their drinks, told their waitress where they were moving and joined the others. Thanks to Liz and Jenna filling them in the moment they arrived, Holly and Gloria already knew the truth about last night's misunderstanding and were enthusiastic in their greetings to Paul.

The group sat for a bit, allowing Paul to get acquainted with everyone, but he and Jillian had not come to talk and after ten minutes, Jillian was fidgeting. When the band began to play *Unchained Melody,* she grabbed Paul's hand, stood up, and said, "Enough talking!"

The rest of the table followed their lead onto the dance floor.

Paul took Jillian in his arms and held her close as they moved to the music. All night they talked, and learned much about each other; about likes and dislikes, family and friends, even some hopes and dreams. Now, they only wanted to dance, to see how they fit together, how their bodies moved with and felt next to each other.

Several times, during slow, romantic ballads, with their bodies pressed close, Jillian was tempted to turn her head up to invite a kiss, but each time, as in the carriage, something held her back. The time still was not right for their first kiss, so they danced, and danced, and danced, and stopped only when the band announced a twenty minute break.

No sooner did they return to the table, than the women all decided a group visit to the ladies' room was in order. Chuck also took off to the men's room.

"I wonder if anyone's ever done a study on why it's impossible for a woman to go alone to the bathroom."

Jamal laughed. "I'm not so sure we really want to know, but my theory is that their bladders are so weak they need to keep their mouths moving to distract them while they're waiting in line." It was Paul's turn to laugh as Jamal continued, "Of course, you know they're all in there talking about *you.*"

"Damn, Jilli, he really is cute," Holly gushed as they waited for the line to move.

"And he can really dance!" Jenna added. "I was watching you two. Are you sure he isn't gay? Straight guys don't dance like that."

That drew laughter from her four friends and a sweet smile from Jillian. "Oh, he's definitely not gay."

"I don't know," Liz said. "Jenna's right. Straight guys usually just shuffle around."

"Yeah," said Gloria, joining in the teasing. "Look at Chuck and Jamal."

"He is *not* gay." Jillian started to blush.

"How do you know?" demanded Holly.

Her blush deepened. "Because I could feel that he's not when we're dancing close."

"Oh yes!" Jenna cried loudly. "Jilli's gonna have a bruised thigh from bumping into wood all night!"

Even the women in the stalls started whooping with laughter as Jillian, mortified, hid her face in her hands.

A few minutes later, as she was sliding down her pantyhose, Jillian realized it had been a very long time since she felt this happy. Her friends liked Paul, he seemed kind and generous and funny, and he was a good dancer. Not the best she ever met, but good. Good enough that with time they could be great together. She would teach him.

But not tonight.

Tonight, she just wanted to be with him, move with him, feel his arms and hands holding her, guiding her across the floor. A part of her wished they hadn't run into her friends, but another part was happy to be showing him off. She thought about what Jenna said and glanced down at her thigh, immediately feeling foolish for doing so.

Then she closed her eyes and formed a mental picture of Paul. She could see him clearly, almost as if he were standing in front of her. In her mind, he smiled at her. A naughty thought came unbidden and she gave in to it. Her mental image removed his jacket and loosened, then pulled off his tie. Slowly, he released the buttons of his shirt and slipped it off. The image then kicked off his shoes, unbuckled his belt and reached for his zipper.

Jillian could feel the heat rising in her face. Even alone, in a bathroom stall, a mere daydream could ruffle her.

A loud knock on the stall door jarred her out of her reverie. "Come on, girl," Jenna said. "The band will be back any minute and I want my dance with coffee guy before you tire him out. Maybe I can get a bruised thigh, too."

Half a minute later Jillian flung open the door to the stall, her eyes blazing.

Jenna saw the fury on her face and backed away. "Hey, I'm sorry. I was only kidding. You know me, Jilli. Sometimes my mouth…" She stopped when she realized her friend was struggling to keep a straight face.

Jillian quickly lost the battle and burst out laughing as did Liz, who observed the whole thing.

Still chuckling, she told Jenna, "That was for embarrassing me before." She looked around. "Where are Holly and Gloria?"

"Back at the table."

"Shoot. Well, come here." She moved to the corner of the room. "I have to tell you what happened.

"Remember Patrick, the guy I was dating?"

"The control freak?" Liz asked.

Jillian nodded. "Well he called me today for a date and I told him I was going out with you guys and then after dinner Paul and I are on this carriage ride and..."

"He took you on a carriage ride?" Jenna asked, a mixture of admiration and jealously on her face.

Again she nodded. "Listen! Anyway, we're on the ride and all of a sudden Patrick sees us."

She gave her friends a blow-by-blow description of the whole incident.

"No way!" Liz exclaimed. "That asshole could've really hurt you. And Paul really defended you like that?"

"I'm telling you, one second Patrick's paw is crushing my arm and the next thing I know, Paul has his other arm behind his back, Patrick is wincing in pain, and he lets me go. I was so scared but so excited, too, to have this guy defending me like that." Her eyes widened and brightened and her voice softened. "He was, I don't know, so manly I guess, I was getting...you know...watching him."

"Hell, I'd be getting hot, too, if some guy did that for me," Jenna gushed. Liz agreed.

"There's something about him," Jillian said wistfully. "Something special. He keeps surprising me."

"There sure is," Liz said. "He drops piles of dough on you, does all this romantic stuff, and then kicks a bully's ass to boot! I wish someone would surprise me like that!"

Jillian and Jenna laughed, but then Jenna's expression turned serious. "You really do like this guy, don't you? I mean, you know, *like* like?"

"I do," Jillian whispered, and the realization startled her. She really did. The feeling she had all night that something inside her changed suddenly coalesced into a word. She shook her head.

It couldn't be, not after one date, a date that isn't even over yet.

She shook her head again and banished it all from her mind. It was time to get back out there.

The band was taking the stage as the girls paraded across the dance floor to their table. Had they really been in there that long?

As he led her onto the dance floor, Paul asked, "Is everything okay? I was about to ask Holly and Gloria to check on you guys."

"I'm sorry, I'm fine. I just, well..."

What could she say? That they were talking about him? That she told her friends how hot he made her feel? That she sat on the toilet undressing him in her mind? Then again...

"I was sort of caught up in this fantasy I was having in there, mentally undressing you and…"

He laughed. "Okay, I get it. Girl stuff I don't need to know about. You could have just said that."

She laughed, too.

Daddy was right. It's always best to tell the truth. Or some version of it.

The band began the set with *The Girl From Ipanema* and seconds later, Paul was leading her effortlessly through the slow-quick-quick steps of the bossa-nova. As she floated in his arms, she caught bits of him singing the words softly, under his breath, and it made her feel special to think she inspired him so.

When the song ended and the band began the intro to Chris De Burgh's *Lady in Red,* Jillian felt a tap on her shoulder. "I do believe I was promised a dance, and what song could be more appropriate than this one, so I'm cutting in."

Jillian gave Jenna a look that said *don't get too carried away* as she stepped away from Paul.

She walked back to the table while behind her, Jenna moved into Paul's arms. She joked a bit with him at first, but then moved close and rested her head on his chest. Paul wasn't sure what to make of it. He kept his own head upright and hoped Jillian would not think he initiated the closeness.

He worried for nothing. Jillian occupied a seat facing away from the dance floor. She knew her friend would not be Miss Prim and Proper as she danced with Paul and if she didn't see it she could pretend it didn't happen.

When the song ended, Liz replaced Jenna, who returned to the table and sat next to Jillian. She leaned close and said, "I am *so* frickin' jealous."

Jillian followed a quizzical look with, "What do you mean?"

Guilt clouded Jenna's face. "You can hate me if you want, but I tested him. Look at the way I'm dressed, and I flirted and plastered myself against him when we were dancing and got nothing. Not even one of those twitches you mentioned." She sounded depressed. "Either I'm losing it, which I'm not, or that boy is so into you it's frightening."

Rather than feeling upset, Jillian found she was elated. "Really? Did you really…"

"I'm telling you, I was all over him and he just stood there and politely danced with me. He didn't even rest his head on mine." She looked contrite. "I really am sorry, but I had to do it. I had to find out if…you know. Liz told me what you said about shaving your legs and, well, I don't want you to get hurt again." She sighed. "Why can't Roy be into *me* like that?"

Jillian could not believe two hours passed when the band indicated the next song would their last of the night. Once the girls had their turns with him, she and Paul spent every remaining minute on the dance floor.

The two guitar players moved their microphones to the center of the stage.

"Thank you all for coming tonight. I'm Jasmine, next to me is Erik, Mickey is on keyboards, Kent is on drums, and we're *Now & Then*. We're here every Thursday through Sunday night and we hope we'll see you again real soon."

She glanced at Erik who said, "We'd like to leave you tonight with an oldie, one of our favorites by Luther Vandross. It's for all you lovers out there."

Jillian smiled. *Wouldn't it be funny if they played...*

Always and forever
Each moment with you
Is just like a dream to me
That somehow came true, yeah

Her smile widened as she remembered how she reacted to the song two days ago. *This has to be a good sign!*

Her eyes met Paul's as she stepped between his outstretched arms and laced her fingers around the back of his neck. Then she softly sighed as his strong arms slipped around her waist to pull her close.

All the night's fancy dance steps were forgotten as they clung to each other, gently swaying to the music, their feet barely moving enough to turn them in place. Their moments in the limo and in the carriage were special, but this far eclipsed both.

As the song wound down, and the final notes faded, they both knew the moment had come. They stopped moving and held fast, each waiting for the other to make the first move. Finally, Jillian felt Paul's hand drift to her chin and tenderly encourage her. She allowed him to raise her head until their eyes met. His eyes asked permission and hers gave it. The rest of the room faded away as, slowly, he began to move his lips toward hers.

A huge crash startled them and they literally jumped apart, stunned, as if awakened from a dream.

Everyone in the room turned toward the bar where a waitress stumbled, sending a tray of empty glasses crashing to the floor.

They watched the commotion for a few seconds before laughing.

"Can you believe that?" Jillian said.

"I know. Talk about bad timing."

Each knew the moment passed, and each was content to wait for the next one.

SATURDAY, MAY 8

1:15 AM

When they settled into the limousine after saying goodbye to her friends, Gary lowered the partition and asked, "Where to?"

"That depends on Jillian." Paul turned to her and asked with a grin, "Have you had your fill of me yet or can you stand a little more tonight?"

More? He planned more? What could he have planned at one-fifteen in the morning? Some after-hours club?

Her curiosity piqued, she returned his grin with a warm smile. "I think I might be able to endure a little bit more of your company."

"Great!" Then to Gary, "You know where to go."

Jillian watched the partition rise as the limo started moving. "Where *are* we going at this hour?"

"'Well, I am partial to food. After that, surprise me,'" he said, an octave higher than normal.

"I did say that, didn't I?"

"Yes, ma'am."

"And you're holding me to it?"

"Yes, ma'am"

"Even if I pout, like this, and ask really, *really* nice, like this?"

"Yes, ma'am"

"You beast, making a poor girl suffer."

"Sorry, ma'am."

They chuckled at the exchange before her voice softened.

"In case I forget to tell you later, Paul, I've had a very nice time tonight."

"Me, too. This night has been so much better than I ever expected. And I was expecting a lot!"

Jillian thought about that, about how Paul created a magnificent evening for them.

A fabulous dinner in the most romantic restaurant in Boston, a romantic carriage ride, and then charming my friends and dancing. Any one of those would have made for a wonderful evening. He really went all-out to impress me!

But he's been going all out ever since we met. Sure, he fumbled some that first morning, but since then, he's been funny, and attentive, and sweet, and forgiving, and generous, and very romantic. Especially tonight. And it's like he can sense my moods. Like now. I smile at him and he just smiles back, like he knows I need some quiet time to think. Does he know it's because I'm thinking about him? Is he thinking about me? Is it really possible he could have known the first time he saw me? But how? That stuff only happens in books and movies. But he knows things about me…knows without even knowing he knows. Damn, I'm making this sound like the Twilight Zone. Calm down, girl. Think of something else.

Her bathroom fantasy popped back into her head and Jillian felt herself growing warm all over. She looked away, not wanting her eyes to betray her thoughts.

I wonder what kind of lover he'll be. Will he be as tender, caring, and attentive in bed as he is out? And passionate? I can sense the passion inside him. I can see it in his eyes sometimes. And I felt it this morning and when we were dancing. Oh no, I'm starting to blush again. What if he notices? But he won't care. He wants me. But do his heart and soul want me as much as his body does?

She met his eyes again, and smiled, suddenly unconcerned about her warm cheeks.

I wonder what kind of kisser he is. He has nice lips. I hope he's not all slobbery or too aggressive or not aggressive enough. Kissing's important. Is kissing important to him, too? Or is it just something he does on the way to getting laid? No, he's been waiting for the right moment, too. I know he wanted to kiss me in the restaurant and in the carriage and when we were dancing but he never made the move until…damn that stupid waitress! That was the perfect moment. But she broke the spell. Even if we'd kissed and it was great, that's all it would have been. The magic would have been gone. Oh! He wants the magic, too!

The insight made her appreciate him even more.

The phone rang and Paul grabbed it "Hello. … Excellent. … I guess that would be a good idea. Are you sure you … Okay then. Thank you.

"We're almost there, but it'll be another few minutes. Gary's going to check things out."

Jillian leaned toward the window, but Paul put his hand on her arm. "Come on. No peeking. I want this to be a surprise."

She restrained her curiosity and settled back into the seat. "What's he checking out? Is this place dangerous?" She felt the car roll to a stop and heard the driver's door open, then close.

"No. It's not dangerous. But it *is* one-thirty in the morning. It never hurts to be careful."

She nodded, but could hardly control her eagerness to find out what Paul saved for the end of their date.

"Thank you for being so nice back at the lounge. I'm pretty sure your plans didn't include spending all that time with my friends."

"Don't be silly. They all seem like really good people." Jillian saw his face cloud. "But...ah...there was one thing."

"Jenna."

"Right. Look, I didn't encourage her or anything. She just..."

"Was testing you. She told me what she did and I'm sorry. She and Liz are very protective and she decided to see if, well...you know."

Paul nodded. Friends protecting friends. He understood that. There was a short knock on the window. A few seconds later, Gary opened the door.

"Everything is fine."

Paul exited the car then helped Jillian slide out. No sooner did her feet touch the ground than she heard it.

I can't believe it! He couldn't have hit on all four.

She lifted her head so her eyes could confirm what her ears already told her. Her heart leapt when she saw it and she threw her arms around him, almost knocking him back into Gary, who was standing behind Paul holding the door open.

"Whoa," Paul cried, regaining his balance while holding on to her. "May I assume from this reaction that you *are* in the mood for a moonlight walk on the beach?"

"I *love* walking on the beach!"

She let go of him, hurried across the sidewalk to the break in the seawall, and took a deep breath of salt air. A slight breeze was blowing in off the water. It felt cool and refreshing. By all rights, it should be downright cold this close to the water at this time of year. But like everything else tonight, some magic was keeping it comfortable for them. Still, she was glad she had the wrap.

Paul caught up with her and they started down the concrete ramp to the sand. As they neared the bottom, Jillian remembered what she was wearing.

"Damn," she said sharply as she stopped short.

"What's wrong?"

"Heels. I can't walk on the sand in heels."

"So take them off."

"I can't. Pantyhose. They'd be torn to shreds in seconds out here."

"Oh." *Crap! What can I do now? When I planned this, I never thought about how she might be dressed.*

"Wait a minute. What was Gary checking before?"

"He wanted to make sure there were no other people on the beach or cars full of kids parked in the area. If there had been, we'd have tried another beach."

"So that means there's no one else around?"

"Just Gary in the car."

"Good. Turn around and face back up the ramp and don't turn back until I tell you to."

Paul turned as requested. "What's going on?"

"You just stay that way for a minute and then you'll find out."

Jillian peered in all directions. The bright moon made it easy to confirm there was no one else around. Then she slid her dress up to her waist and started to push down her pantyhose.

I can't believe I'm doing this. If a gust of wind ever blows this dress up...

The pantyhose was bunched around her ankles now, but she realized it would be impossible to balance on one foot on this incline while she undid the strap and removed the shoe and hose from the other.

She shuffled over to the tapered concrete wall. This far down, it was only about 18 inches high, too low to lean on.

"Damn."

"Are you okay?"

"Don't you dare turn around." It was a command. "I'm fine. Just another minute."

She would have to sit on the low wall. There was no other way. When she put her hand on it though, she discovered the surface was very rough. It would ruin her dress if she sat on it.

Lord, if he ever turns around I will absolutely die. She again pushed her dress up to her waist and rested her bare backside on the wall. In seconds she was barefoot and hurried to stand and return her hemline to its proper location.

"Okay, all done. You can turn around."

When Paul saw her holding her shoes and hose in her hand he said, "Oh, you're barefoot. Good idea. I think I'll join you."

He kicked off his shoes and peeled off his socks. "Give me your stuff. I'll put everything on the seawall so we won't have to carry them."

When he returned, he began rolling up the legs of his trousers. "You know, I've had the pleasure of admiring your legs all night so I think it's only fair that you get to look at mine for a while."

When both pant legs were rolled securely above his knees, he offered her his arm and they walked out onto the sand.

Jillian squeezed his arm before they'd gone ten paces. "I need you to promise me something," she said shyly.

"What's that?"

"Promise me that if the wind starts blowing my dress around, you'll keep your eyes straight ahead."

He started chuckling. "Oh dear. You don't want me catching a glimpse of your lacy under…"

He stopped and moved a step away from her, eyes wide as it dawned on him why she wanted the promise.

"You're not wearing…you don't have anything…"

Jillian heard a long mournful groan escape his lips.

"No. No. Not again! Not two nights in a row. I'm not going to be able to sleep again. Why do they keep doing this to me?"

Jillian remembered what Priya had confided about Paul's reaction to her revelation the previous evening. She started to giggle.

"I'm sorry," she said playfully. "Maybe I shouldn't have said anything. I didn't realize you knowing what I'm not wearing under this dress would cause you such distress." She was teasing him unmercifully, but she couldn't help herself.

He groaned again. "Evil. You're an evil woman to do this to me."

She laughed, moved back beside him, and took his hand. "True, but do you promise?"

He promised.

They strolled for a while in silence, listening to the surf, each wondering what the other was thinking.

Predictably, all Paul could think about was the thin wisp of cloth covering her otherwise bare skin. She was wondering, once again, how he could know so much about her. As wonderful as this all was, it seemed too good to be true, too good to be a happy coincidence. It was a question she could hold in no longer.

"I have to ask you something."

"Anything. Anything you want to know…as long as it's not about underwear."

She giggled, then took a deep breath. Maybe she didn't want to hear the answer to this. But she had to ask.

"How did you decide what to plan for our date tonight?"

"Well, you said that Italian food was your favorite, so I knew we'd be going to a nice Italian restaurant. That it was *Casa de Luna* was serendipitous, as you already know.

"I arranged the carriage ride because they always looked so romantic when I saw them in movies. Then, I figured most girls like to dance, and I hadn't been to the *Candlelight* in a long time. If you didn't like it and wanted more action, I'd have suggested *Platinum* down the street. And this, well, I couldn't think of anything more romantic than a moonlight walk on the beach. And believe me, I tried."

She did believe him and moved closer, feeling guilty now. Her arm slipped around his waist while his angled across her back, his fingers resting on her side.

"I'm such a…I thought you might have talked with one of my girlfriends or something. I know it's silly. You didn't even know them until tonight, but you planned the exact romantic date I've always dreamed about. It was like you read my mind. And it made me a little nervous. I've…"

She hesitated.

Go on, you can tell him. You have to tell him.

"I've had some bad experiences in the past with guys, and it's made me…cautious, I guess. Suspicious. And it's made me doubt you twice, no, three times counting the morning we met. But I won't doubt you again."

Paul snorted. "Of course you will. Doubt is part of life, part of any relationship. And sometimes you might have good cause to doubt. Something like, ohhh, seeing me kiss someone else."

He pulled her tighter for a second to let her know he was kidding.

"And I'll probably have doubts about you now and then. So what? All we have to do is talk when we have doubts. Not much can hurt us if we talk things through. It's the fears and the doubts we hold inside that eat away at us. So from now on, *our* rule number one is 'Ask instead of keeping it inside'. Okay?"

"Okay."

They fell into a comfortable silence again as they moved down onto the wet sand, letting the incoming tide wash over their feet. It was chilly, but they found it stimulating. Her arm was around his waist again and his rested as before, holding her close. Both were aware their conversation alluded to a future together; that they were already starting to define their relationship.

Paul glanced down at the sand and surf. He noticed the shape of her feet and the way the moonlight made her bare skin almost glow. He thought about his feelings for her, how they seemed to have mushroomed since that first, chance meeting a few days ago. He felt the heat of her body pressing against him as they wandered aimlessly along the beach. He did everything he could to impress her, said everything he could think of to help her know him and know how he felt about her. Now, there was nothing left to say and only one thing left to do, the one thing that would let them both know if they were truly meant to be together.

They drifted back onto the dry sand and Paul turned to face her. He glanced up at the sky, then back down to meet her eyes.

"The moon *is* beautiful tonight."

"Yes it is."

"But not as beautiful as you."

Jillian's breath caught as he moved closer. It was time, she knew. On this deserted beach, under a bright, lovers' moon, with the soft sound of the surf behind them, in the most romantic setting she could think of, they would share their first kiss.

She felt his arms draw her to him, holding her gently, but firmly against his muscular chest. She felt one hand slide under the wrap and up to her neck as the other drifted down to the small of her back.

He held her close, reveling in the softness of her body against his. His hands came together below her shoulder blades and he pressed her more tightly to him.

"Mmm, you feel so good."

After a minute, he slid both hands down to her waist, pressing her hips to him as he leaned his head and shoulders back slightly away from her. He craned his neck in all directions.

"What are you looking for?" she whispered.

"Making sure there are no waitresses with trays nearby."

Jillian couldn't help herself. The laugh just burst out of her.

She felt one of his hands bury itself in the hair at the back of her head. The wrap fell open as she raised her arms and laced her fingers across the back of his neck. Both their grins faded as their eyes met and each sensed the time was right.

"I've wanted to do this from the moment I first met you," he said in a throaty whisper.

"Then stop talking and do it," she whispered back, closing her eyes.

She felt his lips, warm and moist, softly touch hers as they tested her response. Then they pressed closer, more firmly, always in motion, tasting her, thrilling her with their tender urgency. Her fingers began to caress the back of his head as his lips continued to fire her passions. A scent mingled with the salt air. Not cologne, but him. It made her head spin as if she had too much wine. His hand moved from her shoulder, slid lower, caressing her back as it moved, pulling her body closer to him. Velvety pleasure coursed through her, centering in her loins, as his tongue touched her lips, then slid inside and toyed expertly with her own. Her passion grew and grew until the whole universe became centered on her desire for him.

She felt his passion, too, growing, pressing against her with its need. This proof of his desire for her was intoxicating, enhancing her pleasure until it nearly overwhelmed her.

They remained locked in their rapturous embrace for long, luscious minutes, until their passion grew so intense it fairly exploded, driving their lips apart and leaving them gasping for air.

It was the most amazing first kiss either of them ever experienced. It had been perfect.

Although their lips parted, their bodies remained fused, as if their molecules intertwined. Both were panting, the heat between them so intense Jillian felt small beads of perspiration gliding down between her breasts.

Her legs were weak and she clung to him as much for support as to feel his hard maleness against her delicate femininity.

Paul was virtually paralyzed by the experience. He could not believe one kiss could contain so much passion, so much raw pleasure, and at the same time, so much tenderness.

He lightly stroked her hair as they held tight, aware only of the surf, the breeze, and each other.

Eventually, he found his voice. "That was…" He couldn't think of the right word.

"Amazing? Fantastic? Unbelievable? Magical?" she whispered.

"Yes. Yes. All that. But so much more. I'm not sure they've invented a word for it."

He felt her head nod against his chest.

"So what are the chances a girl like you would care to spend more time with a guy like me?"

"Pretty good, I think. Pretty good."

Jillian smiled as her eyes grew heavy. The activities of the night, coupled with the intensity of the emotions she just experienced seemed to have drained her.

I think I could fall asleep right here in his arms if he'd agree to stand and support me for the next eight hours.

Paul felt her settling in against him and realized she must be giving in to exhaustion. He looked around and saw they were not far from the ramp that led back to the sidewalk.

"Hold on tight," he whispered as he bent at the knees and lifted her into his arms.

Oh my.

Through a growing haze of sleepiness, she snuggled against him.

Could this evening have possibly ended any more romantically?

3:10 AM

When the limousine stopped in front of Jillian's building, her head rested on Paul's shoulder, her hands clasped between his. She was so tired, but what a wonderful tired it was. The night had been perfect, almost enchanted, from the moment he arrived to pick her up.

She watched him open the car door and extend a hand to help her out. Safely on the sidewalk, he asked her to wait a moment and walked around to the driver's window. A minute later, the car pulled away and he was next to her, again.

She took his arm and they strolled to the entry.

"I had such a wonderful time tonight, Paul." She pressed her shoulder against his as they walked. "It really was the most romantic evening of my life. Thank you so much."

"Me, too. It was…" Again he was lost for words.

"Yes, I know," she sighed.

When they reached the front door, Paul drew her aside, out of the glare of the entry light and pulled her close for one last kiss. As before, Jillian could feel the heat radiating from his body, warming her. She also felt a different heat inside her, the beating of her heart, the dizzying passion. Her lips tingled, desperately wanting to taste him again, but savoring the anticipation. His hand caressed her hair, her cheek. His fingertips brushed across her neck and throat, sending shivers of pleasure down her spine.

Then he took her in his arms.

Their second kiss was everything the first had been, only better. His lips seemed to remember the things that thrilled her the first time and she responded with a fierceness that surprised her.

She pressed herself into him, fusing their bodies, allowing the passion to take control. Again he grew hard against her.

She moved her thigh, sliding it gently against his arousal causing it to throb. She felt as much as heard the low, soft moan vibrate the lips that continued to devour her own. She rubbed her breasts against him and felt him sway, then lean back against the building for support, drawing her with him, never allowing an inch of their bodies to lose contact.

His lips moved down to her chin then further down to her neck, searching for the special spot they seemed to know was there. She almost swooned when they found it, sending sharp sparks of pleasure through her as she moved more urgently against him, her body throbbing with desire.

When his lips found hers again, all hope of restraint was abandoned. She thrust her tongue into his mouth, insistent, demanding more of him. She could feel his entire body responding, as she was sure he could feel hers wanting him.

After what seemed like an hour, their lips parted but their bodies remained glued together. They were breathless, mindless of anything but each other and their arousal.

Her body warm against his, her head rested on his shoulder as her hand reached up to caress his cheek.

"Would you like to come up?" she asked softly, feeling safe in his arms, sure of his answer.

"Yes, I would," he replied, just as softly.

He cupped her face with his hands and leaned back in to kiss her. Again, they reveled in the kiss. Then it was over, and he released her head, his hands moving down to her shoulders, his eyes meeting hers.

She could see his desire and was sure he could see hers as well. But she saw something else as well.

He held her eyes for a few more seconds, then said, "There's nothing in this world I want more than to come up, but I don't think I will."

Jillian was confused and hurt by the rejection. She thought everything went so well. They connected, really connected. She felt it. She knew it.

"Jillian, something special happened tonight. I know you felt it, too. I know you understand now what I meant Wednesday when we first met and I said something clicked."

The intensity of his gaze grew with each word. She nodded. She did understand.

"You know how much I want to come up. A few minutes ago you could feel how much I want to."

She blushed at the memory of his arousal and of her wanton reaction to it. But she was still confused. He wanted her, so why was he rejecting her?

She let his arms enfold her, drawing her gently to him and heard the tenderness in his voice as he continued.

"Jilli, this isn't the first time I've been invited up after a first date. And the thing is, every one of those relationships ended badly. Some ended quickly, some took a while, but…"

He sighed. He saw the hurt on her face when he declined her invitation.

I have to make her understand, but how can I explain this so she won't feel rejected and won't think I'm a wuss?

He released her again, then took her hands in his, kissing them. "Jilli, every one of those relationships that started out in bed never seemed to get beyond the bed. The sex was great, but let's face it, after sex you still have to spend time together, you still have to have something to talk about.

"When my last relationship ended, I realized all those women…well, I shouldn't say 'all those.' There were only five. But none of them ever really got to know me. And I never got to know them. We never really formed a bond outside of bed, I guess, is the best way to put it. And Jillian, I so *do not* want that to happen with us.

"Despite everything we experienced tonight, despite everything we shared and learned about each other, we've only known each other three days. We had one lunch, some pretty interesting drama, and one incredible fantasy of a date.

"But I want more. More of you, more of us. And to get more will take time. I want to take that time, so when we do share that one, final part of ourselves, we'll know it's because it's right and because it's time, and not just because we're horny as all hell."

The hurt drained away as he spoke. Jillian nodded. She did

understand. As soon as he said it, she realized the same thing happened to her both times she issued that first date invitation.

"Look," he said with a mischievous glint in his eyes, "I'm a twenty-first century guy. I know women have, ah, needs and desires like men do, which makes me feel bad that I'm leaving you in the lurch, so to speak. So if you really need something, I know this all-night place where we can get you an excellent vibrator."

She burst out laughing and smacked him on the chest with the palm of her hand. "You jerk. I do *not* need a vibrator, thank you very much."

She threw her arms around him again and he held her close.

"But I have the feeling I'm going to find I need you. A lot."

She tilted her head up to kiss him. She wanted this man so much right now she'd have traded anything, everything to have him. And, once again, she could feel he was feeling the same way.

After a while she broke the kiss and stared into his eyes, into his soul. She had expected to see the longing and desire. And she was happy when she saw the joy, the admiration, and the respect. But she was startled to see something else, something she hoped to see in his eyes one day, something she knew would remain unacknowledged and unspoken for now.

She saw the love.

11:30 AM

A muffled groan drifted from beneath the pale pink satin sheet that covered all but a shock of the dark auburn hair splayed wildly across the matching pillowcase. The alarm's buzzer droned on until a hand crept out from beneath the covers to turn it off. The soft curves outlined by the satin lay motionless once the noise stopped.

After about four minutes, another low groan signaled the owner of the arm had not fallen asleep again.

Jillian rolled onto her back and stretched. A peaceful, happy smile grew as thoughts of her date last night drifted through the still sleepy haze.

"Paul," she whispered. The thought of him, of how he treated her last night, of their first kiss and their last kiss before parting, made her tingle.

She checked the clock on the nightstand. Eleven thirty-five. She would have preferred to remain right where she was for another hour or two, thinking about last night, and him, but she promised she would meet her sisters later and knew Liz and Jenna would be dying for her to call with the details of what happened after they parted last night.

She kicked back the covers. The tingle focused itself as she tried to imagine Paul's reaction were he to see her in this thin white nightie that left little to the imagination. "Enough!" she muttered and slid out of bed.

After a quick stop in the bathroom, she took her cellphone from her purse and checked it as she walked back to the alcove.

Huh. Nothing. Not even a message from Liz. That's curious.

She sat on the bed next to the nightstand that held the alarm clock, a small lamp, and her phone with the answering machine. The light was blinking. Six messages.

Good thing I turned the ringer off or I'd never have gotten any sleep.

The first message was from Paul, left not half-an hour after he said goodbye at her front door.

"I wanted to hear your voice one more time before I fell asleep but I guess the machine will have to do. Sweet dreams." There was a long silence before he continued. "A part of me really wishes I had accepted your invitation. And no, not that part. But my head knows it was better I didn't. For now. Call me when you get up. If I can't go to sleep to the sound of your voice, at least I can wake up to it. Bye."

Jillian pressed the pause button before the next message could play. She closed her eyes, and recalled Paul's face.

How many times has he said just the right thing at just the right time? It's like he's known me all my life instead of only three days.

She reached for the phone to call him, but changed her mind and pressed the play button in case he left another message later.

He did not. There were two messages from Liz and one each from Julia and Joanne reminding her about their shopping date today. The last was from Jenna, who let her know she would be at Liz's place awaiting her call, and if she didn't call pretty damned soon to relieve their suspense they would come over and break down her door. She laughed at that, knowing Jenna would do it!

She picked up the phone and dialed Paul's number. After three rings, a groggy voice answered.

"Mmmmm, ah, hello?"

"Good morning."

"Oh, it's you! Good morning. Mmmmm, I was right. It *is* nice waking up to the sound of your voice. Did you sleep well?" His voice was clearer now.

"Wonderful. How about you?"

"Not so well. I kept having these dreams about a beautiful black dress and what wasn't being worn underneath it."

Jillian's cheeks flushed as she giggled. "I'm sorry. We could have stayed on the sidewalk."

"No, it was worth it. The walk was worth it. And the kiss." She heard a long sigh. "That was worth a thousand sleepless nights."

His words filled her with pleasure.

Always the right thing.

"Any chance you can get out of shopping today?"

"I'm sorry, but I promised. We all have to get dresses for my cousin's wedding in a few weeks."

"What time will you be leaving?"

"Julie's picking up Jo and Jessie and then they'll come here to get me. Knowing Jessie, she'll keep them waiting at my parent's house, so it'll probably be around one when they get here." She glanced at the clock. "And I have to get going or I won't be ready."

She heard him sigh again. "Oh well." He sounded disappointed. "I had thoughts of getting coffee and muffins for us, but I can see that's not a plan today. How long will you be shopping?"

Jillian laughed. "Let's see, four women need dresses and accessories. There's a gazillion places to look for them in town. What are the chances we'll be back before late next week?"

Paul joined in the laughter. "I hadn't thought of it that way."

"That's because you're a guy," she teased. "Actually, it's not just the shopping. We haven't had a sisters' day in a while, so we'll probably have dinner, maybe do something afterward. We sort of play it by ear."

"What about your brother? Doesn't he get included in these outings?"

"James? Sure, that's exactly what a twenty-year-old guy wants to do. Go shopping for dresses with his four sisters."

"Hey, I'd go shopping with you if you asked."

"You mean you like shopping for women's dresses?"

"I didn't say I'd like it, I said I'd go."

"Well then what good would you be?"

"I could help you try them on."

Jillian laughed. "I should have known. Bye Paul."

"Wait. Do you have a cell phone?"

"Well, I usually only give my cell number to special people, never to anyone who might turn out to be someone I might not want calling all the time. And strange guys who yell in my ear in coffee shops sort of fall into that category."

Paul laughed. "I kind of figured that was why I got your land line Wednesday. So, am I still in that category?"

"Hmmm...I don't know. You were kind of nice last night. And you did save me from Patrick. Decisions, decisions..."

After they exchanged numbers, Paul said, "Please, call me in case you get done early or something. I'm not sure where I'll be, but if it's not too late, maybe we can do something. Or if you're too tired, I'll be more than happy to just sit somewhere and look at your face."

"Tell me, tell me, *tell* me!" Liz cried without even a hello. She must have been hovering over the phone with caller ID. Jillian heard a click and figured she was now on speakerphone.

Jenna's anxious, "Yeah, tell us!" confirmed it.

But Jillian was feeling mischievous. "Oh, we went for a walk on the beach then he took me home. So what did you two do after you left the lounge? Did..."

Liz and Jenna were having none of that game. They peppered her with questions so fast Jillian couldn't have wedged in a word had she tried.

"A walk on the beach!"

"Took you home where?"

"What beach?"

"Did you kiss him?"

"What did he say about us?"

"Yeah, did he like us?

"When did you get home?"

"Is he a good kisser?"

"What else is he good at?"

"Did you go swimming?"

"Oooo! Skinny dipping!"

"Did you do it?"

"Does he have a big one?"

"Come on, girl, tell us!"

"Ya, tell us. We're dying here!"

Jillian's hand covered her mouth, holding in the laughter until her friends paused for a breath. "Okay, okay." She gave them all the details of the ride to the beach and what happened once they arrived.

"Oh wow, that is so romantic," sighed Jenna after hearing about their first kiss and how he carried her back to the limousine.

"Is he still there?" Liz assumed they spent the morning in bed together.

"He never was here." She explained what happened when she invited him in.

"I don't believe this guy. He's cute, he works, he's thoughtful, he dances, he's romantic, he treats you like a frigging queen, and now you're telling us he turns down sex because he wants to get to know you first? Either this boy is seriously deranged somehow or..."

"I know." Her voice was soft and serious.

"What?" Jenna asked.

"Or he's thinking about the future. His future with Jilli."

"Oh my gosh, Liz, you're right." Then to Jillian she said, "He likes you that much he's already thinking about..."

"Don't say it. Please, don't say it. I don't want to think about it."

The possibilities overwhelmed her. She did not think through the implications of Paul's refusal last night, and now that her friends followed the logic to its denouement, she was feeling very nervous. But there would be no jumping to conclusions for her.

"Then all I'll say is," Jenna added, "he has it bad for you, girl."

"Oh yeah," Liz agreed, "really, *really* bad."

Next, Jillian phoned Julia to find out what time they would pick her up.

"We're leaving mom and dad's house now so we should be there in about half an hour or so. I'll call you when we get there."

Jillian's parents and her sister Jessica lived in Southborough, about twenty-five miles west of Boston. Julia lived in Northborough, only five miles from her parents. Joanne also lived close-by, in Shrewsbury. Their brother James shared an apartment with three other BU students in Allston, close to the University.

She jumped into the shower, hurried into khakis and her favorite t-shirt and was ready and waiting when her cell phone rang.

1:10 PM

Julia's tan Toyota was double-parked beside two other vehicles. As she approached the car, Jillian saw Joanne in the front passenger seat and an unhappy-looking Jessica in the rear. She slid in beside her and said, "What's wrong now?"

"Well hello to you, too." Joanne made a face at her.

"Sorry," she said sweetly. "Hi Julie, hi Jo, hi Jessie. Now tell me what's wrong." She was staring at Jessie.

"Nothing. It's not important."

Julie, who was taking a sip of water from a bottle, almost choked. "Are you kidding? We've been listening to you for forty minutes and now you tell Jilli it's nothing, it's not important?"

"Yeah," Jo agreed. "Either you tell her or I'll tell her."

Jessie sighed. She seemed to want to cry, but Jillian knew she would not. Her baby sister was an eighteen year old stoic, or at least pretended to be. Growing up, she was never given to tears or emotional displays in public. Where a skinned knee or sprained wrist would send her sisters into fits of weeping, Jessie invariably set her jaw and refused to cry. She saved her tears for when she was alone. The only time anyone could remember her crying in public was when their grandfather had passed away three years ago.

Jillian reached for her hand. "Come on Jess, spill it."

Jessie took a deep breath and let it out with a whoosh. "Ethan and I had a big fight yesterday. My friend Gail saw him making out with Dedee Sidman at the mall. He didn't even try to deny it."

Jillian wanted to throw her arms around her sister and hold her, but she knew Jessie would never allow it, at least not in front of the others.

"I'm guessing you two split up?"

Jessica nodded silently.

"And there's more?"

Again Jessica just nodded.

"Now she doesn't have a date for the prom next week," Julia said. "The little creep is taking Slutty Sidman."

"Oh sweetie, I'm sorry. That really sucks. Isn't there anyone else at school you can ask?"

Jessica's eyes answered before her words. "Sure, if I want to go with a druggie or one of the geeks." She turned away and stared out the window. "I'd rather die than be seen with any of those guys."

"Why don't you go alone and have a good time?"

"We tried that suggestion already," Jo told her.

Jessie glared at Joanne then said to Jillian, "I can't show up alone if he'll be there with *her*. It would be too humiliating. I'll just stay home. And I'm not going with Jimmy. How desperate would that look?"

She was still turned toward the window, but Jillian was sure she could see moisture filling the corner of her sister's eye.

4:20 PM

Jillian and Julia stood side-by-side in front of a mirror wall examining the dresses they tried on. Julie was singing along quietly as Beyonce's *Me, Myself, and I* played over the store's PA system.

At five foot five, Julia was two inches shorter than Jillian, and the ten extra pounds she never lost after having her third child settled in her breasts and backside, much to the delight of her husband Matthew. Still, she only outweighed her sister by five pounds.

Jillian's one hundred twenty-five pounds were distributed perfectly on her frame. She was the only one of the four sisters who really could not find much fault with the way nature sculpted her.

"What do you think?" She turned slowly.

"I think you look great in that."

"I agree. I'm getting this one."

Joanne was the first to find her outfit, in the second store they visited. She combined a thin, black, sleeveless boyfriend sweater and a pink chiffon skirt with black floral embroidery on the bottom half to create an ensemble that was modest, striking, and very pretty. She was the tallest of the sisters at five feet nine and a half inches. Though she ballooned up to 160 pounds during her recent pregnancy, since delivering the baby, managed to shed nearly all the weight she gained. Only her breasts were still larger and she knew they would remain so as long as she continued nursing. Like Julia's husband, Joanne's hubby, Tom, was not complaining at all.

Six stores later, Jillian found hers.

She was wearing a deep burgundy faux wrap dress with a v-neck and three-quarter sleeves. The matte jersey material hugged her just enough to be alluring.

I wonder what Paul would think if he saw me in it.

As she thought his name, Anne Murray started singing *Could I Have This Dance*, the first song they danced to last night. She smiled at the timing.

She was dying to tell her sisters about him, but held back, not wanting to flaunt her happiness in the face of Jessie's misery.

When Joanne and Jessie emerged from the changing room, Jess was wearing a strapless candy apple red tieback sheath that hung perfectly on her model-thin five foot six inch body.

Julia saw her, sighed, and said, "You have no idea how much I hate you for being able to wear that. You look absolutely delicious." Turning sideways, she gazed at her reflection in the mirror. "I don't care how much Matty says he likes the new me, this big butt *has* to go. And if the boobs go too, so be it."

Even Jessie laughed a bit at that.

Six o'clock found them walking back to the parking garage. All found clothes, shoes, and accessories during an afternoon filled with fun and the kinds of news, gossip, teasing, and confidences only sisters can share.

They were a block from the garage when Jessie said, "So Jilli, when are you going to tell us about the guy you were with last night?"

Jillian was confused and it showed. *How could she know about Paul?* "What makes you think I was with a guy last night?"

"Jimmy called me this morning to say hi. He said he saw you getting all cozy with some guy in one of those horse drawn carriages." She flipped open her cell phone. "Shall we call him and find out if he was lying?"

After Jillian explained why she didn't say anything, Jessie assured her it was okay.

"Let's put this stuff in the trunk and go get something to eat and I'll tell you all about him."

7:10 PM

An hour later, the sisters were finishing the last bites of their sandwiches as Jillian recounted the walk on the beach and their first breathtaking kiss under the full moon.

"Oh Jilli, that is so romantic. I'm getting hot just listening to you. No wonder you didn't answer your phone this morning. You were probably doing the wild thing with him for the fifth time or something."

Jillian shook her head and completed the story with details of their parting.

"This guy said he loves you but didn't want to sleep with you?" Julia couldn't believe what she heard.

"No. I said I invited him up and he said no because he didn't want us to end up like all his previous relationships where they jumped right into sex. And he never said he loved me. I said I saw it in his eyes."

Jessica rolled her own eyes. "Seems to me that if he really cared that much he'd want to get naked with you."

"No," said Joanne. "I understand what he meant. He wants to wait until they form other bonds…friendship, respect…that kind of stuff. That way, when they do it, the relationship will be about more than great sex…" She paused for a beat and grinned. "…assuming, of course, the rest of him is as talented as his lips."

"And you really think he could be the one?"

Jillian still did not want to think about what Liz and Jenna alluded to earlier in the day, but her sisters weren't her friends and felt no obligation to let her hide from her feelings. As her story progressed, they badgered her with questions and comments until Jillian gave in and admitted the inexplicable depth of feeling she had for Paul.

"I don't know, Julie. He's just the nicest guy. And it's like…it's like he knows me, like he's known me forever. It was kind of creepy at first, but the more I'm with him the more I'm feeling it, too. A connection of some sort."

Jillian took a deep breath and let it out very slowly. "I don't know. Maybe I'm kidding myself. Maybe it's all because of what happened last night. But I do feel differently around him than I ever have with any other guy. Including you-know-who."

Julian and Joanne nodded.

"Aiden," Jessica said, "right? You know, I'm less than a month away from being legal. Are you ever going to tell me what really happened back then?"

"Shut up, Jessie. You know she doesn't like to…"

"That's okay, Julie. Maybe it is time she knew." She turned to Jessica. "How much do you remember?"

"I remember you were engaged to some guy named Aiden and then you weren't. And nobody would ever tell me why. I mean, I knew that 'they just decided to call it off' stuff was crap. Nobody spends months crying over and years refusing to talk about a mutual decision."

Jillian smiled at her little sister. "I wish you could hear yourself. Half the time you sound like a kid and the other half like a college professor.

You are going to have them scratching their heads for sure, wherever you decide to go next year."

"Yeah, yeah, blah, blah. So you gonna spill it or what?"

"See! But okay.

"You know that he…Aiden…was my first real love, right?"

Jessie's shrug drew a sigh from her sister.

Just start from the beginning.

"We met when I was a freshman and he was a junior. He said he saw me walking on Comm. Ave. with Liz and knew right then I was 'the one.'"

Her fingers made quotation marks in the air.

"He chased after me for, I don't know…it must have been two months before I agreed to go out with him.

"He was handsome, and charming, and smart, and so intense, and I could tell he really, really liked me. And we had a great time He was…" She felt herself starting to blush. "…the first guy I ever slept with on the first date."

Jessica's eyes widened at the revelation.

"Two weeks later, we were living together in his apartment and just before spring break, he proposed."

This time, her eyes nearly popped. "Living together! Does ma know you two were…"

"No! And you better not ever tell her. You know how…"

"Chill, will ya. You think I'm stupid? I still live there. If she ever found out, I'm the one who'd pay for it."

Her sisters laughed.

"Mom would probably lock her in her room so she wouldn't follow your bad example."

"You're probably right, Jo. I'm sorry, Jess."

"Whatever. So keep going."

"Well, except for holidays, we were pretty much inseparable for the next fourteen months, I guess. We…"

"Wait a minute. Were you living with him that summer?"

Jillian nodded.

"But how did you keep ma from finding out?"

"Jenna was taking summer classes so she got to keep the dorm room. I got a summer job at a supermarket and told ma I was staying with Jenna so she wouldn't have to be alone."

"You lied to her! And she bought it?"

An abashed grin scrunched Jillian's face and furrowed her brow.

"Jilli was the good girl," Julie said. "Don't you remember? The new Madonna. And I don't mean the singer. Ma would believe anything her little pet told her."

"Well, you and Jo made it so easy. All I had to do was stay out of trouble. If you two had just…"

"Stop! Finish the story. And will you two please keep quiet."

"I have a better idea. Come on, Jo. I have to pee."

As her sisters stood, Jillian continued.

"Do you remember the wedding was going to be at the end of June, about a month after Aiden graduated?"

Jessie nodded.

"Well, after his parents left, we went to a big party that lasted all night. When we finally got home we…" She felt her face growing hot again. "ummm…fooled around for most of the morning and then fell asleep.

"I woke up a little after five in the afternoon and Aiden was gone. At first, I thought he ran out for food or wine. But once I got out of bed, I found a note leaning against the wine bottle we used as a candle holder."

She didn't realize how much of the pain of recalling that day showed on her face and in her eyes until she saw Jessie's expression change.

"Oh, Jilli. This is really hurting you. I'm sorry. Just stop. I don't need to know this now. Maybe some other time, when it…"

"No. No. I've avoided this ghost for too long. I'll tell you then I'll lock him away forever." Her eyes dropped to her empty plate. "I must have read that letter a hundred times. However many it was, I can remember it like it was yesterday. It said

> *Dearest Jillian,*
>
> *I am sorry, but I cannot marry you. By the time you read this, I will be far away. Please know that it is not you. You have always been my heart and soul and I will always love you.*
>
> *I cannot explain why I am leaving for I don't really understand it myself. I only know that what I thought was true is not and I must search for the real truth or never find a moment's peace.*
>
> *I will return someday, I hope, once I find the answers to the questions that now haunt me. When that day comes, I'll find you, and hope that no matter where your life has led you, you'll have found a way to forgive me.*
>
> *Please think of me now and then, once you stop hating me, for I will think of you always, and hold you in my heart no matter where I am.*
>
> *Aiden*

When she looked up, Jillian saw tears in her sister's eyes.

"Oh, Jilli. How could he do that? How could he hurt you like that? What an asshole. Now I understand why you cried so much. And now I feel even worse for making you tell me. I'm so sorry. I…"

"Jess, it's okay. I wanted to tell you. Really. Just let me finish so I can put an end to him."

Jessica nodded as she wiped her eyes.

"It took me almost a full year to let go of him, of the love and the hate. But I did. I moved on. And now…now it's been five years…and I hardly ever think about him and what might have been."

Jessica heard the words, but could see the change in her sister.

She was so happy before when she was talking about new guy. And now she looks so sad. And it's my fault. No wonder Ethan dumped me. What a loser I am.

Jillian shook her head to dislodge the ghost. She did not want to think about Aiden ever again. A small part of her might still be conflicted about her feelings for him, but now that she met the man who might share her life, she would not allow any phantoms or feelings from the past to mess things up.

"Are you planning to tell Paul about him?"

"Of course. But not right away. I mean, your past lovers aren't something you share on the second date."

She heard Julia chuckle as she and Joanne took their seats. "It seems to me last night could have qualified for at least four pretty fabulous dates."

"That's right," Jessie said, "and now that you've had four dates, it's about time for the horizontal hokey-pokey."

Her sisters burst out laughing.

"Where did you come up with that?" Joanne asked, wiping tears from her eyes.

"Some old romance novel I found in the attic. Mom has tons of them up there."

Julia reached over and touched Jillian's hand. "May we assume the story's over?"

Jillian nodded.

"Good. So when do we get to meet this new dreamboat?"

"Never. Or at least not until I have a chance to warn him. You three would scare the poor guy half to death and I'd never see him again."

"We wouldn't do that. Really!" Joanne almost sounded sincere. "Come on, call him and have him come over here to meet us."

Jillian refused, but her sisters began to protest and whine, promise and beg, wheedle and nag until they convinced her they would be on their best behavior.

"But I don't even know where he is. He said he might be going out with friends." She really did not like this idea but was running out of reasonable excuses.

"Just call him and see," Jessie said. "Come on, how often do Jo and Julie get a whole day off like this? It will be fun. And we promise to be good, don't we?"

Her sisters held up their right hands and crossed their hearts with their left as they did when they were all little girls.

Crap! There's no way out of this.

He answered on the third ring.

"Hey Jilli! What a nice surprise! Are you done with your sisters already?"

He knew it was me. Oh, right, Caller ID.

"Hi Paul. No we're in Delaney's Grille. We had sandwiches and were talking, and I thought I'd call to see where you were."

"I'm at DHL with a bunch of people. Are your sisters there? Did you tell them about me?"

"Yes and yes."

"That's great. I'll bet they've been bugging you to call me so they can meet me."

"Uh, yes, how did you know?"

How does he keep knowing these things?

"It's what I'd do if I were them. Hey, if no one is in a hurry to go home, why don't you all come over and hang out for a while?"

He wants to meet my sisters? He wants his friends to meet me and my sisters?

"Um, hold on a second." She pressed the mute button. "He's with some people in this bar about a mile from here. He wants to know if you all want to go hang out for a while."

"Oooo," Julia said, impressed. "I think I like this boy already!"

7:50 PM

Fifteen minutes, two phone calls to understanding husbands, and a quick taxi ride later, Jillian and her sisters walked through the doors of DHL. Paul jumped up as heads turned throughout the bar to see who came in, then lingered at the sight of the four lovely women.

Jillian was suddenly nervous as she realized she was unsure how to greet him in front of her sisters.

Should I offer my hand or kiss him? If I kiss him, for how long? Maybe I should just say hello?

Paul solved the dilemma by moving right in and giving her a polite kiss on the lips.

She introduced him to her sisters and he hugged each of them in turn.

"I am very happy to meet you all." A mischievous grin crept onto his face. "Jilli's told me so little about you, and to get back at her for the oversight, I'm hoping you'll all spend the next few hours telling me all the embarrassing stories from her childhood she doesn't want me to hear. You know, like the time she decided to streak through the house buck naked in front of a party full of people."

He was going for a big laugh with that, but the four sisters stared at him and then at each other in disbelief. After a few seconds, it dawned on him why and his grin transformed into a look that matched their own. "No way." He turned to Jillian. "I was kidding. You didn't really do that? Did you?"

Jillian's suddenly bright red cheeks were all the encouragement her sisters needed.

"What's the matter, Jilli? You had such a cute little behind back then."

"Come on, that's not half as bad as the time dad caught you playing doctor with Billy Tanner in the garage."

"Don't be embarrassed. He's probably already undressed you in his head a dozen times."

Jillian's face went from red to scarlet, drawing laughter from her tormentors. She turned to Paul, who was grinning broadly, and mouthed, "I'm sorry." Then she turned back to her sisters and protested through clenched teeth, "You promised" as Paul slipped his arm around her waist, and pressed her closer to him.

When the girls realized how upset she was, they hurried to apologize. "We're sorry, sweetie," Joanne said. "We got a little carried away. Please don't be mad. We'll be good the whole rest of the time we're here. Our word to Grampa."

Joanne looked at Julia and Jessica who both nodded gravely and repeated, "Our word to Grampa."

Giving one's word to Grampa was sacrosanct and Jillian began to relax.

Paul led them all to several tables that had been pushed together to accommodate everyone.

"So how *do* parents with five kids get out of the house on a school night?" Lisa was asking Patti.

"Wonderful in-laws," she replied, drawing a chuckle as Paul and the new arrivals reached the table.

Paul introduced Rob and Lisa, Priya, and Tom and Patti Driscoll.

Jillian nodded politely, said hello to everyone, then walked around the table, leaned over, and gave Priya a warm hug.

"Paul said the date went well last night. But he's being awfully cagey about providing details," Priya whispered.

"It was wonderful, so romantic," she murmured back. "Lunch Monday, okay? Lisa, too."

"Absolutely!"

Jillian took a seat next to Paul. She turned to Lisa and said, "I understand you were responsible for arranging the dinner reservation last night. It was wonderful. Thank you so much."

"You're welcome," she replied. "It was my pleasure." Then she reached across Rob and smacked Paul on the arm. "You dope! Why did you tell her I set it up? She was supposed to think you were a magician!"

Paul shrugged. "I couldn't lie to her."

That drew a round of 'oooos' and 'awwws' from the women and rolled eyes from the guys, but it sent a little spark through Jillian, who leaned closer and kissed him on the cheek.

Over the next hour, and several rounds of drinks, everyone got acquainted. Spirits were high all around, except for Jessica, who seemed to have reverted to her pre-shopping depression. Jillian wondered if her sister's funk was due to the presence of three obviously happy couples at the table, plus so many others throughout the room.

Much to everyone's amusement, Julia and Joanne took every opportunity to casually inquire about Paul and his life story as they bantered with him and his friends until, unable to stand it any longer, Jillian all but dragged them into the ladies room and told them to stop.

The Saturday night crowd in the bar was large and in a good mood. As a result, the jukebox steadily cranked out tunes. Several times, Tom, who loved to sing, broke out in song and most of the group joined in. Just before eight-thirty, the bouncy rhythm of the oldie *You Don't Mess Around With Jim* faded away as the group applauded themselves for their performance. It took only a second or two for Jillian to realize the next song was *Always And Forever,* the last song they danced to last night.

She turned to Paul who was only a half-second behind her in recognizing the tune. Their eyes met and a silent message passed from each to the other. Paul stood and extended his hand.

DHL did not have a dance floor, so Paul led her to the small space that opened up when they pushed the tables together earlier.

Her heart was racing and she felt a lump in her throat as she followed him. Was it the song or his very public romantic gesture that was causing her to feel suddenly lightheaded?

When he took her in his arms, she settled herself against him. Memories of the previous night flooded through her as she lay her head on his shoulder, loving the way his strong arms held her close and made her feel warm and desired.

They moved together as they did last night. They swayed and turned more than danced, each lost in the sensation of holding and being held, of moving as one body, feeling as one soul.

All conversation stopped at their table as Paul's friends and Jillian's sisters watched them dance. Priya sat with her hand to her throat, filled with joy for Paul and Jillian and with pride at knowing she played a part in helping them get to this moment.

Tom was getting poked by his wife who whispered, "Why don't you ever do romantic things like that for me?"

Rob and Lisa held hands and watched, happy their friend appeared to have found the girl of his dreams.

Julia drew her two sisters into a huddle. "This guy's good. He wants her so bad you can see it in his eyes."

"And she's just as horny for him," Joanne added.

"Whatever." Jessica was contemplating the scratches on the table instead of the happy couple.

As the song reached its conclusion, everyone saw Paul lean down to give Jillian a soft, tender kiss, a kiss that made her heart flutter and the other five women feel the slightest twinge of jealously mix with their happiness for her.

"Hey dude," Rob said to Paul about an hour later, "Lisa and I are hitting the road. We're heading down to the Cape tonight. Lisa's parents have a summer house in Brewster."

Tom, Patti, and Priya left about twenty minutes earlier.

After the goodbyes, Julie, Jo, and Jessie headed to the ladies room.

"So what's up with Jessie? She hasn't seemed too happy to be here tonight."

Jillian explained about the breakup and how she would miss her prom as a result.

"That really stinks. Guys like that give the rest of us a bad name."

When her sisters returned, Paul turned on the charm, telling jokes, making little comments and observations that had them laughing and feeling good. Without it seeming obvious, he tried to pay extra attention to Jessie. He succeeded in lifting her spirits a little, and sensed the sisters all appreciated his efforts. After polling them about their favorite songs, he asked Jillian to help him play them all on the jukebox.

"So what do you think of him now?" Jo asked her sisters, once Paul and Jillian were at the jukebox.

"He's cute," Jessica said.

"He's great," Julia gushed. "I keep waiting for him to say or do something to make me wonder, but he keeps on being sweet and charming. And it's not even an act, unless he's the world's greatest actor."

"I know what you mean. He's so attentive to Jilli even when he's paying attention to us, or to his friends earlier. And some of the things he says...well...I see what Jilli means about feeling like he knows her. What do you think, Jessie? Is he for real?"

"I guess so. He's been really nice to us all tonight and especially to me. I think Jilli told him about Ethan." Her sisters nodded their agreement. "I get a good vibe from him, you know? I mean, how bad can the guy be if he'll pay attention to the skinny little sister when Jillian's sitting next to him?"

Over at the jukebox, Jillian was using the touch screen to page through menus for the titles they wanted. After she selected Kelly Clarkson's *A Moment Like This* for Joanne, Paul asked, "Would you mind very much if I went out with another woman next week?"

She turned her head to examine his face. This had to be one of his jokes. "That depends. Are we talking about your mother? I wouldn't mind that at all."

He laughed. "No, not mom."

"Priya?" She realized there was an edge to her voice.

He caught the edge and grinned. "No, not Priya. Actually, if you think she'd want to go with me, I was thinking of asking Jessie to her prom."

Jillian was caught completely off guard. That was the last thing she might have expected him to say. "You want to take Jessie to her prom?"

"With your permission of course."

"You don't need my permission to..." She felt his hand squeeze her arm and looked at him. What she saw made her heart skip with joy. The tilt of his head and the look in his eyes under raised eyebrows told her he did indeed need her permission, because he considered them a couple now.

The smile he received in return let Paul know she understood, and the gentle touch of her palm on his cheek told him she felt the same way.

"You'd really do that? Take her to the prom?"

"Of course. She's your sister, and she's hurt, and I know how important proms are to girls her age. And not to appear immodest, I am kind of cute and willing to help her make the little twerp who dumped her realize what a horrible mistake he made."

Jillian chuckled.

"And besides, I was sick and never went to my prom. I think it'll be fun. If she'll go with me. What do you think?"

She had no idea. Paul kept surprising her. "I guess it's up to Jessie."

"But what about you? Would you be okay with it?"

She could tell the slightest reservation on her part would be enough to make him forget the whole thing. "Well," she said playfully, "you're not planning to get fresh with her after the prom, are you?"

"Only if you'll join in," he teased, bringing a pleased flush to her cheeks.

"Okay then. That sounds like fun," she shot back, surprising herself once again by joking about such a thing. "You can go."

As they returned to the table, they decided to let Paul ask Jessie when he thought the time right. Everyone talked for a while as the music played in the background, trading stories about jobs and families. Jessie remained generally quiet, but Paul had noticed earlier she seemed interested whenever anyone was at the dart boards.

"Do you play darts?" he asked her.

"Not very well," she replied listlessly.

"Me either. Priya's great at it, though. She never played darts until she started working here in Boston but now no one at work but me will even play with her, and I only play because it's so amazing to watch her. As for me, I figure I'm doing well if I don't hit people standing at the jukebox."

That drew a half smile from her.

"Want to throw some?" She looked hesitant. "Come on. You can tell me all kinds of embarrassing things about your sister while we play."

"Don't you dare," Jillian cautioned they pushed back their chairs. "You gave your word."

Jessica was better than she let on, but then so was Paul, who kept up a running dialogue, sharing moments from his life as he probed gently into hers. Jessie relaxed more and more as they played, her spirits rising with every well-placed dart she threw, until, when she won the second game, she became almost giddy with delight. Paul thought the girl might have hugged him if he wasn't her sister's new boyfriend.

Boyfriend. That's the first time I actually thought of myself as Jillian's boyfriend. I like the way it sounds. But I think the time has come to broach the subject of the prom.

"Very nice," he said, admiring the result of her last throw.

"Thanks!"

"Hey, umm, I hope you won't be mad at your sister or anything, but a while ago, I sort of asked her about why you seemed so down and she told me about the dung worm and what he did."

Jessie giggled. "Dung worm. I like that. It fits him perfectly."

"Anyway, I had this thought before and asked Jilli about it and I don't know if it's too crazy or what, but here goes. Would you do me the honor of allowing me to escort you to your prom next week?"

Her hand stopped cold in mid-throw. "You want to take me to my prom? Why? You're like, old."

Paul clutched his chest. "Arrgh. You think I'm old?"

Jessica realized she'd been less than tactful. "Well, I don't mean you're *old* old, but your Jillian's age. Why would you want to go to some lame high school prom?"

He turned to face her. "Several reasons. First, you're Jillian's sister and I like you." He saw her eyebrows shoot up. "I like you as her sister, I mean," which drew a grin from the girl. "Second, I figure you're really more upset about missing the prom than about Mr. Slime Mold breaking up with you." He saw her nod slightly and the look in her eyes change from skepticism to interest at what would come next. "Third, let's face it, Jessie, you're a babe, and a guy would have to be nuts not to jump at the chance to be seen with you." That caused her face to start glowing with both pleasure and embarrassment. "Fourth, I never went to my own prom and I think it will be fun. And fifth…" He paused. "…I figure that with a little effort, we can make Ethan so jealous he'll spend the rest of his miserable life asking people to kick him in the butt for being stupid enough to cheat on you."

Jessie was beaming now.

"Since you put it like that, how can a girl possibly refuse?"

She threw her arms around him and hugged him, much to the amazement of her sisters, who were watching them, even though they could not hear what was being said.

"Jillian was right," she said softly after releasing him, "you really *are* the nicest guy."

SUNDAY, MAY 9

7:15 AM

Lisa padded down the wide, carpeted staircase, her feet clad only in a pair of Winnie the Pooh socks. She stopped at the bottom to stretch, then turned down the hall to the kitchen.

"I thought she was done with him."

It was her father. He was asleep last night when she and Rob arrived and she could tell from the tone of his voice he wasn't pleased to hear the news.

She stopped a few feet from the doorway to listen.

"Evidently they made up, Chad," her mother Elissa replied. She didn't appear to share her husband's displeasure, but neither did she sound happy about it.

"I really don't understand her, Lissy. With her looks and brains she could have any man in New England. Hell, there are at least a dozen associates at my firm who'd kill to go out with her. Just last week Morgan Downey told me his son asked about her. Did you know he's clerking for Justice Thomas?"

"No dear, I didn't know that. But I don't think Lisa is really interested in meeting any attorneys, even if they have clerked at the Supreme Court."

"And that's another thing. What the hell's wrong with lawyers? She..."

"Chad. Please. Stop. Must we really have this conversation again? You know as well as I do she wants a man who won't spend all his time working, as we did for so many years. She's told you that at least a dozen times. She's a grown woman and she'll do whatever she wants to do. If she loves this boy then that's all there is to it. We can either accept it, and him, and all be happy, or we can drive her away and never see her. Which would *you* prefer?"

Lisa heard the clink of a coffee cup against a saucer, followed by a long sigh. "But couldn't she at least find someone who's not…I mean, what the hell will the kids look like?"

"Oh for the love of… They're not even engaged and you're worried about kids." Her mother sounded annoyed. "If someday they do have children they'll look however they'll look, and we'll love them exactly as we love her." She paused for a few seconds then said, "You know, Chad, sometimes you make me embarrassed to be your wife."

There was another long sigh.

"I know, Lissy. I'm sorry. I only want what's best for her."

"Well that's for her to decide now. Maybe if you tried to get to know him, you might find he's not as bad as you think he is. Have you ever actually talked to him?"

"What opportunity have I had to talk to him? We've seen him twice in six months, both times at parties."

"Well today is as good an opportunity as you'll ever have. I think I'll wake them in a few minutes. Why don't you cut up some fruit and bagels while I go take a quick shower."

"I have a better idea. Why don't I join you in the shower?"

Ewwww

Lisa grimaced as she turned and hurried back to the stairs and up to her bedroom. She did *not* want to hear any more of *that*!

The sound of the door closing awakened Rob. Still groggy, he asked where she went. She didn't want to admit to her eavesdropping and didn't want to lie, so she jumped back into bed and snuggled up to him. She knew the closeness would take his mind off talking. Several times his hands wandered, testing her interest, but she was too distracted by trying not to imagine what was taking her mother so long. After fifteen minutes, she sent Rob off to the shower, then took one herself when he was done. It was almost eight-thirty when she finally heard her mother knock on their door.

Lisa was nervous about the four of them sitting together around a table, but to their credit, her parents really made an effort to get to know Rob. So much so, she found herself being ignored as they told their stories and listened to Rob tell his.

Only half hearing them, she thought about how close she came to breaking up with him and of his promise to spend the rest of his life making her happy.

That was last Thursday and now, just three days later, she was putting him to the ultimate test. A day with the parents. When she mentioned it, he didn't blink an eye and even suggested driving down last night instead this morning.

"Lisa!"

Her father's voice broke through her reverie.

"I'm sorry, daddy. I was thinking about something. What did you say?"

"I asked you about Tony DiBennedetto. Rob said you talked with him Friday to set up some date for a friend of yours."

Lisa told them about asking if Tony could find some space for her friends, and about his offer to let them use one of the private dining rooms. "He's such an old softy. I should have known he'd do something like that."

When her mom began clearing the table, Lisa rose to help. Rob pushed his chair back and offered his assistance, but Elissa waved him back into this seat. "This time, you're a guest," she told him, then drew a laugh when she added, "Next time, you get to wash."

As the women cleaned up, Chad and Rob continued to talk, or, more properly, Chad asked questions and Rob answered. After listening to almost five minutes of her father's terse, probing questions, Lisa thought he sounded like he was cross examining Rob. She was about to say something when Rob interrupted her father.

"Excuse me, sir." He sounded quite serious. "Before we go any further, don't you think it would be a good idea if I were sworn in?"

Lisa almost dropped the dish she was drying. She turned away so her father would not see her contorted face. She caught her mother's eye and saw she, too, was trying not to laugh.

For almost half a minute Chad stared at Rob, during which time he asked himself if he heard the boy correctly, decided he did, wondered if the boy was being funny or impertinent, caught his wife's struggles in his peripheral vision, decided it was the former, and broke into a broad smile. "Very good. Very good. Not many people can leave me speechless."

That was all the encouragement the women needed as they let loose. Laughing all the way, they walked over to their men and wrapped their arms around them.

The ice was broken, Lisa knew, and when her father caught her eye, she thought she noticed the slightest glimmer of respect for Rob. It wasn't the open-armed, admiration she would have preferred, but it was a start. A good start.

MONDAY, MAY 10

6:45 AM

"Who the heck is calling me at quarter-to-seven in the morning?" Jillian ran from the bathroom, dripping wet, to grab her cellphone. As much as she loved her job, she hated Monday mornings. She invariably kept hitting the snooze button on her alarm until she was late getting started, then had to rush through her shower and dressing so she wouldn't be late for work.

Metro Magazine wouldn't have cared, but Jillian set standards for herself and one of them was to get to work on time. She tried to towel herself off as she moved. She was running late, it was her turn to get the coffee, and now a phone call would eat up more minutes. She would be skipping a leisurely breakfast today for sure.

One hand toweled her hair while the other flipped open the phone. Without even a glance at the display she barked, "Hello, who is this?"

There was silence for a few seconds, then, "Uh, maybe I should call back later." She recognized the voice and immediately felt terrible.

"Oh, Paul, I'm so sorry. Please, can we start again?"

"I...ah...guess so." He didn't sound too sure.

"Ring, ring," Jillian said brightly. "Hello?"

Paul laughed. "Good morning. I was going to ask if you wanted to get breakfast, but from the way you answered before, either the world is about to end or you're running really late."

"The world is not ending." She did her best to dry her legs and feet with one hand as she sat on the edge of her bed.

"Well, if we can't have breakfast, may I at least ride to work with you?"

"Yes! I'd like that very much!"

"When will you be ready?"

"Twenty minutes. I'll meet you downstairs in twenty minutes."

Twenty-five minutes later, she walked through the front door of her building to find him leaning against the side in the exact spot they stood when they kissed goodnight Saturday morning.

"It's still warm," he said with a grin.

Jillian blushed, remembering the heat of their passion as he walked over and kissed her lightly on the lips. "What a great way to start the day."

A shiver of pleasure flashed through her. She wondered for the twentieth time since meeting him if he ever said the wrong thing. It had not happened so far. Paul slipped his hand in hers and they strolled to the subway station.

It took the train twenty minutes to travel the six stops from Fenway Station to Park Street. As they rode, he told her again how much he enjoyed meeting her sisters, and speculated on how much fun he would have escorting Jessie to the prom. He suggested meeting her for lunch, but she already had a lunch date.

"Priya and Lisa! I'm not sure I like that idea."

"Why not? Are you afraid I might learn something you don't want me to know?"

"Well, duh. Who knows what could happen when three women get together to talk about men. It can only mean trouble."

Jillian laughed, but didn't deny it.

The line at Coffey's was surprisingly short for a change and by five minutes before eight they placed their orders.

Two minutes later, Barista Ralph set their coffees and eats on the counter and asked, "Will there be anything else today?"

Paul squeezed Jillian's hand and they said simultaneously, "Whatever you're giving away for free."

They burst out laughing, oblivious to the strange looks coming from Ralph and the other customers. This was the place, and that was the line that brought them together the previous Wednesday morning, and they both knew it would be a joke they would share for as long as they were together.

8:07 AM

Shandra and Marie fidgeted impatiently, anticipating Jillian's arrival.

"Where have you been girl?" they demanded when she finally arrived. "We've been dying to hear about the big date. Hell, that's all everyone has been talking about. But now we don't have time. Cathy called the whole department into a meeting at 8:10."

Inwardly, Jillian groaned. The arrival of the flowers last Thursday followed by Friday morning's drama pretty much ensured she would have no peace today. Everyone would be asking her about Paul and the date and she still had a big ad to finish.

They strolled down to the break/meeting room to find it packed with the other members of the group. Cathy sat at the far end of the long table. When she saw them walk in, she said, "Great. Now we can get started.

"We have two issues to cover today. The powers that be have decided it's time the magazine had a makeover and they want design ideas from us. But even more important than that is the need to resolve something I'm sure we've all been thinking about all weekend."

She stared straight at Jillian, as did everyone else in the room.

"First, we need to find out what happened on Jillian's date last Friday."

12:50 PM

"I was so embarrassed. Everyone was staring at me, waiting to hear the details."

Jillian, Priya, and Lisa were seated around a small table in Coffey's enjoying lunch, which consisted of a cup of coffee each and a Cinnamon-Apple muffin and a toasted bagel with cream cheese, each split three ways.

"How much did you tell them?" Lisa asked.

"Well, I gave them a rundown of the evening, but nothing like what I just told you two."

Priya snickered. "I hope not. I can see the pantyhose story being included in your company newsletter!" She paused for a few seconds then asked Jillian, "So, was I right?"

Jillian knew exactly what she meant. "Oh yes! He is the most amazing kisser. If he's half as good horizontally as he is vertically, I'm not sure I'll be able to stand it! He had me so hot Friday night I'd have done him on the beach, in the limo, hell, in the bushes in front of my building if he asked me to. And I am *so not* that kind of girl."

Lisa laughed. "Jillian, for the right guy we're all that kind of girl. Believe me, I know."

It was Jillian's turn to laugh. "My yoga instructor said the same thing last Thursday after I told her about Paul. I guess you'd both be right if he accepted my invitation. And if you *know*, that means…"

A chance glance out the front window caused a wide-eyed double-take. Both of her new friends turned to see what caught her attention, but there was only the usual stream of people walking by.

"What was that about?" Lisa asked.

"Nothing. I…I thought I recognized someone, but it couldn't be him."

"Him? Anyone interesting? A high school sweetheart, maybe? Or some guy you had a hot one-night stand with?"

"Just someone I knew at college."

And thank God it wasn't him. He's the last thing I need now that I have Paul.

"Now *I* want to know how *you* know that what you said is true."

"Huh?"

"That every girl is *that* kind of girl for the right guy."

"Oh...right."

Lisa was many things, but shy wasn't one of them. She spent the next ten minutes detailing the time she and a local rock star did it between some packing crates behind the stage during a concert at the old Boston Garden while his band-mates played on without him.

"What can I say? I was eighteen and he was so gorgeous I would have done him in the middle of the stage if he insisted. You know how it is when you get *so hot* you just kind of lose control?"

Jillian nodded as she and Priya, who just sat there smiling, shared a quick look.

Lisa's eyes darted back and forth between her lunch companions as she asked, "Am I missing something?"

Priya nodded slightly in answer to Jillian's raised eyebrows.

"Priya's never been that kind of girl."

Lisa stared in disbelief. "Do you mean never as in never *ever*?"

Priya nodded and explained about her vow.

"Wow! I never imagined a girl as pretty as you would still... I mean, I could never... I mean, I can't go two days without jumping Rob. Don't you ever get like, really horny or anything?"

Priya laughed as her head bobbed. "Sure, all the time. But I have this friend who visits me when I take a bath." She held up her hand. "His name's lefty."

Lisa nearly choked on her drink and Jillian turned bright red. That was not a subject she wanted to explore, especially in a public place.

"I have more news," she announced. At that moment, the radio started playing *Could I Have This Dance*.

"That's so strange. Before last Friday, I couldn't tell you the last time I heard this song. Probably years. But Paul and I danced to it Friday, and then Saturday, when I was shopping with my sisters, I was thinking about Paul and the song came on. And now here it is again, just as I'm about to tell you guys something about him."

"That is a little weird..." Lisa was more interested in the gossip than strange coincidences. "...but what's the news?"

"Paul's taking my sister to her prom this Friday."

5:20 PM

The prom was on Paul's mind as he put his computer into sleep mode, stacked the pages of the manuscript he was editing, and reached for the telephone. The receiver almost reached his ear when his cell phone rang. Replacing the handset, he flipped open the cell and smiled.

"Hi, Jilli. I was about to call you. Had the phone in my hand and my finger poised over the number pad. Are you done for the day?"

"Hi, Paul. Actually, no. It looks like a bunch of us will be stuck here for a few more hours at least. There's a development meeting tomorrow and we have to be ready to present the ideas we came up with today. I have a feeling we'll be here until ten or eleven tonight."

"Well that stinks. Now I have to eat alone. I had visions of enjoying a succulent shrimp stir-fry and a salad with a nice bottle of wine for dinner and then savoring some very sweet lips for dessert."

Jillian giggled. "Oh really? And where had you planned to find these lips?"

"They come attached to this absolutely lovely face I found recently. But now I'll have to spend the night dreaming about them instead."

She heard a sigh before he continued, his voice more serious. "You know, I have to call Jessie. I have to make sure my black tux is okay and find out what color her gown is so I can get the right flowers."

"You own a tuxedo?"

"Of course. Doesn't everyone?" When he didn't get an immediate response, he told her, "I bought it last year. I was going out with this girl Krista and we kept getting these invitations to society dinners and fundraisers and such. It was cheaper to buy one than to keep renting them. Fits better, too."

"Well I'm impressed. I think I might like to see you all dressed to kill."

"You will Friday. Aren't you and your sisters planning to be at your parent's house to help Jessie get ready?"

It's uncanny the way he seems to know women

"Yes, of course we'll all be there. I'm taking a personal day Friday so I can head out there right after Thursday-night dinner."

"Speaking of which, I hope you'll be setting the record straight with all those women who still think of me as a worm."

Jillian's sweet laugh tickled his ear.

"That's right! Some of them don't know the truth about you and Priya. They still think the two of you are lovers."

"Lovers? Given the way Marie all but took my head off last Friday morning, I expect they have a wide variety of more colorful words in mind."

Jillian laughed. "You're probably right. So tell me, is she pretty?"

"Huh?" Paul was confused by the abrupt segue. "Is who pretty?"

"The girl you went out with last year. Krista."

Paul covered the phone as he groaned, realizing he broke the Cardinal

Rule of new relationships. Never, ever, ever mention an old girlfriend. He let himself be seduced into indiscretion by the ease of their relationship, by the incredible comfort he felt with her, and forgot that no matter what else she was, Jillian was still female.

Damn, now she'll work on me for days, or weeks or months until she finds out everything about me and Krista. Damn! And Krista would give Priya a run for her money. And she was so smart and... Damn! Too bad she had that one big flaw...dumping me for that six-figure investment banker.

"Would you like me to tell you about her?"

Of course I want you to tell me about her. I want to know everything. Why did you like her? Why did she like you? Who chased who? Who dumped who? And why? Was she prettier than me? Did she kiss better than me? Did you sleep with her? Was she good?

"Only if you really want to."

Had she said yes, Paul would have told her everything she wanted to know right then on the phone. He knew from experience it was so much easier to fess up right away instead of enduring the poking and prodding at odd moments when you least expected it. And he knew she really wanted to hear it all, but probably thought it was too soon in their relationship for her to appear even remotely jealous. But she chose to be coy, instead,, and now Paul would have a little fun.

"Oh. Well, if you feel that way." He paused for a few seconds. "I guess she's okay. Do you think Jessie would be home now?"

It was Jillian's turn for a silent groan.

Damn! Why didn't I just...but it's too late now. And now this Krista person will be bugging me all night.

They chatted for a few minutes longer and said goodbye after she gave him her parent's phone number and promised to call him later.

5:50 PM

Jessie lay on her back across the patchwork quilt on her bed, her head and arms hanging over one side, her feet over the other. The quilt was a 16th birthday gift from her paternal grandmother, Gramma Florie. Jessie treasured it as much as she treasured the woman who made it.

A relaxed, dreamy smile was the outside reflection of the happiness she felt. Paul's offer to escort her to her prom completely banished the blues that plagued her since her breakup with the Dung Worm. She giggled out loud as did each time Paul's name for him popped into her head.

All she could think about since Saturday night was Paul and the prom. He was so cute, so nice, so funny, so sweet, so everything! Her imagination ran full tilt as she visualized the two of them at the prom, making their entrance and walking to their table as the other girls looked on in envy. She fantasized about him holding her close as they danced, what he would feel like, what he would smell like. She even dared to dream about him kissing her right in the middle of the dance floor where Ethan and everyone else could see how much he wanted her. She knew it would never really happen, but it was fun to imagine.

Normally, she would leap to answer the phone when it rang, but thinking about Paul was far too enjoyable, so her eyes stayed firmly shut. Her mother would get it. Jessie was wondering how far she could carry her fantasies without feeling like she was betraying Jillian when she heard her mother yell up the stairs for her to pick up the phone.

It must be one of the girls. But why didn't she call my cell?

"Hello?"

"Hi Jessie, it's Paul."

A blush colored her cheeks.

Cripes! What if he knows I was daydreaming about him?

"Umm, hi! How are you?"

"I'm well, thank you. Have you changed your mind yet about going to the prom with an old guy like me?"

Jessie's blush deepened and spread to her ears as she recalled her comment of last Saturday night. "Uh, no."

"That's good because I'm really looking forward to this."

They made small talk for a few minutes, or rather, Paul made small talk as Jessie found her usually vast vocabulary suddenly reduced to a small series of barely intelligible croaks and grunts. She was grateful when he finally asked her a question that only needed a straightforward answer.

"There are a few things we need to talk over." His voice had changed, deepened a bit. "First, what color is your gown?"

"It's white."

"Okay. What about a ride? Have you made plans to share a limo or anything?"

"Well, Ethan, umm…"

"Say no more. I get it. I'll take care of our ride."

Jessica wasn't used to guys taking charge like this. It was a nice change and she realized she liked it.

"Now, for the most important thing. What do you want to do about Ethan? Will you let me have some fun with him, or will I have to be good all night? I mean, you seemed to like the idea of teaching the worm a lesson. If you still want to, we should think about strategy."

She was still very much in favor of making Ethan wish he never cheated on her. Her vocabulary returned and they chatted for about thirty minutes. She told Paul what she could about Ethan and what to expect at the prom, and they worked out the beginnings of a plan.

After he said goodbye, Jessie flopped back across the bed again and closed her eyes. This time, she imagined Ethan growing more and more jealous, more and more sorry, more and more miserable. When she dozed off, the satisfied smile remained on her face for a long time.

TUESDAY, MAY 11

7:55 AM

Tom and Priya waited quietly at their desks.

Tom was usually at his desk by 7:20 every day. As team leader, he liked to have time to review progress or make adjustments to schedules before the others arrived. Sometimes, though, he just liked to sit with his feet up and daydream. That was his intent today, but when he walked through the door, he realized Priya must have beaten him in by at least half an hour since she was almost finished. She quickly explained what she was doing and he pitched in to help.

They shared a grin, each wondering how Paul would react when he arrived. They were about to find out.

He strolled into the office, coffee cup in hand, froze, and burst out laughing. His stop was so abrupt that Rob, who followed but a step behind, bumped into him. When he realized how the office was transformed, he too cracked up.

Taped to the wall behind Paul's desk was a large homemade pennant that said SOUTHBOROUGH HIGH. On his desk were two cheerleader's pom-poms in the school colors. Red and gold crepe streamers, twisted together, were strung in rows along the ceiling. Thin ribbons and tinsel dangled from the streamers and from the walls.

Priya glowed with pleasure. "Since you'll be reclaiming your youth on Friday, I thought this might help get you in the proper mood."

"How did you know I was going to a prom on Friday?" he asked, once he was able to control his voice again. But before she could answer, he said, "Wait. Let me guess. Jillian told you at lunch yesterday."

Priya's grin was all the confirmation he needed.

"See. I was right. I told Jillian no good would come from you three having lunch together." Paul turned to face Rob and Tom. "Were you two in on this, too?"

"Not me," Rob replied, holding up his right hand.

"All I did was help her put up some streamers this morning," Tom said. "She was almost done when I got here."

Turning his attention back to Priya, Paul grinned and said, "Well thank you. This is very cool." A thought occurred to him. "Say, did Jillian know about this? And Lisa?"

"No, it was all my idea. I didn't even think of it until late yesterday afternoon."

"When you started giggling for no reason."

Priya's raised eyebrows and tilted head told him he was correct and that she was impressed he noticed and put it together.

"So, Tom. Can we leave this stuff up until Friday?"

Word of the prank spread quickly through the company and all morning people stopped by to see for themselves. By nine o'clock, Paul explained so often why he was going to a prom, the story was distilled down to 'Girlfriend's sister's boyfriend dumped her. I'm escorting her to her prom so she won't miss it.' By nine-thirty he was so tired of saying it he printed the words on a large banner and taped it to the front of his desk. From then on, when someone stuck their head in, he just reached forward and pointed down.

At lunchtime, Tom decided to treat everyone to Chinese food from The Golden Panda on Beach Street. While they waited, Paul called New England Coach to arrange for a limousine. The owner remembered him.

When he explained why he wanted the car, Davie suggested he book a beautifully restored white 1931 Bentley 8 Litre, a very impressive ride.

"Will Gary be available to drive?"

"Well, he's already booked that night, but he might want to switch with someone. Let me track him down and I'll get back to you."

Their lunch arrived as Paul finished his call.

Between bites of Kung Pao Chicken, Vegetable Moo Shu, and Shrimp with Chili Sauce, Rob and Tom began to razz Paul about his upcoming date with his girlfriend's little sister. Tom started it all when he offered to chaperone the couple. Then Rob lectured Paul about having the girl home right after the prom.

"And no funny business, mister. She's a good girl," Tom chided.

"But if there *is* funny business you better make sure Jillian doesn't find out," Rob added.

"Unless she goes in for that kind of thing."

"Oh wow, sisters. You lucky bastard."

They kept it up until Priya was laughing so hard she couldn't eat. And though he tried his best to ignore them, Paul, too, soon found it impossible to keep chewing.

WEDNESDAY, MAY 12

4:55 PM

As the hands on the clock approached five, Priya sat at her desk flipping through a pile of photographs. The guys were all on the phone, Paul and Rob talking to their girlfriends, Tom to his wife. She wasn't really paying attention to the photos. She was watching Paul out of the corner of her eye.

Since their kiss on the Common last Thursday, Priya tried to sort out her feelings for him. There was no doubt he awakened something inside her that night, but she still was not sure if what touched her heart and caused this confusion was a result of their friendship or the surge of excitement his lips engendered.

Probably both.

The sound of him laughing at something Jillian said sent a warm glow through her chest.

Priya Kumar you are being silly. You're acting like a schoolgirl with a crush.

She sighed.

But you'll get over it. All these romantic feelings will fade and just the friendship will remain. But until then, I guess it can't hurt too much to enjoy it.

She flipped over another photo and resumed watching and wondering.

Paul was last to hang up his phone. He looked around the room and asked what everyone had going that night. "Jilli still has an hour or so of work to do. Anyone up for a few beers at DHL?"

Rob grunted. "Lisa told me to ask if you and Jillian wanted to meet us there, so I guess we're in." He turned to Priya. "What about you, Pri?"

"Gee, I had this big night planned…head home, eat dinner alone, and then read a book. Hmmm, should I give all that up to go out and possibly have fun? I don't know."

Paul grinned at her. "Priya's in. Tom?"

"I wish," he said, feigning disappointment. "But the madhouse awaits."

Tom often joked about how miserable his home life was, but everyone knew he couldn't wait to get out of work each day and rush home to Patti and their five children.

He was one of those lucky men who married the love of his life and who loved spending time with his family. Patti once told them that when he came home, he usually gave her a quick kiss then hunted down the kids to play with them for an hour or more before dinner. He would have loved to have five more, but she was not one of the lucky women for whom pregnancy got easier each time. The labor and delivery of each child had been long and hard, so when, two days after delivering Kerri, she explained to Tom that he could have a vasectomy and have sex or not have either, he made the appointment the same day.

Now, he told people it was the best move he ever made. "You know," he'd say, grinning from ear to ear, "when you're shooting blanks, your wife can't really tell if you're hitting the target so she makes you practice all the time. And I do mean *all the time!*"

Priya, Paul, and Rob parted ways on the sidewalk in front of the Common. Rob headed off to meet Lisa at work while his friends started down one of the paths that would take them across the Common to the corner of Beacon and Charles.

"Jillian told me you two had a really nice time last Friday," Priya said, glancing over at him.

He met her gaze with raised eyebrows and a lopsided grin. "I bet she told you a whole lot more than that."

Priya nodded, lips pursed in a tight smile, her eyes wide and flashing with merriment.

"Did she tell you about the pantyhose at the beach? And about me saving her from a drunken bully?"

"She did."

"And?"

"And what?"

"And what did she say about me? Was everything really okay? It seemed like it all went well. Did she…"

"Hey, take a break. Remember Friday morning, when Lisa asked how much you wanted to impress Jillian and you said you wanted to knock her socks off?"

He nodded.

"Well think about it. You did it, literally, when the pantyhose came off."

Paul crowed with delight. "That's right! I never thought of that! Man, I am *sooo* good!"

Priya rolled her eyes, but extended her hand and slapped the one Paul proffered.

They walked slowly, enjoying the warm spring air. She was surprised when he changed the subject. She could tell there were questions he still wanted to ask, but thought it best to let him get there in his own way. She only half paid attention as he told her about an art show this coming weekend at a small gallery in Somerville featuring the work of Emma Washington, a woman who dated his brother years ago. Paul always liked her and her art and stayed in touch. One of her early works, a nude in silhouette, hung on the wall of Paul's living room. She gave it to him on his twenty-first birthday but never revealed it was a self-portrait until two years ago. It was the only real piece of art he ever owned, one he knew he would value for the rest of his life.

As he spoke of his old friend, Priya thought about this new friendship of theirs and how comfortable it felt. She liked being with a man and not worrying about the whole sex thing. In some ways it was like having another brother, but in other ways very different. She knew she could tell Paul anything without fear of the judgment or ridicule she could expect from Raj.

"So, she really told you everything about the date, huh?" Evidently Paul had talked through his tangent and was again heading toward the question Priya suspected was coming.

"I think so, but I can't be sure, of course."

"Did she tell you about our kiss on the beach?"

"She sure did. And Lisa and I were feeling quite jealous."

"Jealous?" He was clearly confused.

Priya grabbed his arm and stopped him. She turned to face him and said, "Tell me something, Paul. And I want the truth. When we kissed last week, you weren't really trying were you?"

He began to shuffle his feet, suddenly uncomfortable, but Priya was having none of that.

"If this friend thing is going to work, Paul, we have to be honest with each other. I think I already know the answer, but I'd like to hear it from you anyway."

"Okay, you're right. I guess I didn't want to answer because I thought it might hurt your feelings or something. But no, my heart wasn't really in it when I was kissing you. I'm sorry." His hangdog expression made clear his contrition

"Don't be. I could tell your head, and I guess your heart, were somewhere else. But the point is that even though you weren't trying and even though there was no spark between us..." She laid the palm of her hand on his chest. "…Paul, that was one of the best kisses I've ever had."

He was not entirely sure if she was serious or setting him up, but his look of remorse transformed to one of hesitant pride.

"Now use your imagination. If you could kiss me that well without trying, imagine what Jillian experienced on the beach when I know you were trying. Trying, uh…hard, too, from what I hear."

"Geez, do women always have to tell each other every little detail?"

"Honey, we live for the details." Priya laughed and started walking again. "And now you know why we were jealous."

Paul again steered the conversation to more mundane topics as they reached the corner of Beacon and Tremont Streets. They waited in silence for the light to change, surrounded by other pedestrians who knew it was safer to wait than to play chicken with Boston's aggressive drivers.

Five minutes later, they walked through the door to DHL and Paul noticed many male eyes checking out his companion. He wondered if that sort of thing got oppressive for women or if they enjoyed being the object of so much admiration and lust. It was a question he would have to ask her someday.

After they settled at a table near the middle of the room, he asked, "You feeling lucky tonight?"

"Sure. What did you have in mind?"

"Mystery Beer."

"Yes! Good idea!"

Paul headed off to the bar.

Of the seventy-two brews DHL offered on tap or in bottles, about a dozen selections were perennially popular. The rest were an ever-changing mélange of currently trendy, foreign, boutique, or specialty beers. It was the rare customer who could lay claim to having tried the entire current assortment.

Paul returned with five player lists. "I figured the others will want to play when they get here."

A few minutes later, a waitress arrived with two trays of glasses and the game was on.

As Paul took his first sip, he noticed a bunch of guys sitting at a table along the far wall. One of them was staring so intently at Priya he didn't catch Paul eyeing him.

"You know, next to losing at darts, this is my favorite game."

Priya laughed. "Later on, I'll be happy to help you with the first one, although all that winning does get tiresome."

Paul held his hand up sideways, the back facing Priya, thumb and little finger folded in, with the first three fingers tightly together. "Can you read between the lines?"

That drew another laugh from her. "Well, at least you'll have a chance with this game. Speaking of which, I've been meaning to ask you. Does anyone know where Mystery Beer began? It's such a great bar game."

"As a matter of fact, I do know. Hold on a second."

He jumped up and she watched him go to the far end of the bar. He returned with a fiftyish blond woman.

"Leah, this is Priya Kumar. Priya, this is Leah Guillemin. Leah owns DHL."

"Paul said you were asking about how Mystery Beer got started."

"I was. It's like, the perfect bar game and I've been curious where it originated."

Leah half turned and pointed to a table across the room. "Right there." She chuckled at Priya's surprised reaction.

"Back in '92, an MIT student named Frank DuBois got the idea to hold beer identification contests with his friends. Usually four to six of them came in and would take turns being the beermaster, the person who selected the mystery beer for that round. He or she would tell the bartender which beer to bring and they'd be delivered in mugs, regardless of whether the beer was draft or bottled.

"When each person had a turn at being beermaster, whoever correctly guessed the most was declared the winner, usually of a small pot of bets.

"After the second or third time, Frank made a list of all the beers we were offering and had copies made so players could refer to it and mark their guesses.

"But the game quickly began to get out of hand. Kids were coming in playing two or three rounds and getting way too drunk. It became a liability issue, but it was so popular, I really didn't want to ban it. So I decided the bar would take over management of it.

"I hired two of the MIT students to write software that would manage the game using our existing POS system."

She smiled at Priya's quizzical look.

"POS. Point of Sale. The touch-screens and registers are all computer controlled.

"The system automatically updates the brew lists. I also found these two-ounce glasses and had trays made for them.

"Once all that was in place, each round consisted of six samples selected at random by the computer, which also kept track of how many rounds each group consumed, to prevent people from drinking too much.

"The changeover worked out a lot better than I expected. There were nights when every table was playing. That hasn't happened for years, now, unless we do a promotion. Anyway, that's the story. Enjoy your game."

Priya knew Paul was still edgy. She wished he'd spit out whatever was bothering him since the others would be here soon. She sipped her third sample, savoring the strong, malty flavor and thought it was an ale. But which one? She glanced up and found Paul again focused on something across the room. When she took a quick glance over her shoulder, all she saw was a table full of guys.

"One of them has been watching you."

"Which one? There were seven of them around that table."

Paul looked away for a few seconds. When his eyes met hers again he said, "I'm impressed. Seven it is."

"Want me to describe them for you?"

Paul's obvious incredulity made her chuckle.

"I'm serious."

"You can describe all those guys after glancing over there for less than a second? I don't believe you."

Her head tilted as her eyebrows and lips angled into their 'Are you challenging me?' position. With a confident grin, she stared right into Paul's eyes and began.

"Starting along the back with the guy who's sitting at the left corner and going clockwise — blond, thirties, big nose, full beard, blue shirt; blond, early twenties, moustache, gray t-shirt; brown hair, early twenties, nice smile, white pull-over shirt; black hair, late twenties, needs a shave, pointed nose, white with blue stripes dress shirt; brown shaggy hair, broad shoulders, gray sweatshirt, couldn't see his face; black hair, very thin, dark green t-shirt, couldn't see his face; and the last one is very tall, brown hair, square jaw, straight nose, gray and blue crew shirt."

She enjoyed watching his eyes grow wider and wider as she detailed each one.

"Unbelievable. How?"

Priya shrugged. "Just a talent I've always had. So which guy was it?"

Paul glanced over and saw he was again staring. "The one in back on the right. You said he had a nice smile."

"He wasn't looking when I turned before."

"I know. I think someone said something to him and he turned his head away before you looked. But he's watching you again now."

Priya shrugged, finished the third sample, decided it might be *Road Dog Scottish Ale*, and put a (3) next to it on her list. Paul fell silent and Priya sensed he was deciding how to ask what he wanted to ask.

He reminds me of Raj when he was in high school and needed advice about a girl he liked.

"Did Jillian tell you about our goodnight kiss?"

"Oh yes. In great and explicit detail. Remember how we live for details?"

She was going for a chuckle but his face remained serious, his eyes questioning just how explicit Jillian had been. She blushed as she told him.

"I was getting hot just listening to her."

She noticed a flush creeping into his cheeks.

"And she told you she invited me in?"

Now we're getting to the real question.

Priya nodded. "She did, and she told us what happened."

"She looked so hurt at first when I said no. I thought I'd ruined the best night of our lives."

"She was devastated when you rejected her invitation. Did you know you were only the third guy she's ever invited in on the first date?" Paul shook his head. "But when you explained why, she realized the same thing happened to her the other two times. She understood, obviously. If she'd been upset, do you think she'd have brought her sisters to meet you Saturday?"

"You're right. I know I'm being stupid. But I really don't want to mess this one up. So you think I was right not to go in."

"What I think isn't important. What do you think? How do you feel about her?"

"Priya, when she was in my arms last Friday I wanted her more than, than…I don't know. I was literally aching to take that dress off her. I can't remember ever wanting anyone that much. But another part of me was really scared that if I did go in with her, we'd end up like all the other times." He sighed. "I don't know why I second-guess myself. I know I was right. I think I just wanted to hear someone else say it."

He picked up a sample and took a sip.

"Promise you won't tell Jillian any of this?"

"Of course. What we say to each other stays between us. Isn't that what we agreed to last week?"

He dipped his head once in agreement, then caught her eyes. "I know this sounds crazy. I know I've only known her for a week. I know it's like, impossible, but I really think she could be, you know, the one."

Priya smiled. As much as she cared for Paul, as much as she already knew he felt that way about Jillian, it hurt a little to hear him say the words.

She reached over and took his hand. "Paul, you did the right thing. You and Jillian are great together and it will only get better."

He inhaled deeply and let it out with a whoosh. "I know. But I want to be careful. There's something…I don't know…I think she was really hurt bad once. It's like a part of her is holding back, waiting for the worst to happen."

"If she has been hurt like that, then all you can do is give her time to accept that you won't hurt her, too. And speak of the angel…"

Priya nodded in the direction of the front door. As Paul rose to greet her, he noticed the guy who was watching Priya now casually eyeing him. After giving Jillian a big hug and kiss, he saw the guy's face change and understood. He thought Priya was with Paul, but now realized she was not. He wondered what would happen next.

He asked Jillian about her day and then explained the rules of Mystery Beer as they waited for Rob and Lisa to arrive, which they did, ten minutes later. A signal to the bartender brought three more trays to the table and with everyone now chatting and sampling, Paul soon forgot about Priya's admirer.

It was a few minutes before nine-thirty when Priya returned from the ladies' room to find Rob and Lisa at the jukebox and Paul and Jillian dancing between the tables. She sat down to watch them, a tiny part of her still wishing it were her with him.

"Excuse me," a voice said from behind her. "Are you by any chance a doctor?"

Priya shifted her bottom in the chair and saw it was the guy Paul said was watching her earlier. She glanced over to where he was sitting. The others were gone.

"No," she replied, wondering if he stayed just to talk to her. "Is something wrong? Are you ill?"

"I was hoping you'd be able to tell me why my heart's been pounding so hard since I saw you walk in earlier."

She blinked three or four times, then crooked her finger and signaled him to come closer. When his face was about a foot from hers she smiled, shook her head, and said softly, "I'll make you a deal. If you go catch up with your friends, I promise I'll never tell anyone you just said that."

As soon as the words were out she regretted being so mean. His face turned red and he snapped back upright. His mouth opened as if to say something, but instead he turned and walked slowly back to his table.

When the song ended a few seconds later, Paul and Jillian returned to the table.

"Who was that?" Jillian asked.

"Nobody. Just some guy with a really corny pickup line."

"Well don't look now, but he's coming back for more." As Priya turned to watch him approach, she heard a whispered, "I told you not to look!"

Standing next to her, the guy nodded to Paul and Jillian before locking eyes with Priya.

"I'm really sorry about before. I know it was stupid but my heart really did start to pound when I saw you walk in earlier, and I really wanted to meet you, and I guess my brain just misfired and made me think that was a clever thing to say. Could I possibly try again?"

Priya still felt a little remorse, and he did grovel well, so she nodded. His forlorn expression was replaced by the smile she earlier thought so nice.

"Hi. My name's Brian Jankowski. I'm an assistant network administrator at Northeastern University, I play the guitar and clarinet, I like to cook outrageously spicy food, and I seem to have a real talent for concocting truly horrible pickup lines."

Priya could not help grinning. She could tell he was nervous, but sensed his anxiety ratcheting down a notch at her positive reaction.

Nervous is good. I wonder if he meant what he said about his heart pounding when he first saw me.

"My name is Priya. Priya Kumar." She shifted around and gave Jillian and Paul a mischievous grin as she introduced them. Then she faced him again. "So Brian, do you like to play darts?"

"I think Priya's found a new friend," Rob said about half-an-hour later.

She and Brian were still at the dart board and it appeared they were getting along well.

"It certainly seems that way," Lisa agreed. "He's made her laugh at least three times and she's touched his arm and shoulder more than that."

Rob and Paul turned to stare at her with twin looks of disbelief.

"What? Girls notice those things."

"That's right," Jillian agreed. "And he made her laugh four times, not three. You were talking to Rob and missed one." She caught Lisa's eye. "Ladies' room?"

Once the girls were gone, Rob asked Paul about his plans for the prom.

"Lisa said you and Jilli's sister have some plan to make her old boyfriend jealous?"

"It's more of a hope than a plan. She told me what she could about him, and we kicked around some obvious ideas, but I think we'll play it by ear when we get there unless some inspiration strikes."

"You could pretend not to know the guy and start talking her up."

"We thought of that."

They spent a few minutes discussing it without coming up with anything great.

"I have to be careful, though. I'm kind of restricted in what I can do seeing that she's Jillian's sister."

"No making out, you mean?"

"Making out! Are you nuts? After what happened last Thursday, I'm not even chancing a kiss on the cheek. Jessie's nice and all, and I want to help her, and a kiss or two on the dance floor or someplace where her old boyfriend can see would probably help the effort, but there's no way that's happening. I'm not taking any chances. Jillian's way too important to me and if she ever found out I kissed her sister...hell, I don't even want to imagine what would happen."

"You kissed Jillian's sister!"

Lisa's shocked voice startled him to the point of actually jumping in his seat. He turned to find Lisa, Jillian, Priya, and Brian standing behind them. His face reddened and he almost shouted, "No! No! I didn't kiss anyone. We were just..."

Jillian put her arms around him as everyone broke out in laughter. "Don't worry. Lisa's just being fresh. We heard everything you said, not just the last line."

THURSDAY, MAY 13

12:05 PM

"Hi!"

Jillian arrived at Coffey's early and spent the time watching other customers and listening to the tunes on the oldies station Gil invariably had playing on the radio.

Paul leaned over for a soft, lingering kiss.

"Hi yourself. Is everything okay?"

"Everything's fine," she assured him.

"Well you sounded so cryptic when you called and said you wanted to talk, but not on the phone. I thought something happened."

"No, nothing happened. And it's not a big deal, so relax. Do you...No way!"

He saw her eyebrows arch over a wide grin.

"What?"

"The music."

"What music. There's a commercial on."

"I know, but I've been here for a while and before you arrived, I was listening to the music and I just realized something. First they played *Woman*, then *I Love You More Today Than Yesterday*, then *Because*, and the last one before the commercial was *You Make Me Feel Like Dancing*. Get it? Put the titles together and they make a sentence. *Woman, I love you today more than yesterday because you make me feel like dancing!*"

"Hey, that's wild. That could be about us. Probably a program director having a little fun. So what's up?"

"How about something to eat first?"

They decided to split a cinnamon-raisin bagel and Paul went to fetch it and some coffee.

After each enjoyed the first few sips and a bite of their half of the bagel, Jillian said, "So tell me. Have you made any progress on your plan to make…what did she say you called him…the dung worm jealous?"

"Not really. I'll just wing it, I think."

"Well, Jessie's really counting on you to stick it to him good."

Paul sighed. "Great, just what I need. Performance anxiety."

Jillian blushed at the double entendre. "Well, I was thinking, maybe you *should* kiss her once or twice where Ethan will see."

Paul almost dropped his cup.

Did she really just say that? Is she serious? Is this a game? Or a test?

"No way. Kissing your sister would be too weird."

What else could he say?

"I don't mean *kissing* kissing. Stage kisses, like they do in the movies."

"Jillian, where is this coming from? I know we've only been together a short time, but stage kiss or not…" He couldn't find the right words and settled for, "I can't believe you want me to do that with your sister."

"Well, it's not like I want you to, but you have to admit it would help with Ethan. Jessie is so psyched about you taking her and about getting back at him."

"I know she is honey, but, I mean, how will *you* feel kissing *me* knowing I've kissed your sister?"

Jillian's eyes fixed on his.

"Paul, if I can get past the whole you and Priya thing, trust me when I say you and Jessie pretending to kiss is not a big deal."

Paul did not seem convinced.

"Look, if it really makes you uncomfortable, then don't. But if you two think you can really do stage kisses and some good acting, then a little pretend making out is okay with me."

Paul sat very still, thinking.

"Just promise me two things."

"What's that?"

"Not too much tongue and nothing below the waist."

Paul's eyes widened as blood rushed to his face. Before he realized what was happening, Jillian whipped out her cell phone, snapped his picture, and collapsed with laughter. Tears were running down her cheeks as she held up the phone and choked out, "Oh, lord, look at your face!"

The commotion caused many people to turn their way, and several continued to stare at the dumbfounded guy and the pretty girl who seemed unable to get control of her glee.

When she finally did stop laughing, she dried her eyes and face with her napkin. Paul's embarrassment faded and he sat there now with a wide grin.

"You are so evil."

"That was for encouraging my sisters last Saturday. I never ever forget and I always get even. Keep that in mind next time."

"Geez, I can't believe you played me like that. I really believed you were telling me it was okay to kiss your sister."

"I was." Her voice was steady and sincere. "I was serious about the stage kisses. Not the other stuff, of course. Okay?"

"Jillian, I…"

"Just think about it. It really won't bother me. I trust you, Paul, and I trust Jessie. But you can't mention this to my parents or brother or sisters. They might not understand."

"Jillian I…"

"You don't have to decide now. Call me on my cell tonight around midnight. I should be at my parent's house by then. If you want to do it, then I'll tell Jessie and see what she thinks. But if *you're* willing, I'm pretty sure *she'll* be game."

As he sat quietly, considering it, Jillian became aware of the music in the background.

Oh my word. Again!

The final strains of *Could I Have This Dance* played out, followed by a commercial for a local car dealership.

This is really getting strange now. What is it with this song playing every time I see him or think about him in public?

7:45 PM

"Would you like to tell me what's bothering you or should we just sit here picking at leftover noodles?"

They were sitting in *Sum Thai Taste,* a tiny four table eatery on the fringe of Chinatown. Paul invited Priya to eat dinner with him, then sat virtually silent the whole time.

He seemed distracted when he returned from lunch, but did not volunteer any information to the group. Now she was getting worried. Silence was not Paul's thing. She reached over and laid her hand on his to get his attention.

"I'm sorry," he said and looked it. "Come on, let's take a walk. I don't want to talk in here."

Paul reached for his wallet, but Priya stopped him and opened her purse. "Remember last Thursday? We agreed I would treat next time we went out."

That elicited the first smile of the night from him. "Shoot, that's right. If I remembered, we'd have gone to Jimmy's."

"Well thank Vishnu you didn't because I don't have that kind of money to spend on food."

"Vishnu?"

"The Hindu god of protection. He sure protected my wallet tonight."

She paid the check and they strolled out onto Harrison Avenue. The evening air was cool, making both of them glad they wore jackets. They walked the half-block to Boylston Street in silence, then turned toward the Common.

"I'm sorry I've been such a bad date tonight. I'm just so damn confused I don't know what the hell to do."

"About what?"

Paul could see the concern for him on her face. "I met Jillian for lunch today."

"I know."

"She told me she thinks it's okay for me to kiss her sister at the prom."

Really?!

"And how do you feel about that?"

Paul grunted. "You sound like a psychiatrist."

"Well, I..."

"Don't worry. I wouldn't have known what to say to that either."

"She really said you could kiss her sister?"

How in the world could Jillian be okay with such a thing, especially after what happened last week?

"Well, she said we could do a stage kiss, you know? Not like a real kiss, but still, you *are* kissing."

He explained the whole thing to Priya. When he was finished, they were standing on the corner of Tremont Street, waiting to cross to the Common. Neither said a word until they reached the opposite sidewalk.

"Okay. From what you said, it seems she thinks a kiss is not always a kiss. Actors' husbands and wives deal with their spouses kissing other people at work. Maybe she figures that since you two will be playing a role, it's not really a kiss. Just like...um...a handshake with your lips."

That drew a second smile from Paul.

"Maybe. But the whole thing makes me feel weird. Perhaps if we'd been going out for a long time and I knew all her family better it wouldn't seem so strange. But I can't deny that it opens up so many more possibilities in terms of getting even with the guy who dumped Jessie."

They were approaching a bench. Paul led them to it and they sat amongst the long shadows cast by the soon-to-be-setting sun.

"Tell me about Brian."

"But..."

"I need a change of subject for a bit. So tell me about him. You two seemed to be getting along nicely last night."

"Well, you know what he does, and that he's musically inclined, and that he's lousy at pickup lines."

"I don't know about that. He seemed to have accomplished his goal."

Priya laughed. "Perhaps you're right. I hadn't thought of it like that.

You guys really do see things differently than we do." She paused for a few seconds. "I like him, Paul. He makes me laugh and he's very smart and he claims to enjoy losing to me at darts. Of course, you can't tell much from three hours in a bar, but he said he'd call me tonight. If he does, we'll see."

"Oh, he'll call, don't you worry. I saw how he looked at you. It was not unlike the way I looked at Jillian when I first met her. And everyone saw how you two were with each other when you were playing darts, and afterward at the table. And he does seem like a nice guy."

A wistful sigh slipped through Priya's perfectly shaded lips. "I hope so. It would really be nice to find someone...well...someone like you but who gets excited when I kiss him."

"Someone like me? I'm flattered. How so?"

Crap! Why don't you think before you speak? What am I going to do now?

She stood up and said, "Let's walk some more."

Paul joined her, but after only a few steps said, "Come on. You're not getting off the hook that easily. What is it about me you admire so much you hope to find it in Brian?"

Her voice took on an edge. "No way. I'm not playing that game. If you want an ego boost, go call Jillian."

Damn! That didn't help, you dope.

Paul caught her wrist and stopped her.

"Hey, what's the matter? Did I do something or say something wrong?"

Priya wouldn't meet his eyes. "No, nothing's wrong. You didn't do anything."

"Don't lie to me, Priya. I know something's upsetting you. Please. Tell me."

Priya's heart ached.

I can't. I can't tell you how I feel. But I can't lie to you either. Maybe a different truth will work.

"I've been feeling a little jealous lately."

"Jealous?"

She nodded.

"Of you and Jillian, of Rob and Lisa, of Tom and Patti. Of everyone who has someone, I guess. You all have someone to care about and I can't seem to find anyone."

Having started down that road, her emotions began to overwhelm her.

Oh lord, don't cry, girl. Suck it up.

"The last few days especially I've been really regretting my vow. I see everyone around me in relationships, in love, and I'm so miserable, sometimes I can't stand it."

Damn!

The tears broke through and began to roll silently down her cheeks.

"Tell me the truth, Paul, please. You're my best friend and I need you to tell me what's wrong with me. Why can't I find someone? Is it the way I look? The virginity thing? I thought men *wanted* to marry virgins. That's the great ideal, isn't it?" Her voice became bitter. "So why do they all keep leaving me? Why doesn't anyone ever want me except to try to fuck?"

She was crying openly now and Paul drew her into his arms to comfort her.

Holy crap! I never heard her use that *word before. She doesn't even curse. And now she's crying. What do I do? What can I say?*

She stood there, her face buried in his chest, his arms making her feel safe and cared for.

I can't believe I lost it like that. He must think I'm a total girl, sobbing like a baby.

She moved away and wiped at her face with her fingers. "I'm sorry," she said quietly.

"Sorry? Sorry for what?"

"For being such a girl. The crying and…"

"Oh stop. You *are* a girl. Girl's cry sometimes." His voice lowered to a conspiratorial level. "You can't ever let on that I told you this because it could get me kicked out of the Real Man club if other guys knew I let it slip, but…" He paused half a second for effect. "…guys really don't mind it when girls cry…unless we caused it, of course…because it lets us be strong and manly and hold you and comfort you. That's like hugely good karma, comforting a crying woman." He rested his hands on her shoulders. "But even if it wasn't, Priya, I'm your friend. Remember? That means you get to laugh, or scream, or complain, or whine, or anything, even cry, whenever you feel the need. No apologies necessary."

Priya's eyes began to tear again as she reached up and touched his cheek. "That right there. That's what it is."

Paul was confused. "That's what what is?"

"That's the thing about you I want to find in a guy. You get me, you understand me, you really care about me, and don't, you know, expect anything in return except the same kind of friendship." She wiped at her face again then stood up straight, her composure mostly recovered. "Please, tell me the truth, Paul. Am I being stupid with this vow? Am I really killing my chances with guys by not sleeping with them?"

Paul thought about the questions for a minute before answering.

"I guess the truth is…yes and no. Guys who dump you because you won't sleep with them aren't really interested in you anyway. They're only interested in your body and in making a trophy out of it.

"The problem with being as beautiful as you are is that guys you meet see the outside first and start drooling. Then they get so focused on getting into your pants, they don't pay attention to all the other things you have to offer.

"So with guys like that, and I admit at our age that may be most of them, your vow probably is hurting you in the sense that guys aren't sticking around long enough to find out who you really are. But that may be a blessing of sorts, too."

"A blessing?"

"A blessing.

"You've never actually said this, but I'm guessing you're ultimately looking for the home and family thing, the golden anniversary, and all that?"

"Well, of course."

"Then think about this. Do you really want to spend your life with a guy whose values are radically different from yours? Do you really want to marry a man who was more interested in your body than your mind and heart and soul? Who wasn't willing to put aside getting laid long enough to discover who the real Priya Kumar is?

"Let's face it, unless you date a blind man, any straight guy you're with will definitely respond to your looks. But there are guys to whom sex is not the be-all and end-all of a relationship. Look at me. Last Friday I wanted Jillian so bad it took every last smidgen of willpower to keep from tearing her dress off on the beach during our first kiss. And frankly, I'm not sure where I found the will not to sleep with her when she invited me in. But I did it. And I did it because…" He stopped and took a breath. "I did it because from the moment I first saw her I had the feeling she was the woman I'm meant to spend my life with."

Wow…did I really just say that out loud?

He looked sheepish. "I know it sounds crazy. Maybe it's hormones, maybe I'm really nuts, but the feeling keeps getting stronger and stronger every day. When I'm talking to her, I have to stay conscious of what I'm saying so I don't slip and say something that might make her think I'm some kind of love-sick psycho."

He paused to order his thoughts.

"I know you see it in movies all the time, but I never really believed this love-at-first-sight thing was real. Maybe it is."

He shrugged and shook his head as they started walking again.

"Or maybe it *is* just hormones. I don't know. But the point of telling you all this is to show you that the kind of guy you want is out there. And if keeping your virginity until marriage is really important to you, and I think it is or you wouldn't have made it this far, then I really believe you'll always regret giving it up to some guy just to find out if he'll stick around.

"So no, I don't think you're making a mistake. Even though it may be making things harder for you, in the end I think you'll be better off. You'll have found someone who you know wants you for who you are and not for how nature sculpted you."

It was Priya's turn to grab Paul's wrist and stop him. When he did, she moved right in and hugged him.

"Thank you. I really needed to hear that. I don't know what happened before to make me lose it like that, but I'm glad it happened when you were around to help."

She gave him a quick kiss on the cheek.

"This friend thing works pretty well, I think."

She let them walk in silence for a few minutes before she asked, "So, what will you do about Jessie?"

Paul groaned.

"I don't know. I'm supposed to call Jilli tonight and let her know. I've been trying to reason this out, but I'm not having much luck. I can make good arguments for not kissing her, and good arguments for doing it. And neither side is more compelling than the other."

"Well, forget about reason for a minute. How do you feel?"

"Confused. I told you, one part of me thinks we could really get to Ethan if we kissed, but the other part is really uncomfortable with all the things that could go wrong."

He shook his head quickly from side to side, trying to shed his troubles like a dog sheds water.

"What do you think I should do?"

"I can't tell you what to do, Paul. All I can say is, if I was you, I'd listen to my gut rather than my head on something like this."

After a minute of silence, she glanced over and could tell from the set of his brow he was thinking. A few seconds later, when his lips curled into a half-smile, she knew he reached a decision.

8:25 PM

"Hmmm."

I think I'm in the mood for lavender and bubbles tonight.

Priya sprinkled scented salts into the inch deep water, then added the bubble bath. Immediately, a white pillow formed and began to grow in the deep, old, claw-foot tub.

The tub was one of the reasons she rented this apartment when she moved to Boston. Another was its convenience to public transportation – one block off Commonwealth Avenue in Brighton. The one bedroom apartment was not the most modern she saw, but it *was* one of the least expensive.

She was about to remove her robe and step into the tub when the phone rang. She dashed out to the living room and grabbed it on the fourth ring.

"Hello?"

"Hi, Priya. This is Brian Jankowski. From last night."

"Hi, Brian. How are you?"

'Well, not so good, actually. I think I may get fired from my job."

"Brian! I'm sorry! What happened?"

"Well, I spent so much time thinking about you today I didn't get much work done. My boss wasn't very happy."

Priya grinned. "Me? Why would you be thinking about me?"

"I don't know. Maybe it was your smile, or the way you laugh, or your deadly aim with a dart, or how easy you are to talk to."

"Flatterer."

"Not at all. It's not flattery if it's the truth, and you mean it. It was, and I meant every word."

Priya smiled again. She enjoyed the time she spent with Brian last night and was happy he called, but prior experience taught her not to get too hopeful about any guy who seemed interested. Chances were he would be gone as soon as he found out he would not be getting laid.

"Well thank you, then. So what are you doing, or what were you doing before you called?"

"What I usually end up having to do when I want to get out early. I was working late. We had a network glitch that had to be fixed and it took us forever to track down the problem.

"Say, I haven't eaten yet. If you haven't either, can I interest you in some pizza and beer, or anything else for that matter?"

"If I hadn't already eaten dinner and wasn't in the middle of…"

Of what? I can't tell him I'm taking a bath.

"…something I have to finish tonight, I would have loved some pizza. But thank you for asking. I…oh shoot, hold on a minute please."

Priya forgot the bath water was running until she turned and saw a mountain of bubbles threatening to spill over the rim. She pressed the hold button on the phone and ran to turn off the water. When she returned to the living room, she stretched out on the sofa.

"I'm back. Sorry about that."

"Everything okay?"

"Sure, I just had to avert a minor disaster."

She giggled a bit, hoping he'd believe she was joking. He did.

"So tell me. Are you a professional darter? I've never met anyone who could throw like you do."

Priya shared her brief history with darts and could tell he wasn't sure whether or not to believe her. But they moved on to other subjects and as the minutes passed, the bubbles popped, and her bathwater grew cold.

"You see? I was right," he said after pointing out that it was almost eleven o'clock.

"Right about what?"

"About you being easy to talk to. I called over two hours ago and it seems like only ten minutes."

She heard him clear his throat.

"I know this is a bit presumptuous of me, but would you consider canceling whatever plans you might have made for tomorrow and have dinner with me? I'd really like to see you and I'm not sure I can stand to wait longer than that."

Despite her head reminding her about the past, she felt fluttery as she agreed to the date. And when they said goodbye a few minutes later, she realized how purely happy she felt, and how long ago it was since she last felt that way.

Back in the bathroom, she pulled the drain plug and perched on the side of the tub.

He was as easy to talk to as he claims I am....and as funny and charming as last night. What did we talk about for two hours? I can't remember half of it...but it was a nice two hours. I can still hear his voice in my head, the way it cracks a little when he laughs, and the way it seemed to soften when he was talking about me.

She began filling the tub with hot water again, adding new salts and bubbles, and swirling the water with her hand as the bubble cloud grew for the second time that night

I really do like him. But are the feelings genuine or fallout from what happened earlier with Paul? Or maybe the gods have sent me someone to help me forget Paul.

She sighed as she stepped into the bubbly, scented water.

Maybe I'll get lucky like Paul and this will be the one for me.

She shrugged and smiled.

I don't know. All I know is my fantasy lover has a new face again tonight.

FRIDAY, MAY 14

4:30 PM

Gary rolled down his window, snatched the ticket he would need later at the toll booth, and started down the ramp to the Massachusetts Turnpike. Sitting next to him in the front seat, resplendent in his tuxedo, Paul was entertaining him with how he met Jillian and about much of what had happened since then.

"And now you're taking her sister to a prom? That's wild!" Gary glanced over at Paul with an appraising and envious eye. "Does she look anything like Jillian?"

"She's a little shorter and a little thinner, but I think she's just as pretty. You'll see for yourself soon enough."

"Man, you have to be the luckiest guy alive. Were you a saint or something in a previous life?"

Paul grinned. "I don't think so. Why?"

"Come on. Last week you stumble onto what sounds to me like the love of your life, and this week you get to take her sister out, too. And she tells you its okay to make out with the sister to make some guy jealous. And the sister's a fox!" He grunted. "And you wonder why I think you have a golden horseshoe nailed to your butt?"

"Hey, what can I say?" Laughing, Paul pulled out his cell phone to call Jillian.

"Hi, hon. I thought I'd check in. Is it total pandemonium over there?"

"No. Actually, everything's going smoothly and almost calmly. Where are you?"

"Sitting next to Gary. We're on the Pike."

"Already? You'll be way too early. You aren't supposed to leave here until quarter past six. How far away are you?"

"Hold on." He turned to Gary. "ETA?"

"If the traffic stays like this, twenty, twenty-five minutes."

Paul relayed the time estimate.

"That means you'll be waiting around for an hour!"

"I know, I know. But it's Friday and I thought the traffic would be heavy, and I wanted a little time to rehearse with Jessie."

"Well you'll have plenty of time now."

"Don't worry. This way I can take some time to meet your parents and fill them in on all the details of our little plan."

"Don't you dare!"

Paul could hear her sisters in the background asking what was wrong. Laughing he said, "I'm kidding, I'm kidding. You think I want your father coming after me with a meat cleaver or something?"

After saying goodbye, he dropped the phone into the breast pocket of his tux. "So what do you do when you're not driving me around? And why do you look as good as I do tonight?"

"Davie makes us wear a tux when we drive this and the other Bentley. For the regular limos we wear the outfit you saw last Friday. I guess he thinks it makes the ride more elegant or something. As for what I do, I mostly go to school and study. I'm a sophomore at Tufts University."

"No kidding. I went there. And I grew up in Medford near Tufts. On Adams Street. My parents still live there."

"I live on Boston Ave across the street from that little convenience store on the corner of Hillside Ave."

"Hey, you're only two blocks from my parents. Talk about a small world. But wait a second. You look too old to be a sophomore. Were you in the military or something?"

Gary grinned. "No. I look old for my age. I bet you thought I was as old as you, twenty-four or twenty-five, right?"

It was Paul's turn to grin. "Well, you're right about what I thought, but I'm twenty-eight."

"Really? Well, I just turned twenty-one last month."

"Hey, congrats! Did you go out bar-hopping to celebrate?"

"Actually, no. I have a hypersensitivity to alcohol. My brain doesn't react normally to it, so one drink and I'm flying. Two drinks and I'm falling down drunk."

"I never heard of that."

"Neither did my parents when I was sixteen and they let me have a glass of wine with the meal at a wedding. They actually grounded me for a week because they thought I snuck at least two or three more glassfuls. After the next time it happened, they took me to the doctor.

"At first I was bummed, you know, but now it's kind of fun being the sober one watching all his friends make fools of themselves."

They traded school stories for the next ten miles or so until Paul asked if the girls at Tufts were still as brainy and beautiful as when he was there.

"They certainly are."

"You go out with any of them?"

"Nah, not really. I go to parties now and then, but studying and work keep me pretty busy."

"Sure, but with all those great women available, how can you pass that up?"

"I date a little, but to tell the truth, I'm sort of waiting to meet the love of *my* life again."

"Again?"

"Uh-huh. A little over a year ago, I was going with this girl, Claire. One Saturday she talked me into taking her shopping at the Gallaria Mall in Cambridge."

Paul nodded. "Girls love that place."

"Sure do. Well, after an hour or so of wandering in and out of stores, I'm getting tired of it but she's getting her second wind. So I told her I'd wait for her in the food court and she promised not to be too long." He grunted. "I knew that would never happen, but I didn't mind. I like sitting around and watching people.

"Well, I'd only been there about five minutes when this big, loud, obnoxious guy and this really pretty girl sit down next to me. She has a small drink and he's pissing and moaning about having to buy it for her, how these places rip you off, and on and on. Then he starts in on her, how stupid she is for buying stuff here, and this fault and that fault. And the girl just sat there, embarrassed, taking it all.

"After about ten minutes of that treatment, during which the girl is looking more and more miserable by the second, he jumps up, literally commands her to stay put until he gets back, and stalks off. No sooner is he out of sight than the girl starts to cry. Not loud, just sort of weeping, like all the embarrassment and shame was leaking out.

"Man, I couldn't imagine why the hell she was with him and I felt so bad for her that after a minute I leaned over and said softly, 'Excuse me, but I wanted to apologize.'

"She sort of stiffened when she heard me and snapped, 'For what?' I told her, 'For being the same gender as that asshole you're with.' Well, that got about half a smile out of her and we started talking.

"I could tell she was a little shy, but once she figured out I wasn't hitting on her, she warmed up. She was quick, and sweet, and funny, and so easy to talk to that I found myself really liking her. And I definitely had the feeling she was into me, too. Of course, she was only a junior in high school, but I didn't care. We were really connecting, you know?"

Paul nodded, not wanting to interrupt.

"Anyway, in the back of my head, I start wondering what Claire will think if she shows up and sees me having a great time talking to another girl. So I checked my watch and forty-five minutes had gone by! And of course, just then Claire showed up. What could I do? I thanked the girl, told her to find a new boyfriend, and said goodbye.

"Well, Claire and I are in the garage walking to my car when I realize I never even asked the girl her name. And suddenly, it was real important to find out who she was. So I handed Claire my keys and told her I forgot a small bag at the table and ran back to the food court."

Gary let out a big sigh, and Paul could tell what was coming next. "She was gone. I was so bummed I almost forgot to stop and buy something so I'd have a bag when I got back to the car."

Gary glanced over at Paul. "You know how you said that when you met Jillian something seemed to click. Well, that's how it was. When Claire and I were driving home, all I could think about was that girl. We really made some connection." He paused and sighed. "Since then, I've been waiting to meet her again. I figure we were fated to meet so it'll happen when the time is right."

"You have no clue who she is or where she lives or anything?"

"Nope. Not even a hint. So I spend much of my free time in the mall hoping to run into her again." He shrugged. "If it's really meant to be, I'll find her."

"Sure, but how long do you keep…"

Paul's cell phone rang before he could finish. It was Jillian, who wanted them to stop at the convenience store on Main Street to pick up a bottle of orange soda.

"I've been craving it all day and mom doesn't have a drop in the house."

"So, you get cravings for orange soda. Any other potential cravings I should know about?"

"Actually, yes! For three days I've been craving that slice of *Zuccotto* we left in the limo last Friday! Gary probably tossed it out. What a waste!"

Paul told her to hold on and turned to Gary. "Hey, did you find a paper bag in the limo last Friday?"

"You mean the one with that incredible dessert?"

Paul grinned. "He found it and ate it. And judging from the smile on his face, he enjoyed it as much as we did."

Ten minutes later, the limo turned onto Sears Road, and they were at the house. Jillian was waiting for them and waved as they pulled into the semi-circular driveway.

Gary sat behind the wheel, glancing in the side mirror as Paul and Jillian embraced and kissed. Then she walked toward his window so he rolled it down.

"You know I may never forgive you for eating my extra dessert."

"I'm sorry." He tried to look contrite. "I had no idea how valuable it was."

"Well, I should make you sit out here for punishment, but I forgive you, so come on into the house."

"That's okay. I'm used to waiting in the car."

"Nonsense. They won't be leaving for over an hour, and if you don't come in now, my mother will be out in two minutes to drag you in. I guarantee it. Come on. The parlor is way more comfortable than out here. You can even have some of my orange soda!"

5:10 PM

Priya was wondering if Paul reached the Marshall home yet when Rob voiced the question.

"Unless they hit heavy traffic on the Pike he should have been there ten minutes ago," Tom told him.

"I still can't believe he's really taking her sister to a prom."

"Why not? It's a nice thing for him to do," Priya said. "Proms are important to girls and even if they don't succeed in making her old boyfriend jealous, she'll remember how nice he was to her for the rest of her life. Take my word on that."

Tom and Rob shrugged. Both attended their high school senior proms and neither understood the big deal. You had to get dressed up to eat rubbery chicken and dance to whatever lame music would be approved by the school. As far as they were concerned, the best thing about their proms was the all-night parties after.

"I'll always take your word, without question, on any girl thing," Rob assured her. "So what time is Brian picking you up?"

"Seven-thirty. What do you think, should I dress up or dress down?"

"Where's he taking you?" Tom asked.

"I don't know," she replied, then added with a grin, "but it's probably not Casa de Luna."

That drew matching grins from the two guys.

"Just because Paul's nuts, doesn't mean all men are," Tom quipped.

"That's right," Rob agreed. "Brian seemed like a pretty steady sort of guy. Reasonable. Not given to undue extravagance, but he'll want to impress you with his gustatory sophistication. Hmmm. Yes... I'm guessing he's taking to you Sal's"

"Sal's? Where's that."

"You know Sal's."

Priya shook her head.

"Sure you do."

"I'm telling you I don't. Where is it?"

"Right near Park Street station.

She shook her head again, her face blank.

"The sausage cart."

Tom saw it coming and burst out laughing.

"You moron!" Priya searched her desktop for something to throw at him. Then she stopped and wagged a finger at him. "I'm going to tell Lisa you did that. *She'll* make you pay."

Rob was about to reply when Priya's phone rang. It was Brian.

"Are we still on for seven-thirty?"

"Absolutely. Do I need to get dressed up?"

"Priya, I can't imagine anything you could wear in which you wouldn't look fantastic. Be comfortable so we can relax, okay?"

Brian couldn't see her pleased smile at the compliment.

"Okay."

"I, ah, well, I didn't know what kind of food you like, so I made reservations at three places; The Union Oyster House if you want seafood, Little Vietnam over on North Beacon street if you want something Asian, and Giacomo's in the North End if you're in the mood for Italian."

"Are you serious? You made three reservations?"

She grinned as Rob's and Tom's eyebrows shot up.

"Hey, I was a Boy scout who became an engineer. Being prepared is in my blood. Actually, that's really why I called you at work. I didn't want to leave the two losers holding reservations on a Friday night."

Priya laughed. "The two losers?"

"Sure. The two places that won't have the prettiest girl in Boston sitting at one of their tables tonight."

Again, the pleased smile curled her lips.

5:20 PM

Paul, Gary, and Jeff Marshall were seated in the living room. After making introductions, Jillian and her mom vanished upstairs to assist Joanne and Julia in completing the transformation of Jessie from high school girl to prom queen.

For the most part, Gary sat back and enjoyed listening to Mr. Marshall tactfully but pointedly extract from Paul the story of his life, plans for the future, political and social outlooks, and plans for after the prom.

"Well, sir, I hadn't really thought about after the prom. With your permission, I suppose I'll leave that up to Jessie."

Her father's pleasant smile never wavered.

"All well and good, but please remember that Jessie is not old enough to drink. She's also somewhat shy and given to going along with the crowd, so I'll consider it a personal favor if you would take special care of her tonight and make sure nothing happens that shouldn't happen."

Then, always the good host, he turned his attention to Gary. "Are you happy at Tufts?"

"Yes sir."

"It's a very good school. Their economics program is world class, but I never realized they offered chemical engineering as well."

"So far it's a great program. I don't get heavily into it until next year, of course, but everyone I've talked to in the program had only good things to say about it. They…"

Three sets of feet pounded down the stairs, followed by a fourth at a more leisurely pace. Joanne and Julia both held cameras as their mother stood by, on the verge of tears.

"Ladies and gentlemen," she announced, "may I present Miss Jessica Anne Marshall.

Paul and Jeff Marshall moved to the archway separating the living room and foyer so they would have an unobstructed view of Jessie's entrance. Gary hung back, but could see the stairs over their shoulders. He remembered being in Paul's position a few years earlier as he waited for his own prom date to descend.

Paul's nervous anticipation amazed him. After all, Jessie wasn't really his date. He was doing the girl a favor. But he realized this is how he would have felt many years ago had pneumonia not prevented it.

His first glimpse of a white-clad foot and slender, stocking-clad calf did not prepare him for the delicate, radiant beauty that followed. Could this possibly be the same, skinny, sullen girl he met last Saturday? This Jessie looked fantastic!

She was dressed in an ankle-length, silk, one-shoulder white gown. The front had an overlapping slit at an angle from the hemline at her right foot to about the middle of her left thigh, with soft ruffles outlining the hem and slit. The delicate beadwork across the bodice sparkled as she descended. Her hair was pulled into a French twist in back, then brought up and curled on top. Wisps of her bangs hung down to frame her face. White pearl earrings and a single teardrop pearl necklace completed the ensemble. The only word Paul could think of was breathtaking.

Jessie caught Paul's eye as she descended. Wide-eyed, he placed his hand over his heart and mouthed the words 'Oh my,' filling her with pleasure. She returned his appreciative smile with one of her own that seemed to make her face glow. Her mother was weeping quietly now as her sisters snapped photos as fast as possible. Even her father had a lump in his throat and moist eyes as he realized for the first time his baby girl had truly become a woman.

Four steps from the bottom, Jessie noticed someone standing in the living room. Her eyes flicked away from Paul's for a moment, then grew wide with disbelief and she almost stumbled. Her sisters rushed forward, ready to catch her if she fell, but she recovered. Her eyes again looked past Paul and her mouth formed an "O' as her hand came up to cover it. Her sisters had not yet caught on, but her parents and Paul turned to follow her stare.

Gary stood there with a look of shock and awe, his eyes fixed on Jessica. Blinking rapidly, he shook his head as if to clear it.

The sisters now realized something unexpected was happening. Julie and Joanne turned to follow Jessie's stare. Jillian put her hand on Jessie's arm, urged her down the last three steps, and asked "What's wrong?"

Unable to tear her gaze from Gary, Jessie could not find her voice.

As if choreographed for a comedy routine, heads wagged back and forth between Jessica and Gary, who only had eyes for each other.

Gary recovered a bit of composure as he slowly walked toward Jessica. Once through the archway, he asked, "Is it you? Is it really you? From the..."

"Mall," Jessie said, completing the sentence.

"I can't believe it."

He moved up right in front of her, oblivious to Jillian who was still at her sister's shoulder.

"I've been trying to find you. Ever since that day...I've been back to the mall a hundred times."

Jeff Marshall cleared his throat. "Would someone please tell me what's going on."

Jessica tore her eyes from Gary and faced her father. "Daddy, this is...Oh..." She turned back to Gary. "What's your name?"

"I know his name. It's Gary Wilmore. But how do you know him, and why do you two look like you've each seen a ghost?"

With her focus again on Gary, Jessie told him.

"Daddy, remember last year when you had to drive into Cambridge to pick me up?"

She didn't see her father nod, but continued anyway. "That was the day I left that jerk Byron. I left because a really nice guy felt sorry for me because of the way Byron treated me. That guy talked to me and made me feel better. He was so nice and charming and funny and we talked like we'd known each other for years. He made me feel really special that day just by being kind to me and he never even asked me my name. And when his girlfriend came back to get him, the last thing he said to me was to dump Byron and find someone who'd really appreciate me. So I did.

"Daddy, this is the guy."

Fifteen minutes later, Gary and Jessie were huddled at the dining room table talking. Joanne, Julie and their parents were in the living room, marveling at the incredible string of events that brought the two together again.

Jillian was talking to Paul in the kitchen. He kept glancing into the dining room, only half hearing her as he watched Gary and Jessie become reacquainted. He, too, was nothing short of flabbergasted at this development, and from the bits he caught of what Jillian was saying, she felt the same way. His head was spinning, at first with the improbability of it all, and then with an idea. He turned back to Jillian and the look in his eyes caused her to stop what she was saying and ask, "What's wrong?"

"Nothing. I had an idea. What do you think of this?"

When he told her, she broke out into a big smile. "That's a wonderful idea! But you'll have to ask my father."

So they did, and to their delight, he needed only a nod from his wife to agree.

Jessie and Gary were seated next to each other, so close their noses almost touched as they spoke in whispers. The conversation came so easy, it was like they met at the mall yesterday. He told her about coming back for her that day and she told him how his remark gave her the courage to jump up and leave before Byron returned. He shared his frustration at not finding her at the mall again and she explained she was there only because Byron took her to the Museum of Science around the corner but parked in the mall because it was cheaper than the museum garage. They shared tidbits and stories from the past year, neither really noticing when Gary's hands reflexively sought hers.

Each was so into the other they missed Paul's knock on the doorframe to get their attention. Neither did they hear Paul's soft chuckle as he grinned at Jillian before turning back and loudly clearing his throat. That brought them back to the real world and they looked up to find the pair smiling at them.

"You guys catching up?" Paul asked.

Gary nodded. "I still can't believe this isn't a dream."

"I know what you mean.

"Look, it seems pretty clear you two have lots to talk about, but there *is* a prom tonight and only a few minutes before we have to leave."

Disappointment at the prospect of having to part so soon after meeting again clouded the young couple's faces.

"However," he continued, "I think I have a solution." Looking straight at the chauffeur he said, "Since you're already dressed for it, how'd you like to take Jessie to the prom and I'll be your driver for the night?"

Gary could not have been more stunned. He turned to Jessie and raised his eyebrows, his eyes asking the question she answered by jumping up and shouting, "Yes! Yes! This is perfect!" She was almost dancing with joy.

"I think Jessie likes the idea. But are you sure about this? Is her dad…"

"Okay with it? Absolutely. And I already talked with Davie. He had to hire me for the night for the insurance and liability stuff so I'm now an official, professional chauffer."

He turned to Jessie. "We'll have to fill him in on the Ethan thing."

"Who? Oh, him. Forget it. Forget it. I don't care about him anymore." Then something occurred to her. "Oh, Paul. Now you won't get to go to a prom. And you'll have to sit out in the car all by yourself."

"Don't worry. Jillian will be riding shotgun with me tonight, so it's not a big deal. We'll think of something to keep ourselves busy while you two are inside having fun." His grin and wiggling eyebrows brought color to Jessie's cheeks as she imagined what he might mean. "You two go back to catching up. I'll let you know when it's time to leave." With that, he and Jillian turned toward the living room, but after only a step, Paul felt a hand grab his.

"I need him for a minute," Jessie told her sister, and dragged Paul out through the kitchen onto the back porch.

She stood facing him, silent for a few moments before she said, "Thank you, Paul. Thank you so much for everything. I never thought I could feel any happier than I did when you asked me to the prom last week, but now you've proved me wrong."

Tears were gathering at the corners of her eyes, threatening to run down her face and ruin her makeup, but she didn't care.

"You are the nicest, sweetest guy I've ever known and if Jillian doesn't fall in love with you and marry you I will never speak to her again."

Her eyes widened. "Oh! I, I umm…I guess I shouldn't have said that. But I don't care. I mean it."

The tears broke free and ran down her cheeks as she threw her arms around him and hugged him close.

"I'll never forget everything you've done for me," she said softly through her tears. "Nobody's ever been this nice to me that didn't have to 'cause they raised me. I…I…"

"Hey, come on." Paul held her gently. "You'll spoil that beautiful makeup and Jillian will blame me."

A short laugh escaped her lips, but the tears kept flowing. "I don't care. I am *so happy*." She lifted her head from his chest, looked into his eyes and whispered, "I've thought about him every day since that day in the mall. And I thought I'd never see him again. But here he is. And it's all because of you."

She squeezed him again and Paul leaned down and kissed her on the forehead. "I think he really likes you, Jessie, so go easy on him. Don't let who you've imagined him to be get in the way of finding out who he really is. And of letting him discover the real you."

He watched her smile grow as her tears stopped.

"Now go do a little touch-up on that pretty face. I'll keep him busy for a few minutes.

"And have fun tonight!"

9:45 PM

"You know, you're not making this easy on me."

The taste of her lips lingered and the soft scent she was wearing continued to leave Paul lightheaded, as if it were a drug designed to break down his will.

He was seated in the back of the Bentley, gently stroking Jillian's hair. She lay across the seat, her head in his lap, her shoeless feet dangling out the window.

With the radio playing softly in the background, the past two hours were spent alternately talking and making out. The conversation ranged from a discussion of Jessie's and Gary's incredible good fortune to places they wanted to visit before they died to which song they liked best on a variety of recent CDs. Periodically, they found themselves drawing closer and closer as they talked, until they could no longer stand the heat building between them and their lips pressed together with a tender, urgent passion.

"I'm sorry." She sounded like she meant it as she tilted her head back until her eyes met his. "I can go sit in the front seat if it would make the waiting easier for you."

It would, but there's no way I'm letting you go anywhere right now.

When Paul declined Jillian's invitation to come up to her apartment after their first date last week, he did not realize how hard a task he was setting for himself. Every time he saw her, he wanted to rip her clothes off, but he was determined not to give in. He would take the time to know this woman, to let her know him, before they shared that final, most intimate of pleasures.

Determined as he was, though, Jillian seemed equally determined to test him tonight. Remarks, little jokes, and innuendo made clear to him her desire and her willingness. Half an hour ago, as they steamed the windows for the third time, Paul's hand drifted down to her breasts, then wormed its way inside her blouse, popping the top two buttons as he caressed her. He stopped after less than a minute, but Jillian never re-buttoned the blouse. Since then, it flopped open each time she moved. The sight of her cleavage, even contained in her lacy white bra, sorely tested his resolve.

"No, I like you right where you are. Besides, I don't want to spoil your fun."

"Fun? Whatever do you mean?"

"You know exactly what I mean. All night long you've been coming on to me, testing me, to see if I really meant what I said last week. Am I wrong?"

Jillian was silent for a bit, then made a short, soft humming sound as he felt her head shake. Her feet drew back into the car and she turned on her side, facing away from him. "You're right. I guess I have been sort of testing you. And I'm sorry. I…"

She paused and he felt her body tense, as if steeling itself for something unpleasant. With a small sigh, she continued.

"You've been nothing but sweet and kind ever since we met, not only to me, but to everyone. Look what you did for Jessie! Without even trying, you may have brought her back together with the love of her life. And…"

Again she paused, unsure if she should continue down this road.

"And the truth is I am so attracted to you it's scaring me to death. I told you I've had some bad experiences before, especially one, and I know you're not those guys, but I can't help feeling…I don't know, like the sky is waiting to fall in again. I mean, we haven't even known each other two weeks, and I feel as comfortable with you as I do with my sisters and my brother. And look at how I'm acting. Look at the things I said tonight, the jokes, the suggestive remarks, sitting here with my shirt half open. That's not me, Paul. I've never acted like that with a guy before and it scares me."

Jillian sat up and faced him, intent on trying to read his face in the dim light. "It scares me because I feel so strange, so different and I don't know how to deal with it. I honestly don't know why I was teasing you tonight, why I had to test you. But I'm sorry. None of this, none of it is who I thought I was."

"Maybe this *is* the real you. Maybe the person you thought you were was a face you learned to put on, part of a wall you built inside because of whatever happened with those other guys. Maybe the comfort you feel…and do you know how flattering it is to hear you say that? But maybe this comfort has started to let out the Jillian who's been lurking inside.

"Hey! Maybe you'll turn out to have seventeen different personalities and I'll get to go out with all of them!"

Jillian smiled at the joke, which only encouraged Paul to go on.

"Imagine! One of you might be a truck driver, or a contortionist. I could really get into her! There might be a middle-aged mom, a teen drama queen, and a drag queen, and a New Jersey hairdresser who pops her chewing gum and says 'Oh…my…gawd' all the time!"

Jillian was laughing now and she leaned over to kiss him on the cheek. "You really are strange, you know."

"I do know, but isn't that one of the things you l…ah…like about me?"

He almost said the word both of them studiously avoided ever since their goodnight kiss last Friday, the word neither would even admit to thinking, much less feeling this soon into their relationship.

"Yes, it is. But even that scares me. You know what makes me laugh, what makes me feel mushy, what…it's like you can see into my soul. And one part of me finds that exciting and reassuring, but another part feels uncomfortable that you can know me that well so quickly. I…"

"Jillian, I don't know you at all. Not really. Every day I learn something new. For example, today I learned you make a little humming noise after you've been thinking about something and before you say what it was. It's not magic, honey. I just pay attention. As for the rest, I'm being who I am. I told you right from the start there was something special between us. Maybe it's that we really *are* compatible, that we complement each other even as we have so much in common."

"Maybe, but it's more than that. You…you seem to know things. Like the Calla lilies you gave me last week. Did you know they're my favorite flower? Ever since I was a little girl. The first memory I have of my life is toddling along a path lined with white Callas at my grandmother's house in North Carolina. I couldn't have been more than two or three years old. And for as long as I can remember, white Callas have been my favorite. Of all the flowers you could have picked, you chose them. How could you know? And the date you set up. It was so wonderful, Paul, but you chose the four things to do that I've always found most romantic. It was like you read my diary or something. Do you see? Do you see why I feel nervous at the same time I'm feeling so happy?"

It was Paul's turn to think and he sat quietly for a minute, processing all she had said.

"I guess I understand. I suppose it should worry me, too, but honestly, it just reinforces what I've felt since the moment we met.

"I don't know what the future will bring for us. I have some thoughts on the subject, but honestly, for now I'm happy just to be here with you, to be anywhere with you.

"If you have doubts or fears, that's okay, too. Remember our conversation on the beach last week? About not keeping doubts and fears inside? I really believe what I said, then. If we talk about things, none of them can hurt us."

"I know, and to be honest, I guess this conversation was another test, to see if you really meant it. I'm sorry I keep doing this, I…"

"You need to stop apologizing, Jilli. Stop apologizing for being who you are. If something bothers you, talk to me about it. That's what couples do, or what they're supposed to do." He let out a short chuckle. "Can I ask you a question that might make you a little uncomfortable?"

"Of course." She could hear the hesitancy in her voice. "But only if I can ask you one later."

"Deal. Okay, here goes.

"Given all these feelings you have, the doubts and the fears and all, why did you invite me in after our date last week?"

Jillian considered the question, not sure whether to answer and whether to tell the whole truth if she did. Then she felt a twinge of guilt.

How can I not be honest with him? He's all but opened his soul to me from the day we met.

"I guess it was because at that moment I wanted you more than anything. I mean, the whole night was so wonderful, and you were so nice and generous and romantic. And when we kissed on the beach it made me feel so...you know."

She felt the color rising to her cheeks.

"And then, when we kissed goodnight, and it happened again, I didn't want to let you go. I wanted you with me so much I blocked out everything else." She paused. "I can't believe I'm telling you this."

"You know I felt the same way. But think about this, now. How would you be feeling today if I came up, if we slept together? Would you be happier? Less scared? Or more? Would you be feeling any of this, or would you have kept that block in place once you gave yourself like that?"

"I don't know. I think...I guess I probably would have blocked all these feelings out, so I could enjoy being with you."

"But the feelings, the fears and doubts, they'd still be there, right?"

She nodded. "Right."

"Do you think you could have kept them suppressed forever?"

"No. Of course not. Eventually they'd have broken through, only...only we'd have grown comfortable together. But we wouldn't have any real depth of understanding of each other to help us get through it. It could easily have broken us up."

"But what's different about dealing with it now? They're the same fears, the same doubts."

"Because we're still learning, still figuring out who we are together. We haven't formed any bonds, don't have any expectations we have to defend to ourselves or each other. We get to find out about each other at the same time as we figure out who we are together, so any bonds and expectations will be based on who we really are, not some fantasy we constructed to justify having slept together."

Last week, in the heat of the moment, when he tried to explain his reason for not sleeping with her, she understood in a general way. But now, after his questions forced her to think it through and actually detail the reasons, she realized she really did see it, really knew in her head and her heart why he wanted to wait, and why it was the right thing, the smart thing to do. And she realized the knowledge made it all seem a little less scary.

It's true. It's always been true. I've always been afraid of getting hurt again the way Aiden hurt me. It's been like barrier between me and guys ever since. But it's different this time. Ever since that first day in the coffee shop it's been gone and I can't bring it back. And I don't want to bring it back.

Her heart was open and unprotected again and that was what truly scared her.

He can hurt me. He can hurt me more than Aiden did. But he can love me more, too. I know. I saw it in his eyes last week. I hear it every time we talk. I feel it every time we're together.

She sighed.

I'm so tired of being scared all the time. I'm tired of holding back, of not letting myself feel too much. I want to let go, really let go. But I think it's going to take more time. And I know Paul will give me that time and help me unpack all the crappy baggage I've been lugging around since Aiden.

She looked at him with a new respect.

"Oh, you think you're so smart now, don't you?"

"So smart? What do you mean?"

"You know what I mean, and thank you."

She re-buttoned her blouse.

"Now, this seat looks wide enough so we can lay down side-by-side. I think I really want to hold you for a while, okay?"

Paul smiled. It was more than okay. They settled in and shared a soft, tender kiss before he said, "I guess it's your turn now. What do you want to know?"

Jillian hugged him close, her head resting on his biceps, their faces inches apart. Even in the dim light, her eyes glowed with anticipation as she said, "Tell me all about Krista."

10:35 PM

"What's the name of the guy who made it possible for us to meet again?"

They were sitting at their table, waiting for the DJ to return from his break. Not once did the dung worm cross Jessie's mind all night. Her thoughts were all of Gary, and of the extraordinary good fortune that brought them together again.

"You mean Ethan?"

"Yes, good old Ethan. I'll bet that's him sitting two tables over to the right, next to a girl in a green dress."

Jessie glanced over and caught him looking her way. "That's him. How did you know?"

"He's been watching you all night. Or maybe he's been watching me, but I don't think so. And I don't think the girl he's with is too happy about it. Every time she catches him, she glares, and I've seen her smack his arm twice."

Jessie shrugged. "Who cares. Ethan is so yesterday. He and Dedee deserve each other. And that's the last time his name will come up tonight."

"Yes, sir...ah...ma'am!"

Gary watched her scowl melt into a grin as he tilted his head and made eyes at her. He thought about Paul and Jillian waiting out in the limo and wondered if they were having as good a time as he was.

Impossible. Jessie's incredible.

He quickly learned he only scratched the surface with her that day in the mall. She was smart and forthright, with a quick wit and an encyclopedic knowledge of music. She seemed to be able to talk about anything and when she smiled, the whole world faded away. He wondered how that guy could possibly have left her, though he was very grateful for what had to be the guy's bout of temporary insanity.

"He must be a frigging moron!" he muttered, not realizing he vocalized the thought.

"Who's a moron?" she asked as the DJ started spinning another disc. They were so into each other, neither of them noticed his return.

"Shoot, did I say that out loud? I'm sorry. I was thinking about something."

"So who's the moron, and why?"

"Him. The person who's name we are not mentioning again tonight."

"Oh. Well, I agree. But why were you even thinking of him?"

Gary hesitated. "I, umm, I don't know that it's really appropriate. We're having such a good time tonight and I don't want to embarrass you or dredge up anything unpleasant."

"Boy, you don't know much about girls, do you? That only makes me more curious to know what it is. Come on, out with it or I'll torture you all night to find out."

"Okay, then. I was thinking about how great you are, and I wondered how he could have been so stupid as to let you go." He shrugged a half-hearted apology.

Jessie smiled at him, blushing slightly at the compliment. She leaned over and gave Gary a quick hug, feeling surprised she wasn't bothered any more about the breakup with Ethan. Then she sat back and said, "I wouldn't sleep with him. He wanted to have sex and I didn't. So he went and found someone more willing than I was."

"Well, I, for one, am very grateful he did. But I'm sorry you had to get hurt."

"Don't be. He did me a favor and one of these days, when I stop hating him a little more, I might even thank him. And now I wanna *dance!*"

With that, she jumped up and started moving to the driving beat as she danced her way to the floor, looking to Gary like an angel, a sweet, soft, undeniably sexy angel.

The dance floor was packed with young bodies losing themselves in the rhythms, the sounds, and their partners as the DJ kept the music loud and fast for almost fifteen minutes. Gary and Jessie were no exception. They shared looks and smiles as they twisted and turned, each showing off for the other, building an emotional heat that rivaled the physical heat of so much exertion. Then the DJ took pity on the dancers and slowed things down.

Happy for the chance to get close, Jessie and Gary moved together as Bryan McKnight started singing *Back at One*. They danced to slow songs earlier, but this time it was different. The feelings between them kept growing stronger all night, and now neither could hide how much they wanted the other.

Jessie moved right into him, her whole body pressing against him as her arms went around his neck. They danced slowly, hardly moving, the music only an excuse to hold each other close.

After a minute or so, she felt Gary's hand move from the small of her back to caress the nape of her neck, sending shivers of pleasure down her spine. Then, as they continued to dance, she felt him lean his head back, so she lifted her own off his shoulder to see what was wrong.

He stared into her eyes for almost a minute, then smiled and said, "Jessie, I really need to know something."

"What?"

"Are you gonna, like, freak out and start screaming when I kiss you in a few seconds?"

"When you…"

His lips cut her off as his hands pressed her closer. They danced as one body now, slowly turning as they tasted each other for the first time. It was everything Jessie hoped it would be - soft, tender, and wonderful, and when it ended, she looked up and answered his question.

"I guess I won't," she sighed with a dreamy smile, "but maybe you better try again. Just to make sure."

SATURDAY, MAY 15

12:10 AM

When the taxi pulled up in front of Priya's building, Brian slipped out and helped her from the back seat. Then he leaned in and asked the driver to wait, a signal to Priya he wasn't expecting to be asked up.

"I had a really nice time tonight, Brian," Priya said softly. "Thank you."

"No," he replied, as softly, "thank *you*. I thought I was only going out with the prettiest girl in Boston tonight. Imagine my surprise when I discovered I was dating the smartest and the funniest, too."

"Oh stop it," she told him, pleased at the compliments. "It's getting late and I have to get up early in the morning." She leaned over and kissed him quickly on the lips. "Goodnight, Brian."

She started up the steps as he drifted back to the waiting taxi. Her fingers had closed around the keys in her purse when she heard, "Priya, wait."

Brian hurried to the bottom of the stairs. "You know, I really meant what I said a minute ago. You were so *not* what I expected. I...I think you're amazing and I know the dating rules say I'm supposed to wait a day or two before I call you, but I don't want to wait that long. I'd really like to see you again tomorrow. Your choice. Whatever you want to do." His eye twitched as a thought crossed his mind. "Assuming you weren't just being kind before to get rid of me."

Priya chuckled. "No, I wasn't just being kind. But my father and brother are coming tomorrow for the weekend. Their flight arrives in about five hours."

She saw the disappointment on his face.

"Oh, well, okay. They'll be here all weekend?"

She nodded. "Until Sunday night. Their flight back leaves at ten-thirty. Maybe we could get together for lunch Monday?"

"Sure, Monday lunch. That's perfect. No, no it's not. I have an all-day seminar in Springfield on Monday. Can I call you when I get back? There's, well, there's something I need to tell you but it will take a while and it's too late now."

"Are you sure? If it's important…"

"No, it'll keep."

She watched him walk back to the taxi. With his hand on the door, he looked back and smiled at her, but in the yellow glow of the streetlight, it seemed different than earlier in the night, as if something were hidden behind it.

She waited until the taxi turned the corner onto Commonwealth Avenue before unlocking the front door.

Something's wrong, I can feel it. He was so sweet, so attentive all night, but then the happy, fun Brian was replaced by…someone else. Someone who thinks I'm not going to like what he wants to tell me. Crap, is he married or engaged or something? No, I didn't get that vibe. And I don't think he's gay. Maybe he's been in prison. That might make him act that way. Damn! Why didn't I insist on talking right then? Now this is going to bug me all weekend!

SUNDAY, May 16

7:10 AM

Paul was making love to Jillian on her sofa. Her lips pressed hungrily against his while his hands roamed to places he previously only imagined. He moaned when she touched him and again when his fingers found her furry softness. Through all of it, their lips never parted. Long, luscious minutes passed as they each grew hotter and hotter. Still, their lips remained locked until, unable to stand it any longer, Paul tried to break the kiss so he could undress her and consummate their passion, but found he could not. Their lips seemed to be glued together. He strained to pull away, to wrench his lips from hers and...

His eyes opened. He blinked a few times, still able to feel her lips against his own. Then he realized the ceiling looked wrong. And those were not lips touching his.

"Good morning, sweetie."

He turned to find Jillian sitting on the coffee table, a sweet, loving grin lighting her face.

"Have a nice snooze?"

"Good morning. What time is it?"

"A little after seven. I've been up for an hour, but you looked so peaceful I didn't have the heart to wake you. Plus, I figured you needed the sleep."

"What time did I nod off?"

"I'm not sure. I noticed about 10:30 when I paused the movie to go pee. Do you even remember what we were watching?"

Paul sheepishly shook his head.

"Groundhog Day. You picked it out. Didn't you get any sleep at all yesterday morning?"

"Not really. We dropped you off about, what, six-thirty? Then Gary and I sat in the car comparing notes for a while. And then Steve called as I got home. Marcus will be coming for a visit next month and my parents are planning a cookout. Your cousin's wedding is the thirteenth, right?"

Jillian nodded.

"Good, because the cookout is the twelfth. Will that be a problem?"

"Shouldn't be, now that you thought to mention it to me."

Her reproving glare made him laugh.

"Hey, I found out yesterday, I told you today. What's wrong with that? Besides, I was obviously out of my mind with exhaustion. And by the way, did you kiss me or something right before I woke up?"

"I was sort of lightly rubbing your lips with my fingertip. I wanted to see if it would get you talking in your sleep. Why?"

"How long were you doing it?"

"About ten or fifteen seconds."

"Well it made me have the most incredible dream."

His detailed description caused her to glow with a combination of pleasure and embarrassment.

"Let me run in the bathroom and then you can jump in the shower. When you're dressed, we can walk over to my place so I can shower and change. Then we can get some breakfast. How's that sound?"

"If I wasn't so hungry it would sound great. How about you take care of business, then go home and get ready while I get ready here. Then I'll walk over and meet you. That'll save at least thirty minutes."

An hour later they stepped out of a taxi and into Coffey's Coffee. "Oh my lord! What is that incredible aroma? I never smelled that in here before." She took a second deep breath.

"That's Gil's Sunday Strudel. He must have just taken a batch from the oven. Go grab a table and I'll get us some."

A few minutes later, Paul returned with two cups of coffee, two plastic forks, napkins, and two paper plates with large, thick squares of strudel that looked as fabulous as they smelled.

Jillian grabbed a fork and tried a bite. "Oh! That is *sooo* good! It's almost as good as the Zuccotto! What's in it?" She hacked off another piece without waiting for the answer.

"Apples, raisins, apricots, plums, butter, sugar, cinnamon, and I'm not sure what else. It's Gil's secret recipe. I guess it takes a while to make because he only sells it on Sunday. Hence the name, Sunday Strudel."

"Oh Paul, we have to come here every Sunday. Only we'll have to jog both ways to burn off the calories. But it'll be worth it."

Their table by the window afforded them a nice view of the mostly empty street. Jillian marveled at how different the shop felt on Sunday from the weekdays when there were invariably lines and noise inside that rivaled the crowds and cacophony outside. They chatted between bites and sips, talking about nothing in particular and having a wonderful time of it. What they said and what they did wasn't really important. They were just happy to be together and it showed.

Jillian was laughing at one of Paul's terrible double entendres when she turned her head and glanced out the window. Her laugh died as the forkful of strudel slipped from her hand.

Paul was cutting another slice of his own strudel when her fork hit the table. His head snapped up and he could see her face had drained of all color. "Are you okay, Jilli? You look like you've seen…"

"A ghost," she said, completing his cliché.

Did I just see a ghost? It was only a glimpse from the side as he turned away. It couldn't be. It had to be someone who resembled him. Right. It can't be him, not now. Not after all this time. Not when Paul and I…

"Are you sure you're okay? Who did you think you saw?"

Oh, no. Look at his face. He's so worried. But I can't get into this now. It's too soon. But I have to tell him something.

"I thought I saw someone I used to know when I was in college. Someone…someone who hurt me a lot. But it couldn't be him."

She reached across the table for one of his hands.

"It was a very painful experience, Paul, and someday soon I promise I'll tell you about it, but right now I can't. I'm sorry, but it's just…"

"Hey, don't worry about it. You'll tell me when you're ready. Let's forget about it and enjoy the day."

She forced a smile.

"Yes. Let's enjoy the day."

She did her best. But no matter how hard she tried, she couldn't drive the ghost from her thoughts.

11:17 PM

Paul lay in bed replaying his first full day with Jillian.

We had so much fun today. But underneath all the jokes and smiles and laughs something was bothering her. Ever since she thought she saw that guy outside Coffey's. I wonder who he was…what he did. Cripes, I hope he didn't beat her up or something. If he did I'll…

He grunted.

…I'll what? Hunt him down? Hurt him back. Why not? If she asked me to, sure. But I don't think it was physical. She didn't look scared this morning, just, I don't know, flustered…or troubled.

He shrugged.

Whatever he did, it's clear the pain is still haunting her.

He sighed.

I wonder if I should be worried.

MONDAY, MAY 17

12:50 PM

Lisa, Hector, and his assistant, Nadia, slid into a booth at Papa Gino's. The three were taking a late lunch after a morning meeting ran long.

The pizza shop was crowded when they sat down, but soon began to empty as people headed back to work. By the time their food arrived, only a few tables and booths remained occupied.

Sometimes, Lisa enjoyed the hustle and bustle of a busy place, but other times, like today, she was grateful when the noise subsided enough to hear without straining and be heard without having to yell.

As they waited for the pizza to cool enough to eat, Hector told the girls about his latest argument with Frank.

"It's like he doesn't even hear me sometimes. He wants to know what's bothering me but then he doesn't pay attention when I tell him."

Nadia was fascinated but Lisa heard it all before. Though Hector was a good friend, his troubles with Frank seemed to be never-ending. As she pulled a slice from the tray to start eating, she found herself half-listening to Hector and half to some of the conversations at tables close to theirs. Eavesdropping was one of her guilty pleasures. Often, she would take lunch alone so she could sit and listen to the conversations around her.

Today, the only people within earshot were two college students, sitting two tables to the left and the four guys in the booth directly behind her. The students seemed to be discussing classes but it sounded like the four guys were in full bragging mode.

There was deep voice number one, who just finished telling his friends about the funny noises some girl named Susan made in bed. They all laughed as high voice guy started imitating the noises. Soon, deep voice number two and raspy voice joined in.

Good lord, what's wrong with them? They sound like a bunch of sixteen-year-olds.

Their conversation continued in that vein for the ten minutes it took Lisa to consume two slices of pizza. Then it took an unexpected turn.

"Hey Mike," the higher voice said, "what was the name of that Indian girl you were trying to nail a few months ago?"

"You mean virgin girl?" the second deep voice answered. "Her name was Priya. Why?"

"You know Brian over in networking?"

"Is he the geeky guy with the black glasses?"

"Aren't all those computer guys geeks?" asked the first deep voice, which drew laughs from all four.

"No, the other guy."

"Yeah, I know who you mean. What about him?"

"I think he's trying his hand with her."

"Oh yeah?"

"A bunch of us were drinking over at DHL last week when she walked in and Brian was like, mesmerized or something. All night he was staring at her. I knew who she was and started to tell him about you and her, but he'd already figured it out and it didn't make any difference to him. When the rest of us left, he stayed. Said he wanted to meet her."

"Why? He's not gonna get laid. She's some kind of religious nut or something."

"I told him that, but I guess he thinks otherwise. He took her out last Friday."

"What happened?"

"I don't know. I haven't seen him to ask. But he's a pretty smart guy. And he has that innocent thing going, you know? If anyone can figure out a way into her, it'd be him."

I can't believe what I'm hearing. Can they be talking about the same Brian I met last Wednesday? It has to be.

The shock on her face caused her companions to ask what was wrong, but she just shook her head.

Poor Priya. Should I tell her? I have to tell her. I can't let her be taken in by this bastard.

She took a deep breath and let it out slowly.

Guys can be such assholes.

2:10 PM

Rob was working on the layout for chapter three of their current project when his cell phone rang.

Damn, always at the wrong moment.

He had a great idea he did not want to lose so he flipped open the phone, saw it was Lisa and said, "Hold on for a minute."

He quickly scribbled his thoughts on a piece of scrap paper then snatched up the phone. "Hi baby. Sorry about that. I had to get an idea down before I forgot it. What's up, and why are you calling on the cell instead of the office phone?"

Tom was out of the office until four, so only Paul and Priya saw Rob's face cloud over as he listened to his girlfriend. They saw him nod, then glance up at both of them. "Hold on a minute," he told Lisa, then to Paul and Priya said, "I'll be back in a few minutes. I think she wants me to talk dirty to her." He forced a grin as he rose and hurried out of the office.

"I wonder what that's about?" Paul asked.

"Obviously something he doesn't want us to hear. But he looked funny. Did he look funny to you?"

"Yeah, he did. I hope they're not having problems again."

Priya nodded as they went back to work.

Twenty-five minutes later, she stretched and said, "Where the heck is Rob?"

"Maybe he was serious and they're having phone sex."

She rolled her eyes and changed the subject. "I still can't get over what happened Friday. I mean, what are the odds of Gary and Jessie meeting again like that?"

"It *was* pretty amazing." A thought popped into his head and he started to frown. "You know how I've been saying Jilli and I were fated to meet? Well, I hope it wasn't just to get Jessie and Gary back together again. That would suck if…"

"Don't be stupid. Jessie and Gary are just a happy coincidence. You and Jillian are the real thing." She thought for a second then continued. "Well, maybe Jessie and Gary are the real thing, too, but don't start doubting what you and Jilli have."

Paul grinned. "I know, I know, but…"

At that moment, Rob, Lisa, and Jillian walked into the office. None of them appeared happy.

"Jillian! Lisa! Hi! What are you two doing here?"

"Hey Paul," Rob said before Jillian could answer. "Take a walk with me. It's important."

Paul and Priya were clearly confused by all of this. What were the girls doing here in the middle of the workday? And why was Rob dragging Paul out of the office?

Concern flashed through Priya.

Something horrible's happened. Is it dad, or Raj? But how would Lisa and Jillian know?

She saw Paul cast a bewildered glance over his shoulder as Lisa closed the office door.

Out in the hall, Paul turned to Rob.

"What the hell is going on? Why are the girls here?"

"Remember Brian, the guy who hit on Priya last week?"

"Sure. She went out with him last Friday. Oh shit, he didn't get hurt, or killed?"

"Worse."

Rob related the gist of what Lisa told him.

"That rotten bastard."

"Indeed. But, ahh…"

"But what?"

"But didn't we used to be like that once?"

Paul flinched, realizing Rob was right. Both of them were exactly like that in high school and college, more interested in the sex than the person with whom they were having it. Both played girls the way Brian was evidently playing Priya. Both flattered them, feigned interest in whatever they liked, and played the game well, scoring often. Now, as he imagined what Priya must be feeling as Lisa told her the truth about Brian, he felt himself growing warm with embarrassment and humiliation at his past.

Silent tears were rolling down Priya's face.

After verifying Brian was a network guy, and Priya dated a guy named Mike a few months ago, Lisa repeated the conversation she overheard at lunch. As she talked, Priya sat quietly, listening attentively. It was only after Lisa was done, and Priya's silence caused the other two to mistake it for depression and start to console her, that tears began to flow.

"Don't cry, sweetie," Jillian said, "there are lots of guys way better than him."

Priya smiled through her tears. "I'm not crying because of Brian. Who cares about Brian. I only went out with him once, and believe me, I'm used to guys like him trying…well, you know."

"Then why…?"

"I'm crying because you two were concerned enough for me that you came here in the middle of the day. I've never had friends like that before. Never had friends who worried about me getting hurt. Friends who cared enough to do this kind of thing for me. I'm not crying because I'm sad." She jumped up to hug them. "I'm crying because I'm happy!"

7:15 PM

When she arrived home after work, Priya dropped her jacket and purse on a chair, stood in the middle of her living room, and hugged herself for almost a full minute. Then she threw her arms into the air and let out a long, loud whoop of joy.

I have girlfriends! Real girlfriends who aren't threatened by me, who don't want something from me, who like me as much as I like them!

Another happy shout filled the air as she started to dance around the room.

It's coming together. My life is finally starting to come together. I worried so much about moving here and it was for nothing! It's the best decision I ever made. I have a great job, a really special friend in Paul, and two real girlfriends. All I need now is someone to share it all with. But that'll come. I know it. The fates have smiled on me and all I have to do...

The shrill ring of her telephone interrupted her reverie. A second later, her cell began to play the *Oompa Loompa* song from *Willy Wonka and the Chocolate Factory*, her favorite childhood movie.

That might be Brian on the regular phone. No way I'm talking to that jerk. But he doesn't have my cell number.

She turned down the volume on the answering machine and fished the cell out of her purse. She didn't recognize the number and hesitantly said, "Hello?"

"Hi Priya, it's Jillian. I hope you don't mind but I kind of coerced Paul into giving me your cell number."

"Hi. No, that's okay. I'd have given it to you next time I saw you anyway. When I saw a number I didn't know, I was afraid it might be Brian and I didn't want to talk to him."

"And that's why I called. I, uh...well, Paul said to leave you alone, but he's just a guy and I wanted to make sure you were okay. I know you said you were okay this afternoon, but I was kind of worrying that you'd get home and start feeling bad about what happened."

"Well thank you." She smiled as she flopped onto her sofa. "But Brian is already a distant memory. I suppose if we'd gone out for a while and I started having feelings for him it might be different, but I've learned not to let myself get hopeful about any guy. It cuts down on the pain when they stop calling."

Jillian didn't respond for a few seconds as the implications sunk in.

"Oh, Priya, I'm sorry. I know how hard it is to shelter your feelings...to, umm, not let yourself hope too much too fast. I was hurt really bad once. And it left scars. And I kind of get the feeling you've had more than your share of hurt, too."

If you only knew how much I'd like to share my past, to tell you about the loneliness, about the guys I let myself care for, about the girls who never let me get close, but it's much too soon to dump all that on a new friend. The last thing I want is to make you think I'm some pathetic, needy drama queen.

"Well, sure, we've all been hurt. That's part of life, I guess. But I like to think about positive things. Like making new friends!"

She hesitated a few seconds before continuing.

"There is one thing, though, that we really need to talk about, but I'd rather do it in person."

"Tonight?"

"Whenever you're free."

"Tonight then. Mind if I come over, or would you rather meet someplace?"

"Oh, you don't have to come all the way out here. I can come to your place. Besides, don't you and Paul have plans for the night?"

"Paul's having drinks with a few of his friends as we speak. He said he'd call me later, but…" She giggled. "…I think it will do him good to miss me a little. There's no reason I have to sit around waiting for him to call. If I'm not home, I can't answer the phone and can't answer the door. And it's perfectly reasonable to put my cell on vibrate and then forget to take it out of my purse. Don't you think?"

Priya laughed. "Jillian! All this time I thought you were so sweet and demure! Well I think you're right. Let him wonder and worry a little."

She arrived about twenty-five minutes later bearing a shopping bag full of gifts.

"What's all this?"

Priya watched Jillian unpack two bottles of wine, a pinot noir and a chardonnay, some cheese and crackers, a bag of carrot sticks, a bag of chips, and two small containers of dip.

"I wasn't sure what you like, so I bought a bunch of stuff and hoped for the best."

"Well thank you! But you didn't have to do that."

"Oh yes I did. If my mother ever found out I went to someone's house for the first time without bringing something, I would never hear the end of it. Years from now, she'd be like, 'Remember the time Jillian went to visit her friend Priya for the first time…empty handed? I was *so* embarrassed when I found out. Priya must have thought the girl was brought up by wolves. Can you *imagine*! A daughter of mine couldn't even bring a bottle of wine. Lord knows what else she does that I haven't heard about. Her sisters probably know, but they won't tell me. They don't want to upset me. Oh, the years I spent teaching her manners and that's the thanks I get. To find out she couldn't even be bothered to buy a bag of chips. I bet her *friend* never showed up someplace empty handed like that."

Jillian's performance had Priya doubled over with laughter.

"You think I'm exaggerating, don't you?"

Unable to stop laughing, Priya could only nod.

"Well, maybe I am. A little. But only a little. Manners are everything to my mom."

She opened the chardonnay while Priya, still chuckling over the floor show, arranged the carrot sticks and cheese on a tray and brought them into the living room. Then she flipped on the radio, turned down the volume to conversation level, and settled in on the sofa next to her new friend.

They chatted aimlessly for a few minutes until Jillian said, "If you don't tell me soon what you wanted to talk about I'll burst from curiosity."

Priya smiled, put her glass on the table, kicked off her shoes, and pulled her legs up so she could turn and sit cross-legged on the sofa facing Jillian, who followed suit.

"A few weeks ago, I didn't have any real friends here in Boston. The guys at work were sort of friends, work friends, but not real friends. Know what I mean?"

"Yes, of course." She thought of Shandra and Marie, her closest work friends and how different their friendship was from what she had with Liz and Jenna.

"But now I have Paul, and you, and I hope Lisa. It's great. I mean, I really like you all and I don't want anything to mess that up. I don't want to ever get in the middle of things because then I'd end up losing one of you and I don't want that to happen."

"I'm not sure I understand what you mean."

"Well, if you confided something to me, would you want me to tell Paul about it?"

"No, of course not."

"And I feel the same way. If I told you something, I wouldn't want you to tell Paul. But what if Paul confides something to me? Would you expect me to tell you about it?"

"Oh, I see now what you mean about being in the middle. But in a way, you'll always be in the middle."

"I know. But I really do like you. And I really like Paul. He's become, I don't know, sort of a brother but...more than a brother. I don't know if I can explain it better than that. But he and I have an agreement that anything said between us stays between us. And I'd like you and me to have the same agreement."

When she finished speaking, Priya noticed Jillian's expression change as a commercial ended and *Could I Have This Dance* started playing.

"What's wrong?"

"Nothing, really. It's just that when Paul took me dancing on our first date, this was the first song we danced to. And since then, it seems like every time I'm with someone and we're talking about him, this song comes on. It's starting to get a little weird."

"Maybe it's an omen."

"That's what I've been thinking." Worry lines creased her forehead. "But which kind, good or bad?"

"Oh sweetie, it has to be good. That first date was so amazing the fates want to keep reminding you of it."

"I guess so. I hope so."

The memory of yesterday's ghost flashed across her mind, but she pushed it out, determined to enjoy her time with Priya.

"I… But I'm sorry, my little drama interrupted you. Please, go on."

Priya grinned. "Don't apologize. I love little dramas like that. Anyway, I was saying that I want us to be able to trust each other when it comes to keeping confidences.

"In many ways, I'm a very private person. As time goes on, there might be things I'd want to talk to you about that I might not want Paul to know. And I'd want you to be comfortable talking with me without having to worry I'd be blabbing it to your boyfriend. I know you have Liz and Jenna, of course, but there might be times where I could provide some insight into Paul. I don't know. I just…I just want us to be friends and don't want a guy, even Paul, to mess it up."

Jillian was touched at how much this woman seemed to care about her and their budding friendship. She remembered the first time they met and how Priya told her she would do almost anything for a friend. Jillian realized this was part of the same thing. She understood now how important friends really were to her and could see her one day becoming as close as Jenna and Liz.

Of course, she consented to the agreement, but before she could say anything else, the phone rang again. Priya reached over and turned the volume back up on the answering machine. *Hi, this isn't really Priya. Please leave a message after the beep.*

"Hi Priya. It's Brian again. I was really hoping to see you tonight. There's something kind of important I need to talk to you about. The seminar was pretty much a waste of time today, but it did give me the opportunity to daydream about you. I'll be home all night so please call me when you get in and maybe we can set something up for tomorrow. Bye."

"Boy, what a jerk," Jillian said. "He sounds so nice and sincere, so worried about whatever it is he has to tell you. And it's all a stupid game to him. What makes guys do that? What makes them so twisted they can't see how they hurt people?"

"I don't know, but there are way too many of them out there. You're very lucky to have found Paul. And Lisa's lucky, too. Did you know Rob used to be a huge player? I mean, I don't think he was as cold and calculating as Brian, but from what I've heard around the office, until Lisa came along, he had a new girl every few weeks."

"Paul told me. I thought he was kidding at first because Rob seems so devoted to Lisa."

"He is. Just as Paul's devoted to you."

Priya noted Jillian's contented smile and let out a short sigh. "You two really are lucky. Now, if only I could get lucky, too."

TUESDAY, MAY 18

6:05 PM

Liz rummaged through the bin in the grocery store, squeezing oranges as she tried to figure out if they were juicy enough.

Peeling one with the orange plastic citrus peeler her mother gave her when she moved into her first apartment, then standing over the sink and biting into it as if it were an apple was one of her guilty pleasures. The juice would explode into her mouth and run freely over her lips and out the corners, dripping down her grinning cheeks and chin into the sink. As she dropped the third orange into a plastic bag, her cell phone rang.

"Could this really be Jillian? I thought she forgot about me. Why, I can remember a time when I talked to her almost every day, when we hung out all the time. But now I only see her at Yoga class. It's sad, really."

"Oh, Lizzie. Stop exaggerating. I'd never forget about you. I've just been a little busy."

"I'll bet. And you're not even getting any. That's even more sad."

"Tell me about it. So what are you doing?"

"Shopping. Buying fruit. What about you?"

"Standing on the corner watching all the guys go by."

Liz laughed. "Really?"

"Actually, yes. I'm leaning against the light pole at the corner of West and Tremont. You-know-who had to work late so I stopped in the coffee shop and now I'm waiting outside for him. He said he'd be out around six-fifteen so it shouldn't be too long. We're walking home."

"Aren't you two ambitious?"

"Well, like you said, we're not getting any so we have to work off all this pent up energy *some* way."

"Jillian!"

"I know. Will you listen to me? I never used to say such things and now it's like, I don't know, I'm a whole new me. Paul thinks this is the *real* me and that I've been hiding it because of all the stuff in the past."

"You told him about Aiden? Already?"

"Sort of…well, no, not really. But…"

There was silence for a few seconds, then Liz thought she heard Jillian whisper, "No, no…no, no, no, not again."

"Jillian, what's wrong?" When she didn't get an immediate answer she almost yelled into the phone, "Jillian! Answer me! What's wrong!"

Shoppers around her turned to stare but she didn't care.

"It's him again, Lizzie. I see him again. I must be going crazy."

"Who?"

"He's standing near the T station on the corner of Park and Tremont. He's watching me."

"Jilli, who? Who do you see?"

"Aiden."

Liz couldn't have been more shocked. "Oh my g…are you sure?"

"Yes, Lizzy. It has to be him. Or his twin. He's looking right at me, but I don't think he knows I've seen him. That's what I was about to tell you. I thought I saw him Sunday. And now again. What am I going to do, Lizzy? Paul will be here any minute."

"Jillian! Calm down. Wait until Paul arrives and tell him you changed your mind and want to take the subway home. Then the two of you start walking toward the station."

"I can't, Lizzy. I don't want to drag Paul into this."

"Then when he shows up, turn around and walk the other way. If you can't confront him, Jilli, then forget about him. But maybe it's someone who just resembles him from a distance. The Aiden I remember would walk over and say hello. He wouldn't be watching you from a block away."

"Maybe. But he looks so *much* like him. Why now? Why is this happening now? I'm…I have to go, Liz. I see Paul. I'm going to meet him halfway."

"Call me later," Liz said, not sure if her friend even heard her.

The moment Jillian stepped off the curb to cross West Street, the man turned and hurried into the subway station.

That clinches it. He's run away twice when he realized I saw him. It has to be Aiden. The odds of a look-alike stalker are just too huge.

"What am I going to do?" she muttered as Paul noticed her and waved. "Please God, help me. Tell me what to do."

WEDNESDAY, MAY 19

10:00 PM

Brian sat back in the recliner and stared at the blank TV screen. An hour of reality television did nothing to take his mind off Priya, who haunted his thoughts almost continuously since last Friday.

I have to talk with her. But she won't return my calls. Damn! This is making me crazy. I should...okay, stop. You're an engineer. Calm down and think this through.

Okay, now. You did your best to reach her. You called Monday as you said you would. No answer, left message, no return call. You called yesterday morning and twice last night. Same result. And three times today. So, what are the possibilities?

One, she's not interested and is avoiding me. Under different circumstances, maybe. But I don't think so. There are too many holes in that theory. First, we had a great time Friday. Second, she kissed me. Third, she agreed to see me Monday. Man, she was nothing like what I expected. That idiot Mike had no idea who she is or what she's about. How could he miss how sharp and funny she is? And how smart and sweet and sassy and sexy and forthright, and...stop, calm down. You're getting carried away again. Okay, so we had a great time Friday and unless Priya was acting, she liked me. I'm sure of it. And unless I completely misread her, if she wasn't attracted to me, she would have just told me when I dropped her off. She wouldn't be playing some avoidance game. So much for that one.

Two, something happened to her father or brother when they were here. But wouldn't she at least have called just to let me know?

Three, she's sick. But why wouldn't she answer the phone? Unless she's in the hospital. But how do I find out?

Four...what else would keep her from returning my calls? Am I kidding myself here? Was Mike right after all about her being a psycho? No, I can't believe that. I won't believe that. But something isn't right.

His eyes lost focus as he pondered his next move. He toyed with the idea of going to her apartment and ringing the bell, but what if she didn't answer? Maybe he should just wait outside her building, but that seemed too creepy. He sighed, and smiled as an image of her smiling popped into his head.

His hands massaged the armrests as his mind's eye focused on her face. *You'll reach her soon*, he told himself, and returned to remembering her smile.

10:22 PM

Jillian glanced at the clock when her cell phone rang.

It has to be Paul. He just went home a little while ago, but who else would call at this hour? Is he missing me already? Or did he think of another goofy pun? Or maybe...

She knew her funk of the past few days worried him. He kept it to himself, but she noticed the way he studied her sometimes. A surge of guilt coursed through her.

Why can't I tell him?

She flipped open the phone and saw it was not him at all.

"Hi!"

"Are you alone?"

"Yes."

"Good. Buzz me in. I'm standing at the door downstairs."

"Wha..."

Liz had disconnected.

When she opened the apartment door, Liz walked in carrying a bag and her jacket. She hung the jacket on a peg, pointed to the sofa, and said, "Sit."

"Liz...

"Just sit."

Confused, Jillian shrugged and sat. Liz settled down next to her, so close their hips and legs were touching. Then she reached in the bag and removed a bottle of Irish Mist and two shot glasses.

"Ohhh." Jillian understood now. It was Truth Time. "But Liz..."

"Quiet. You know the rules."

The ritual developed over several years. It began when the girls were seventeen and Liz snuck a half-full bottle of her mother's Irish Mist up to her bedroom during a sleepover. By freshman year in college, the rules were set.

Whenever one of them realized the other was depressed, or had a big problem, she arranged for some private time and a bottle of Irish Mist. No words were exchanged until each downed their first shot. Then, the initiator spelled out why she arranged a Truth Time. Then they talked. The glasses were refilled every fifteen minutes, or if one person thought the other was not being truthful, until the whole truth came out, the problem was resolved, or the bottle was empty. Only absolute openness and truth were permitted and neither could carry a grudge over anything that was said. In eight years, the ritual was invoked many times, but the bottle emptied only once.

Liz poured the first shots and the two friends clinked glasses before downing the sweet liquid.

"There are three problems we need to address tonight. First, what to do about Aiden if he's back. Two, what to tell Paul, when, and how. Three, why my best friend in the whole freaking world has left me hanging, worrying about her twice in the past two weeks. I'd prefer to deal with the last one first."

She glared at Jillian.

"*How* could you *not* call me back last night or today?"

Jillian put her glass on the table and hugged her.

"I'm so sorry, Liz. I'm so messed up over this ghost I can't think straight. I know I should have called you, and I really am sorry, but the truth is, I didn't think of it. All I can think about is…is him."

She sat back up, feeling miserable.

"I saw him again this morning. When Paul and I were on the train, I glanced out the window and there he was, standing on the platform near the steps.

"I can't get him out of my head, Lizzy. And I don't want him there. I can't stand him there. It's making me remember things, feelings, good ones *and* bad. Even when I'm with Paul he keeps pushing into my thoughts. And I know Paul can tell something's wrong. But what can I say? I'm with you, sweetheart, but I'm thinking about this asshole who ran out on me years ago?"

Tears cascaded down her cheeks.

"I don't know what to do, Lizzy. He won't go away and it's ruining things."

She was sobbing now as all the emotions of the past few days came spilling out.

"Damn him. I hate him, I hate him, I hate him!"

Liz took her hand and held it for a minute until the tears stopped.

"Okay, let's back up for a minute. Do you really think it was him you saw?"

"Yes. It has to be him. If it had only been once, I could believe it was someone who resembles him. But three times? And each time he's watching me?"

Liz nodded. "I think you're right. Let's assume it is him, that he's back." She saw a shiver run through Jillian. "Do you really hate him?"

Jillian nodded silently.

"But do you still love him, too?"

"No!" Jillian paused and looked away. "No…I don't know."

Liz refilled the glasses and handed one to Jillian. Again they touched glasses and downed the shots.

"Do you still love him?"

"I don't know." It was a whine more than a statement, prompting Liz to refill the glasses yet again.

"Do you still love him?" she asked for the third time when both glasses were back on the table.

This time, Jillian sat quietly for almost three minutes before she answered. "Lord help me, Lizzy, I think a small part of me still does. I think that may be why I've been so confused, why I can't get him out of my head." From the corner of her eye, she could see Liz nodding in agreement. "Most of me wants to scream at him and hurt him for what he did. But another part, a tiny part, wants to hold him again. How can that be? How can I feel *anything* for him?"

"You never had any closure with Aiden. Maybe that's why he's still haunting you. You know about that fine line between love and hate, Jilli. Maybe you're confusing the two. But whatever it is, you have to be careful. Paul is a really great guy. Even on your first date I could see how much he cares for you. Somehow, you have to find a way to let go of Aiden for good. His memory has been ruining things for you for too long. I think you have to tell Paul the whole story, sweetie."

"I know. I know I should tell him, but we haven't even been together two weeks. I don't want to dump my miserable past on him so soon. It's not fair."

"Maybe so, but if it *was* him, chances are Paul *will* find out. He should hear it from you, first."

Liz heard her friend sigh again.

I wish I had some magic words to banish that asshole and his memory forever so she can finally move on with life. If only the bastard had the guts to face her that day. But he didn't and she's been paying the price ever since.

"But what if I'm wrong? What if it wasn't him? Then I look like some paranoid fool. Or worse! Like I'm trying to manipulate Paul into feeling sorry for me. I can't do that, Lizzy. I can't take that chance. Especially not after I spied on him before we even went out."

She closed her eyes, took a deep breath, and held it for a few seconds. By the time she slowly released it, her decision was made.

"I have to handle this on my own, Liz. Well, not on my own. With your help. But I can't inflict it on Paul. I know he'd want to help, but he can't.

"I think you're right about my needing closure. If it *is* him, he'll eventually find the nerve to approach me. When he does, I have to deal with him as an equal. Whatever happens, it has to be me, alone, making the decisions, and me, alone, suffering the consequences if there are any."

"Are you sure about this, Jilli? Paul…"

"Paul is a wonderful guy. But he's not my husband and he's not my fiancée. He's my boyfriend. I'm not going back to how it was with Aiden, him being the leader, the strong one, and me just following along. Paul and I are equals, and if we're to stay that way, I can't expect him to shelter me from life. He can beat up a bad guy now and then 'cause he's stronger, but the rest of it is my responsibility. Does that make sense?"

The gleam of admiration and pride in Liz's eyes let her know it made perfect sense.

Jillian picked up the bottle and poured them both another shot. This time, truth having been told, they sat back and sipped.

THURSDAY, MAY 20

9:25 AM

Priya clicked *Save* and closed the graphic for the back cover. She glanced at Paul, watching for a few seconds as he poured over the final draft of the manuscript, searching for errors.

I wonder if he knows how much he's changed these past two weeks. Probably not. But I can see it.

She could see the undercurrent of joy that made his step a bit lighter, his smile a bit brighter, and made him act like a man in love.

I wonder if it's the same with Jillian? She certainly seems happy whenever I see her. Not that I see her all that much with him taking up all her time. But Monday was great. Talking, joking, sharing for hours. It's been so long since I've had a friend to do that with.

Paul stretched, caught her eye and smiled before continuing with his work. He was still in her heart, but not as strongly as before.

I wonder if it's a fear of messing things up with Jillian that's causing my feelings for Paul to fade so quickly.

Any doubts about how Jillian felt were dispelled when she arrived home last evening to find a card from her in the mail.

I don't know if we'll be friends forever

But I'm looking forward to finding out

Then, not an hour later, she called to invite her to join the Thursday dinner group.

Priya examined her feelings as she eyed Tom and Rob. She was more than a little nervous about dinner tonight. Jillian assured her all the girls knew the truth about what happened two weeks ago, but even still, Priya could not help feeling apprehensive. For too long she shied away from such gatherings, having too often experienced the looks, the subtle cattiness, and backhanded compliments other women seemed to feel she deserved by virtue of her appearance. But Jillian really wanted her to go and Priya, having tasted again the joy of having a real girlfriend, would endure a roomful of scorn, if necessary, to make her new friend happy.

Yes, that has to be what's damping the romantic feelings for him. Jillian likes Paul...more than she admits, I think...and I want to make her happy. Which means I don't want to make her sad. And if anything romantic ever happened between me and Paul it would make Jillian very sad. So the only way to ensure that never happens is to not have any romantic feelings for him. Which is why the feelings are fading.

She was smiling at the insight when a new thought popped into her head.

What would have happened if I'd realized my feelings for him and let him know before he met Jillian? Who would he have chosen?

"I guess we'll never know," she muttered unconsciously.

"Never know what?"

Tom asked again a bit louder when Priya didn't respond.

Startled, Priya said, "I'm sorry. What did you say?"

"I asked you what it was you guess we'll never know, but you were somewhere else so I said it louder and you still didn't hear me. I think I speak for all of us when I ask again what we'll never know."

Oh great. What do I say now? I'll have to lie to my friends again. Or will I?

"I was thinking about, well, someone, about how I'll never know how things would have worked out if..."

Priya's phone rang.

Talk about good timing.

She reached for the receiver. "Hold that thought."

"Priya Kumar."

Tom rose, muttered he would be back in ten minutes, and started for the door.

"Priya! Hi! It's Brian! I'm so glad I found you!"

"Oh. Hello, Brian." Her voice was flat, devoid of emotion. "I'm pretty busy right now."

At the mention of Brian's name, Tom turned on his heal and returned to his desk where he perched on the corner and joined the other two who weren't even pretending not to listen.

"I know I shouldn't have called you at work, but I was worried something might have happened when I didn't hear back from you. I thought we had a pretty good time Friday, and there was something I needed to tell you, and..."

"Brian, stop. I know what's going on, okay. I know about your little game and I really don't have the time or the inclination."

"What are you talking about?"

"About nailing the…" She'd almost said 'virgin' but caught herself. Tom and Rob did not need to know that about her. "Look, someone heard two of your friends talking about you and me. I know the whole thing and I don't appreciate being played like that, okay? You took your shot, it didn't work out, so move on. Please don't call me again."

"But Pr…"

Priya hung up the phone, reached to the side of the base, pulled out the cord, and turned back to her work. "I'm out of the office for a while."

9:40 AM

"What the *hell* just happened?"

"What's up? Did the network crash?"

Ralph Witherspoon was one of those uber-focused, incredibly smart guys who considered the label *geek* a compliment. So it was no surprise he was so completely absorbed in his work he did not hear Brian on the phone. He turned his head away from his monitor to find Brian pacing in front of his work station rather than sitting at it. Most people would have realized the problem was not one that could be solved at the keyboard, but Ralph was not most people.

"I asked if the network crashed."

Brian came to a halt and snapped, "Ralph, what the hell? If the network crashed, would I be standing here or would I be online trying to fix it?"

Most bosses might have been annoyed at the insolence, but Ralph was not most bosses. "Oh. Yes. I see." He started to turn back to work but caught himself. "Uh, then what *is* wrong?"

Brian was so startled Ralph actually showed unprompted interest, he told him.

"Remember last Friday, I said I was going out with this really great girl? Her name is Priya." He knew better than to expect a response. "Well, we did go out and had a great time. A really great time. And when I dropped her off, we made plans to talk on Monday. But when Monday rolled around, she never returned my calls. Same thing Tuesday and yesterday. So today I call her at work and she blows me off with some story about me playing some game, something about nailing her. Why the hell would she say that?"

Again, Brian was not expecting a response and so was unprepared when Ralph asked, "Were you?"

"What?"

"Were you playing some game to nail her?"

"No, of course not."

Ralph arched his eyebrows high over the frame of his thick glasses.

"I swear. I really like her. She's the girl Mike Conyers dated a few months ago. Remember when he came around every day bragging about how he was going to fuck this Indian girl?" Ralph's blank stare was followed by a slight shake of the head. "Well he did. I saw her in a bar last week and I wanted to find out if she was as crazy as Mike said. But she turned out to be great, really great. So I asked her out. And I should have told her about knowing who she was right up front, but I didn't. I wanted to tell her the next day, but her family was in town and by Monday, somehow she got the idea I was messing with her head. Oh man, this really sucks."

"Perhaps Mike was right and she *is* crazy."

"No. It's not that. She said she heard people talking about me and her. But who? You're the only one I… Ralph! Did you tell Mike I was going out with her?"

"I don't know. Maybe." He sat and thought for several seconds. Brian knew he was playing the days back in his memory. "Friday afternoon I was in accounting and one of the guys there asked how you were doing. I don't know his name. I told him you were fine. He asked me if I was getting any pussy. I think he was making a joke because when I told him I wasn't he laughed and said computer guys never get any pussy. Then I told him you were going out with a beautiful Indian girl that night. He asked me her name, but I wasn't sure. He asked if it was Priya and I recognized the name and said yes.

"Perhaps this guy in accounting knows Mike. Maybe they were the ones talking about you."

Another boss might have been annoyed when Brian spun around and raced out of the room without a word, but Ralph was not another boss. Before the door finished closing, he was back to writing code, the conversation with Brian already forgotten.

7:50 PM

Priya stood nervously outside the entrance to *Ginza* on Hudson Street, hoping she made the right decision.

After work, she splurged on a taxi to ensure she would have plenty of time to pick just the right outfit. The plan was to look good, but not too good. No tight sweaters, low-cut blouses, or short skirts. She wanted to make friends tonight, not scare off people.

By the time she stood in front of her mirror, satisfied, half her wardrobe lay scattered on the floor. The rest lay in piles on her bed. The outfit she settled on – a cream-colored silk, square-neck shirt under a long, salt and pepper colored cardigan sweater, flare-leg black pants, and her black Steve Madden ankle high, low heel boots – was perfect. She looked good; feminine, but not sexy.

Now, she bounced on her heels as she waited, trying to burn off some of her nervous energy, when a voice to her left said, "Hi! Are you Priya?"

She turned and saw a pretty, almost boyishly thin, thirtyish woman smiling at her.

"I'm Maggie." She extended her hand as her eyes flashed with amusement. "You hiding out here waiting for Jillian?"

Priya blushed and nodded as she shook hands. "I thought I should since I wouldn't recognize anyone in the group."

Again Maggie's eyes flashed. "You shouldn't have worried. *Everyone* knows what *you* look like."

Priya's blush deepened and discomfort crept into her eyes.

Maggie noticed and immediately apologized. "Hey, I'm sorry. I was kidding around. I didn't mean to make you feel weird. When Jilli told us last week that she was thinking of inviting you to join the group, everyone was very enthusiastic. Really. I mean, we all sort of hated you for a week when we thought you were stealing Jilli's new guy, but when she explained it all, well, everyone got over it. Believe me, you can expect nothing but friendly faces tonight. And if anyone gets out of line, smack 'em with some sushi."

Priya laughed and found herself relaxing. "I *was* a little worried about the reception I'd get."

"I can imagine. And with your looks, I bet you have to put up with a lot of crap from other women."

"Sometimes." *If you only knew.*

"Well not to worry. Nobody here is insecure, nobody likes to be nasty or catty without cause, and nobody will give you a hard time about being a hooker."

"Wh...what! I'm not..."

"A hooker? Really, it's okay. You don't have to pretend. Jillian told us that was why you were with Paul that night. That his friend had hired you as a gift for him. To tell the truth, we've all been anticipating some great stories about the guys you've been with. Most of the girls are relatively tame – the ones who are into the relationship thing and all, but a couple of us can get a bit raunchy sometimes talking about the guys we've had. Especially me. I'm sort of the group slut."

Priya's head was spinning. "Excuse me?"

"I like guys, I like sex, I like variety, and I like a lot of each. Give me a nice stiff dick on a guy who knows how to use it and I'm set for the weekend. Of course, I suppose being a professional, you don't really get into it much. Or do you?"

Priya's color deepened. She was speechless.

Did Jillian really tell these women I'm a whore? Was it all an act? Has she been setting me up for some kind of humiliation?

"Oh, look at you. Blushing like a virgin. Your clients must love that. But come on, let's go in and get settled. Jillian, Jenna and Liz will be here soon." She checked her watch. "Their yoga class should be wrapping up right about now."

"Wait a second," Priya barked, her eyes flashing with fury. "I don't know what's going on here but I am not some kind of prostitute. I don't know who told you people what but there is no way…" She stopped as she realized Maggie was collapsing with laughter. Her fury became confusion, then understanding.

"This was all a joke?" The anger was returning.

"Oh, lord, I'm sorry," Maggie managed to get out as she forced herself to stop laughing. "I really am sorry. That was so bad, even for me. Please don't be mad, Priya. Jillian made us all promise to be on our best behavior at dinner 'cause this was your first time and she really likes you, but when I saw you standing there, I don't know, something came over me and I couldn't help myself. Please don't hate me. I swear I never would have done it if any of the others were around. It's just that Jilli told us you were like really sweet and nice and innocent, and, well, you know, and the thought of you being a hooker was so polar opposite to who she said you really are that I…"

Priya's fury cut her off. "I don't believe this! Jillian told you all I was a virgin?"

Maggie started and shook her head, suddenly at a loss for words "What? A…did you…are you…oh my go…" It was her turn for incredulity.

It took only a second for her reaction to make Priya realize she jumped to the wrong conclusion. *How can I have done this again?* She paled as she realized that now everyone in the group would know.

"Oh Priya, I'm so sorry. My stupid joke made you say something you obviously didn't want…damn." She moved in closer, until the two were only inches apart. "I know you don't know me yet but you can trust me. I swear I will never speak of this to anyone. Not even Jillian. Please believe me. And please forgive me for being such a bitch. Damn! I feel terrible now."

Her agitation seemed to spin out of control. She moved back a step and smacked her forehead three times with the heel of her hand, just like in the movies. "Stupid, stupid, stupid! Look, I really am sorry. I'll just go. Don't even tell anyone you saw me and they'll all just think I couldn't make it this week." She turned to leave.

Priya was suddenly unsure what to make of it all. Clearly the woman was upset over what happened, but she could not let her leave like this.

"Maggie, wait. Please don't leave. Someday, I promise you I'll get you back big-time for that joke, but the rest was my fault for assuming something instead of finding out for sure. It's really not that big a deal that you know, although I *would* appreciate you not saying anything to the others. If we all get along and I start coming regularly, I'll probably eventually tell them. But for now, it would just make things weird. Okay?"

There was no mistaking Maggie's relief. "Okay. And thank you so much. Maybe this will teach me a lesson. Then again, knowing me, probably not. But thank you for being so nice about it." She chuckled. "What a pair we are. The virgin and the slut." In response to Priya's surprise, she added, "Oh, I wasn't kidding about that part. I've been with more guys than I can remember. Hundreds."

"But why?" Priya asked.

"I told you. I like guys, I like sex, and I like variety."

Priya's eyes focused on Maggie's as she pondered her explanation. She saw something, felt something, but was unsure of what it was. After a few seconds, she shook her head slightly and muttered, "No, I think it's more complex than that."

"What?"

"I'm sorry, it's nothing. Just thinking out loud. Why don't we go in so I can meet the other girls."

Maggie was introducing Priya to Gloria, Marissa, Holly, and Shandra as Jillian, Liz, and Jenna arrived. The women took turns asking Priya questions about her background and work. Everyone was polite, almost to a fault, but something was wrong. Despite Jillian's assurance that Priya was a regular person, there was tension around the table. The usually open and free banter was missing. Nobody was telling jokes, nobody was ragging on anyone. It felt more like a gathering of old society mavens than a night out with the girls.

Soon, Maggie could stand it no longer. "What the hell is going on here tonight?"

Everyone turned to stare without responding.

"We're all acting like some kind of pod people because Priya's here? A really pretty girl comes along and all of a sudden we're all so insecure we can't relax and be ourselves?"

Again no one spoke.

"Well that sucks."

She turned to their guest. "Priya, I'm really sorry about this. Usually we're a pretty wild bunch but obviously some of us find you intimidating. So screw it. If we can't have fun tonight, I want to at least learn something. Do you mind if I ask you something personal?"

Priya wasn't sure what to expect, but anything was better than the strained geniality of the past fifteen minutes.

"Not at all. Ask away."

"Look, this isn't the kind of thing I'd normally ask someone I just met, but I'm *sure* everyone here is *dying* to know the answer."

She paused for a few seconds as all the girls fidgeted with curious expectation. Then, when even Priya had leaned forward slightly in anticipation, she pointed at Priya's chest and asked, "Are those real?"

Priya blinked twice, then broke into a gleeful smile. She flashed on the day a few months ago she used a similar shock tactic to make a point with her new co-workers. Then she took in the expressions of the girls around the table, met Maggie's eyes again, and said, "One hundred percent real. Why? Do you want to feel them or were you looking for a referral?"

The entire table erupted with laughter. All it took was that one simple exchange to prove she really was one of the girls. The ice was broken and the conversation began to flow as, now, everyone *really* wanted to get to know her.

Ten minutes later, as the waiter was taking orders, Priya caught Maggie's eye. A slight smile and nod of her head conveyed her thanks. Maggie's return grin and raised eyebrows told her she was welcome and the look in her eye told her something more. She made another new friend!

11:40 PM

"Ohmygod," Rob panted. "That was amazing."

His breathing slowed but his eyes remained closed, his face contorted. After a minute or so, he blinked his eyes open to find Lisa watching him, beaming with pleasure and satisfaction.

"What are you grinning at?" His hand reached out to caress her cheek, then drifted lower to her breast.

"I was just watching you. Your face was all scrunched up and you were making those noises and you seemed to be in such pain. Maybe we should stop doing that." A soft, "Mmmmm" escaped her lips as his other hand joined the first.

"Stop? Sure we can stop. Want to stop this, too? Or this?" His right hand drifted lower.

Lisa squirmed and lay forward on his chest. Her arms snaked around his neck as her lips sought his. Rob tugged his hands out from beneath her, hugged her close and began to lightly scratch between her shoulder blades as they kissed.

A few minutes later, as her head rested on his shoulder, he asked, "Where did you learn to do that? What you did before. Should I be getting jealous? Or worried?"

"You bet. I found a guy who knows lots of new tricks."

"Oh really? What's this new guy's name?"

"Hector."

"Hector? You mean Hector from work? Gay Hector?"

Lisa laughed and leaned up so she could see his eyes. "Yes, gay Hector from work."

Rob looked doubtful. "How does Hector know about, you know, girl parts and what to do with them? Especially something like that!"

Lisa cocked her head to the side and said, "I don't know. I never thought to ask him. But from your reaction, it sure seems like he knew what he was talking about!"

Rob's arms drew her back down. Her head settled back onto his shoulder. "So this is the kind of thing you two talk about at work, eh?"

"Sometimes. It's just girl talk."

Rob chuckled as he rolled them both on their sides. "Girl talk? With a guy?"

"A gay guy. A *very* gay guy."

Rob continued chuckling as Lisa grabbed the sheet and dragged it over them. When she settled back down, he began to gently stroke her hair. "You know...I've been thinking."

"Always a dangerous activity."

Rob faked a scowl but it quickly turned into a smile. "Seriously. Do you love me? I mean, really love me?"

'Don't I tell you I do every day?"

"You do. But please answer the question."

"Yes, Robbie, I love you." Then, dramatically, "I really, truly, deeply, *madly* love you."

His face lit up with a grin. "Ah, you're only saying that because you're still horny."

Lisa feigned indignation. "So what if I am?" She reached under the sheets and took him in her hand. "A fat lot of good this guy will do me. He won't be ready again for an hour."

"Is it any wonder after what you just did to him?"

They both started laughing. Lisa marveled at the ease with which their intimacy came. There were no head games, no needy reassurances necessary. Rob was a good lover and he knew it. He knew how to please her and was willing to try almost anything to make her happy. She leaned in and kissed him softly on the forehead. "I do so love you, Robbie."

With a satisfied sigh, he said, "And I love you, too."

They settled in, arms around each other, and simply enjoyed the feel of skin against skin. They fit so well together even their breathing soon synchronized, one inhaling as the other exhaled, and the gentle rhythm lulled them to sleep.

FRIDAY, MAY 21

12:05 AM

"Thank you for inviting me," Priya told Jillian as she hugged her. "I had a really nice time. The girls are all great. I hope you'll have me again sometime."

Jillian laughed. They were standing inside the door to the restaurant, waiting for Liz and Jenna, who stopped by the ladies room. "What are you talking about, 'have you again'? You're part of the group now...if you want to be." She reached out and touched Priya's arm. "I hope you'll want to be."

"I do! But I thought you all had to vote or something."

Again Jillian laughed. "No. If anyone had any reservations about you, they'd have let me know. Now, you heard Jenna say we're going to Sabatino's in the North End next week?"

Priya nodded.

"Jenna always picks a place in the North End when it's her turn. She loves Italian even more than I do. As the newest member, you'll get to pick the spot for the following week. That is, if you come next week."

"I don't know if I'll come, but I'll definitely be there."

It took almost a second to sink in. "Priya! I can't believe you said that!"

It was Priya's turn to laugh. "I know! I think it's this town. Lately, I've been surprising myself with some of the things I say. But you know what. I like it. It feels good to let go, even if it *is* just with words."

A minute later, Liz, Jenna, and Maggie emerged from the ladies room and joined them.

Jenna's head tilted. "So?"

"She's in."

"Excellent!" Liz turned to Priya. "You know, some of us were a bit nervous about the prospect of you joining the group."

"I sort of had that feeling when Maggie and I walked in earlier."

"Well, Jillian kept telling everyone what you were really like, but I think most of us couldn't get past how friggin' beautiful you are."

Jenna agreed, and added, "But when you came in dressed like that and you sort of blew everyone away with being, I don't know, just a girl like the rest of us, well, all I can say is everyone would have been very disappointed if you hadn't wanted to join us."

Priya was pleased, but slightly embarrassed. Women never before treated her like this. She said a quick, silent prayer she would not wake up and find the night was all a dream.

Liz yawned loudly and asked, "Anyone want a ride?"

Jillian nodded and Priya said, "Sure, but I live out in Brighton."

"Where in Brighton?" Maggie asked.

"Royce Road. It's the first street on the left after the intersection with Harvard Ave."

"I'm going that way if you don't mind riding with me."

"Not at all. That would be great."

Ten minutes later they were sitting in traffic waiting for the light to change.

"You know, you were very impressive tonight."

"Thank you. I was pretty nervous going in and it got worse when everyone seemed so uncomfortable. But what you did, what you said, that was perfect. It really was inspired. I don't know how to thank you."

"No need. Let's call it even for the joke I played when we…Son-of-a-bitch!" Maggie jammed on the brakes as a small car flew out of the side street just after the light changed, cutting her off.

Priya could see five heads in the car jerking around as if they were laughing or partying. "That's why I don't drive in this city."

They talked about Boston drivers for the few remaining minutes it took to reach Royce Road.

Maggie stopped the car in front of Priya's building, shifted into *Park*, but left the engine running. "Can I ask you something personal?"

"Sure." Priya turned to face her.

"You don't have many girlfriends, do you?"

Priya tried to see into Maggie's eyes in the dim light from the streetlamp and what reflected from the car's headlights, but the shadows were too deep. "What makes you ask that?"

"Your nervousness early on, and then you seemed so happy everyone liked you. Little things you said and did, or maybe more the way you said and did them. Plus, I don't know, a little undercurrent of loneliness, I guess. Forgive me if I'm wrong. It was just a feeling."

Priya was impressed this woman read her so well. "You're right. Jillian's my only real girlfriend, and that only happened recently." She grinned and snorted. "I guess you probably knew that. And there's Lisa. She's Paul's best friend's girlfriend. We've sort of been getting friendly."

"Can I ask you something else?"

"Of course."

"What did you mean earlier, when you said you thought it was more complex?"

"Huh?"

"Before we went into the restaurant, I told you I was the group slut and you asked why and when I answered, you hesitated for a second and muttered, 'No, I think it's more complex than that'."

"Oh." Priya fidgeted a little.

"Please, you won't hurt my feelings or anything. What did you mean?"

"I...well, I had the feeling you were putting on a face, playing a role and saying what you thought I expected to hear, or maybe what you wanted me to hear, rather than the truth. I...never mind. It's nothing."

"Say it. Please. You what?"

"Maggie, I'm certainly no authority on sex. Heck, I'm as far from it as you can get, but I can't believe any girl sleeps with so many men simply because she likes sex. Surely you've been with many men who were great lovers. If good sex was all that mattered, why not stay with one of them? Or a couple of them? No, there's something more going on. Something happened to you. I don't know what, but something made you want to or need to hide part of yourself from the world. Something hurt your heart and..."

Priya saw silent tears glistening in the dim light as they ran down Maggie's cheeks. "Oh, Maggie, I'm sorry. I don't know what I'm talking about. Please don't cry. I wasn't trying to hurt you."

"No. No, you didn't hurt me. You...you're right." The tears flowed full force now. "You...nobody's ever seen that before. Nobody's ever wondered or cared enough to even ask."

Priya leaned awkwardly across the center console and put her arms around the distraught girl. "It's okay. It'll be okay."

"No it won't. It'll never be okay. You know how I could tell you were lonely? Because I'm so lonely I want to scream sometimes. Everyone thinks ol' Maggie's life is all fun and games. But it's not. Some women eat and some women throw themselves into meaningless work. I fuck a lot. I do it so I can feel someone next to me, so I can feel alive, so I can..."

She started shaking as she cried and Priya realized the girl who was so lively, so much fun at dinner really *was* a façade.

Inside is a woman who's desperate for companionship and love, but doesn't know how to find it. Or won't let herself find it.

"Maggie. Would you like to come in and talk for a while? Why don't you park over there and come in."

"No," she replied between sobs, "you have to get up for work in the morning. I don't want to burden you with all this."

Priya leaned back and rested a hand on Maggie's arm. "You are not a burden. I'd like to think of you as my friend. And when you know me better, you'll find out I am always there for my friends. Please, you need to talk. You need to tell someone what's bothering you, what's haunting you."

Maggie didn't accept, but neither did she refuse. Priya sensed she wanted to be convinced. "I have beer and vodka and coffee and... Hey! We can have a grownup pajama party. Come on, we can both call in sick tomorrow if necessary, but this is way more important than work."

An automobile horn honked behind them.

Maggie smiled and wiped at her eyes with her fists. "You're not just being kind? You really want me to come in?"

"Yes, I really do."

"Well, I suppose I do know your secret, so it's only fair that you know mine."

12:35 AM

Paul hit the mute button and grabbed his cell. "Hi sweetie."

"Hi yourself. I thought you'd be sleeping."

"Nah. I decided to watch *The Tonight Show* and wait for you to call. So how'd it go?"

"Fine. Priya was a big hit and now she's part of the group."

"I'm almost sorry to hear that. I was getting used to hanging with her on Thursday nights. Maybe I'll take up bowling or something."

They chatted for a few minutes about their workdays, which were uneventful, and Paul's evening, which encompassed some web surfing, some television, some laundry, and some beer. Jillian gave him a few more details about the dinner and everyone's reaction to Priya.

When a pause in the conversation stretched out, Paul decided it was time to get some answers. "Jilli, can I ask you something?"

"Of course."

"What's wrong? I know something's been bothering you all week. It's like part of you has been somewhere else whenever we talk, even when we've been together. Is it that guy you thought you saw Sunday? Is there some problem? I mean, that's when it seemed to start. Whatever it is, I want to help."

Jillian heard the worry in his voice and felt terrible as she listened to him all but plead with her to talk to him, to let him be there for her.

"I'm sorry, Paul. You're right. A part of me has been somewhere else this week.

"Sunday morning, well, it dredged up some very unhappy memories. Memories I buried because they were too painful. But I know I can't keep hiding forever. Painful as they are, the time has come to face them."

She paused to collect her thoughts.

If Aiden's really back in town, telling Paul will only make him worry more. But I can't lie to him. I won't. I've been hurt too many times by lies and I won't start a new relationship with a lie.

"I've been avoiding my past for a long time, Paul, building walls and dodging hurt. But meeting you changed everything. Somehow, without even trying, you've reopened a part of me I kept closed off and it feels wonderful. Just knowing you'll be there for me if I need you has given me strength I forgot I had. This ghost or demon has been with me long enough, and now it's time to deal with it. But it's something I need to work through on my own."

"So, you're telling me I can't fix this for you?"

He sounded like he was pouting, which drew a short laugh from her. "You probably could. I've started to believe you could do almost anything. But you've already beaten off one bad guy for me." Her voice turned serious again. "Paul, I have to know I can face this myself, on my own. If I don't, I'm not sure I'll ever be the girl I see reflected in your eyes. And I want to be that girl, Paul. I want to be her for you, but I *need* to be her for me.

"There'll be lots of things in the future we'll have to face together, but this one I have to do alone, to know I *can* do it alone. But I can't talk about it until it's done. Okay? Please?"

Ten minutes later, after saying goodnight, Paul sat and stared at a silent beer commercial.

Something doesn't feel right. Whatever it is, or whoever it is, it's huge...maybe big enough to change everything. But she didn't sound worried. Scared maybe, but sure of herself, of what she thinks she has to do. I guess I should feel good about that. But I hate not knowing. Or maybe I hate feeling helpless. But she knows she can count on me. She knows how I feel about her. I guess all I can do is take her at her word and carry on as if nothing's wrong and hope it's enough.

4:10 AM

Rob woke with a start, still locked in the arms of his best friend and lover. Her head rested on his left arm, her cheek nestled against his chest. As usual, her left arm and leg were thrown over him, maximizing body contact as they slept. He wanted to lean his head back and watch her sleeping, but in this position, he could hardly move.

A dream awakened him, one he found both exiting and disturbing. In the dream, he was in bed with Lisa, much as he was now. They talked some as usually happened at bedtime and they made love. But then…

He shook his head. Was this a sign? Were the fates telling him something? Or was he trying to tell himself something? As suddenly as he woke, he knew what he wanted to do, what he had to do. And right now.

Gently, he began to caress her cheek and neck until she began to stir.

"Lisa."

"Hmmmmm."

"Lisa, wake up baby."

She groaned and asked, "What time is it?"

"I don't know. You're head's on my arm and I can't move to look at the clock. Lift your head up a little."

Without opening her eyes, she complied. Rob extricated his arm then turned to check the time. "It's almost quarter past four."

"Ohhhh. What are you waking me up now for?"

"Come on, honey, please. Open your eyes. I need to talk with you about something."

"Now?"

"Yes." He ran his fingertips along her side and hip.

Lisa scooted away from the tickling fingers, but opened her sleepy eyes. "What's wrong, Robbie?"

"Nothing. Nothing's wrong. I had a dream, and it started me thinking, and I need to talk to you about it right now."

Lisa rubbed her face with both hands and leaned up slightly on one arm. She regarded him with a mixture of curiosity and amusement, unable to imagine what had him so riled up at this hour.

"Remember last night, after we made love, we were talking about how much we love each other?"

"Of course."

"Well, I've been thinking. In the two weeks since we've been back together, I've stayed over here every night but one, and that night you stayed over my place. And in the month or so before the break, it was pretty much the same thing. And two people who love each other as much as we do, who get along the way we do, who have so much in common yet complement one another as well as we do, well, I think those two people should be considering their future together. Don't you?"

"I don't know," she said cautiously. "I guess so. But at four in the morning?" Through the fog in her still-sleepy brain, she wondered what this was all about. Waking her at this hour to talk about anything, much less their future was not like him.

Rob jumped out of bed and started to turn slowly around. "Lisa, this is me, standing naked before you. Not just naked in body, but in mind and heart and soul.

"You are the best person I've ever known and I love you so much that sometimes I think I'll burst from happiness. When I walk out the door each morning, all I can think about is walking back through it after work so I can see you again and talk to you again, and hold you again. When I think of how close I came to losing you…" He visibly shuddered at the thought, then fell to his knees at the side of the bed.

Lisa's eyes widened.

Oh no! He's not…he can't.

"Lisa, the break made realize I don't want to live without you, that I can't live without you. You're my sunshine, my music, my sugar and spice. You're everything I could ever want."

"Robbie…"

His hand came up.

"I know I'll never be the best looking guy, or the funniest guy, or the richest guy who wants you. And I'll never be the smartest, the buffest, or the best read. But Lisa, I swear that no guy will ever love you as much as I do. No guy in this world will ever care for you the way I will. And no guy will ever be as thankful as I'll be each morning when I wake up beside you."

Please, Robbie. Don't.

"Lisa, I want to love you and care for you and make you happy for the rest of my life. I…I never thought I'd ever ask a girl this, but Lisa…will you live with me?"

Oh thank you, lord. Live with him.

"Live with you?"

"Yes. Live with me. After."

"After? After what?"

"After we're married, of course. Please, Lisa. Please. Will you marry me?"

6:12 AM

Priya glanced at the clock as she lay a blanket over the sleeping form on the sofa. There was no way she was going to work today. She left a message on Tom's voice mail then walked into to the alcove that held her computer, removed two sheets of paper from the printer tray, and wrote two notes.

The first she placed on top of Maggie's purse.

Good morning, unless it's afternoon in which case, good afternoon.
If you're reading this, I'm still asleep. I'm really glad you stayed last night. In case you don't remember, you called in to work about 2:30. I called in, too, so we both have the day off.

I took your clothes out of the bathroom and folded them. They're in the plastic bag next to the sofa but they're pretty messed up, so don't try to wear them. I have some things that should fit you.

Please come in and wake me. I'm guessing we'll both need strong coffee when we get up.

Priya

The second, written in big red letters, she taped to the door to the apartment, over the lock.

Don't you DARE leave this apartment without waking me first.
Please.
I want to talk with you.

Priya

She returned to her bedroom and slid under the covers. As she reached to turn off the ringer on the phone, she noticed the message indicator on the answering machine was blinking. She pressed the play button and heard

"Hello, Priya. Please, I really need to talk with you. I don't know what..."

She hit the delete button, not bothering to listen to the rest of the message. She was tired. And happy. And even Brian and his games couldn't get her down today.

A sigh escaped as her head hit the pillow, her mind reviewing the previous hours with Maggie. She felt her eyes fill with tears as she remembered Maggie's story of a lost first love, of almost unbearable pain, and of the unfortunate method she fell into for ensuring she would never feel that pain again. The tears ran down her cheeks with the memory of the agony and emptiness, the longing and suppression, the denial and acceptance.

She thanked the gods for her father and the talk that led to her vow. She shuddered at the thought the same thing could have happened to her had she not eschewed sex.

"Poor Maggie," she whispered, wiping her eyes with the sheet. She really liked the woman. They were so different, the virgin and the slut, as Maggie said. But they were alike in many ways, too.

They were both bright and quick. They both liked stylish clothes but hated shopping alone. They both desperately wanted someone with whom they could share their lives. And sex was making it harder for both of them, though in diametrically opposite ways. Physically, they were as different as could be, but both were comfortable with their bodies.

Around three-thirty, when the vodka she consumed proved too much for her and came back up all over her clothes, Priya led Maggie to the bathroom to clean up. After getting her a facecloth and towel, she fetched a nightgown and robe only to return to find her sitting naked on the edge of the bathtub, not the least concerned with her nudity.

"What do you think?" She stood and, a bit unsteadily, turned slowly around. "Think I could pass for a boy."

"Oh stop. You're lovely, just a little thin. I bet if you put on ten pounds you'd have some nice curves."

"Maybe. But nothing like yours."

Priya conquered her own body shyness as a teenager in public school locker rooms. In those days, she enjoyed showing off her physical gifts to make the mean girls jealous. Were circumstances reversed tonight, she could see herself doffing her clothes exactly as Maggie had.

"The virgin and the slut," she said softly. If this developed into a real friendship, it would be a most interesting one indeed.

She rolled on her side and settled in, smiling, as she drifted off to sleep thinking it was a very long time ago since she felt this content with her life.

10:40 AM

"Will somebody *please* shoot that fucking phone!"

Tom and Paul looked up from their work, over at Rob, then at each other. Paul could read Tom's eyes. He wanted him to find out what was bugging Rob.

"Hey Rob," he said casually, in between rings.

"What?" his friend snapped.

"You want me to check Priya's desk and see if I can find some tweezers to pluck out that hair across your ass?"

All morning, Priya's phone rang about every fifteen minutes. Her voicemail always picked up on the fourth ring, but the constant interruptions were becoming an annoyance, especially for Rob who was distracted enough when he walked through the door earlier. He shot Paul a withering glance as he jumped up and grabbed the receiver of Priya's phone.

"Hello," he said forcefully, as if daring someone to be on the other end. "She's not here. She took the day off, so stop calling. And take a frigging hint, will ya? She doesn't want to talk to you."

He slammed down the handset, shaking his head in disgust. "Brian."

Paul glanced at Tom and nodded toward the door. "Hey Tom, did we ever get those proofs back?"

Tom smiled. "No. We should have had them yesterday. Let me walk down and see if I can find them."

As soon as the door closed behind him Paul turned to Rob. "Okay, Rob. What the hell is going on with you today? Did you and Lisa have a fight or something?"

"A fight? No, no fight. A fight would have been easy to deal with. No, she stabbed me in the gut and twisted the knife, that's all."

"What are you talking about?"

"Last night, or this morning, I proposed to her and she said no."

Paul was not sure if he was more stunned by the news Rob proposed to Lisa or that she refused him. "You really asked her to marry you?"

Rob nodded, his face growing more grim by the second.

"And she said no? She said 'no I won't marry you'?"

"Just about."

Paul took a deep breath. "Rob, what exactly happened and exactly what did she say?"

"You know, I've been like a whole new person since we got back together. I've been everything she wanted me to be. Everything *I* wanted to be. And we've been great together. And then last night, I had this dream about us and I knew it was time to do it so I did. I woke her up and proposed."

"And..."

"And she just looked at me. Then she started crying. She said not to ask her that now. It was too soon. She said to take it back and ask her again in six months. Six months! Six fucking months! Am I supposed to love her more in six months? Is she supposed to love *me* more in six months? *What the hell happens in six months?*" He was almost shouting again.

"Did you ask her?"

"Of course, and she kept crying and saying it was too soon." Rob was pacing now, furiously moving back and forth between the desks, unconsciously trying to dissipate his anger and hurt.

"So?"

"So I got dressed and left."

"You what? Are you crazy?"

"I couldn't deal with it, man. I mean, I was expecting her to be all happy and to jump up and hug me and...man, I freaked out. And then she started crying harder and begging me not to leave, but I couldn't face her. I felt so small, so humiliated. I guess I found out how big a loser I really am."

"What are you talking about? How are you a loser? Why the hell did you even act like that? Why…"

"Aren't you listening? She doesn't want to marry me. She doesn't want me. She…"

"Stop, you moron. Just stop! Don't you *ever* listen?"

"I listened. I heard her. Six months. You know what six months is? It's code for 'I don't want you.'"

"You really *are* nuts. And you really *don't* deserve that girl. She never said she didn't want to marry you. All she said was not to ask her now, to ask her later. So what? Maybe she has a problem, maybe she…who knows. But man, you walked out on her and left her crying like that. Are you *trying* to lose her for real? You better get your ass over to the Ritz right the hell now and find her and beg her to forgive you for being such a humongous dick. I mean, this is way beyond the pale even for you."

Paul glared at Rob, who could only look back, dumbfounded.

"What the hell are you standing there for? Go. Now. I'll tell Tom you had an emergency."

Rob didn't move. He appeared dazed, unable to process what happened and what Paul was telling him. He shook his head to clear it.

"But what if…"

"Rob, if you blow this with her you *will* regret it for the rest of your life! You'll end up drinking yourself to death or something over it. Man, if you blow this, you really *will* be a loser. The biggest loser of all time. You have to find a way to deal with this. You have to go talk to her. You have to apologize. And you have to do it right now!

"Tell her you freaked out. Tell her you felt like a loser. And tell her it was no excuse for leaving. Do whatever you have to but you better do it now. My God, Rob, what the *hell* were you *thinking*?

"Now go. Get out of here."

Rob's previous anger and misery could not stand up to the fury of Paul's diatribe. He looked up at his friend and almost cringed at the disappointment he saw on his face. That was when he knew how wrong he'd been. He nodded once and headed slowly for the door.

"I said hurry! And don't forget to grovel. On your knees if you have to. And bring flowers. Lots of them!"

12:10 PM

Jillian stood at the window in the lobby of her building and scanned the crowd on both sides of the street. She was looking for Aiden.

She was certain he was stalking her. Or if not stalking, then watching. She saw him five times since Sunday, always from a distance, always watching her until he realized she noticed. Then he vanished.

It just doesn't make sense. Liz was right. Stalking wasn't Aiden's thing.

Maybe it's some sort of game. Now that would *be like him. But what game? If he wants to see me or talk to me, why doesn't he just call 411? Or ring my bell? He must know where I live by now. Could something have happened to him? Five years is a long time. People change and not always for the better.*

She glanced at her watch. It was almost twelve-fifteen. As she turned away from the window, the air in the lobby filled with an instrumental version of the song that had been had been dogging her for two weeks now. She stopped and listened for a minute, letting the music wash Aiden right out of her head.

Then it was time to go. She was meeting Paul at Coffey's and after last night's conversation she was determined to focus all her attention on him.

There is no way I'll be thinking about Aiden today.

She pushed open the door.

At least not during lunch.

12:35 PM

Rob was frantic. He couldn't find her anywhere. After leaving the florist with four dozen roses, the most he could carry, he rushed over to the Ritz only to discover she called in. Then he tried her cell phone, but she didn't answer, so he went to her apartment. She wasn't there, either. He started calling friends and family.

Nobody's seen her. Or maybe she just asked everyone to tell me that. No. I can't believe that. I know her. She'd never ask someone to lie for her. She'd just tell me to my face to fuck off.

On a whim, he headed to his apartment, hoping she might either be there or have left a note or a message on his machine, but again, no Lisa. He tried restaurants and coffee shops, everywhere she might hang out. Finally, he ran out of ideas.

His arms were aching from carrying the roses as he crossed Tremont Street and found a bench on the Common where he could put them down, rest, and think.

What a jerk I was. Paul was right. What kind of man would walk out like that?

He glanced at his watch and muttered, "Lunchtime. Where would she..."

And it hit him. He gathered up the roses had headed for the Public Garden.

As he approached her favorite bench from the rear, he could only see the right side of her face, but even at a distance he could see it was puffy from crying. His heart sank into his stomach.

What can I do? What can I say to make this right?

He stood watching her for a few minutes, desperate for inspiration. He thought about saying a prayer, and the thought gave him an idea.

He extracted one rose and lay the rest down on the grass. Then he quietly moved up behind her, knelt, and began to pray out loud.

"In the name of the Father, and of the Son, and of the Holy Spirit."

He saw her stiffen at the sound of his voice, but she didn't turn around and, thankfully, didn't get up and walk away.

"Dear Lord, please help me. I did a very stupid thing this morning, perhaps the stupidest thing any man's ever done. And I don't know if I can make it right on my own.

"I think I really hurt the most wonderful woman you ever created, Lord. I did something I shouldn't have done, and then reacted so badly when I didn't get the response I expected.

"I know there's no excuse, Lord. I know I'm stupid and weak. But Lord, I love this woman more than my own life. Please help me find the words to take away her pain, to make her smile again, to make her happy again. Please help me find the words to let her know how sorry I am. Please help me find a way for her to love me again. And if the only way you can make her love me again is to take my life, then do it now because I'd rather die knowing she loves me than live in a world without her.

"But if the only way she can be happy is to never see me again, then please give me the strength to accept it. All I want, all I ever wanted was to make her happy. And now I've acted the fool and hurt her again.

"I know I don't deserve your help, Lord, but…"

"Enough already." Lisa turned enough to catch his eye. "Come over here and sit."

Rob bowed his head and said softly, genuinely, "Thank you, Lord. However this works out, thank you." As he sat down next to her, he offered her the rose.

"Only one?"

"The rest are back there." He hooked his thumb over his shoulder.

At her raised eyebrows, he said, "Wait," ran to retrieve the other roses, and hurried back to present them to her.

"Oh, Robbie," she said with a mixture of tenderness and regret. "They're beautiful. Thank you."

He sat down again, afraid to speak, but more afraid not to. "I'm so sorry."

"Why did you leave? Why did you leave me there like that?"

This is it. Whatever I say next will determine whether I live the rest of my life with this girl or spend it regretting my stupidity. There's no magic words. All I can do is be honest and hope it's enough.

He looked into her eyes. "I was scared and hurt and confused and overwhelmed and I didn't know what else to do."

"Scared?"

"Scared you were telling me you didn't want me anymore. Scared you were being kind and that the six months thing was a way to let me down easy.

"When I woke you up, when I jumped out of bed, I honestly believed you'd be happy I asked you, that you'd say yes, and you'd be crying tears of joy, not anguish or sadness or, or whatever they were. I thought you'd want to marry me. And when you didn't, I..." He let out a long sigh. "I felt like a fool, a loser. Suddenly, the dream I was having turned into a nightmare. You didn't want me and all I could think to do was run away from it, run away from the pain and humiliation. I couldn't face you anymore."

"Then why are you here?"

"Because someone who wasn't blinded by self-pity pointed out that what you actually said did not necessarily lead to the conclusions I'd drawn. And then I realized I broke the promise we made a few weeks ago, the promise to talk things out. The first test, the first time I was faced with a problem and I failed miserably. I am so ashamed...and so sorry."

Rob dropped his gaze to the bricks in front of them. He could not face her, could not bear to take the chance of seeing the wrong answer in her eyes when he asked, "*Were* you just trying to give yourself time to break it off?"

"Oh Robbie." He heard tenderness in her voice. "I've handled it all so badly. It's me who should be sorry."

She put her hand on his shoulder and asked him to look at her. "Robbie, I *was* trying to give myself time, but not to break up with you." She saw relief flood his eyes. "I was so unprepared for you to propose to me. It never occurred to...I mean, I hoped one day you'd ask, but I never thought it would be so soon. And you'd just woken me and I wasn't thinking straight and..." She took a deep breath. "Robbie, I love you. But there's something I have to tell you, something I should have...would have told you about if I had any idea you were thinking of proposing, something that only four other people in the world know.

"I would have told you someday, after...well, that doesn't matter now. You deserve to know, and you may not feel the same about me afterward, but no matter what, I need you to promise me you will never tell this to anyone. Not Paul, not my parents, not your priest, no one. Will you promise?"

"Promise? Lisa, what...? Yes, I promise. But, what did you do? Were you in jail? Did you kill someone?"

Lisa closed her eyes. It was she, now, who did not want to chance seeing the wrong thing in Rob's eyes as she confessed, "I'm married."

1:15 PM

Priya was not an especially heavy sleeper and was awakened by the motion of the bed as Maggie sat on the edge.

"Hi." She rubbed her still-heavy eyelids, then ran her fingers through her hair. "What time is...oh Maggie...you've been crying. What's wrong?"

"I was going to leave, but when I opened the bag I almost gagged. I'm so embarrassed about last night. I had no right to burden you with all that stuff." She shook her head. "I can imagine what you must think of me, but please, promise you won't tell the other girls. I...I really enjoy the dinners each week and I couldn't stand for all the girls to know about...you know."

Priya swung her legs off the mattress and put her arm around the woman's shoulder. "No one will ever know anything unless you tell them. Is that why you were crying? You were worried my mouth is as big as my boobs?"

That drew a faint smile to the sad, puffy face. "No. I..." She let the thought trail off.

"What?"

"Nothing. I'll be okay. All I need..."

"Bullshit!" Priya spat it out with such force she could feel Maggie's shoulders twitch. She removed her arm and turned so she was facing the sad woman. "Unless you're prepared to open that bag and put on those clothes, or leave here wearing that nightgown, you better start talking." Her voice softened. "Please, Maggie, talk to me. Whatever it is, please let me help."

Maggie didn't answer, but neither did she move. After a minute of silence, Priya started bumping her with her hip as she chided playfully, "Come on, you know you want to. And I'm really pretty experienced for a virgin."

That drew a second smile, but it quickly faded. Sensing she needed to think, Priya sat quietly with her, hip to hip, until finally Maggie asked, "Do you have any coffee?"

"I never told anyone what I told you last night." Maggie shifted slightly on the kitchen chair, then added a teaspoon of sugar to her cup and stirred slowly, thoughtfully.

"Then I'm truly honored."

Her eyes shot up, expecting to see mocking or amusement, but instead found only sincerity and respect.

"I was crying before because when I woke up and realized what I said and what you now knew, well...it scared me. It made me see myself through your eyes and…and I hate what I see."

Tears threatened to spill down her pale cheeks.

"I'm so tired of being sad and lonely like…like some shadow of a woman who uses sex to hide from life." She caught Priya's surprised expression. "You thought I didn't know what I was doing?" Priya nodded. "I do. I realized a long time ago and I've hated myself for it for years, but I don't know how to stop."

"Maggie, you just stop."

"You don't understand. It's an addiction, like a drug. Maybe worse. Something inside me is so frightened of being hurt again the way Billy hurt me that no matter what I do, no matter who I'm with, I can't open my heart. So I open my legs and it makes me feel good for a while, even though I know I'll feel bad again later on.

"Maybe I could have changed things ten years ago, but now?" She shook her head. "And even if I could change, who'd want me? Who'd want someone who's slept with hundreds of men?" The tears overflowed. "What decent guy would fall in love with a slut like me?"

Priya let her weep for a bit before she said gently, "You're right, Maggie. No decent guy wants a slut. But don't you see? You *have* the power to change who you are. The moment you decide to change, and accept the change in your head and in your heart, you'll become a new person. Then, no one can call you a slut. No one can call you anything but who you'll be – a bright, desirable woman.

Priya's confidence was answered by a simple, "I can't."

"You're right again. If you believe you can't, you'll never change. But with a different attitude, you certainly can. People kick drug habits all the time. Did you know that it's harder to quit smoking than to give up heroin? Yet people do it every day. Somehow, they find the strength to do it."

"Sure, and lots of people go back to it."

"And lots of people don't. You're a smart, personable, funny, beautiful woman, Maggie, and…

The doorbell cut her off.

"Who the heck is that?" She went to the front window. A delivery van from a local florist was double parked. She walked over to the intercom, pressed the button and said, "Hello?"

"Hi. I have a delivery for P. Kumar."

Priya met the girl at the door, not the least self-conscious about the ratty bathrobe she had on.

"They're beautiful," Maggie said as Priya placed on the table the huge vase full of Orange Asiatic Lilies, Belladonna Delphinium, Blue Iris, Orange and Yellow Germinis, Burgundy Matsumoto Asters, and Leather Leaf. "Who are they from?"

"We'll find out in a second." She opened the envelope and removed the card. "Oh." The card dropped to the table.

Maggie reached for it.

Dear Priya,
I heard you called in today. I hope you're feeling well.
Whatever you think I've done, please give me the opportunity to explain or make it right.
Please call me. 617-555-3274
Brian

"Whoever Brian is, he must really like you. He spent a bundle on these."

"Brian's nobody."

She told her the whole story.

"Ouch. That sucks. But I can see why he keeps trying. To a guy like that, a virgin your age with your, umm, gifts, would be one humongous trophy to brag about. I wonder how much effort he'll put in before he gives up."

Priya shrugged. "Who knows and who cares. But speaking of effort, let me ask you something. When you're at dinner with the girls, or with other friends, and you're all smiling and joking about screwing this guy or bragging about how many guys you've had, like you were doing last night, is that easy for you to do?"

"I don't understand."

"Is it easy to pretend you're not miserable? Is it easy to pretend you don't hate who you are? Is it easy to make everyone believe you love being promiscuous?"

Maggie dabbed at her eyes with her napkin as she thought about it for a few seconds. "No. No it's not. I mean, it's easy to joke around and all, but even as I'm doing it a part of me wants to scream, wants to tell them all the truth. Holding that in is the hard part."

"I'll bet it is. Think of how disciplined you must be to do that. Now consider this – what if you put all that effort into changing what you hate instead of hiding it."

"Priya, I've tried, I really have. More than once. But it's too hard. I can't bear being by myself. It's too lonely. Once, I went a whole month, but most of the times it only took a week or two."

"And who did you have to talk to those times? Family? A girlfriend?"

Maggie shook her head. "Nobody."

"And you're surprised you failed? Would you try to pick up a sofa and move it by yourself?"

Again her head shook.

"Of course not. It would be too difficult. So why in the world did you imagine you could change your whole life without any help from anyone?"

"It's really not the same thing."

"Yes, it is. Both are things for which anyone would need help. Maggie, please look at me." She waited until her new friend met her eyes. "Maggie, I don't know much about sex addiction, but I do know that overcoming any addiction is very hard without someone to support you, someone to help you be strong when you feel weak. So I swear to you right now, that if you're willing to make the effort, I will learn all there is to know about it. Actually, we'll both learn about it together. And I promise you I will be there for you any time you need me."

"But why would you do that. You don't even know me. Why would you want to make that kind of commitment to someone you've only just met?"

"Because I like you. Because you're someone I'd like to have for a friend. Because you need someone, and *I* can't bear the thought of someone I like living in such pain and misery. *And* because it'll be *incredibly* good Karma, and I *really* need the points."

When Maggie didn't answer for a full minute, Priya rose and dumped the old filter and grounds, rinsed the pot, set it all up again, and flipped the switch. Then she sat back down, folded her hands on the table, and waited.

She could tell Maggie was thinking. Probably weighing the chances Priya was on the level.

How hard it must be for someone who's lived with such hurt for so long to trust someone.

As she waited, she said a silent prayer, asking the gods to deliver her friend from anguish and help her start a new life.

Neither spoke as the coffee dripped. When it was done, Maggie rose, filled both their cups, and returned the pot to its place. Then she leaned against the counter and watched from behind as Priya toyed with her teaspoon.

Had Priya been able to see Maggie, she'd have noticed a calm come over her a moment before she picked up the cups and walked back to her chair. She stopped next to Priya long enough to set down her cup and touch her shoulder. Then she returned to her seat, smiled, and said, "Well, if you really *need* the points…"

MONDAY, MAY 24

7:50 PM

"Mmmmmmm. That was nice. May I take off my jacket now?"

Paul laughed. "Hey, I haven't seen you since this morning. And besides, I would think you'd like it that I can't wait to kiss you when you come home."

Come home?

Jillian still couldn't decide if Paul was aware of saying things like that, things that meant so much and gave such insight into his thoughts and feelings for her.

Come home implies he thinks of his apartment as my home, too. Of course, he said the same thing last week when he got to my place after work. Evidently he thinks wherever we are together is home.

The thought sent a wave of warmth through her.

He was especially attentive over the weekend. She was sure that because she would not let him help with her problem, he decided to make all their times together special, to let her know he would support her any way he could.

She mentally flogged herself again for allowing even a tiny part of her heart to want Aiden. She saw him again Saturday afternoon, but not Sunday or today.

Maybe he realized I'm with Paul now and went away again. Forever.

Her head hoped so but her heart was conflicted. It still wanted closure, wanted to hurt him and hold him at the same time. She realized she was dividing her attention again and felt guilty as she watched Paul walk back into the kitchen. Something smelled great. "What's cooking?"

"A curry recipe I stole from a friend in California. How about opening that bottle of wine? I just remembered something." He turned the flame under the curry to low, walked out of the kitchen, through the living room, into his bedroom.

As the cork came free, he reappeared holding a small package wrapped in aluminum foil, shaped suspiciously like a CD case. "This is for you. Sorry about the wrapping. It was either that, or a piece of old newspaper."

"What is it?"

"A little gift. Open it and find out."

She tore the foil off and saw it was indeed a homemade CD. She flipped it over to read the handwritten song titles. "This looks familiar."

"It's a copy of the one Gary had playing for us in the limo on our first date. We both seemed to like it so much, I called him over the weekend and asked if he could burn a copy. Then I burned another for me so we can have one here and at your place, too."

"Paul, that's so sweet. Thank you." She leaned over and gave him a kiss more suited for dessert than a simple thank you.

"Delicious. I'm definitely giving you gifts more often." He stirred the curry, then held out a spoon for her to taste.

"Oh wow! That's fantastic!"

Paul grinned, pleased at the praise. "So how was your day?"

"Same old, same old. I put together a two page ad for *Charles Clothiers*. They're having a big sale next month. What about your day?"

"Un-be-lievable." He picked up one of the glasses of wine and took a sip. "You really are *not* going to believe what happened today. But the curry's ready. Let's get settled and then I'll tell you all about it."

Jillian set the table while he scooped rice into each dish and ladled generous servings of curry over it. He set one at each place and sat down.

She began to eat, but her attention was on Paul. She let him consume two spoonfuls before insisting he tell her the big news.

"Remember this morning when I said it was strange Rob didn't meet us outside the subway station and didn't answer his cell when I called?"

"Yes."

"Well, he never showed up for work."

"So you never found out what happened with him and Lisa?"

"Oh I found out. But relax. All in good time. Anyway, he didn't show up for work and Tom seemed a little miffed given that he ran out Friday morning and didn't come back. So he was not in the greatest of moods around noon when the call came in."

"Not Brian again!"

"Nope. He called a little after nine, as usual, and Priya hung up on him, as usual. This time, it was Rob. As soon as he heard Rob's voice, Tom started in on him. It really wasn't like Tom. He's usually so steady and calm. Not today, though.

"After a minute, Tom paused for a breath and that was when Rob apparently apologized for not calling in, told him he was at the airport, and would be there with an explanation and lunch for all of us as soon as he could get a taxi."

He reached for his wine glass.

"The airport? What was he…"

"Just wait. About forty-five minutes later Rob walked through the door with bags from DelFlorio's."

He paused for a sip of wine, more curry, and another sip of wine to wash it down. Then he continued with how Rob had searched for and found Lisa.

"Married! Are you serious?"

Paul grinned. "Didn't I *say* you wouldn't believe it?

"It seems that when she was nineteen, she spent Christmas break in the Bahamas. Three days into the vacation, she fell for this rich French kid who was also on vacation. One thing led to another and ten days later they decided to get married.

"A week later, he told her he had to fly home so he could pick up some things he needed. She wanted to go with him, but he convinced her to stay and enjoy the sun since he would only be gone a couple of days. Then he'd be back, they could finish out the vacation together, and he would come to the US to live with her while she finished school.

"They'd pretty much been living in Lisa's room since they were married, but most of his stuff was still in his own room. The day he's going back, he told her he wanted to check out of his room and move his stuff to her room. So he goes upstairs to pack and take a shower. While he's in the shower, someone comes into his hotel room and steals his watch and jewelry, his wallet with all his credit cards, his return ticket, and all his cash.

"First, he makes a big scene with the hotel, then confides to Lisa that he's terribly embarrassed because he probably forgot to lock the door when he went in to shower. Plus, his father is constantly accusing him of being irresponsible and he's mortified at having to call him for money to get home. Naturally, Lisa wouldn't hear of her husband doing such a thing, so she whipped out her credit card, paid his hotel bill, bought him a first class round trip ticket, and gave him a few thousand in cash. The next morning, with the shuttle to the airport waiting, he kissed her goodbye with tears in his eyes at having to part from her for even a few days.

"Four days later, after not hearing a word from him, discovering the phone number he gave her wasn't in service, and that the address he wrote down didn't exist, she realized she'd been conned."

"Oh no. That's horrible."

"True, but it gets worse."

"She was so humiliated at having fallen for the con that it never occurred to her the marriage might be legal. She hadn't told anyone she knew, not even the friend she went with because the friend had latched onto a local guy the first day and she hadn't seen her since. So she decided to bury the whole thing. What she didn't do was file a police report, or for an annulment or divorce."

"Okay. But all that still doesn't explain why Rob was at the airport this morning."

"I'm coming to that. Evidently it did occur to Lisa a couple of times over the years that she should do something about it, but she was always afraid it would get back to her parents. Last week, she made an appointment with a lawyer for this Wednesday to start the process of an annulment, if possible, or a divorce if not. The big problem was, of course, she didn't know where the guy was and if Marcel Portanier was even his real name.

"She was hoping she'd never have to tell anyone about what happened. If an annulment came through, it would be like she was never married at all. I guess that was why she sort of freaked out when Rob proposed. She knew they'd get married one day, but never expected him to pop the question so soon. And then *he* reacted as badly as *she* did and, well, you know."

Jillian nodded.

"Anyway, when Rob heard all this, he decided this was his chance to make up for everything he'd screwed up with her since day one. First, he convinced her she had to tell her parents about it. After all, they're both big-time lawyers with big-time connections. And those connections paid off. It took him most of the weekend to talk her into it, but Sunday morning, they drove to the Cape, met with her father and mother, told them the story of her marriage, and asked for their help.

"In true lawyerly fashion, her dad called a friend in the State Department who put him in touch with someone in the American Embassy in Nassau who was owed a favor by someone in the Registrar General's office who promised that first thing this morning the documents needed to get the ball rolling here in Massachusetts would be ready.

"Then her mother volunteered the company jet to go pick up the documents. She intended to have one of her assistants make the trip since Lisa would be needed here as they prepared all the legal papers, but Rob offered to go. He left about six this morning. Someone was waiting at the airport with the papers when he arrived in Nassau and Lisa was waiting at Logan when he returned. From what he said, annulment papers were filed in court this afternoon."

"That really *is* incredible. So how long before she gets the annulment?"

"Rob wasn't sure, but he figured it would take considerably less time than usual."

Jillian shook her head, trying to assimilate it all. "I guess you did have quite a day."

"But that isn't even the end of it."

"There's more?"

Paul nodded. "But not about Rob and Lisa. About Priya."

"Priya?" *Priya's my friend!* "Well tell me!"

"After Rob told us everything that happened, he took off after promising Tom to be in early and work late for the rest of the week. So it was just Tom, Priya, and me for the rest of the day.

"We all left together about five-thirty. No sooner did we step off the elevator than Priya said 'crap!' and nodded toward the front doors. Brian was waiting there.

"I asked her if she wanted me and Tom to go break the guy's legs, but she only wanted me to make him go away. So I told Tom to take her arm and walk out with her and I would stop Brian. I walked ahead and right up to the guy, but all the time he was fixed on Priya.

"I told him she didn't want to talk with him, but it was like he didn't even hear me. As she and Tom approached he tried to go around me but I stayed in front of him, so he said loud enough for her to hear, 'All I want to do is talk to you. You owe me that much. You...' He never finished because she'd gone through the door. He tried to go around me again so I grabbed his arm and when he tried to shake me off I pinned him, which, in hindsight, wasn't too smart because he probably could've had me arrested for assault or something. But it got his attention. I tried to look menacing and told him again to leave her alone, but, well, who knows?"

"Did you catch up to Priya and tell her?"

"Nah. I hung around near the front door for a few minutes until I figured she had time to get to the subway. I'll talk to her tomorrow and explain what happened. Maybe she should talk to him, if only to get him off her back."

"Why don't you call her after dinner?"

"No, I don't think so," he said, his eyes sparkling. "I have other plans for my lips tonight."

THURSDAY, MAY 27

9:15 AM

When the phone on Priya's desk rang at 9:15, Tom barked at her not to touch it. Everyone in the office knew it was Brian.

He called every day at 9:15, and every day, Priya hung up as soon as she heard his voice. They all knew about the flowers he sent last week, the singing telegram on Sunday morning, the candy that was waiting for her when she arrived home Monday, and more flowers Tuesday. There was no gift yesterday, but the phone calls kept coming. Paul and Rob thought it was funny the guy kept trying so hard on such a lost cause, but Tom did not share in the humor. In fact, all week, he did not see humor in much of anything and grew more choleric by the day. Yesterday, when Rob decided to take a chance and ask if he was okay, the glare he received in response left no doubt in anyone's mind that Tom wanted to be left alone with whatever was bothering him.

He pressed the line button on his phone, picked up the handset and said, "Hello" in a voice that was on the verge of boiling over with anger.

As soon as he knew it was Brian, Tom erupted like a volcano that could no longer withstand the pressure of the magma boiling inside.

"Look you asshole," he yelled, "what the hell is wrong with you?" He then spent two full minutes telling Brian what he thought of him and threatening everything short of murder if he ever called the office again. None of the team ever before heard him use such language. Priya actually cringed at some of the things he was yelling into the phone.

When he finished and slammed down the receiver, he sat still, glaring at nothing as his co-workers watched, unwilling to even breathe too loud. After a few minutes they saw his eyes come back into focus. Seconds later he stood, said, "I uh, I need to take a walk," and vanished out the door.

The three sat wide-eyed for a few seconds before Paul said, "Holy crap!"

Leftover tension still charged the air in the room, so much so Priya started laughing quietly in response. "Holy crap indeed! Can you believe that?"

"Pri, I know you said Tuesday that you wouldn't see him again, and that you don't want to talk about him anymore, but maybe you really *should* just talk to the guy and put an end to this. Either that, or get a restraining order." Paul shrugged apologetically but could see the determination in her eyes never wavered.

Tom returned thirty minutes later and apologized to everyone for losing it, especially to Priya for cussing as he did in front of her.

"I've had a lot on my mind this week," he told them as he took his seat. They all started to reassure him but he cut them off. "I have to tell you guys something. She won't let me talk to any family or neighbors or anyone, and I suppose that includes you three, but it's starting to affect my work and I...damn!" He shook his head and sighed, "Patti found this lump in her breast. A big one. And we're freaking out about it. She has an appointment with the doctor this afternoon, but then they'll have to do a biopsy and, oh shit, what if it's...it's...I can't even say the word." He appeared to be on the verge of tears.

Rob and Paul were speechless, but Priya jumped right in with words of sorrow and comfort.

"I know the chance of it being...bad is small," he told her, recovering his composure, "especially at her age, but what if it is? What if..." He was afraid to voice the possibility, as if doing so might make it happen.

She stood and walked over to his desk. "Tom, I can't imagine keeping that inside all week. You poor guy." When he didn't look up at her, she crouched down so she could see his face. "Go home. Go home right now and take Patti to the doctor this afternoon."

"But she made me come to work. She said she didn't want me to..."

"Baloney. She's just trying to be strong and not show you how scared she is. I know it's confusing, but sometimes we really *don't* want you guys to listen to us. Of course, you idiots invariably pick the wrong times. But think about this. If *you're* this upset, imagine how *she* must be feeling, regardless of what she says.

"You know all the stuff you've been imagining, all the stuff you keep trying to drive from your head before it takes root and becomes real? Well she's struggling with the same things. And if she's like most women I know, she's not telling you half of the things she's imagined because she doesn't want *you* to worry more.

"So get out of here before I make Paul and Rob drag you out. We can take care of things here. You go home and be with her. Be strong for her. And listen to her.

"You can't be a guy and solve this problem. You *can* listen if she wants to talk and hold her if she wants to cry or scream or rant.

"And don't even think about coming to work tomorrow. You stay home and do family stuff with her and the kids. Have a long weekend together. Get her out of the house and do something so she won't dwell on all the bad possibilities. If it turns out to be nothing, you'll have goofed off a little. And if it turns out to be something, you'll have had some important time together before all the crap starts. So no excuses. Go. And *don't* tell her you told us."

"Priya I…"

"I said go!"

Tom smiled. "I just wanted to say thank you…"

Priya blushed. "Oh!"

"…but I'll go now." He slid some papers into his briefcase, grabbed his jacket, and started to leave, but paused at the door and said to Priya, "You know, it's strange sometimes how you almost read people's minds. Someday, you're going to make a really scary boss."

SUNDAY, MAY 30

5:10 AM

Rob turned the corner onto Beach Ave. as the edge of the sun peeked over the horizon.

When he awakened at four, he rolled on his side to watch Lisa sleep while he thought about all that transpired over the past ten days. Almost immediately, her foot reached out in her sleep to find him. They often slept entwined, but even on those nights when tossing and turning moved them apart, whenever he awoke, some part of her, an arm, a foot, or her marvelous backside, would be pressed against, draped over, or touching him somewhere.

He felt an ache in his chest as he reached out to stroke her hair. She was so beautiful, so peaceful as she lay curled in the fetal position. At least she looked that way when she wasn't snoring.

The memory of her indignation the morning, several months ago, when he suggested she might want to invest in some of those breathing strips to cut down on the decibel level made him chuckle. Then, unable to fall back to sleep, he decided to go for an early morning run.

He was headed back, now. Another ten minutes and he would be in a nice warm shower. He wished he could wake her and make love, but she was funny about that. Although her parents never seemed to have a problem getting it on when Lisa was around, he discovered the last time they stayed over that she could not get comfortable having sex with them in the house, even if they were sound asleep.

"Might have to make it a cold shower," he muttered, watching the waves stroke the beach as he ran.

He and Lisa drove down right after work Friday, expecting to have the house to themselves until Saturday morning, but when they arrived, her parents' Mercedes was parked in the drive. Fortunately for Lisa's psyche, they were engaged in nothing more than some cuddling and kissing on the sofa in front of the fireplace when they walked in.

All weekend, both parents were very pleasant toward him. Not the gracious and courteous he was used to, but downright nice. It was almost as if they suddenly liked him.

He shivered, partly from the cool air, but mostly because it felt strange for them to be treating him like…like…he couldn't find the right word and so shrugged and plodded on.

As he approached the back door to the kitchen, he noticed the light was on. He was pretty sure he turned it off when he left, but maybe not. The mystery was solved when he opened the door and was greeted by Lisa's father.

"Good morning, Rob. Have a good run?"

"Good morning, sir. Yes, I did. The air was cool, with a light breeze coming off the water."

"That's great…" He was smiling. "…but, I think it's time you stopped calling me sir. Chad will do fine."

Wow! This friendliness is getting spooky.

"Yes, sir, I mean, okay, Chad. Do you do any running?"

"I jog a bit, but nothing like when I was your age. Did you know I used to run track in high school and college?" Rob shook his head. "I was okay, even won some races, but I was a little too stocky to ever become a great runner. After law school, most of the running I did was on company treadmills to help stay in shape. But now…well, Lissy and I sometimes take early morning jogs. Or walks."

"Well, walking is good, too. I hope I didn't wake you when I went out earlier."

"No. I'm always up this early. Force of habit from too many years of having to review case files before going to court. I just made some coffee. Want a cup?"

Oh no. He makes terrible coffee. But he obviously wants company.

"Sure." He went to the fridge for the cream.

Cups in hand, they sat at the kitchen table for only a few seconds before Chad said, "Rob, I want to say something to you."

Oh-oh. What is this about?

"I don't think it's any secret that when you and Lisa first started dating, Lissy and I were not exactly thrilled about it. No, that's not fair. Lissy was happy that Lisa was happy.

"I, on the other hand, had somewhat stronger opinions. I always thought Lisa would someday marry a lawyer like her dad. And for years I've literally hated the men she ran with. Most of them were nothing but pretty boys or self-styled studs whose only interest in my daughter seemed to be her body and her trust fund."

Rob's eyes widened in shock and his reaction was not lost on Chad.

"Did you think a father doesn't know when his daughter is beautiful and sexy? Trust me, it's a nightmare that begins at puberty and never ends, at least not until they get married and then it's for the husband to worry about. Anyway, as I said, I never liked anyone she brought home, and that included you."

Geez. Why don't ya say what you really mean?

"Lisa has always been a rebellious girl. Even as a child, she had a mind of her own and it made things very difficult. You see, her mother and I had her life mapped out before she was even born. Good schools, on to Harvard or Yale, then to law school, a brilliant career, maybe a judgeship, maybe even the Supreme Court.

"She put an end to that dream a week before her eighth birthday when she announced she wanted to be an astronaut. Or was it a goat herder? No matter. The point is from that day on, she never had the slightest interest in the law. It took us a very long time to get over that. We saw it as a rejection of who we were, of everything we stood for. Stupid, I know, but such are the joys of parenting.

"When I finally came to terms with her not wanting to be a lawyer, I switched to wanting her to be happy. But the kind of happiness I saw her pursuing, the partying and pretty boys...well, I knew that was partly her youth. But another part was because she knew we'd disapprove. It was as if she wanted to send us a message that she was willing to be anything, as long as it wasn't like us. That hurt the most. I think I understand it better now, in light of what I know about the marriage. She must have been devastated when she realized what happened, but we were so alienated then, she never even gave a thought to telling us and letting us help. I'm sure she believed we'd have...well, all that's in the past. Even now, she doesn't think we understand or approve of her. And maybe we...maybe I'm to blame for that.

"I was always quick to express my disapproval of her lifestyle and the men she dated. I knew none of them ever really made her happy. They were playthings and I found myself rejecting each new one out of hand. It was clear to me from the moment she hit puberty that nobody would ever be good enough for my little girl. But then, suddenly, she wasn't a little girl any longer and she wouldn't let me take care of her and protect her."

He gazed out the window as he spoke, but turned his head to catch Rob's eyes. "I know you can't really understand those feelings, even if you think you do. But someday you will, if you ever have a girl of your own."

He paused again and shook his head. "I can't believe how I've been rambling. I had this all planned out before you came back, and now...well, if I ever did this during a summation in court, I'd lose the jury for sure."

Again he paused, this time for a deep breath. "As I was saying, now for the third time, I never thought any of the men she dated were good enough for her. Until now."

Rob's stomach sort of turned over.

Did he just say...?

"This past week or so, I've learned something about your character. Many men, certainly those who preceded you, would have run from a mess like the one Lisa created. But you stood by her, apparently unfazed. You influenced her to do what was smart and right, and you supported her in every way she needed. And unless I've severely misjudged you, you'll continue to do so regardless of what or how long it takes. Am I correct?"

"Yes, of course I will."

"And what she did doesn't bother you at all? That she could have been so rash, so impetuous, and then so foolish in letting it go on?"

Rob shrugged. "We all have a past."

And thank God you're not privy to the details of mine.

"My own might not hold up too well under cross-examination. But it's our pasts that made us who we are today. In a way, I'm happy about what happened back then. Because if she hadn't been so impulsive, who knows where life would have led her. Probably not to me, though."

Chad saw how the boy physically reacted to the thought. "You really do love her, don't you?"

"Sir, Chad, I don't know that I have the words to tell you how much I love your daughter. She is the most amazing woman I've ever met."

He paused, and Chad could see he was weighing whether or not to say something.

"Chad, I...I know I'm no prize. I know who I am and what I am and that I'll never be the richest or most successful guy she could be with. But sir, whatever I am today, whatever I'll be in the future, it will be because Lisa brings out the best in me. If she dumped me tomorrow, I'd still be a better man for having known her. She makes me want to be more than I am, more than I think I can be. And I don't mean just job- or money-wise."

Chad was nodding. "I understand. It was like that with Lissy and me when I was your age."

Rob started to say something, but Chad held up his hand.

"Rob, the real reason I wanted to talk to you this morning, is that I wanted to thank you for everything you've done for Lisa recently. Getting her to come to us for help...well...I know that couldn't have been easy. Not at all. And I also wanted to apologize for the way I misjudged you. At first, I thought you were another one of the party boys. I never took the time to try to discover what she saw in you, even when it became clear you were more than a casual fling. But I'm starting to see it now, and I find myself very impressed."

This is surreal! Her father who used to hate me is thanking me! And apologizing to me! Lisa is not going to believe it!

"Rob, I know for a fact the annulment will be granted. It might take some time to work through the system, even with the prodigious amount of grease Lissy and I applied, but it will happen."

"That's great news!" Rob was clearly excited. "Uh, did you want me not to say anything to her?"

"No, you can tell her. Hell, you'd better tell her." He shifted in his chair to face Rob full on. "One thing you should know, in case you don't already, is never try to keep secrets from your wife. She'll *always* eventually find out, and *you'll* always pay for it, one way or another."

My wife? He just called her my wife!

Chad caught Rob's expression and laughed out loud. "No, you *really* better not try to keep secrets from her. Or lie. *Ever.* You're way too easy to read."

Then, as if he *had* been reading his mind, he said, "Lisa told Lissy about your proposal. Perhaps she could have left out some of the details…" Chad saw embarrassment flood the boy's face. "…but we're thankful she's talking to us again about her life.

"Rob, understand that I'm speaking for Lissy, too, when I tell you how sorry we are your proposal didn't go as you planned. But it's our sincere hope that when this unpleasant legal mess is resolved, you will once again ask her to marry you, and that this time, she'll have the good sense to say yes."

He extended his hand across the table. "And I want you to know that when she does, I will be very happy to know an exceptionally good man will be taking care of my little girl."

MONDAY, MAY 31

6:05 PM

"I guess that's good news all around then."

Paul drained the last of his Rodenbach Belgian Red Ale.

"Man, it's hard for me to imagine you as a married dude. You realize the day's gonna come when the only time we'll be able to sit here drinking beer like this is nights like tonight, when Lisa's working late and Jillian's at the theater with her friends."

"Yeah, well, I'm not married *yet* so drink up. But once *she's* not married anymore, I'm goin' for the gusto as my old man used to say."

"And you weren't exaggerating a little about what her father said?"

"I swear. By the time her mom came downstairs, he and I had been trading stories about college for over an hour. Turns out he was one wild dude.

"You know, I think this thing with Lisa really rocked them. I think it made them look at how they lived their lives, working all the time and such. I think it made them realize that as much as they love Lisa, when she was growing up, they let her down as parents by substituting things for time. I..." Rob frowned for a second, then nodded toward the door. "Isn't that the guy who was playing Priya?"

He turned and sure enough, Brian stood near the front door surveying the room. When he noticed Paul, he headed directly for him.

"What the hell does he want now? Is he never going to give up?"

Seconds later, Brian stood facing him.

"Hi. This will probably seem weird, but I need to ask you a favor."

Paul's obvious incredulity didn't faze him a bit.

"I know you're good friends with Priya. She told me so the night we went out. I need you to ask her to let me talk to her."

"Look man she really doesn't want to talk with you. Frankly, I don't blame her."

"But why? What did I do? We hit it off so well that night. And then she avoids me and the only time I talked with her she accuses me of playing her. She didn't even tell me how or why or anything. She never gave me a chance to say a thing. And it is *not* true."

That neither of them believed him was again obvious, but again, Brian seemed unconcerned.

"Paul, I know she liked me that night, just as much as I liked her. Well, maybe not *just* as much, but enough. When we said goodnight, everything was cool. We were both looking forward to talking on Monday. But something happened and I have to find out what it was. All I want is a chance to explain or make it right. Do *you* know what happened?"

"Brian, whatever's going on between you two is between you two. It's not for me to say anything. She's my friend, and even if I knew her thoughts, I wouldn't presume to tell them to you, or Rob, or anyone else."

Brian sighed. "I understand. Can I sit down for a minute?"

Paul nodded toward a chair and Brian perched on the edge of it.

"I know I must have been coming across as a freak or some kind of stalker for the past two weeks, but I *really* like her. She's someone special, and I'm not willing to walk away with her thinking I'm some kind of scumbag.

"If there hadn't been any chemistry, then it would be different. But there was. It felt like, I don't know, like I knew her that night. It was the best date I ever had.

"All I want is one chance to talk to her, to find out what happened. Then, if she really doesn't want to see me any more, I'll never bother her again. I swear. But I can't give up and walk away without knowing why. Can you understand that?"

Paul didn't say anything at first.

Yeah, I understand. And it sure seems like you're telling the truth. Reminds me of me a few weeks ago. But...damn!

"Okay, Brian. I want you to listen to me very carefully because I mean every word I'm about to say literally."

He paused a second to let it sink in.

"I think I believe you. And so I'll talk to Priya, let her know what you've said, and what I think, and I'll probably end up convincing her to see you. Now this is the part you should really pay attention to. Priya means a lot to me. So if I do this, and I ever find out you're a good actor and that you've been playing some game with me and with her, there is nowhere you'll be able to hide. I will find you and I will hurt you. And I don't think I'll have any problem recruiting a few friends to help me." From the corners of their eyes, they both saw Rob nodding vigorously. "This is not a joke. If you are not one hundred percent on the level, and you hurt her in any way, you had better relocate to another country before I find you. Do you understand?"

"Yes, yes, thank you. Really. Thank you."

"Does she have your phone number?"

"She did, but she probably tossed it."

Paul pushed a napkin across the table. "Write it down. If she's willing to see you, she'll call you. If she hasn't called by Friday, you can safely assume she won't and that it's time to get on with your life. Understand?"

"Yes. I understand. But please, do your best. I just can't lose her over a misunderstanding."

9:10 PM

"Hey Jilli, listen. Isn't that the song?"

Over the din of the crowd milling around the lobby during intermission, Liz caught faint strains of an instrumental *Could I Have This Dance.*

Jillian was telling her friends about how nice Paul was lately, despite her preoccupation. "Yup. See. Every time I'm talking about him."

She last saw Phantom of the Opera three years ago. This would be her fourth time but was the first for both Liz and Jenna.

"You were right," Jenna said. "The music is so much better in person. I'm really glad you talked me into coming. And the guy who's playing the Phantom. Did you see his picture in the Playbill? I think I may want to have his children."

"Stand in line," Liz told her. "I get first dibs 'cause I'm older."

"No way. Five weeks doesn't entitle you to anything but waiting your turn while I make that man reach notes he never dreamed of."

They argued back and forth over who would ravish him first until, after a minute or so, Jillian said, "*Both* of you can stand in line. Seeing as *I'm* the oldest, *I* should get to do him first."

"Woo-hoo! Wait 'till I tell Paul about this." Liz was wearing her evil grin.

"Woo-hoo is right!" Jenna said. "You getting tired of coffee boy already? Or are you getting frustrated 'cause he won't give you any?"

Jillian laughed. "Well, I have been feeling a little frisky lately, especially the last week or so. Even with the way I've been…preoccupied…he's been so damn sweet and attentive that sometimes I just want to jump him."

"You realize he won't stay that way forever if this Aiden thing keeps dragging out," Liz said. "No more sightings?"

Jillian shook her head. "Nothing for over a week. It doesn't make any sense. Honestly, I'm grateful it's stopped, but now I'm thinking about him even more, wondering if he'll appear again."

"Maybe *that's* his game," Jenna said. "He stalks you for a while to let you know he's back and to get you thinking about him. Then he vanishes for a while, which he figures will confuse you and make you think about him even more so when he does reappear, you've almost conditioned yourself to want to see him again."

"That *would* be like him," Liz said. "He was always good at manipulating people and situations. I bet Jenna hit it right on the head."

"I'd like to hit *him* on the head," Jillian grumbled. "This game of his is *not* amusing."

The lights in the lobby flickered to let patrons know the play was about to resume. She turned to Liz as they walked down the isle to their seats. "As for you blabbing to Paul, go right ahead. Maybe it'll make him jealous enough to finally take off his pants!"

9:25 PM

After Brian left, the conversation reverted back to Rob and Lisa and stayed there for the better part of two and a half hours. Rob seemed to have undergone an astounding transformation. Paul never before saw his best friend so excited, so enthusiastic, so willing to talk about his relationship with Lisa, and his plans and dreams for their future together. He was happy for him, but the happiness he felt for Rob and Lisa only underscored his reservations about *his* relationship with Jillian.

He was doing his best to be supportive, to help her in the only way she would let him – by being there and making their time together special. But more and more, he noticed her attention was off somewhere. More and more, he wondered who or what was so engaging her. And more and more, he worried she might be drifting away from him.

Maybe I should have screwed her when I had the chance.

"Nah."

"Huh? Nah what?"

"Nothing."

I don't want meaningless sex with her. I want it all. But Rob's not the one to talk to about this, at least not tonight, when he's so high on himself and Lisa. Maybe I'll call Priya later.

When Lisa arrived a few minutes later, Paul was just starting on a Sam Adams Double Bock. "Hi. How're you doing? It feels like I haven't seen you for weeks."

Lisa searched his face for a few seconds then turned to Rob and said, "You two have been talking about me all night, haven't you?"

Rob just blinked. Paul shook his head a little, as if to clear it. "How the heck did you know that?"

"Feminine intuition. Don't you know you can never hide anything from us?" She laughed a bit before she turned to Rob. "And you, mister, will be well served to remember that."

The guys joined in the laughter and Rob flagged the waitress as Lisa settled in. After her Harpoon Summer arrived and she emptied half the mug in a few seconds, she asked Paul how things were going with Jillian.

"Everything's fine."

"Sure it is. Now tell me the truth. I know about what's been going on. Did you think Rob would keep it to himself?"

Rob's rueful grin let Paul know Lisa did, indeed, know everything. He sighed.

"Honestly, I don't know. Sometimes it's like the first two weeks, but more often than not, it's like she's somewhere else inside her head. I'm starting to think there might be someone else."

"Really? Another guy?"

Paul shrugged. "All I know is this started two weeks ago when she saw someone she described as a ghost from her past. If she'd tell me what's going on I could deal with it, even if she won't let me help. But all this silence is really making me think she wants to hide something."

"Or someone," Rob added.

"Yeah. Or someone."

"What'll you do?" Lisa asked.

"What *can* I do? I suppose I could follow her around, or make a scene and demand she tell me what's going on, but neither of those is my style. If she's telling me the truth, then she'll resolve the issue and clue me in one day. If she's not, well, I guess I'll find that out soon enough. But I have to believe she's being straight and going through something that'll make her stronger, make us stronger. Maybe I'm kidding myself, maybe it's wishful thinking, but the feelings I've had since the day I met her haven't changed a bit. So I guess I'll wait it out and hope for the best."

TUESDAY, JUNE 1

5:40 PM

"Mmmm. The sun feels great," Paul said as they crossed to the Common.

"Sure does. Where's Jilli?"

"Still at work, I think. I told her I had to talk to you. I'm seeing her later."

Once on the familiar paths, they strolled slowly, silently. After a few minutes of quiet togetherness, Priya couldn't stand the waiting any longer. "Are you going to tell me what the big mystery is or do I have to get tough with you?"

Paul chuckled. "Sorry, I was going over something in my head one last time. I wanted to make sure I'm doing the right thing." He paused for a second. "Guess who I ran into last night?"

Priya's face clouded over. "Not him, I hope."

"Yup. Him."

Paul gave her a rundown of everything that was said, including the threats he'd made.

"And you really believe him?"

Paul nodded. "I do, Pri. Maybe he's a really great actor, but last night I looked into the guy's eyes and he really looked miserable, almost haunted. He did not look like any player I've ever known. And when you think about it, and look at everything he's done, I mean, what guy would go through all of that, would humiliate himself like that, just for a piece of ass. Even one as nice as yours."

Her hand shot out and smacked his shoulder. "Hey, my ass is worth way more than a little humiliation!"

Paul laughed. "Maybe so, but seriously, the things he said, the way he said them, the things he's done…add them all up and maybe you should give him his chance to talk."

"Do you think Lisa could have misunderstood? Not heard what she thought she heard?"

Paul shrugged. "I don't know. But maybe the guys she overheard didn't know what they were talking about. Rumors fly around all the time in workplaces and not all of them are true. And people do sometimes misinterpret things."

Priya nodded, remembering her own recent involvement in a grand misinterpretation.

6:15 PM

Jillian sat at her desk, alone, unmoving, and unhappy. Her forehead rested on the palms of her hands, all supported by elbows planted on the desktop. Silent tears squeezed between closed eyelids, some following the profile of her cheeks as they ran down, some simply letting go to fall on the stack of papers below.

She was startled when a voice said, "Are you okay, Jillian?"

Her hands dropped to her lap, but her head remained bowed. "I'm okay, Cathy. I thought everyone left a while ago." She heard her boss walk into her space and felt the hand on her shoulder when Cathy stopped next to her.

"Jillian, sweetie, you are obviously not okay. Can I help?"

She turned and could tell from Cathy's reaction how she must look. "It's all such a mess. It started out so wonderful, so unbelievably wonderful, and now I've gone and messed it all up."

Her tears flowed freely now as Cathy sat on the stool in front of the drawing table.

"What did you mess up? Paul? Has something happened?"

Jillian wiped her eyes and took a deep breath before telling Cathy everything that happened since the day she first thought she saw Aiden. She talked about her confused feelings and of Paul's reaction to her distance. And when she was done, her tears began anew.

"He's been so great the whole time, but still I feel like I'm losing him," she sobbed, "and it's all my fault."

Cathy let her cry for a bit, then gently urged her to blot the tears and talk.

"Tell me the truth, now. Do you love him? Or at least like him a lot."

"Of course. If I didn't I wouldn't be so upset. But is it fair to Paul to be with him when part of my heart is somewhere else? Having Aiden in my head makes me feel like I'm cheating on Paul. It's crazy, I know, but I can't help it."

The time for crying was passed. They talked about Jillian's problem for most of an hour. It was clear to Cathy the girl was deeply conflicted about her feelings for this Aiden. She suspected the feelings were due more to the mysterious nature of his reappearance than to any true affection for him. But she knew from things she experienced in her own life they could be real, too.

"It seems to me you need to stop worrying so much about *how* you're feeling, and start thinking about *why* you're feeling that way. Why do you feel as you do about Paul? Why do you feel as you do about Aiden? You really need to get to the root of it all, to figure out what it is, and who it is you really want."

Jillian nodded.

It all comes down to what and who, what and who. If only I knew.

8:10 PM

"You've been quiet tonight," Elissa said as she replaced her wine glass.

The Robertsons were dining, as they did nearly every Tuesday, in the parlor of L'Espalier.

"I know. I'm sorry."

"Big new case?"

"No. I've been thinking about how happy we've all been for the past week or so now that we have our daughter back. And about the past, and how bad a job I did being her father."

"No worse than I did as her mother."

Chad shook his head. "Do you realize between us, we have over 300 IQ points and despite all that intelligence we spent nearly her entire life not having a clue about what she really needed and wanted from us."

His wife nodded.

"How could we have been so wrapped up in our careers, in ourselves, in our certainty of being right, that we never understood Lisa is a marriage of our genes, not a clone. You would think all the rebellion, all the arguments, all the acting out would have given us a clue. But we never saw it." He took a sip from his own glass. "How?"

"Arrogance? Hubris?"

"Indeed. And stupidity. Lissy, when I think back on some of the lectures I gave her, when I think of the number of times she tried to tell me who she was and who she dreamed of becoming, and when I think of how I simply dismissed it all as the ramblings of a child who'd not yet seen the light..." A deep sigh completed the thought.

"I know. But I was no prize either. I'm her mother. I'm the one who *should* have listened."

A shiver ran up her spine.

"I'm just thankful she didn't end up like some of her friends. Between the drugs and abortions and...you know the Cushman's daughter

Rachel?"

Chad nodded.

"Last week I heard she had her third abortion. My lord, didn't anyone ever teach the girl about birth control? And how many times have Mort and Grace had to bail her brother out of jail? When I think of all the things that could have happened, Lisa getting conned and married really isn't so bad. We are very lucky, Chad."

"*Unbelievably* lucky."

He drained the last of his wine, then poured more for both of them.

"You know when it hit me that I might sometimes be a bit full of myself?"

Elissa's arched eyebrows preceded a simple, "When?"

"Three weeks ago, when she brought Rob down to the summer house. We were all having breakfast Sunday morning…"

"Ahh."

She knew what was coming.

"…and he had the audacity to imply that I was cross-examining him. Everyone had a good laugh, but it started me thinking. I realized I *was* treating him like a hostile witness and I wondered how many times in the past I've treated people that way and if that's the reason we have so many acquaintances and so few really close friends. Have I been such an ass my whole life?"

"Pretty much."

She said it with a grin.

"Then why in the world did you stay with me?"

"Because for a long time I was just as big an ass." Her smile softened. "And because I love you."

Chad reached over and took his wife's hand. "I'm a pretty lucky man. I have an amazing daughter, and a future son-in-law who I know will take good care of her. And I have an incredible wife who's not only the most beautiful woman I've ever known, but who's the smartest and funniest, and who inexplicably loves me despite all my faults. I don't believe my life could get any better."

"Oh, I don't know. Perhaps you should get the check so we can head home. I think you may be getting even luckier tonight."

9:35 PM

Is it possible?

Before heading home after work, Priya spent more than an hour walking around the Common with Paul, talking about Brian.

He's clearly convinced Brian is sincere. And his arguments make sense. If it was just a play, would he really have carried it that far? Risked harassment charges and stalking charges?

"Hmmm."

Paul said he looked desperate, but desperate for what? To win some bet? To satisfy his ego? Or is he really that desperate for me not to think badly of him? Does he really like me so much after one date he'd humiliate himself just to raise my opinion of him? Is it possible I've done the same thing Jillian did to Paul the night she saw us together? Did I assume the worst instead of confronting him?

"I did, didn't I?"

But Lisa heard them talking. There's no reason to think she wasn't being truthful. Was she mistaken about what she heard that day? Even if she wasn't, Paul was right. Rumors are sometimes wrong. But she said they used my name. And his name.

"It just doesn't add up."

I did like him before all this. He made me laugh. And we did have fun on the date. And he held his own when we talked. And...oh! Talk. He wanted to talk the next day. About what? If I hadn't discovered...no...been led to believe he was a player, I would probably have gone out with him that Monday and...what? What did he want to tell me? Would it have explained what Lisa heard?

The uncertainty troubled her.

This is not good. This is bad karma, very bad. And if it's true I've misjudged him, I have to make it right.

She wavered back and forth a few more times, but in her heart she knew she had to do it.

I can't condemn him without giving him a chance to defend himself. But I already did, didn't I? I let my past dictate what I did in the present. Just like Maggie's been doing.

I have to call him. I have to give him a chance. But what if Paul was wrong? Do I really want to be alone with him if it plays out badly? Maybe I can ask Paul to be with me when I talk to him. Or I could ask Jillian and Lisa. Or Maggie. She's certainly seen enough players to be able to spot one. Maybe...

An interesting idea popped into her head, but before she let it excite her, she had to make a few phone calls.

When she pressed the *END* button nearly an hour later, Priya was smiling. Everything was set.

She picked up the napkin and dialed Brian's number.

"Hello?"

"Brian, it's Priya."

"Priya, I..."

"Don't talk, listen. You wanted a chance to talk to me. It's Thursday at my place. Eight-thirty sharp. Okay?"

"Priya, I…"

"Okay?"

"Okay."

"Good. I'll see you then. Goodnight, Brian."

THURSDAY, JUNE 3

8:30 PM

When the doorbell rang at precisely eight-thirty, Priya pressed the buzzer and opened her door. She waited until Brian's head rose above the landing so he could see her, said, "Come in and close the door behind you," and vanished back into the apartment.

"Damn. I hope she's not waiting for me in there with a gun."

Brian pushed open the door and stepped into the vestibule. As the door clicked shut, he heard her say, "You can hang your jacket in the closet if you want."

So far so good. If she planned to shoot me, she probably would have preferred the jacket stay on to sop up some of the blood.

"Hi, Priya," he said as he walked through the doorway to the living room. He was prepared to face an unhappy, even hostile Priya, but he wasn't prepared for a room full of unhappy, hostile women scowling at him as if he were the anti-Christ come to steal away the soul of a newborn child. He froze as he caught sight of the group. Two were familiar faces from the night he met Priya. But the rest!

Staring at him from around the room were Jillian, Lisa, Liz, Jenna, Shandra Lewis, Marie Kavanagh, Holly Washington, Maggie Sayer, Marissa Kim, and Gloria Kneeland.

His eyes darted from one to another

So many women. So many angry women! What's going on here?

"Come in, Brian. These are some of my friends. Everyone, this is Brian, the guy you've heard about. Brian, this is everyone."

He blinked a few times, trying to figure out what he should do. The tension level in the room made the air feel thick and difficult to breathe. "I, uh, I thought we were going to talk."

"Well, technically, you've been saying you wanted to talk *to* me, not talk *with* me. So here's you're chance."

"But…"

"These are my friends," she repeated, anticipating his objection, "and they know everything. You came here to tell me something so give it your best shot. But it's not just me you'll have to impress. You'll have to convince everyone. If that's a problem for you, well, you know where your coat is."

Brian saw in her eyes she was serious.

Is she really that special that I put up with weeks of rejection? Do I really like this girl enough after only one date to be willing go through this to be with her?

Yes!

He walked to the center of the room and looked around. Not one person smiled. Moving forward, he stopped about six feet from where Priya was seated. Her eyes bore into him.

"Okay. Here's the thing. A few weeks ago, we went out on what I thought was a really great date. When I brought you home and we said goodnight, I was sure you wanted to see me again. Was I right about that?"

Priya's stare never wavered.

"At that moment, I mean. At that moment, when I brought you home and *you* gave *me* a kiss, you wanted to see me again as much as I wanted to see you. Right?"

She nodded slightly.

"Right. And we made plans to talk Monday night because there was something I needed to tell you. But when I called, I got your machine. Twice. Then I called on Tuesday and on Wednesday but you never returned my calls. At that point, given what I thought I knew about you, I figured you had to be sick or injured or something else bad happened. If it was anyone else, I'd have given up after Tuesday. But I didn't believe you were the kind of person who played the silence game. If you didn't like me, if we hadn't clicked, I knew you'd have told me when I dropped you off. Correct?"

Again Priya dipped her head slightly.

"So I called your work. And you blew me off without giving me a chance to find out what you were talking about.

"After that, any sane guy would have decided you *were* some kind of a loony-tune. But I guess I'm not sane because I couldn't let go of the most incredible woman I've ever met without first finding out what was going on. So here we are. You're pissed off, hell, the whole room here is pissed off at me and I think it's only fair you at least tell me what you think you know about me and how you think you know it."

Priya's eyes narrowed, as if she were trying to see into him to discover if this was real or part of his act. He returned her stare until Lisa cleared her throat, walked over to Priya, and whispered something in her ear.

Nodding, Priya said softly, "You're right."

Lisa straightened up and turned to Brian. "Since you've put so much effort into getting here, you do have a right to know what happened. And since I'm the one who started all this, I'll tell you."

She proceeded to repeat, almost verbatim, the entire conversation she overheard during lunch that day. As she spoke, his eyes grew wider and wider. Periodically, his head would nod or shake the slightest bit. And when she was done, he stared at her for almost ten seconds before shifting his gaze to Priya.

Priya watched closely as Lisa confronted Brian. She expected to see him crumble or grow defiant, but when Lisa finished and he looked again to her, she was completely unprepared for what she saw in his eyes – disappointment.

That startled her, though she remained as she was, her expression unchanged.

"And you believed that?"

He looked around the room at all the girls.

"You all believed that? On the strength of hearsay from a bunch of boneheads you believed that I..."

He closed his eyes and bit his lower lip as if he was trying to restrain himself from saying something. When he opened them again a few seconds later, Priya saw pain now accompanied the disappointment.

His eyes locked with hers as he moved within three feet of her. Then he crouched down, so they would be on the same level.

"Maybe I can sort of understand why you might believe what you did. What I *don't* understand is why you wouldn't have confronted me with it. But, you know something, I don't care right now."

He paused for a second to gather his thoughts.

"When I saw you walk into DHL that night, it was like I was looking at an angel."

He shook his head.

"I know that sounds trite, but honestly, I...I'd never seen anyone so beautiful before in my life. I thought for sure you had to be a model or an actress or something. All I knew was that you were way, waaay out of my league. Still, I couldn't stop looking at you. And then I remembered something. Two or three months ago, Mike Conyers, who works in the same building as I do, by the way, and is *not* a friend, had been going on and on about this incredibly beautiful Indian girl he was dating. Mike's one of those guys who, ah...seem to get more pleasure from bragging about his conquests than he does from the conquests. Know the type?"

Priya nodded, as did most of the women in the room.

"Well, for two weeks or so, Mike would come to work every day with stories of how he was going to nail this beautiful Indian girl. It was only a matter of time, he'd say. Then one day, no bragging. So somebody asked him about you and he started with this story about the virgin ice queen, this religious nut who was saving it for marriage. I mean, he made you out to be…well, trust me when I say you don't want to hear all the details."

He shook his head slightly before continuing.

"The more I thought about it, the more I believed you might be who he was talking about. Certainly you were beautiful enough. Then at some point, I caught your name and knew you had to be the one.

"I really wasn't interested in going out with a crazy virgin, but I'd been watching you and you didn't seem like the head case Mike made you out to be. The people you were with seemed okay and they all seemed to like you and I started to get curious. After the other guys left, when I approached you, all I really wanted was to find out if Mike was full of shit about you being nuts. When you blew me off the way you did, I almost decided he *was* right. But then I realized the line *had* been a little lame, so I figured I'd try honesty.

"Well, we hadn't been playing darts more than ten minutes before I was convinced Mike either lied outright or hadn't a clue about who you really were. Like I said, I didn't intend to ask you out, but by the time you creamed me for the second time Priya, getting to know you better was all I could think about. And then on our date Friday, you were so amazing. You were not like any woman I'd ever dated before."

He paused for another breath, his pupils now boring into her.

"It was at ten-fourteen – I actually looked at my watch because I wanted to remember the exact moment – it was at ten-fourteen when I realized how incredibly special you were, when I realized I didn't care if you were a virgin, I didn't care if I wouldn't be getting laid. I just wanted to be with you. I just wanted to make you feel about me the way I was starting to feel about you."

He sighed.

"But there was the Mike thing."

"I hadn't lied to you, but I wasn't entirely honest either and I didn't want that standing between us. But I couldn't bring myself to chance ruining a great first date by telling you right then. *That* was why I wanted to talk to you Saturday. If you couldn't forgive my omission, well, at least I had the one date. But your family was in town all weekend and when I called Monday, you never called back."

He shuffled a foot closer.

"Priya, I don't care if you're a virgin. I'll never find another woman like you. And I know you liked me, at least a little, when we said goodnight that night. All I'm asking for is a chance, a chance to date you, a chance to get to know you and to let you get to know me. All I want is a chance to see if there might be something there for us.

"And if you say yes, I promise right here in front of all your friends that I will never, ever lie to you. No, wait. If you ever ask me something like 'Does my new hairdo make me look fat' I might have to lie out of self-preservation, but never about anything else."

The girls all tried to restrain their laughter, but a few giggles broke through. Even Priya couldn't help but smile.

"But if you say yes, it has to come with the same promise not to lie to me, and with the same exception, of course. But you'll also have to promise never to judge me again without talking to me first.

"And I know there'll be no sex and there'll be no making out. There'll be nothing beyond the goodnight kiss you gave me after our date. I don't care. No, that's not true. I do care. But I'm willing to accept it because I think you're worth it."

Brian crouched there for a few more seconds then shrugged as he stood up. "That's it. If that's not enough then I'm sorry for both of us. Tell me now and I'll never bother you again."

None of the girls said a word as all heads turned toward Priya, who again seemed to be trying to tap into Brian's soul. She thought about everything that happened, everything she felt, and everything he just said.

Paul was right. He did sound sincere. But wasn't that what players were good at? Making girls believe in them?

She sighed softly. Brian's gaze never wavered. After almost two minutes, the corners of her mouth twitched, then curled into a smile.

"Well...I wouldn't say there'll never be *any* making out."

FRIDAY, JUNE 4

6:40 PM

"What a dope I am." Rob was headed toward Lisa's building carrying two big bags of groceries.

He was getting ready to quit for the weekend when she called him at work with the list. He hated grocery shopping, especially on a Friday night, but she promised him a night he would never forget if he did her this one favor.

When he emerged from the store, he tried to grab a taxi, even though it was less than half a mile to her place. Unfortunately, every taxi in sight seemed to be occupied, so after two minutes of standing there trying to hail one, he gave up and decided to walk.

I wonder what she has in mind. Maybe she bought some new lingerie and she's gonna model it for me. Yeah. I bet she got some of those baby doll things I like. The see-through ones. And after the show I get to take them off her. Nice and slow. And...oh crap. Down boy. That's all I need now is to have to walk down the street with two bags of groceries and a woody.

One block from his destination, his arms began to ache, but he was determined to make it at least to the lobby before he had to put down the bags.

As he approached the building, the doorman pulled wide the heavy brass and glass door. "Quite a load there, Mr. Tello."

"Thanks Phil. And it's Rob, remember. Mr. Tello's my father."

"I'll try to remember that next time, Mr. Tello." They both grinned at the familiar exchange. "Let me call the elevator for you."

By the time the doors reopened, his arms were throbbing. He almost ran down the hall to Lisa's door and pressed the bell. Ten seconds later he saw the peephole darken as she checked who it was before she flipped open the lock. Then the door swung open and both bags almost went crashing to the floor.

Lisa stood in the foyer, wearing a pair of red spike heels and a red, sheer silk wrap with strategically placed panels designed to not hide much, but just enough.

"Well don't just stand there. Close your mouth and come in before one of the neighbors comes by."

She didn't have to tell him twice.

She followed him into the kitchen where he set the bags on the counter. Then she took his hand and led him to the living room sofa. "Sit."

He sat.

She settled down next to him and said, "First, I'm sorry I made you go shopping. We really don't need most of that stuff, but I had to make sure I got home before you so I could get the surprise ready." She blew him a kiss as her hands slid down the front of her wrap. "How's it going so far?"

His hands and lips tried to answer at the same time, but she gently pushed them away.

"None of that. Not yet, anyway."

"Yes, dear."

He didn't know where this was going, but he was more than willing to wait to find out.

"Second, I know I've said it before, but I really want to thank you for everything these past two weeks. I was stupid to try to hide what happened and even more stupid not to do anything about it for so long. And I especially want to thank you for making me tell my parents."

"I didn't exactly make you."

"Okay, but you convinced me. And somehow it's brought us closer together. They've been acting so different since..."

There were tears in her eyes that threatened to spill over.

"You know my mother has called me every day to chat! It's...it's wonderful! I wish they were like this when I was growing up. But I'll take it now and it's all thanks to you."

She leaned over and gave him a short, sweet kiss.

"Next, I talked to my father today, too."

She looked like she'd burst with excitement.

"It's done. I'm a single girl again."

"So fast? He said it would take weeks, not less than one!"

"I guess it pays to have powerful parents!"

"This is great! This is really great!"

She's free now. She's free! Maybe tonight I should...

"And finally..."

She kicked off the heels, jumped up, and threw off the wrap.

"Rob, this is me, standing naked before you. Not just in body, but in mind and soul. You are the nicest, kindest, most decent guy I've ever known. Every day I wake up happy because I know you're with me, and that somehow, you'll find a way to make me feel special.

"I know I'm not the prettiest, or the sexiest, or the smartest girl you could be with, and I'm certainly not the easiest to live with, but there is no other girl in the world who will love you and care for you like I will."

She fell to her knees, took his hands, and stared right into his soul.

"Roberto Tello, love of my life, will you marry me?"

SATURDAY, JUNE 5

9:45 AM

Paul stood preening in front of the bathroom mirror. He was so nervous he nicked himself twice shaving. Today would be a very big day, perhaps one of the most important of his life.

It was his and Jillian's one month anniversary, which was important enough. But today was also the day he would tell her how he felt about her. Not that he imagined she did not already know, but today he would say the words.

I love you.

A flash of insecurity surged through him.

Will she say it back? Of course! I hope. With everything that's been going on lately maybe she's not ready to say it out loud. But she's been better this past week. Whatever's been bothering her doesn't seem to be consuming her like it was. Or maybe she's getting better at hiding it. Hmmm. I guess it doesn't matter. It's time I staked my claim. She's my woman. She's the one. I know it. If she still has doubts, if she's trying to choose between me and this…this ghost, then it's up to me to make her pick me. And if whatever's been bothering her has nothing to do with another guy, well, it's still time for this relationship to move forward. I love her, I'm pretty sure she loves me, and today's the day we say it. And if things go as I hope they will…

"Damn!" A quick glance at his watch showed it was almost ten o'clock and he did not want to start this day off late.

He peeled the bits of tissue from his chin and neck, checked his hair again, grabbed his wallet, cell, and keys, and headed for the door.

Halfway through the three hundred and sixty seven yard walk between his place and hers, his cell phone rang.

"Hey hon, what's up?

"Did you leave yet?"

"Sure did. I'll be there in a few minutes."

"Then I'll wait. I'm running late and…"

"Late! Here I am on time and you're running late!"

"Well it's not *my* fault someone kept me up until three AM."

"Poor baby."

"Darn right. I was about to take a shower, but I'll wait until you get here first."

Paul wanted to tell her he'd be happy to join her in the shower, but didn't want to give even a hint of his plans.

They chatted for the few minutes it took for him to reach her building. After buzzing him in, she told him the apartment door was unlocked, blew him a phone kiss, and headed for the bathroom.

Paul settled in on the sofa, reviewing again his plans for the day.

So we start with a nice leisurely walk along the Charles. Then we grab a light lunch somewhere. Maybe Coffey's. Sure would be appropriate. Then we head over to Fenway. Too bad the Sox are in Kansas City. But the park tour is nice. We can get a picture of us kissing in front of the scoreboard. That'll be cool. Crap. What if she's done that before? Oh well, she hasn't done it before with me. After that we can…

The doorbell snapped him out of his reverie. He could hear the hairdryer running, so he walked over to the intercom.

"I'm sorry," a man's voice said. "I must have the wrong apartment. I'm looking for Jillian Marshall."

"You have the right place."

Behind him, the whine of the hairdryer ended.

"Hi. I'm an old friend of hers from college. I haven't been in Boston for a while, so thought I'd look her up. But I don't want to bother her if she's busy. I guess I should have called first."

"Don't worry about it. She's in the bathroom. Come on up."

He pressed the buzzer to release the downstairs door lock. He started toward the bathroom door but then thought it would be fun if she came out and was surprised by whoever it was.

"I'll be out in a minute. You did say casual, right?"

"Yup. Jeans and whatever will be fine."

There was a light knock on the door. Paul opened to it find a tall, blond guy.

"Come on in."

"Thanks. It's been a long time since I last saw Jillian. If she hadn't been in the phone book I don't know how I'd have found her."

Paul grinned and thought he seemed nice enough. He extended his hand.

"Hi, I'm Paul DiLorenzo."

The guy shook it with a grip as firm as his own.

"Nice to meet you, Paul. I'm…"

"Aiden!"

At the sound of Jillian's voice both men spun to face her.

A six-headed green monster devouring her boyfriend could not have shocked her more than the sight of the man who shadowed her and haunted her thoughts for three weeks shaking hands with him.

"Hello, Jillian. You haven't changed a bit. Well, maybe just a bit. Your hair is different."

I don't believe it. Aiden and Paul in the same room. What does he want? Was Jenna right? Was the stalking part of a plan to get her ready for this? Oh crap, does Paul know who he is?

"I was about to tell Paul we were friends in college, before I took off for five years, never to be heard from again. Until now, of course."

He looks older, more mature. But that self-assured smile hasn't changed. That's what made me…oh…I have to say something or Paul's going to…

"Hello, Aiden. It's been a long time. What are you doing here?"

She tried to keep her voice light, as if he was nothing more than an old classmate. She did not want to get into it in front of Paul.

This must be the guy, the ghost. Why else would she react like that? Damn. I'd feel a lot better if he was a short, fat guy with bad teeth instead of looking like one of those underwear models. He's gotta be at least six-two. Looks like he works out, too. Felt like it, too, from the handshake. If he really is the competition, he certainly beats me in the looks part of the contest. Damn! Bet I could whip his ass in a real fight, though.

"I came to see you, of course. I was overseas most of the time since I graduated. But I can see I'm intruding. You two are going out, yes? Perhaps I can call you tomorrow? We can have lunch soon and catch up."

"Umm, sure. That would be fine. But we really do have to get going now."

She was so focused on Aiden she almost forgot about Paul. When her eyes shifted, she could tell he suspected something was happening below the surface pleasantries, but all he did was raise his eyebrows and give her a reassuring smile.

10:20 AM

"I almost called you last night."

Maggie and Priya settled in at Coffey's, each with a large cup in front of her. Between them sat the single blueberry muffin they agreed to share. This was Maggie's first time at Coffey's. As she lifted the cup to her mouth, Priya was anticipating her friend's reaction to her first taste.

"Why didn't you?"

She grinned as Maggie's eyes widened a bit.

"Wow! You weren't kidding. This is spectacular! Is the muffin this good, too?"

"Try it and see."

Priya loved bringing new people here. So far, no one was disappointed.

"Wow again! How did I never hear about this place?"

Priya shrugged.

"You've obviously led a sheltered life, caffeine-wise."

Maggie laughed.

"That may be the only-wise."

"Hey. I thought we agreed there'd be no negative jokes or comments. So why didn't you call last night? You didn't..."

"No. It's fifteen days and counting. But I came close."

"How close? Tell me."

"I was out with some girls from work. We went up to the Palace in Saugus. One of the girls knew someone in one of the bands that are playing there."

She saw the question in Priya's eyes.

"No, I was not drinking. Strictly diet soda all night. But there was this guy. He asked me to dance a couple of times, then we started talking, and Priya, he was hot. Not just a face and a body, but funny, too. Then, about midnight, both of the girls I went with told me they were leaving with guys they picked up.

"I could see in Eddie's eyes that he wanted me. And I really wanted him."

Her voice became a whisper so people are nearby tables wouldn't overhear what she said next.

"Priya, I was so wet I felt like I was dripping, even when I was sitting."

She closed her eyes and sighed

"Anyway, he asked if I wanted to leave and I almost said yes. But instead, I told him I had to pee and walked to the ladies room, intending to call you so you could convince me not to go with him. But the strangest thing happened. By the time I reached the bathroom, I realized that just knowing I *could* call you made me think of how you'd feel if I gave in and slept with him. And suddenly, it was more important not to disappoint you than it was to have him close to me that night. I never had that feeling before, Priya."

"Lord, Maggie, I'm so proud of you. That was your first real test, and you kicked ass. But I wish you *had* called me so I could have been happy for you last night, too!"

"If that hadn't happened, I would have. But I knew you were out with Brian and I didn't want to bother you."

"Don't be ridiculous. I told you when we began, this is a twenty-four/seven thing. How do you think *I'd* feel if you needed to call me and didn't because you thought it would bother me and then…"

She left it unsaid.

"Please promise me you'll call if it happens again. I don't care if it's four in the morning."

Maggie felt a surge of warmth as she gave Priya the assurance she wanted. She marveled at how close to her she felt after only two short weeks. They talked every day, met for lunch when they could, and hung out even when Brian was around. She learned just how serious Priya was when she promised to help her and to always be there for her, for as long as it took to get her head, and her life, to where she always dreamed they should be.

I wonder if this is what it's like to have a sister.

It was much too soon for her to trust her emotions. She knew *that* confidence would be a long time coming. Still, she could tell Priya really cared about her and knew she felt the same way.

The sound of children crashing through the front door caused many heads to turn, including their own.

"Hey, that's Tom and Patti and the kids! Tom's one of the guys I work with."

An evil grin crept across her face as she reached for the empty foil muffin cup and crumpled it into a small ball.

"Have I ever mentioned my incredible hand-eye coordination?"

Tom was still by the door, his back to them, about fifteen feet way. Priya half-turned in her seat, brought her arm back, and let the ball fly. And fly it did, bouncing dead center off the back of Tom's head.

"What the hell…?"

He turned to find Priya and another woman sitting at a table laughing.

"I should have known."

He herded his family over to their table.

"You know, in some companies, assaulting the boss gets you all the boring, rinky-dink work for a month or more."

Priya laughed.

"It was worth it to see the look on your face when you turned around."

Priya introduced Maggie and Tom did the same for Patti and his kids, Justin, Katie, Louisa, Frank, and Kerri.

"What are you guys doing in town?"

"Taking your advice. Having fun with the family. The kids wanted to see where dad worked."

Patti snorted.

"Advice? The way I heard it, it was more like an order."

Priya's eyes flicked from Tom to Patti and back again.

"Yes, against your orders, he confessed to telling you all. I'm glad he did. He needed to unload and I was so…well, it wasn't fair to make him keep it all inside. Thank you for being there for him. And please thank Paul and Rob, too."

Priya smiled.

"I will. Umm…is everything okay?"

"Yes! The doctor called yesterday. It's just a cyst. They're taking it out next Thursday."

"That's wonderful news! No wonder you're celebrating!"

They all chatted for a few more minutes until it became obvious the kids were approaching their tolerance level for standing around quietly. After buying coffee for themselves, juice for the kids, and pastry for all, Tom and Patti said goodbye and led the kids out for a picnic on the Common.

"Are you and Brian going out, tonight?"

"Not really. I'm meeting him later for a few hours, but he's off to some seminar in Dallas tonight. He won't be back until late Tuesday night. Why? Want to do something?"

"Maybe. Do you like old movies? Old love stories?"

"You mean like the old black and white things with Gretta Garbo and Lauren Bacall and such?"

Maggie nodded.

"Sure. I love those things."

"Well I rented *Roman Holiday* with Audrey Hepburn and Gregory Peck, *How to Marry a Millionaire* with Marilyn Monroe, Betty Grable and Lauren Bacall, and *An Affair to Remember* with Cary Grant and Deborah Kerr. Want to come over and watch them with me?"

Priya thought for a minute.

"Brian's not leaving for the airport until six-thirty. I can pick up a pizza or something and be there between seven and seven-thirty. Okay?"

"Okay. But no anchovies."

"Were you planning to watch all three movies?"

"Well, yes. I had nothing else to do. You don't have to stay for all of them, though."

"Don't be silly. Those are three classics. I'm thinking maybe I'll bring some clothes and sleep on the couch."

"Yes! I owe you a sleepover. But no barfing all over yourself like I did."

Priya laughed.

"I promise. No binge drinking tonight."

Maggie joined the laughter.

"So you know those are classics. Does that mean you're a movie buff?"

It was Priya's turn to lower her voice as she said with a grin, "You may not know this, but we virgins spend a lot of time alone in our apartments. We watch lots and lots of movies. Especially love stories, so we can dream of the day we're *not* virgins anymore."

11:25 AM

Jillian and Paul lay on the grass in front of the Hatch Shell on the Esplanade, site of the annual Boston Pops Fourth of July concerts. They were on their backs, feet pointed in opposite directions, heads touching ear-to ear.

They strolled the mile and a half from her apartment to the Esplanade, stopping frequently to watch sailboats on the Charles or kids playing on the wide strip of grass that lined the shore.

As they relaxed, Paul laid out his plans for the day with the exception of the two most important events. Although they chatted about work and friends most of the way, he noted she never brought up old friend Aiden.

From the way she reacted when she saw him and the way she's that little bit distracted again, that guy Aiden has to be more than just a classmate. He has to be the ghost, the guy who hurt her. Damn him for showing up today of all days. Hmmm. If he can distract her that much, maybe I should rethink the plan for tonight. Or maybe it'd be better just to stick to it.

As they lay there, his mind churning like an out-of-control washing machine, he realized he was making himself crazy with worry and could stand it no longer.

"Are you going to tell me about him? He's the ghost, isn't he, the guy you've been thinking about for the past few weeks?"

Jillian knew the question would be coming. She dreaded it from the moment Aiden walked out her door, reiterating his promise to call her tomorrow. Thoughts and questions swirled through her almost faster than she could register them.

Why did I agree? Why didn't I yell and scream at him, as I've wanted to do for so long? If I really love Paul that much, why didn't I throw Aiden out? Why am I hiding all this from him? But I do love him. He's everything I ever wanted in a man, and more. Isn't he? Why am I acting like this? Why, why, why? There are too many whys. And now I have to tell Paul about him.

As the silence dragged on, she became more frantic.

What should I tell him? The truth, of course, and all of it. But how? It doesn't matter. Just say it before he starts imagining the worst.

"I'm sorry for the way I've been acting, Paul. Seeing him like that sort of threw me."

She rolled over on her side to face him.

"Aiden and I lived together when I was in college. He was the first man I ever really loved. We were together for two years. We...we were engaged, but he ran out, ran away, really, the day after he graduated."

Paul rolled over to face her.

"Do you still have feelings for him?"

"No!"

She knew she said it too quickly, too forcefully, as if she was trying to convince herself instead of him. But it was a lie and it was clear Paul suspected from the way his eyes probed hers.

This can't be happening. He doesn't believe me. And why should he? I don't believe it myself.

Abruptly, she jumped up.

"Paul, I loved him for so long. And then I hated him for so much longer. And I thought I'd put it behind me. All of it. But...but...seeing him again dredged up all these feelings and I don't know... Please. Please wait here for a few minutes."

Then she turned and walked quickly toward the river bank.

As he did the say they met, Paul watched her hair swing back-and-forth in a gentle counterpoint to the sway of her hips. He smiled at the memory, but with each step away from him, the bad feeling that started the moment she said 'Aiden!' grew stronger and stronger.

As he waited, he replayed in his mind the night of their first date.

What a fool. I should have slept with her. I should have grabbed her heart and filled it so full of me that there'd be no room left for this Aiden guy. Maybe it would have worked out. Maybe.

She stood rooted to a spot by the shore for almost five minutes, so he lay on his back again to enjoy the fair weather clouds in the baby blue sky. As much as he wanted to go to her and lobby for himself, he knew whatever she needed to think about, whatever she needed to decide, she had to do it alone.

No sooner did he settle down, though, than a shiver ran through him, a premonition. He turned his head and saw someone approaching her from the left. It took a few seconds for his eyes to refocus and realize it was Aiden.

"What the hell is *he* doing here?"

By the time Paul leapt to his feet, Aiden reached her and said something that caused her to start. Before he could take two steps, Jillian turned away from Aiden and faced him. Even from a distance, he could see the tears in her eyes as she held up both hands, palms forward, and shook her head, asking him to stop, to not get involved. It took more will than he expected, but he did as she asked.

The next twelve minutes were the most difficult of his life.

"I hope those tears aren't for me," Aiden said.

"What are you doing here?"

She pulled a tissue from her pocket to blot her eyes. "Were you following us the way you were following me two weeks ago?"

His confident grin never wavered.

"I figured you knew it was me. I'm sorry about that. I wanted to learn a little about who you'd become before I contacted you. To see if you were married or a nun or something."

He hoped that last line would elicit a smile, but it didn't.

"What do you want, Aiden? After all this time."

His smile faded. He started to reach out to touch her, but held back.

"I owe you an apology, Jillian. And an explanation. I know both are long overdue, but you deserve to hear them, if you want to."

The hardness in her eyes softened a little, encouraging him to go on.

"Jillian, I am more sorry than you will ever believe for the horrible way I treated you. I was young, and confused, and so full of myself that I didn't really see how my decision would affect you. I knew you'd be hurt, but at the time I was too much of a coward to face the hurt and the betrayal I knew I'd see if I told you in person.

"Not a day has gone by since then that I've not been ashamed of what I did to you. And to myself. I had a wonderful girl who loved me, who was ready and willing to share her life with me, and I tossed it all away like an old laundry ticket.

"I don't know how you could ever forgive something like that, but I hope, I pray you've found a way and that the pain and hate have not been with you all these years."

Jillian never before saw shame and sorrow on Aiden's face and it took her a minute to recognize them. The realization tugged at her heart.

"I need to know why, Aiden."

"Yes, of course. You have a right to know why I left as I did."

He paused for a few seconds, taking deep breaths and releasing them slowly, not unlike what Jillian did to relax and prepare for her yoga class.

"Do you remember Christmas break of my senior year? I wanted you to come home with me, but you said it would be our last chance to have a special Christmas alone with our families."

"I remember."

"Do you remember I didn't call you for a week and that when we returned to school..."

"You were acting strange."

"That was because the day after New Year's, my parents decided that since I was getting married soon, it was time to tell me I was adopted."

She flinched a little, not expecting such a revelation, but she remained silent.

"It seems the daughter of one of my mother's cousins in Sweden got pregnant. My parents had been trying unsuccessfully to have a child for ten years, so she came to stay with them, had the baby, signed the adoption papers, and returned to Sweden.

"When they told me, I, uhh, I didn't take it well. My reaction hurt my parents, I know, but I couldn't help myself. I railed at them for letting me grow up without knowing my true heritage. I was very mean and very hurtful and they didn't deserve it, but I was young and stupid and it didn't matter they promised Hanna not to tell me until I married. Hanna's my birth mother. Hanna Giertz.

"So I took off for a week. I crashed with friends and spent the time thinking. When I calmed down and went home again, I apologized to them, but I could see they were still hurt. And inside *I* was still hurt. And confused. Suddenly, my whole life was a lie. I felt like I didn't know who I was anymore.

"After the break, I knew you could see the change in me. But you accepted my 'nothing's wrong' and went on loving me. And that's when things really started getting crazy inside my head. Suddenly, there were all these fears, all these questions.

"How could I love you if I didn't know who I was? How could you love me? What if our love was based on a fantasy, on who we thought I was, but it wouldn't even exist once I discovered who I really was. I know it sounds crazy, but that was just a small part of what began to consume me. If it wasn't for you being there to ground me, I don't know how I would have finished the year and graduated.

"Then, as graduation, and the wedding day approached, I became convinced the only fair thing for me to do was to go away and find out who I really was. I had to find my birth mother, but more than that, I had to discover my whole heritage. I couldn't make a life with you when I didn't even know who I'd be once I searched out the truth. When I left, when I wrote that note, I honestly imagined I'd only be gone a few months, at most."

She listened quietly, patiently, almost hypnotized by this Aiden who was so unlike the man she remembered, who opened himself up in a way he never had during their time together. "But..."

"But why didn't I tell you? Why didn't I share the burden? Why didn't I trust you, let you help, or at least be there for me?"

"Yes!"

"I told you. I was young and stupid and confused. And without realizing it, I was in the midst of a nervous breakdown. What I really needed back then was not to find my birth mother, but a psych ward to get me thinking straight again.

"You have to know it wasn't anything to do with you, Jillian. I didn't leave because I didn't love you. In my mixed up head, I was leaving because I *did* love you. Because you deserved to know who I really was before tying yourself to me. And then, by the time I came to my senses and realized what I'd done to you, it was too late. Too much time had gone by. I knew you would have moved on."

"Then why..."

"Have I come back now?"

The tiniest of smiles curled the corners of her lips.

At least that hasn't change. We always were good at completing each other's sentences.

"Yes."

"I did find my birth mother. Thankfully, screwed up as I obviously was, she and her husband welcomed me, introduced me to all the other relatives, and let me live with them most of the first year. And they insisted I keep in touch with my parents. Between all of them, they helped me return to sanity, I guess, is the best way to put it. And by the way, I don't know if you contacted my parents after the first few months, but it was almost a year before they knew where I was. So please don't hold it against them if..."

"I only called them a couple of times after the first few weeks. I hated you too much after that to care."

It was Aiden's turn to flinch. Certainly he knew how she must have felt then, but it was hard to hear it from her own lips. He sighed and nodded.

"During that first year, as I was recovering and learning about who I was, I learned Swedish and found a job teaching English.

"Almost eighteen months went by before I went home to visit for the first time. I've been going back a couple of times a year since then. Twice, I arranged a stopover in Boston for a night, so I could check the phonebook to see if you moved, maybe get a glimpse of you going in or out.

"Then a few months ago, I realized I had settled into a life there. And it was a good life. But a part of me still missed my old home in Indiana. Or so I thought. It took a few weeks of introspection, but I finally realized what I really missed most was not my old hometown or my parents. It was you.

"*Du var min stora kärlek, min vackra blomma, och jag har tänkt på dig varje dag. Varenda dag.* You were my great love, my beautiful flower, and I have thought about you every day. Every single day."

He ran his fingers through his hair as he used to do whenever he was about to say something important.

"I realized it was time to decide whether or not I'd stay there and make it my home. But I also realized the thought of never seeing you again was more than I could bear. So I had to come back to see if there was any chance of rekindling what we had together. I found this beautiful life, Jillian, but it's empty because you're not in it. I wanted you to see it, to be a part of it.

"So I took a sabbatical and came to Boston. But when I arrived, I found I was incredibly nervous, that I had no idea what to say to you after all this time. And it occurred to me you probably hadn't even thought about me for years. Or if you did, there was a curse of some sort attached. I figured if I just showed up, you'd probably throw something at me, so I watched you for a while.

"At first, I wanted to figure out if you were with someone and if it was serious. Then, when you noticed me that day through the coffee shop window, I realized it might be a good thing if you started thinking about me before I actually showed my face, to sort of give you time to get used to the idea of me again. But as I was following you, trying to give you just the occasional glimpse of me, I felt more and more foolish. So I went home to visit my parents for a while and think about how to approach you. And by the time my flight landed yesterday, all I wanted to do was to see you, take whatever I had coming, and hope for the best. There was really nothing else I *could* do.

"So now you know it all. I realize none of it is an excuse for what I did, but it's the truth. And you deserve to know."

Paul was watching them, unable to tear his eyes away. Aiden seemed to be doing most of the talking, his hands often moving about to emphasize something while Jillian stood still for the most part, occasionally shaking or nodding her head. Twice, she glanced over at him, perhaps to make sure he was still there. But she did not seem at all upset with Aiden and that worried him.

Then, when it seemed as if the dread filled him to overflowing, he saw them turn and walk toward him. Aiden did not look happy, but neither did he look sad or upset. Suddenly, Paul was not sure he really wanted to hear what would come next.

They stopped four feet from him and Jillian moved to form the third point of a triangle.

"I have a lot to say, and I want you both to hear it all, but I'd appreciate it if neither of you said anything until I'm done. Okay?"

Both men nodded.

Facing Paul first, she said, "Some of this may not be easy for you to hear, but I owe it to you to finally be completely honest. You deserve to know what's been going on.

"Over the past month, since I met you, I've come to realize what a special person you are. You've opened me up in a way I would not have thought possible after what Aiden did. For that alone, I'll always be grateful to you. And I think I know how you feel about me. I think I've known since our first date.

"But knowing all that was part of why I've been so distracted lately. Ever since our first date, I wanted you so much. But when I started thinking about Aiden again, it felt like a part of my heart still wanted to see him, despite the way he hurt me, despite his abandonment, despite everything. And I knew that wasn't fair to you. I felt like I was betraying you. You're such an incredible guy that you deserve a woman whose only thoughts are for you, who has no reservations about anything, who can make a commitment to you without harboring feelings for a lost love."

She turned to Aiden. "What you did to me was inexcusable, but thinking I saw you again made me believe a part of me really did want to see you. So I guess your little game worked even though it confused and distracted me. More than that, really, it consumed me. And Paul paid the price for it these past weeks. But you showing up this morning, and then again, here, made me understand I was right. I did want to see you. I *needed* to see you."

She shifted back to Paul. "I hope you can forgive me, Paul. I know my distance and distraction hurt you. I told you the night you asked me about it that there was something I needed to sort through on my own. I don't know what you might have imagined or suspected, but I'm sorry. I'm so sorry for putting you through it. But now the time has come to do what I need to do. I *have* sorted through it, and I have to do what's right for me, do what will make my life right again."

Turning again, she said, "Aiden, I don't think you ever really understood the depth of my feelings for you. I don't think you really knew how completely I loved you. And so I don't think you can possibly imagine how much you hurt me, how devastating it was for me to find that note you left, to have to read about your abandoning me instead of hearing it from your own lips.

"For months afterwards, my whole being wanted you to come back, wanted you to take me in your arms again and tell me it was a joke, a cruel, drunken joke. And though I believed I was over you, I realize now that all this time, a small part of me still wanted you to return.

"When you appeared again it scared me. I told myself I didn't want to open old wounds, relive old, buried feelings. But try as I might to stop them, all the old feelings came flooding out, confusing me, but also forcing me to think about what I really wanted. And over the past few days, that's all I've done is think, really think. And seeing you now, talking to you, listening to what you had to say, now I know.

"I want a man who will love me as unconditionally as I'll love him, a man who'll stand by me and help me, who'll let me help him. I want a man who'll share with me, not just his life, but his thoughts and feelings, his very soul. I want a man who'll laugh with me when I'm happy, who'll take care of me when I'm sick, and who'll let me care for him when he's hurting. I want a man who sees who I am on the inside, deep inside, where I don't let anyone else look. I want a man who'll let me be who I am, who won't try to change me, or expect me to change him. I want a man who makes me laugh, who surprises me, who gets me. I know that sounds like a lot, but it's what I want.

"I'm happy you came back, Aiden. Happy to hear you've made a life for yourself. Happy you still care for me and want me back. It completes the circle of our relationship."

Her eyes bore into his. "For so long, I wanted to hurt you, to yell and scream and humiliate you, to give you a taste of what it was like for me back then. But now that the opportunity is here, after listening to your explanation, I just feel sorry for you."

When she shook her head, her whole body appeared to shiver.

"My god, Aiden! You found out you're adopted so you abandoned the people who loved you, who cared for you, who would have done anything for you? You tossed away two years of our lives because you freaked out?"

She took a step toward Paul.

"You see this guy. Take a good look. Here is a man who is all the things I said I wanted a minute ago, a man who saw the person inside me before I even knew who she was. Here is a man who's been nothing but sweet and kind and loyal despite all the doubts he must have felt about the way I was acting these past weeks. Here is a man, Aiden. A genuine, strong, loving, caring man. And he cares about me. I'm still not entirely sure why, but he does. You must have been experimenting with some pretty powerful drugs for five years to think I'd actually leave someone as wonderful as Paul for anyone, much less someone like you."

Without even meaning to, she had succeeded in humiliating and humbling Aiden. He caught her eyes, then Paul's, then returned to Jillian.

"I...I guess I knew this is what would probably happen. But I had to make amends as best I could. And I had to try. I had to know for certain."

He started to leave, but after three paces, turned back and said to Paul, "Jillian was an amazing girl in college. And I can see she's become an even more amazing woman."

He shook his head, a rueful half-smile curling one corner of his mouth.

"You know, I chased her for two months before she'd go out with me. I can't even tell you why. Something just drew me to her. And after our first night together, I was sure I'd found heaven on Earth.

"I'll regret my stupidity for the rest of my life. Hold onto her and make her happy. You'll never find another like her."

With that, he turned and walked away.

Jillian and Paul stood quietly, unmoving, as they watched Aiden for the two minutes it took him to reach the sidewalk and lose himself in the crowd.

"I'm sorry, Paul. I'm so, so sorry. I'm sorry for everything I've put you through these past weeks. But even more, I'm sorry for not telling you. Even though I wanted to take care of it on my own, I should have told you. I can only imagine what you must have been…"

Paul interrupted. "Does this mean you're not breaking up with me?"

"Breaking up with you? Breaking up with you!"

She threw her arms around his neck and kissed him. Then she buried her face in his neck and said, "Don't you know how much I love you?"

He pressed her to him, his head suddenly light with joy.

"I thought I did. But then he showed up, and…and everything else that followed seemed…damn!"

"What's wrong?"

"Oh nothing." He sounded forlorn even though he was grinning. "It's just, I had all these plans for today. And all of it was to surprise you, to find the right moment, the perfect moment to tell you how much *I* love *you.*"

His grin turned into a pout.

"And now you've gone and said it first."

The rest of the day was spent talking about anything and everything except Aiden.

They stopped by Coffey's, where, to their delight they were able to use their favorite 'whatever you're giving away for free today' line. Then they took a taxi to Fenway Park and had their picture taken kissing in front of The Green Monster. Souvenir in hand, they walked the three blocks to the Fens and strolled from one end to the other, stopping frequently, once for an hour to watch the end of a little league game.

As evening approached, they talked about what to do next. Neither really wanted to go out to eat or to a club or wanted people and noise around them, so Paul suggested they stop by the market for some groceries. Since he cooked for her several times, she could cook for him tonight.

"Are you sure you want to take that chance? I've tried to tell you over and over I'm not much good in the kitchen beyond boiling water."

Paul put his arm around her. "My stomach has complete confidence in you."

Five minutes later, as the automatic door to the grocery store swung open before them, Paul asked, "Do you have *any* food in the house?"

"Coffee and tea. Maybe some crackers. And probably some moldy leftovers in the fridge."

He shook his head and laughed.

"Sad. Really sad. Look, I obviously shop here more than you do and I know where everything is. Why don't you go next door to the deli and get some cheesecake for dessert. I'm really in the mood for cheesecake. I'll get what you'll need to cook dinner and meet you outside."

"But what if I don't know how to…"

"Please, trust me. Everything I buy will be geared to your skill level."

Ten minutes later, Paul emerged from the market with a bag of groceries. Across the top was a thick loaf of Italian bread.

"What'd you get?"

"You'll see. Wait 'til we get home. This bag is heavy."

Jillian's cell phone rang as Paul unlocked his front door.

"Let me have the cheesecake and you can grab that."

"Happy anniversary," Priya said when Jillian answered. "I thought you'd have your phone turned off and was going to leave a message on your voicemail. Why aren't you out with Paul?"

"Thank you! Actually, we've been out all day. We're at his place now. He wants me to cook him dinner."

"But you..."

"I know. I told him, but he assured me I'd have no problem cooking what he bought."

"Which is?"

"I don't know. He's in the kitchen unpacking the bag now."

"Then I won't keep you. You two have fun tonight. And don't do anything I haven't done yet."

"I should be so lucky!"

Jillian closed the phone, walked through the kitchen doorway, and stopped cold. "You jerk!" she exclaimed, laughing.

True to his word, everything Paul purchased was geared toward Jillian's non-existent cooking skills. Laid out on the small counter were the loaf of sliced bread, a family-size heat and serve meatloaf, a can of brown gravy, a package of frozen mixed vegetables, a box of boil-a-bag rice, and two bottles of wine.

"Think you'll need some help?"

He received a playful glare as an answer.

"Then I'll go put on some music."

When he returned, the meatloaf was in the oven and two small pans of water and an empty sauce pan were on the stovetop for later use in heating the rice, vegetables, and gravy.

Paul uncorked one of the bottles and poured two glasses of wine.

"How long before you have to start the veggies and rice?"

"Forty-five minutes or so."

"Good. Want to sit down?"

He nodded toward the small table and chairs.

"Wait."

Jillian set the timer for forty-five minutes.

"Let's sit on the sofa."

Once settled in, Paul reached over and took Jillian's hand.

"Remember how we agreed that if something is bothering us, we should talk about it?"

"Of course."

She knew what was on his mind.

"Aiden."

Paul sighed.

"Aiden. How is it that he suddenly appeared on the Esplanade like that? And what, exactly, were you two talking about for so long?"

"Evidently, when he left my apartment this morning, he hung around and followed us."

"What!"

"It doesn't surprise me. Propriety was never a strong suit of his. It was one of the things that attracted me to him back when I was young and foolish.

"He said he wanted to know how close you and I really were, and when he saw me walking away and you didn't come after me, he thought perhaps we'd had a fight or something and that it was a good time to approach me."

"By the way, why *did* you walk away like that?"

"Because I was upset at myself and had all these feelings I didn't understand and I knew I was about to cry and you'd been so sweet and I didn't want to ruin things by letting you *see* me cry."

"But…"

"I know. It was stupid. If I can't cry in front of the man I love…"

"And who loves you."

"…and who loves me, then what's the use of it all? I think it was the shock of seeing him after all these years."

Paul nodded.

"As for what we talked about, actually, he did most of the talking."

She snorted.

"Same as when we were together, come to think of it. First, he tried to apologize for running out on me. Then he explained about being adopted and going off to find his roots, then he told me he wanted me back, that he'd made a huge mistake, and blah, blah, blah."

"And what did you say?"

"You heard what I said. That was when I brought him over and made my little speech.

"I wanted to hit him and hurt him for so long, but taking the high road like that, well, it finally released all the misery and anger I've carried around for so long. And it felt *really good*.

"You know, if he hadn't shown up, I think his memory would have haunted me for the rest of my life. Today finally gave me closure."

Again, Paul nodded. She was on a roll and he did not want to disturb it.

"I've been thinking about something else, too, all afternoon. It turns out you really were smart to say no that first night. If we *had* slept together, I don't think I'd be feeling the same as I do right now. I don't think you would, either. Aiden's reappearance would have really upset things."

She shrugged.

"Who knows? All I know is I want more wine. You want some, too?"

"Sure."

Again he reveled in the rhythmic sway of her backside as she went to fetch the wine from the fridge. After filling the glasses, she asked, "What are the eggs and crescent rolls for?"

"Breakfast."

"You know I have to get up at seven to meet my sisters."

"I know."

"You want me to get up that early to come over here for breakfast?"

"No."

He stood up in front of her. She looked confused. Then he pulled her to him and kissed her. It was a kiss not unlike the first one they shared on the beach. When it was over and she looked up at him, she saw it in his eyes.

She sighed with anticipation as her arms encircled him and pulled his lips back to hers. At some point, shoes and shirts and pants were discarded and Paul lifted her in his arms and carried her into the bedroom. He set her down gently, and within seconds, the last wisps of clothing were crumpled on the floor.

He gasped at his first sight of her lithe, sensuous beauty and she stared for a few seconds, pleased at the sight of what she'd only previously felt pressing against her thigh. Then she was stretched out on the bed and he was next to her, his lips devouring hers as their hands began their long awaited, much anticipated explorations.

She shivered at the soft, knowing touch of the fingers that started at her ear, traced their way along the curves of her neck and chest, and began teasing her breasts. The lips that planted soft kisses all over her face drifted lower and she moaned as they reached the special spot below her ear that redoubled her shivers. His hand cupped first one, then the other breast before the palm rubbed over and around her nipples, stimulating them to hardness, causing thrills of exquisite pleasure. Then his fingertips explored the contours of her stomach while her hand sought out his manhood.

When her fingers closed around him, his deep, low groan thrilled her. His hand continued to move lower, circling, teasing, building the passion inside her until she could no longer stand it and pleaded softly, "Touch me. Please touch me."

So he did, and she wanted to scream with the intensity of the pleasure, but all she could manage were incoherent moans.

She was ready, so ready, as she knew he was, too. His hand abandoned its ministrations and he moved over her. Leaning on his elbows, he cupped her head with his hands, leaned down, and kissed her, his body lightly pressing against her own. And when he entered her for the first time, he seemed to fill her completely, not only physically, but emotionally and spiritually. He truly became a part of her as they began to move, slowly at first, but then faster and faster as their urgency expanded and consciousness contracted until only the two, as one, remained.

Neither of them heard the timer's bell when it rang a while later, as they lay in each other's arms, sweating and panting, enjoying the afterglow together for the first time. Neither of them heard much of anything for the next sixty-seven minutes except loving whispers, sighs, and moans of pleasure, until, as they were sharing their love for the third time, the smoke alarm began to shriek.

EPILOGUE

THURSDAY, MAY 5, 2005

6:15 PM

"It's me."

Priya pressed the buzzer and opened her door.

"Hey girlfriend."

Maggie usually picked her up on dinner nights so they could spend some time chatting before heading to that week's restaurant.

She grabbed an open bottle of wine from the fridge and poured two glasses. She handed one to Maggie and waited for her to give what had become their traditional toast.

"To the virgin and the slut, the most unlikely best friends in Boston."

They clinked glasses and sipped the wine as they did every week, then, completing the ritual, put down their glasses and hugged.

"Congratulations on another week."

"Thank you." Maggie squeezed her friend a little harder than usual before letting go and retrieving her glass.

"Do you realize that in two weeks it will be a whole year?"

Priya looked as sad as she sounded.

"I know, but why the long face. I thought you'd be happy for me."

"I am, of course. But I figure that after a whole year of you not sleeping with anyone, we can't be the virgin and the slut anymore."

"Why not? Are you planning to fuck Brian's brains out now that you have that rock on your finger?"

She may have given up men for almost a year, but Maggie was as uninhibited as ever with her language. The look Priya gave her made her laugh.

"Of course not! I've waited twenty-four years. You think I can't wait another two months until my wedding night?"

She stuck her tongue out at her friend who returned the favor.

"It's just that, on the one hand, I like that private joke we have. But on the other hand, I don't want you to keep thinking of yourself that way. Because you're not a slut, and…"

"Oh, Pri."

Maggie hugged her again, almost spilling her wine in the process. Since the night she drank herself sick, threw-up all over herself, then slept it off on Priya's sofa, they truly had become the very best of friends.

At first, their relationship was tentative. Despite everything, it was hard for Maggie to accept Priya could be so selfless, so willing to help her overcome her addiction without expecting anything but friendship in return. That doubt vanished in July when Priya dragged herself out of bed at two-thirty in the morning and took a taxi almost forty miles to Pelham, New Hampshire to rescue her. She actually had her panties off that night when the thought of Priya's disappointment sent her into the guy's bathroom with her cell phone. Priya told her to lock the door and not open it until she arrived.

Back at Maggie's apartment, Priya sat up with her as she cried and talked and realized she finally found a real and true friend. She never looked back after that day. She decided to make her friend proud of her and she did. Each week, hearing Priya congratulate her gave Maggie a sense of accomplishment and pride that was better than anything she achieved at work. Even better, she found a peace that all those years of non-stop sex were never able to provide.

"Sweetie, I stopped thinking of myself as a slut long ago. I only say it because it's special to me, special to us."

Tears began rolling down her cheeks.

"And I'll still be saying it someday when you and Brian are married and me and somebody are married and we both have a pack of kids, and everything's starting to sag, and life will be driving us crazy, but I'll know the virgin will always be there for me, just like the slut will always be there for her."

9:45 PM

"Now, I won't guarantee Jilli and I will, ahh, be able to spend too much time with you guys."

Jessie reached over and patted Gary's thigh. "Oh, that won't be a problem, Paul. I'm sure we'll think of something to amuse ourselves."

Gary reddened as Jessie made suggestive faces, then giggled at his reaction.

"I love it that he's so easy to embarrass."

"Stop or I'll tickle."

Gary wiggled his fingers. If they were alone, she would have continued to tease him until he did start to tickle. Then she would attack him the same way and they would squirm and laugh until one or the other called a truce and make love. But they *were* with Paul at his condo, so they just shared a quick kiss.

"I know Gary's already said this, but thank you so much. This is going to be a great time. I can't believe you're taking her down the Cape for four days and then paying for us, too."

"Well today *is* the one year anniversary of the day we met. And Saturday *is* the anniversary of our first date. And what was I going to do, have Gary drive us all the way down to Orleans and then come back here and then come back to get us in a few days? Besides, the way things are going with you two, and with me and Jilli, we'll all be related someday anyway."

That drew a blush from Gary *and* Jessie, who decided to change the subject.

"What time do you want to leave?"

"Well, these Thursday night dinners usually run until midnight, but I thought I'd show up around 11:30 or so to surprise her."

"And she has no idea?"

"I don't think so. I arranged with a couple of the girls to make sure she stays until I show up, but she never leaves early anyway.

"Say…this won't create any problems at school for either of you, will it?"

Both shook their heads.

"Jessie doesn't have any classes tomorrow. I have one, but I cleared it with the professor."

"And we're both bringing books and stuff for studying."

Jessie ran her fingers through her hair.

Paul slapped his thigh.

"That's what it is!"

His guests' quizzical looks made him smile.

"Well, I haven't seen you guys since Easter and something's been bugging me and I just realized Jessie cut her hair."

"Oh, the haircut." Gary said it without much enthusiasm.

"He hates it."

"That's true…" He caressed what was left of her beautiful locks. "…but I still love you."

10:00 PM

"You know, this was a great idea," Jenna said as she turned to Cathy. "I'm really glad you thought of it."

Two weeks previous, Cathy O'Hara was invited to dinner with the group. Everyone liked her as much as she liked them, so, as the newest member, it was her turn to choose the location for tonight. When she asked if there were any rules requiring it be a regular restaurant, no one could think of any, so she suggested eating dinner in the Franklin Hotel restaurant and spending the rest of the evening in the Candlelight Lounge.

Jillian hesitated only because she suspected Paul might be taking her there as part of their first anniversary celebration Saturday, but everyone else embraced the idea so enthusiastically, she would not have felt right nixing it.

So here they were and it turned out to be a special evening for another reason. For the first time in months, all the members made it to dinner. Perhaps it was the novelty of dancing after dinner, or perhaps it was simple serendipity, but everyone was here -- Jillian, Liz, Jenna, Priya, Lisa, Maggie, Marissa, Gloria, Holly, Cathy, Shandra, and Marie.

"I've wanted to come here ever since last year when Jilli went on *The Date*." Cathy turned to her. "You know, I really should be mad at you."

"Why?"

"Because that date was so damn romantic, so fantastic, Mike will never be able to top it. You've absolutely ruined it for the rest of us."

Agreement floated in from all around the table.

Laughing, Jillian protested. "Wait. That's not fair. *I* didn't set it up, Paul did. He's the one you should be mad at."

"Oh no. It's your fault alright. You're the one who inspired him."

Everyone ragged on Jillian for a while but the conversation soon turned to other light subjects like music, clothes, husbands and boyfriends - the usual.

"So Lisa," Holly said, "we haven't seen much of you the past few months. It was nice having someone else in the group who could appreciate all the stuff married women have to put up with. Of course, now we have Cathy, too."

Lisa's and Rob's October ninth wedding was the social event of the year for most of the group. Her parents spared no expense, flying in family and friends from around the world, setting up a huge tent at the Country Club filled with toys and TV's and babysitters for those with children, and hiring a caterer who was required to spend ten days training with the chefs at Casa de Luna.

"That's right," Marie said. "Ever since you found out you were pregnant you've been avoiding us. How far along are you now?"

"A little over four months." Lisa glowed with happiness as she did every time someone mentioned the pregnancy.

"Is it true ol' Rob hit the target on Christmas morning?" Maggie asked. When Lisa blushed and nodded, she added, "Well I think it's way cool, the perfect Christmas present."

"Huh," snorted Holly. "She may not think so when July and August roll around and her belly's out to here and the humidity is making her melt."

The girls all laughed and Jillian and Priya offered to stay by her side with lemonade and fans to keep her cool.

11:25 PM

All night, the girls took full advantage of the music and parquet floor, dancing off and on, in pairs or groups. They had so much fun, they jokingly booed each time the bass player, Jasmine, announced the band was taking a break.

It was almost eleven-thirty when Gloria noticed them making their way back to the stage. She, Liz, Maggie, Marissa, Shandra, and Holly were seated facing the stage. The rest of the girls had their backs to it. She poked Shandra and nodded toward the stage.

"Hey, wait a minute," Shandra bellowed, stopping all conversation at the table. She turned to Jillian. "Isn't today the anniversary of the day you and Paul met?"

Jillian smiled and nodded.

"Then why aren't you two out somewhere fancy or curled up in bed tonight?"

This time, Jillian sighed and pouted. "His brother Marcus is in from Japan and I guess every year the brothers all take their father out for a guy's night and tonight was the only night Marcus could make it so I told Paul not to worry and to go and have a good time."

"Well that stinks. He should have made his brothers pick a different time."

A chorus of 'yahs' and 'that's rights' emboldened Shandra. "What *is* the matter with that boy? You're his woman and you should come before everything else. Why I have half a mind to…"

"Stop! Please!" Jillian blushed. "He and I had a very nice, umm, breakfast this morning and we met for lunch and he brought me some beautiful flowers and he met me with a taxi after work and we…ummm…held hands on the ride home."

"Sure you did," Maggie said, her eyes wide with merriment. "And what did you have for breakfast? A six inch tube-steak?"

Blushing Jillian shot back, "Why no, it was much larger than that. And it was so filling I only had coffee for lunch." That sent the whole group into fits of laughter.

When things calmed down, Gloria asked, "So seriously. Are you two going out tomorrow to celebrate?"

"No. Saturday. That's the anniversary of our first date. I told him to surprise me and…" She hesitated, not sure whether to tell them.

"And what? Marie asked.

Jillian looked at Liz and Jenna and Priya and Lisa, all of whom were nodding and making encouraging faces.

"He's been acting kind of funny lately. He's been, like, extra sweet and, well, for the past couple of months, he's been asking questions and we've been having these conversations."

"What questions? What conversations?" Marissa and Gloria asked simultaneously.

"Things like, would I like to stay in the city or move to a suburb or the country someday...you know, working moms versus stay-at-home moms...how many kids I want...stuff like that."

"You mean...?"

Shandra left the question unfinished.

Jillian nodded.

"I think he plans to propose on Saturday. He won't tell me anything about it other than I have to wear the same dress I wore last year."

"You wearing pantyhose this time?"

Priya's question brought more laughter. Everyone remembered what had happened last year.

Jillian blushed furiously, but said, "Actually, I thought I'd surprise him and not wear anything at all under it."

"Jillian!"

Five shocked voices rang out at once. She had all she could do to answer the barrage of questions they were throwing at her. Behind her, she heard Jasmine thanking everyone for hanging in during the break and explaining they had a special guest who wanted sing for them tonight, but Jillian was too caught up in the verbal sparring to pay much attention.

The band began the opening chords of The Fifth Dimension's *Wedding Bell Blues* as she said, "No, he is not a bad influence. On the contrary, he brings out the best in me."

Jill, I love you so, I always will

It took her a second to realize it wasn't Jasmine singing, but one of the guys.

Wow. He almost sounds like...did he just say Bill or Jill?

I look at you and see the love I found last May,

Those aren't the right words. And that voice.

She started to turn toward the stage and noticed the gleeful grins on the faces of all the other girls. Then she saw him. It was Paul! And he was singing to her!

Ohhhh,
But now I think it's time to plan our wedding day.

She started to laugh but then began to process the words. "Oh my!" she whispered, though no one could hear her over the music. Her hands came up to cover her mouth.

You've been in my heart Jill now my love's ruling
And I've never schemed or lied Jill there's been no fooling
But kisses and love won't carry me unless you marry me Jill
I love you so, I always will.

She was standing now, tears of love and joy streaming down her cheeks.

And in your voice I hear a choir of carousels. Ohhh,
But now I really want to hear our wedding bells.
I was the one who came fumblin' when you were lonely
And I haven't lived one day not lovin' you only
But kisses and love won't carry me 'til you marry me Jill
I love you so, I always will

Her girlfriends were expecting a few jokes and an announcement about the anniversary and trip. They crowded around, hugging and patting her on the back. Gary and Jessie, who were hiding near the door anticipating the same, also rushed over. And Rob, the only person other than the band who knew what was really going to happen, strolled around with a huge grin on his face, capturing everything on two video cameras.

Jillian was oblivious to it all. She only had eyes for Paul, who stepped off the stage and walked across the dance floor to her.

And though devotion rules my heart I take no bows. Ohhh,
But Jill it's time we stood and took those wedding vows

He was in front of her now. She was beaming through her tears as he fell to one knee.

Come on Jill
Ohhh, Come on Jill
Come on and marry me Jill
I've got the wedding bell blu-u-es
Please marry me Jill

I've got the wedding bell blu-u-u-ues
Wedding bell blues, ya, ya,
Marry me Jill
I've got the wedding bell blu-u-u-ues

Jillian stood there, silent, transfixed, as the final chords faded.

"I know," he said as he rose and faced her with a grin that beat Rob's. "I always go overboard. But if you think you can stand a lifetime of this kind of thing, Jillian Marie Marshall, love of my life, will you marry me?"

"Yes," she whispered.

"What?" Jasmine asked into one of the microphones. "We can't hear you in the back."

The whole room erupted as Jillian threw her arms around Paul and yelled, "Yes! Yes, I'll marry you!"

The laughter turned to applause as they embraced and shared a long, passionate kiss.

Behind them, Jillian heard the opening chords and words to *Could I Have This Dance* the song that seemed to attend every conversation this past year about the man who was kissing her, the man who loved her from the first moment they met, the man who would share her life for the rest of her life.

She broke the kiss and stared at him. "Did you ask them to play this, too?"

He shook his head. "Maybe they remembered from last year or...or..." He shrugged, then held out his hand. "May I have this dance, my love, for the rest of *my* life?"

She sighed, a contented smile on her face.

I guess it was *an omen after all. A good one.*

She moved into his arms and rested her head on his shoulder. The whole world contracted, closing in around them until only the two of them and the music remained. This was it. This was the feeling for which she waited so long. This was the beginning of the life she dreamed of.

As they moved to the music, his arms holding her close, Jillian remembered the pains of the past and marveled at how they led her to the magic of the last year, to new friends, new feelings, new challenges, and to this wonderful man who loved her more than anything in the world.

And as the song came to a close, and Jasmine asked for the final time if she could have that dance for the rest of her life, Jillian closed her eyes, snuggled closer to Paul, and sighed.

Yes, it's going to be a wonderful rest of my life.

– The Beginning –

Dear Reader,

Thank you for reading Coffee in Common.

If you enjoyed it, please stop by Amazon or Goodreads and leave a comment or review. It can be just a sentence or two or as long as you like. Reader opinions really do matter, and are very much appreciated!

Thanks again!

~ Dee

~ ~ ~

Also by Dee Mann:

Beginnings – Seven short stories that prove you never know where and when love will strike.

Plain Shane - With the help of her new roommates, and a new special friend, Shane overcomes her shyness and finds life leading her down paths she only once imagined.

Available at www.masonmarshall.com and amazon.com

Acknowledgements

Always And Forever
Words and Music by Rod Temperton
Copyright © 1976 RODSONGS
Copyright Renewed
All Rights Administered by ALMO MUSIC CORP
All Rights Reserved Used by permission
Reprinted by Permission of Hal Leonard Corporation

SOMEONE TO WATCH OVER ME (from "Oh, Kay")
Music and Lyrics by GEORGE GERSHWIN and IRA GERSHWIN
© 1926 (Renewed) WB MUSIC CORP.
All Rights Reserved
Used by Permission of ALFRED PUBLISHING CO., INC.

Wedding Bell Blues
Words and Music by Laura Nyro
© 1966, 1976 (Renewed 1994, 2004) EMI BLACKWOOD MUSIC INC
All Rights Reserved International Copyright Secured Used by permission
Reprinted by Permission of Hal Leonard Corporation

www.ingramcontent.com/pod-product-compliance
Lightning Source LLC
Chambersburg PA
CBHW030018180626
46810CB00001B/98